Home & Away

Samantha Wayland

Also by Samantha Wayland

Home & Away

Published by Loch Awe Press
P.O. Box 5481
Wayland, MA 01778

ISBN 978-1-940839-09-7

Edited by Meghan Miller
Cover Art by Caitlin Fry

Dedication

For Renee, dearest sister in my family of choice. You've stuck by me through every damn thing. I'm sure this doesn't begin to express how grateful I am for your friendship through all these years.

Acknowledgements

I must begin by thanking Marc for emailing me a list of quaint terms from bygone eras. And thanks also to his lovely wife for asking if I thought there was a way I could work "fadoodle" into one of my books. I'm not sure if this is what you had in mind, Kari, but I enjoyed the challenge.

This book would simply not exist were it not for Stephanie Kay. When she decided to try her hand at NaNoWriMo, I assured her I would rather stick a hot poker in my eye than join her. She then went on to successfully completed NaNo, while I was doing, roughly, nothing. This led to my not-altogether brilliant idea to set the same word count goal in December (because what, Christmas? Pshaw) and, well, it worked. Then Steph took the time to read my chapters as I wrote them, give me good feedback, *and* to learn to love hockey as much as I do (okay, maybe more), making her the best coach, cheerleader, and terribly enabling hockey-addict this writer could ever hope for.

As always, I must thank Victoria Morgan. She is my rock, and ever patient with me. In particular this go around, since I wasn't always able to get her read-throughs back to her as quickly as I should have. I don't deserve her at all.

Many thanks must go out to Caitlin Fry, who has done a

wonderful job with all my covers. She never complains about my inability to get back to her in a timely fashion, nor my hatred of all things tagline-related. Her patience, kindness, and creative genius will serve her well in all her future endeavors, not the least of which will be motherhood. Many congratulations, Caitlyn.

As always, I must thank Meghan Miller. First, of course, for her brilliant editing. But mostly for not throat-punching me when this book took twice as long as it should have and I sent her endless texts freaking out about it along the way. She is a saint and an angel and I really don't understand why she won't move to Massachusetts so I can install her on my couch forty hours a week for unfettered access to her calming influence. Oh, wait...

Chapter One

Rupert was fond of many things. Callum Morrison was not one of them.

Rupert had suspected the man was a pain in the arse after the first time they spoke on the phone, and more or less confirmed it on a group Skype a week later. Callum's biting tone and rampant arrogance perfectly suited his scarred lip and obviously repeatedly broken nose.

He was precisely the sort of man Rupert used to make an effort to avoid. But, sadly, that wasn't going to be possible now that he'd foolishly agreed to take over the management of the Moncton Ice Cats.

He, Rupert Smythe, quiet, thoughtful business man and total wimp, was going to run a professional hockey team. As his life had reminded him on an almost daily basis for the past month, this wasn't the most brilliant idea he'd ever had.

But the Ice Cats needed him, and it had been the best way to convince his best friend, Reese, not to sell the team. Why on earth it had mattered so much to Rupert, he was still trying to work out. He was English, for Pete's sake. No one gave a shit about ice hockey in England. But sometime during the past decade, in the course of helping Reese with the business side of owning a team, Rupert had fallen in love with the game.

Not the players. Or even the staff. Not at first. God's truth, they were a brutish lot and, more often than not, still scared the shit out of him.

He'd only started watching hockey out of some perverse notion that it was research. That, in spite of his strong distaste for the violence that often went along with the sport, he should learn more about it before he started making decisions that would impact the team. But he found he couldn't resist admiring the fluid motion of the game. The agility and power on the ice. The strategy. The cycles and special teams and all those wonderful statistics. Plus-minus scores, shots on goal, ice time, save percentages.

Rupert had found himself rooting for not just the team, but his favorite players. He was disappointed to see some traded away, excited to bring others aboard. He'd had grown to admire the reflexes of the goalies, the Ice Cats' own Alexei Belov in particular. And, if he were going to be honest about it, Callum Morrison as well. He'd watched Callum's Olympic performance with the same slack-jawed awe as the rest of the world. He'd been a superstar of the NHL for a lot of years now, a household name—at least in those houses that followed hockey.

Unfortunately, none of that made Callum any less of an arsehole, as evidenced by the way he barged, wholly unwelcome and unannounced, into Rupert's office. The heavy door ricocheting off the cement wall sounded like a thunder clap.

Until that moment, Rupert had been having a perfectly pleasant meeting with Garrick LeBlanc, former captain of the Ice Cats and now part-owner of the team. He was also Rupert's friend, and Rupert would be lost in this crazy endeavor without him.

They both leapt to their feet.

"Don't you answer your fucking phone?" Callum barked into the shocked silence.

Callum hadn't called Rupert recently, so he could only assume the drama was for Garrick's benefit.

Garrick, generally a socially adept and quick-witted man, was obviously flummoxed. "Callum, what are you doing here?"

"I'm saving your bacon, buddy," Callum said with something that was less of a smile so much as a baring of teeth. He kicked Rupert's door shut.

Suddenly, Rupert's small office felt very, very full.

He stayed where he was, safely ensconced behind his desk, as the two men shook hands, the meeting of their palms a loud crack in the air. Garrick was a large man, but somehow, even though Callum was few inches shorter, he took up more space.

Rupert surreptitiously wiped his damp palms against his trousers.

Garrick remembered his manners. "Callum, you've met Rupert over Skype a time or two, I believe," he offered, waving a hand at Rupert by way of introduction.

Callum barely spared him a nod, which was *rude*. Then again, Rupert should be perfectly happy not to be the focus of a possibly deranged hockey player who'd taken one too many pucks to the head.

Callum glared at Garrick. "You're going to Boston."

Garrick appeared to be rendered speechless by this pronouncement.

Rupert's mouth fell open. "*What?*"

Callum spun, pinning Rupert with the full weight of his bright green stare. Sweat broke out across Rupert's entire body, but he held Callum's gaze. Of course, he still had the desk between them, so this wasn't exactly a towering act of bravery.

Rupert felt sorry for Garrick, he really did. Not just because both his lovers had moved to Boston for their new jobs. Or because he was forced to stay here in Moncton to help with the sheer volume of work that needed to get done this summer. But because the fool was in love with Savannah Morrison, and was probably going to have to deal with this rampaging arsehole for the rest of this life because of it.

"I'm here to help," Callum declared. The fact that he needed to state that should have been his first bloody hint that he wasn't doing a very good job. "Garrick has to go."

Garrick looked concerned. "What happened? What's wrong?"

"Garrick can't just leave," Rupert said, as calmly as he could manage. "He has a lot of work to do here."

Callum's grunt dismissed Rupert completely.

"Goddamn it, Callum," Garrick snapped. "What the hell is going on?"

"Nothing. I don't think. I don't know." Callum threw up his

hands, the unhelpful prick. "Look, as far as I know they're both fine. But I also know is my sister is up to her eyeballs in her new job *and* taking care of Rhian, and you need to get your ass to Boston and help her."

Garrick grabbed Callum's arm. "But what—"

"Get your business in order!" Callum barked, yanking his arm free. "I have no idea what that will look like, and I don't give a shit. Just go!"

Garrick looked stricken.

Rupert saw *red*. He slammed his hand down on his desk. "Just who the hell do you think you are, barging in here and telling him what he has to do?" he shouted, surprising even himself. "We are in the middle of draft negotiations *and* a major construction project. He can't just hie off to Boston because you demand it."

"Who the hell am I? Who the hell says *hie*?" Callum returned, his face flushing red. "I'll tell you who the fuck I am. I'm his future brother-in-law, if he doesn't fuck it up, and I'm part owner of this team. That's who!"

Both those things were technically true—as was the fact that as part-owners, Garrick and Callum were Rupert's bosses—but none of that mattered in the face of Callum's unpardonable arrogance. "Well, I don't give a rat's arse," Rupert shot back. "You don't get to throw this organization into chaos because you've unilaterally decided to be a bloody-minded arsehole!"

Garrick stared at Rupert in awe.

Callum, on the other hand, appeared utterly unimpressed. He sneered at Rupert. "You're going to have to get over it, *duchess*, because I'm staying and he's going."

Duchess?

Garrick made a poor attempt at masking his laughter with a cough. Rupert narrowed his eyes on Callum, who glared right back.

"Listen, *Daniel Boone*," Rupert snapped, his accent more clipped than usual. He couldn't help it when he was this worked up. "Maybe you think your brash new-world style is charming, but I'm bloody well not impressed. We can call a meeting of the owners and discuss this like the civilized businessmen *some of us* are. Until then, we need Garrick here."

"How about this?" Callum shot back. "We send Garrick to Boston and hold off on the meeting until you've had a chance to decide if I can actually help around here, instead of assuming I'm just some dumb hockey player with a big bank account and pucks for brains."

This was, in fact, precisely what Rupert thought of Callum. He lifted his chin higher. "You couldn't possibly jump into the draft at this stage. You have no idea what's needed."

"Screw you, too, Smythe. I've read every report, and I know a good hockey player when I see one, on ice or on paper. I've studied this team for months. I know the Hamilton kid will fill out our defensive line and why. I know Belov is thinking about retiring and we need to sign strong goal talent who will last past a few seasons. I know every damn thing you know, and I have the advantage of actually having played hockey, which I would bet my last fucking dollar you've never done in your damn *life*."

Rupert ground his teeth, foolishly stung by the accurate assessment of his non-hockey-playing past, and furious at the insinuation that he was anything less than fucking amazing at his job. A job Callum Morrison had no fucking idea how to do, and that no amount of time in the net, or an Olympic fucking medal, or even being one of the Morrison clan, could possibly have prepared him for.

"Fine," he bit out, deciding that if nothing else, he'd have the pleasure of watching Callum fall on his face. "Let's see how we do. You stay, Garrick goes. And when next season you're not pleased with the results, you'll have no one to blame but yourself and your monstrous ego."

Callum lunged forward and Rupert's temper, along with the delusional fit of bravery that had come with it, deserted him utterly. He stumbled back until he slammed against the filing cabinet in the corner.

"Callum!" Garrick barked, but Callum was already frozen in place.

Rupert's ears rang with the clang of metal at his back and the harsh scrape of his breathing. His face burned with humiliation at the stunned look on Callum's face as he hovered on the other side of Rupert's desk.

He'd never come close to Rupert. Hadn't even tried, Rupert realized with a sinking heart. Callum just moved so bloody *fast*.

Rupert swallowed, more disgusted with himself than anything Callum Morrison had managed so far. He stood and stepped away from the filing cabinet, clinging to what few shreds of his dignity remained to him. He looked at Garrick. "Go."

"What?" Garrick asked.

"Go. Go to Boston. Your mind has been there for months anyway."

"But, Rupert—"

"Shut up before I change my mind," Rupert said, trying for humor and failing miserably. He took a deep, steadying breath. "As much as it galls me to admit it, Callum is right. You're needed in Boston. You can work your ass off from there. I doubt we could prevent it if we tried, which, frankly, I won't."

Garrick glanced at Callum meaningfully before searching Rupert's face. "Are you sure?"

Rupert was grateful to Garrick for his friendship. For his protectiveness, and obvious concern that Rupert might not feel safe. That Garrick didn't laugh at him for being weak or afraid, though he was quite obviously both.

The least Rupert could do was give him this.

"Yes. Go. Send my love to Savannah and Rhian. Tell them I'm sorry you've had to stay here as long as you have."

"What about—"

"I assure you," Rupert said, arching one eyebrow at Callum, trying very hard—and failing—not to sneer, "if he's not up for the task, you'll be the first to know. Let's hope he's capable of more than high-handed douchebaggery and can pull his weight."

Callum's eyes widened but, remarkably, he held his tongue. Even *he* had enough brain cells to realize Rupert was about to succeed in getting Garrick out the door and on his way to Boston.

Garrick still hesitated. "But—"

"Go," Callum and Rupert said in unison, their eyes locked on each other.

The door opened, then slammed, but Rupert didn't see Garrick leave. He was too busy trying to stare Callum through the floor.

Callum was willing to admit he could have made a better first impression with Rupert. Probably.

He was perfectly aware that at some point in the past few years, he'd become a grumpy bastard. It wasn't on purpose, it was just—well, *life*. Fortunately, he didn't have that many people *in* his life, so he only got to inflict his own special brand of warmth and joy on a select few, most of whom were members of his family and wouldn't put up with that shit for more than ten seconds before putting him in his place.

He kind of liked that Rupert had done it within minutes of meeting him.

They stared each other down across Rupert's desk. The cool, businesslike image Rupert had projected over Skype was lost to the high color on his even higher cheekbones and the clench of his fists.

Callum could recall perfectly the first time he'd seen Rupert. His computer screen had blinked once, then there was this man—blue eyes bright even in low-res, crisp English accent, shirt and tie at what had been ten o'clock at night in Nova Scotia. Callum had allowed himself to stare, knowing the webcam would obscure who he'd studied, while Rupert had run through the deal to purchase shares of the Ice Cats from Reese Lamont. Back then, Rupert had been Lamont's business manager, a title Callum normally associated with someone a lot more staid and boring than Rupert. But as Rupert had spouted out numbers and projections and enough legalese to put anyone off their supper,

Callum had been embarrassingly enthralled. When the negotiations began and Rupert had consistently, flawlessly, arrived at every calculation within the blink of an eye and without the aid of any machine, Callum had been downright grateful the webcam only showed him from the chest up.

His best friend Michaela had laughed her ass off when he'd confessed his little problem to her later. And would laugh her ass off again if she could see him now. Or she would have, right up until the point he'd sent Rupert staggering back in fear. She would be furious at him about that part.

He was kind of furious at *himself,* actually.

He hadn't meant to frighten the guy. Hadn't for one moment thought he *could.* Jesus H. Christ, Rupert managed a professional hockey team. This was not an occupation for the faint of heart. And until that moment, Rupert had been happy to lock horns, his cheeks red and accent clipped, practically radiating prim British outrage. It had been kind of adorable—not that Callum was ever going to admit that out loud. To anyone. Ever. He had only intended to get in Rupert's face and make his point. He would never lay a hand on someone in anger.

Well, okay, he'd never lay a hand on someone in anger *off the ice.*

Now Callum was left with Rupert looking like he had a very large and profoundly uncomfortable poker up his butt. He was glaring at Callum like if he tried hard enough, he might be able to light Callum on fire.

There was probably something wrong with Callum that this didn't make Rupert any less attractive.

Could long-term celibacy lead to the early onset of dementia?

Rupert's lips pursed, and Callum realized he was about to get another tongue-lashing—of the uptight, bitchy variety, not the potentially more fun kind.

"What do you want me to do?" Callum asked, hoping to forestall the lecture he probably deserved.

"Pardon?" Rupert asked haughtily. His tone made it clear

that Callum was the equivalent of something stuck on the bottom of Rupert's shoe. The accent helped, too.

"Where do you need me? What should I do? I said I would help, and I will," Callum said. He'd come here because he loved his sister and wanted to help her—with or without her permission—but he also wanted to learn more about the team he'd bought into, and the people who were running it.

That included Rupert Smythe, even if the other man obviously wished Callum were several thousand miles away and never to be heard from again.

Rupert studied him dubiously and Callum forced himself not to fidget. He tried to think how he could present himself as helpful. Which, okay, was probably a little late, but whatever. "I need to check into my hotel at some point, but otherwise I'm ready to start now. Whatever you need."

"You came directly here?"

"From the airport. Yes."

Rupert lost his bitch face long enough to look worried. "Is everything okay in Boston? I know you told Garrick that nothing had happened, but you seemed to be in a hurry to get him out of here."

Callum grimaced. "No, they're fine. I mean, as far as I know. And I don't want to know more. Because any further discussion about what may or may not be happening in Boston may or may not get into the details of my sister's love life, which may or may not involve more than one man and—*ugh*. Yeah, *no*." He shuddered.

A hint of a smile curled Rupert's lips. "Fair enough."

Callum stared at Rupert's mouth. "So, where do you want me?"

Rupert's frown returned, and with it the efficient, controlled businessman. "There is a meeting of the construction team at one o'clock." Rupert thrust a massive binder across the desk. "This is my copy of the project information. Garrick has another. Learn it."

Callum knew an olive branch when it was waved in his face. Or smashed over his head, as the case may be. "Great."

He didn't miss how Rupert stepped back, putting himself more than arm's distance away again. What the fuck was up with that?

"It's still only part of what you'll need to know, but perhaps if you learn something, you'll get through the meeting without embarrassing yourself. Or me."

Seriously, the dude was such a *bitch.*

"I'll see what I can do."

Callum had been traveling for a living for longer than he cared to remember, so getting settled at the hotel took all of fifteen minutes, even with his hockey equipment bag and his hastily thrown together luggage. He had no idea how long he would be in Moncton, so he'd packed for the long haul. He usually spent his summers training in Denver, but he could do it just as well here. Better, possibly.

Denver knew him. Or thought they did. But Moncton? Not as much. Even in a nation full of hockey fans, he hoped he would only occasionally be recognized, since no one expected him to be in New Brunswick and ninety percent of his television time was spent beneath a mask.

He loved his job, was proud of his career, but what he really wanted was to be anonymous. Just for a while. That wasn't going to happen, of course, but even a little less attention on him would be welcome.

He decided to unpack his clothes into the closet and drawers, something he never did while traveling during the hockey season. When he was done, he thought he could comfortably ride out a couple months in this generic room as well as he could at home.

He wasn't sure what that said about his apartment in Denver.

Settling down with the ream of paperwork, he soon realized

why Rupert had been happy to dump it on him. It was an overwhelming amount of information. Quotes, projections, project plans, contractors, sub-contractors. Callum's head was going to explode. Instead of trying to learn it all, he focused on that day's meeting agenda and anything he could find that correlated to that. He was just about to call Garrick and beg for mercy when his phone rang.

He didn't recognize the number. Normally he wouldn't answer, but it might be Rupert, which shouldn't encourage him to answer either, but—

"Hello?"

"Uh, hi. Is this Callum Morrison?"

Definitely not Rupert. Callum waivered, considering hanging up on the unfamiliar voice. "Yes?"

"Um, this is Jack Chevalier. Garrick LeBlanc gave me your number. I hope that's okay."

Callum hadn't been able to make a lot of sense out of the tome on his lap, but he *had* managed to learn the name of the project manager. "Hi, Jack. I was just reading about you."

There was a long silence on the other end of the line. "You have?" Jack said finally.

"Sure. Rupert gave me the project plan. I see your name all over it—and everything else in this binder."

"*Oh!* Okay," Jack said with what sounded like a relieved chuckle. "That's what I'm calling about. Garrick says you're going to take over for him here in Moncton. He seems to think Rupert might not be inclined to help you get settled?"

Jack's obvious confusion was yet more evidence that Callum's sparkling personality had brought out the very best in Rupert.

"There's an understatement. And yes, I'm stepping in for Garrick. I hope that's okay with you."

"That's great. G needs to be in Boston right now."

Callum wondered, again, what the hell was going on in Boston and if he should ask. He promptly discarded the idea. He still didn't want to know.

"Yeah, well, I should probably apologize. It's going to take me a while to get up to speed."

"How would you like a crash course before our meeting at one? You know there's a meeting at one, right?"

Callum chuckled. "I do. But that's about all I know."

"Okay, we can fix that. Where are you? I'll come pick you up."

After having his morning ruined by Callum Morrison, Rupert's day continued downhill at such a remarkable trajectory, he could only hope to hit bottom soon. He'd briefly looked forward to the meeting at one and Callum's inevitable comeuppance, but now he wasn't as certain it was a good idea to throw Callum to the lions.

Not that he gave a rat's arse about Callum, of course. It was the lions that were giving Rupert trouble.

Each day, about mid-morning, Garrick would walk through the arena with Jack and check on the construction. And, more specifically, on the contractor. The project was coming along well, with some small delays, but Jack and Garrick's vigilance kept them to schedule as much as possible.

Unfortunately, Jack was nowhere to be found. And making Callum do the walk-through would be a complete waste of time. He was clueless, and god forbid anyone recognized him—it would bring the entire site to a halt. Not that Callum was much to look at, but this was Canada. And Callum was, as much as Rupert was loathe to admit it, very good at his job. His *real* job, playing hockey. No self-respecting hockey fan would pass up the opportunity to fawn over him a little.

Except Rupert, of course. He would rather poke his own eye out than give that man another minute of his attention.

What would it take to force Callum to go back to Denver and his perfect life with his perfect supermodel girlfriend? Whatever it was, Rupert was willing to do it. Posthaste.

But in the meantime, in an effort to keep things on track in spite of Garrick's departure, Rupert was conducting a quick walk-through alone. He *hated* doing this, and to date had successfully managed to avoid the responsibility, along with most aspects of the construction project. But no matter how much Rupert relished the idea of Callum being knocked down a peg, he wasn't going to let this project get knocked down, too.

He walked briskly, mentally checking the work being done against his memory of the project plan, nodding at the men who acknowledged him, ignoring those who didn't. So...mostly ignoring everyone.

He'd survived almost the entire experience when a bellow of rage erupted from the mezzanine bathrooms, followed shortly by a huge man stumbling backwards. He crashed into Rupert, slamming them both into a stack of drywall along the railing.

Rupert's head spun as he crumpled to the floor. Before he could figure out what the fuck had just happened, or even suck any air back into his lungs, four men stormed through the bathroom door, bearing down on them fast.

Rupert's stomach plunged, and he scrambled backward as the man who'd landed half on top of him was hauled to his feet. Rupert shook his head, struggling to understand what the men were yelling about. It took him far longer than it should have to figure out that was because they were yelling in a coarse Quebecoise French.

Forcing his brain to shift gears, he was able to determine someone had cheated at cards, and another man's mother was of questionable morals and profession. Oh, and these men didn't use the term "cocksucker" as a compliment.

Rupert knew what Garrick would do, were he here. He'd step in, shove the men apart, and get everyone back to work. The men weren't much bigger than Rupert—some were actually shorter than he was—but they were strong. And they knew each other.

They were, for all intents and purposes, a team. A potentially unified front. Rupert was only one man and an outsider, to boot.

Hating himself more than a little, he scanned the corridor for an escape. He let out an undignified yelp when one of the workers wrapped a strong hand around his arm and yanked him back onto his feet. He'd no more than caught his balance when his original assailant and another man lunged for each other, fists flying. They barreled into Rupert, shoving him back, his arms pinwheeling, his wingtips useless against the layer of dust on the tile floor. His back slammed into the balcony railing, forcing the air from his lungs with a feeble, terrified sound. He grabbed the railing with both hands and planted his feet, holding on for dear life and refusing to look over his shoulder to the drop below.

He was so focused on the men fighting in front of him that he didn't see Jack and Callum running toward them until Callum's voice boomed throughout the arena.

"What the fuck is going on here!?"

Everyone, including the fucking idiots fighting practically on top of Rupert, froze.

In the time it took everyone to take a deep breath, Callum managed, barely, to wrestle himself back under control. He'd nearly had a fucking heart attack when Rupert had gone reeling backwards toward that railing.

Callum glanced over at Jack. They'd been laughing and joking around as they'd arrived to do the daily walk-through, Callum feeling so much better about his odds of proving to Rupert that he could pull his weight around here. Jack had helped him cram for the meeting later, making Jack just about Callum's favorite person in the world right now.

It didn't hurt that he was also, quite possibly, the best-looking human being Callum had ever laid eyes on. Even now, when his face was a mask of anger.

"You got this, Jack?" Callum asked.

Jack dialed his phone with one hand, glaring at the fucking idiots in front of him. "Yeah." He pressed the phone to his ear. As soon as someone picked up, Jack started shouting in French and the workers all cringed in unison. Callum barely spoke the

22

language, but he understood half of what Jack said based on years of listening to the colorful cursing of his French-Canadian league-mates. Jack liked the word *tabarnak* a lot.

Callum went to Rupert. "Are you okay?"

Rupert looked at him, pale, his pupils tiny black pinpricks lost in a sea of blue, and nodded. He ran a shaking hand through his hair. Callum swept his gaze over the men surrounding them, and swore to himself that if he saw a single one of these guys on their site again, he'd fire the construction company first and figure out how to unfuck the project schedule later.

He moved to put himself between Rupert and the assholes Jack was currently dressing down at great volume. Rupert flinched.

Jesus Christ. It was one thing to be terrified, another altogether not to hide it in front of these assholes.

He grabbed Rupert's arm, ignoring the way his eyes widened, the barely audible whimper, and pulled him away from the railing. Callum would have nightmares about that fucking thing for weeks. He marched down the corridor toward the Ice Cats' offices with Rupert in tow.

When Rupert opened his mouth, Callum squeezed his arm. "Just shut up."

Rupert sucked in furious gasp. Callum had no illusions—Rupert wasn't just going to ignore his suggestion, but do so loudly.

"Please," Callum added quietly.

That, at least, shut Rupert up long enough to get around the corner. As soon as they were out of sight, Callum dropped Rupert's arm.

Rupert practically dove out of reach.

"You are the most highhanded, arrogant bastard I've ever met," Rupert snapped. The color returned to his face, glowing hot on his cheeks as he brushed plaster dust off his perfectly tailored, wildly expensive suit.

Callum knew he looked like a bumpkin next to all that

sartorial splendor. Then again, this was a construction site, and it wasn't like Callum wanted to get into a fashion competition with Rupert. If Callum ever tried to wear a suit like that, he'd look like a gorilla stuffed in a leotard.

Callum sighed. "I was trying to help," he said, knowing it was pointless.

Rupert's head jerked up, his hand frozen mid-swat above his shoulder, a cloud of plaster dust hovering around him. "How was that, exactly? By dragging me off like a naughty child?"

Callum barely bit back an offer to spank Rupert. Probably not appropriate right now. Or ever.

"Never let them see your fear."

Rupert stood straighter, his suit forgotten. "What?"

"Look, it's none of my fucking business why, but you're a really skittish dude and it's totally fucking obvious. Which is..." *Ridiculous. Bizarre.* "...not really ideal around a bunch of guys like that." *Or hockey players, for that matter.*

"I am not *skittish*," Rupert said, his pride obviously stung in spite of it being the plain fucking truth.

Callum arched an eyebrow and took one quick step in Rupert's direction.

Rupert jumped back and almost lost his balance in those stupid shoes. Jesus Christ, how did he not know to wear work boots on a construction site? It was a miracle he hadn't stepped on a nail and given himself tetanus. Yet.

Rupert glared. "You are an insufferable bastard."

"Well, you're going to have to find a way to suffer me, because I'm not going anywhere. And while you're working on that, how about you explain to me how the hell you ended up here, doing *this* job? Because it doesn't seem to suit you at all."

Rupert drew himself up to his full height, which left him at eye level with Callum. "I'm very good at my job, thank you very much, and it suits me perfectly. Moreover, I don't need your approval to do it."

"Uh, yeah. You do. I own this team."

"You own one quarter of this team. I assure you, Reese and Garrick understand fully what I bring to this position. Perhaps not all of us are blessed with a burning desire to beat the piss out of other people for fun or money, but that doesn't mean I can't manage this team as well or better than anyone else ever has or could."

The hell of it was, Callum agreed. Management took brains, not brawn, and Rupert had plenty of those. Getting some *balls* sure wouldn't hurt, though.

Callum was saved from having to come up with something appropriate to say, let alone something that wouldn't get Rupert's panties in an even tighter twist, by Jack jogging around the corner. He immediately went to Rupert and put a hand on his arm.

No flinch. In fact, Rupert didn't seem to mind in the least. *Fucking figures.*

"You okay?"

"Yes, thank you," Rupert said, prim once again. "Your timing is appreciated."

"I'm sorry we didn't get here sooner."

"It's quite all right, Jack. I'm fine."

Jack didn't look like he believed it, but, being a far more diplomatic person than Callum, refrained from making any comment.

Rupert smiled grimly. "In any case, I think this has proven that my talents are better employed elsewhere. Going forward, I will leave overseeing the construction to the two of you."

Callum's brain stuttered. "Uh, what?"

"Normally, Garrick would have done the walk-through with Jack, and then run the meeting this afternoon. I'll jump in today so you don't screw up the whole project, but I won't be available for tomorrow morning's conference call. Nor Thursday's team meeting. Think you can handle it?"

Callum glanced at Jack, alarmed to find him staring at Rupert like he was out of his mind. Callum almost laughed. He really had to admire Rupert's willingness to go right for the throat. Maybe the guy had some balls after all. But if he thought Callum would run back to Denver with his tail between his legs, he was going to be sorely disappointed.

Callum had Jack. He'd have Garrick to call for help once he arrived in Boston. And he'd be damned if he was going to let Rupert Smythe beat him.

Smiling serenely, he shrugged, as if having a multi-million dollar construction project dumped in his lap was no big deal. "Sure, duchess, I can handle it."

Jack made a strange choking sound.

Rupert's eyes narrowed dangerously. *"Really?"*

"Really." Callum made sure his grin was of the shit-eating variety.

Rupert appeared, for fucking once, to be speechless. He spun and stalked off toward his office.

Callum swallowed back another parting shot and silently mouthed *bitch* at Rupert's back instead, because he was a grown up.

Chapter Two

Within a week of Callum's arrival, Rupert was going out of his mind. By the end of week two, he was just about to lose his shit.

First there was the draft and preparing for the coming season—a ton of work in the best of circumstances, and with the players they'd lost this year and the changes in management, it was nowhere near the best of anything.

Then there was all the extra time he spent babysitting Callum Fucking Golden Boy Morrison, which would be a monumental pain in the arse if Rupert could do it out in the open. But, no. He had to sneak around when Callum wasn't looking, just so he could reassure himself the stubborn jerk wasn't fucking things up.

And don't even get Rupert started on the *duchess* bullshit.

At this point, Rupert wouldn't blame Jack if he up and quit on them. Callum was Jack's constant shadow during the day, so Rupert had taken to pestering Jack in the evenings for an update when Callum wasn't around. When Rupert had stopped by Jack's apartment at ten o'clock last night, Jack had suggested that if Rupert expected them to spend their nights together, he ought to put a ring on it.

Jack had been joking, obviously, but Rupert had gotten flustered, and Jack had taken one look at his face and cracked up. Rupert wasn't even certain Jack was gay. Or if Jack knew Rupert was gay. Or, well, whatever. The point was, he and Jack were spending a lot of time together.

Rupert was perfectly aware he was being a control freak. He hadn't been all over Garrick like this when he'd been in charge of the construction, but Garrick had proven to be an adept businessman and leader. Rupert had no reason to believe that Callum was either of those things.

Except he sort of was.

Within days of his arrival, Callum had charmed everyone at the offices and the arena. Workers, staff, management. Hell, Callum practically had Sheila, the battle-axe who ran the box office and who scared the pants off Rupert, eating out of the palm of his hand. And it wasn't just her. Rupert had been stunned the first time he'd come out of his office to find a grinning Callum surrounded by half of Rupert's team, everyone listening raptly as he recounted some practical joke they'd pulled in the Olympic Village.

Until that moment, Rupert hadn't realized Callum knew how to smile, let alone how it lit up his eyes, framing them with a fan of little lines that absolutely should not have been as attractive as they were.

Callum's successes weren't just limited to his people skills, which he remained wholly incapable of employing when Rupert was involved. It was the work he'd accomplished, too. Jack had clearly helped a lot for the first few days, but then Callum had figured out which end was up and slid into the leadership role with an ease that would be admirable, if Rupert were willing to admire anything about Callum Morrison. Which he wasn't.

So he kept checking on Callum, waiting for him to screw up, and running himself into the ground in the process. He was so out of sorts, he arrived at Jack's doorstep that night without having warned Jack he was on his way. Marvelous. Rupert was now rude, in addition to a pain in the arse.

This was also Callum's fault, Rupert decided as he hesitated outside Jack's door. He supposed the worst Jack could do was tell him to fuck off. Or not be home at all.

The door swung open before Rupert even knocked.

Callum. And he didn't seem the least bit surprised to find Rupert loitering on Jack's doorstep.

"Hello, Rupert."

"What are you doing here?"

"Visiting with a friend," he said mildly. "And you?"

Rupert scrambled to come up with an explanation for stopping by Jack's home at night. There weren't a lot of believable options that would leave his dignity intact, and Rupert had lost all capacity for bullshit anyway.

"I'm here to check up on you. As I do most evenings," he announced.

Callum smiled and opened the door wider. "Well, alrighty, then. Come on in."

Jack greeted him kindly and offered him a drink, as he always did. Rupert normally declined, but somehow he knew Callum expected him to, so for the first time, he accepted a beer.

He tried to relax, to shake off some of the tension from his day, but it was impossible with Callum watching him with one eyebrow lifted in sardonic judgment.

Rupert threw back almost half the bottle on the first go. Unwise, but needed.

"You all right, Rupert?" Jack asked.

Rupert's face heated, and he hoped they could pretend it was the alcohol and not his embarrassment at feeling so damn frayed at the edges. He liked control. Order. He had lists and he worked his way through them and things got done and that was good.

But this job, the draft, the way his blood pressure soared whenever he found himself surrounded by hockey players or construction workers—which was all the damn time—was taking a toll. And that wasn't even the *worst* of the shit in his life right now.

His phone rang and he frowned at the screen, discovering it was indeed possible for this day to get even more stressful.

"I'm sorry," he said to Jack. "I have to take this."

Jack shrugged and waved him toward the living room. "Go ahead. This can wait."

This being tonight's pile of paperwork for review. Lovely.

Rupert answered his phone, grateful when Nick dispensed with the niceties and got right to the point.

More bad news. Rupert told himself to listen and breathe and sit calmly on the couch, but soon he was leaping to his feet and shouting into his phone. "What do you mean you found

Lydia but not Oliver?"

"I'm sorry, Rupert. She's in Monaco, but she didn't bring Oliver with her."

"But he's only four years old," he said uselessly. He caught a movement out of the corner of his eye and turned his back to the door. "You said he isn't with Lydia's parents. That she hasn't spoken to them in years. Does she have any other family?"

"Not that I've been able to find, no."

Rupert rubbed his forehead and reminded himself, not for the first time since this ordeal had begun, that panicking wouldn't help.

Fuck.

"I can approach her, if you like," Nick offered.

"Do you think you can do it without tipping our hand?" Rupert would do anything to find Oliver, but he feared letting that gold-digging, conniving bitch know Rupert was onto her would hurt more than help.

"I can try. I don't exactly have access to the same parties she does. She's running with a pretty wild crowd, but an exclusive one."

Rupert's stomach churned, fearing what that might mean for Oliver. "Okay. Keep me posted."

"Will do. I've still got a guy in London, working on a lead there. If she didn't bring Oliver along on her party tour, then my guess is he's somewhere closer to home—and the source of the money."

By which Nick meant Rupert's bank. Until he knew Oliver was safe, he couldn't cut the bitch off.

He sighed. "Contact me the minute you learn anything."

"Of course."

Rupert hung up and pressed his phone to his forehead. Hard. He had to keep it together. He would not embarrass himself in front of Jack and Callum.

But what if something had happened? What if Oliver was

sick, or hurt...

His head snapped up when a hand touched his elbow.

"Why don't you sit down?" Callum said gently, nudging him toward the couch and handing him the beer he'd left in the other room.

Rupert studied Callum suspiciously. "Don't be nice. It's freaking me out."

Callum rolled his eyes. "Take it easy, duchess. I promise not to make a habit of it."

Rupert almost smiled, reassured that there was still order in the universe. Still some things he could count on. Callum Morrison being an arsehole was one of them.

Callum watched Rupert collapse onto Jack's couch and melt into the cushions, all the starch gone out of him. It was, frankly, alarming.

This wasn't Rupert. Rupert was stiff upper lips and crisp accents. Callum was sure Rupert had never worn clothes that weren't tailored exactly to his trim body, left the house with a single silky hair out of place, or chugged half a beer—from the bottle, no less—in his life.

It was only mildly reassuring that the hair and clothes were still just as they should be. The rest of Rupert very clearly wasn't.

Callum perched on the other end of the sofa, putting as much space between them as possible, even folding his hands non-threateningly in his lap. Jack slid into the arm chair on the other side of the coffee table.

Rupert eyed them both warily.

"What's going on?" Callum asked, trying to sound neutral.

"Nothing," Rupert said before taking another slug of beer.

"Who were you just talking to?"

"It's nothing you need to be concerned with," Rupert snapped.

"Could you please stop being so fucking uptight for ten

seconds? I'm trying to be nice."

Rupert huffed out a laugh and took another gulp of beer.

Callum took a deep breath and tried again. "I apologize."

Rupert's eyes widened comically, obviously mocking him.

"Did something happen at the arena today?" Callum continued, determined not to rise to the bait. He wasn't really worried about the team. Sometime in the past week, he'd accepted he would never worry about the team with Rupert in charge—a fact that irritated him to no end.

"No, everything is fine."

"You get that we know you're lying, right?" Callum asked.

Rupert grimaced, then turned to Jack. "How was your day?"

Jack smiled pleasantly. "If you mean did Callum and I break anything, piss anyone off, or force anything off schedule, then no, and our day was fine, thank you."

Twin spots of color bloomed high on Rupert's cheekbones. He smiled was rueful. "I've been a bit controlling, haven't I?"

Jack held his smile, arched a brow, and remained diplomatically silent.

"Yes, well," Rupert continued, adorably prim as he sat up. "I should go, then."

"Wait," Callum blurted, trying to come up with a reason for Rupert to stay. To trust them. He kept hearing how gutted Rupert had sounded when he'd said *but he's only four years old.*

Jack bailed Callum out. "Finish your beer, at least. You do look like you could use it."

Rupert sat back and closed his eyes. "Okay. Thank you."

Callum took the rare opportunity to study Rupert. What should have been milk-pale skin under his eyes looked bruised. His normally plush pink lips were pressed in a tight white line.

"You look stressed," Callum observed, then held up a hand to ward off Rupert's glare. "I just want to know if there is anything I can do, okay? Don't go all *duchess* on me."

Because saying shit like that was definitely going to help.

Sometimes Callum wanted to punch himself in the face.

"There is nothing you can do," Rupert said, resigned, then appeared to change his mind. "Actually, I may need to go out of town at some point. To London. So, yes," he conceded, "I take it back. I may need your help."

It obviously killed Rupert to admit it. Callum decided to be an adult and not point out Rupert was still being super pissy.

"Garrick, Jack, and I can cover whatever you need," Callum said with more confidence than he felt. Rupert was covering all the player trade negotiations *and* the logistics for next season. Callum had no fucking idea how to do that, but whatever, he'd figure it out. "Will you be gone long?"

Rupert sighed and ran a hand over his face. "I don't know. I don't even know if I'm going. I've—well, if you must know, I've lost my brother."

Callum's heart stopped and he sent Jack a helpless look.

"Lost?" Jack asked carefully.

"Oh, no!" Rupert said, bolting upright, clearly horrified. "Not that. Not dead. Dear god, no." If Rupert got any paler, he'd be transparent. "Oliver, my brother—well, half-brother technically—is just four years old, and his mother appears to have left him behind while she parties her way across Europe. But I don't know where he is. Or who is looking after him. And I haven't been able to reach him—or his mother—for months."

Callum recalled Rupert missing a handful of meetings. "Weren't you over there a few weeks ago?"

"Yes. The investigator I've hired thought he had a solid lead, but it turned out that we were either too late or it was the wrong child. We never figured it out for certain."

Callum would be tearing his hair out if one of his siblings went missing, and they were all grown adults. "Why didn't you say anything?"

"Because of that whole thing where you've been an insufferable bastard?"

Jack let out a startled laugh.

Callum threw up his hands. "And why do you suppose *that* is?"

"I haven't the foggiest idea, Callum. Maybe because I'm not what you pictured in a team manager. Or because I've never played hockey. Because I'm British, perhaps? What is it you call me? Duchess? Or maybe it's because I'm a better dresser than you. Or gay, or—"

"What the fuck!" Callum leapt to his feet, appalled and furious, arms flailing as if he could ward off Rupert's accusation. "Fuck that. *Fuck you.* I'm an asshole, but I'm not a bigot, and if I've given you a hard time it's because *you're* an asshole. Not because you're gay, for Christ's sweet sake. So really, fuck you. Fuck you *a lot.*"

Callum stopped to catch his breath while Jack and Rupert stared at him, agape.

Rupert was the first to recover. "I apologize," he said, and he actually sounded sincere.

Callum gifted him with the same wide-eyed surprise Rupert had mocked him with earlier. Rupert acknowledged it with a nod and something that almost passed for a smile.

For one crazy moment, Callum felt the urge to blurt out the truth. He sat down until the feeling went away, scowling at Rupert the whole time.

Eventually he muttered, "I didn't even know you were gay."

Rupert sent him an extremely skeptical look.

Callum rolled his eyes. "Fine. It's not like you...errr...hide your light under a bushel."

Jack clapped a hand over his face and shook his head.

"What?" Callum said, wincing. "I'm not judging."

"Sounds like it from where I'm sitting," Rupert said, obviously amused.

If Callum were in Rupert's shoes, he wouldn't find it funny at all to be judged—which he wasn't doing. But still. He tried to explain. "No, I mean, I...I admire it."

"You admire me being gay? How delightfully patronizing."

34

"I don't admire you for being gay, asshole. You either are or you aren't. That would be like admiring someone for their shoe size. What I *admire* is that you're so, you know, honest about it. Open. That you don't care who knows or wonders or guesses, or whatever. Which is," Callum rushed to clarify, "as it should be. But in this business it's just...hard. I'm guessing. I mean, I don't know."

Callum bit his lips, determined to stem the tide of verbal diarrhea.

Rupert arched one brow. "I'm overwhelmed by your support. Perhaps we should sing Kumbaya now."

Callum flopped back on the couch, refusing to smile. "Ugh. Shut up. I hate you."

Jack stood. "I think we need another round of drinks."

Rupert strode into the arena the next morning, not regretting, but still aware of the beers he'd drunk on an empty stomach the night before. He wasn't a complete lightweight, as a rule, but it had been a while since he'd had even a single drink. It had been unexpectedly nice to sit and relax for a while, even if the conversation had focused on work and Callum had still been a royal pain in the arse. Still, it had been pleasant enough that he'd not wanted to end the evening in order to go in search of food.

Now, though, Rupert was feeling the repercussions of that decision. He'd slept better than he had in weeks, but woken up with a fuzzy head and the burning desire to drink a gallon of water. A very large cup of tea and his granola-bar breakfast had taken the edge off, but he needed some quiet time in his office to get him the rest of the way there. He had two separate lists of tasks he wanted to tackle today, and another he'd been drafting in his head that needed to be transferred into the app on his phone he kept for these things.

"Good morning, Rupert," Sheila said as soon as he entered the team's offices.

"Sheila."

He noted Jack and Callum were already ensconced in the conference room they'd annexed sometime over the past week. Callum rose and came to the door as soon as he saw Rupert.

Rupert felt his muscles tightening, a knee-jerk reaction apparently not cured by one night of friendly drinks.

"Good morning," Callum offered, pleasantly enough, and Rupert told himself to chill out. "Any news?"

Rupert paused in his retreat to his office. "Pardon?"

"About Oliver—that's his name, right? Your brother?"

Rupert blinked at him stupidly for a moment before answering. "Nothing."

Callum frowned. "I'm sorry."

Rupert would have believed Callum capable of many things, but empathy would not have made the list. He'd been wrong, it seemed.

"Thank you," Rupert said. "For asking."

It struck Rupert that this was the first time either of them had been the least bit gracious with each other. He was a bit ashamed of himself, really.

That was the first day in the two weeks since Callum had arrived that Rupert didn't check up on the construction project once. It was also the first time Callum and Jack sought him out in the afternoon to give him an update.

It was the start of a détente of sorts. Each morning Callum would ask after Oliver, and sometimes do so again later when he and Jack stopped by or Rupert poked his head into their conference room on his way out. By a week in, Rupert only had to shake his head as he rushed to his office one morning before an important call, seeing Callum waiting in the doorway, the question on his face. Callum's responding frown was fierce. He looked as frustrated as Rupert felt.

Shaking off a ridiculous flash of warmth, Rupert dashed to his desk and grabbed his ringing phone. An hour later, the Ice Cats were down a seasoned defensemen but had a new, desperately needed left wing to fill out their second line, and a draft pick.

In spite of the thrill Rupert got from the challenges of the work, the negotiation and back-and-forth, he never forgot that, in the end, these were *people* he was dealing on and off the team. It made it hard. Still, he was unprepared when, later that afternoon, the freshly traded defensemen came barreling into the Ice Cats offices, bellowing his name.

The entire room fell into shocked silence. Rupert froze where he stood in front of the new trainer's desk, his heart jackrabbiting into his throat.

"Smythe! What the fuck have you done?"

Rupert turned on unsteady legs as the man turned toward him and squared off, as if intending to check Rupert clear into the next province.

"Can I help you, Derek?" Rupert asked, wishing his voice was stronger but pleased he'd managed to say anything at all.

"You son of a bitch. What did you do?"

"I traded you," Rupert said baldly, betrayed by the quaver in his voice. "Your agent said he'd let you know."

"Yeah, he told me," the man sneered, striding closer.

Rupert stepped back, furious with himself for it but too aware of the fists clenched at the other man's sides. He forced himself to look Derek in the eyes. "Did you have a question, then?"

"I've been good for this team, and this is the thanks I get? Traded to some shit team in East Bumfuck?"

The people of North Bay would probably disagree with that designation. Also, it was to the west, but Rupert carefully refrained from sharing these observations. "It's a good team, Derek, and they're paying you well. You'll do them a lot of good, and we needed to make some changes."

"Make some changes? How the fuck would you know, you little—"

A hand clamped down on Derek's shoulder.

"Think carefully before you speak," Callum said in a deadly

calm voice.

The cold, furious look on Callum's face was terrifying, but it wasn't directed at Rupert. In fact, Rupert now realized he'd been getting off easy when it came to bearing the brunt of Callum's anger.

"You're going to defend him?" Derek asked, gesturing at Rupert dismissively. "He doesn't know shit about hockey. I can't believe you're letting him ruin this team."

Rupert noticed that some of his colleagues and staff looked offended on his behalf, and tried very hard to ignore those who appeared to agree with Derek's assessment.

Callum moved to stand with Rupert, their shoulders brushing as Callum crossed his arms over his chest. "He knows as much about hockey as you or I. And he knows a hell of a lot more than both of us combined about how to run a business, which is what this is. If you don't like it, get out of the game. But if you want to keep playing, *anywhere*, I suggest you shut the fuck up."

For the next several seconds, Derek did a perfect imitation of a freshly landed carp. Rupert probably didn't look much better. He pinched himself to be sure he wasn't dreaming the whole thing.

Without another word, Derek spun on his heel and stormed from the room.

"Well," Jack said from the conference room door, breaking the heavy silence, "that was unpleasant."

"You have a gift for understatement," Rupert said. He nodded at Callum. "I thank you for your help."

"You're welcome," Callum said, his voice as gruff as his manners.

They stared at each other in the ensuing, increasingly awkward silence. Rupert's phone buzzed in his hand and he looked down automatically to see a text message on his screen.

Found him. 37 Chiltern, W1, London. Apt 3b. Above the wedding shop.

"Oh my god," he breathed, his stomach plunging to the floor. His hands, already unsteady from excess adrenaline, now shook so badly it took him three tries to enter his passcode.

"What?" Callum demanded. "What's happened?"

"I think they found him."

Jack was suddenly at his side. "Let's go in your office. Come on."

Rupert let himself be herded through the door. Callum closed it behind them.

"What going on? Is he okay?"

"I don't know," Rupert cried, still trying to get his hands to cooperate enough to hit the correct icon.

With a growl, Callum snatched the phone from Rupert's hands. Callum was a presumptuous bastard, but Rupert couldn't be bothered to get upset. He gestured at the phone. "Check the text messages."

"All I see is an address. Tell me what to write back."

"Ask if it's Oliver. Ask if they have him. Is he okay?"

Callum manipulated the phone with remarkable dexterity, and Rupert wondered inanely if it was an unintended benefit of goalie training. When the phone buzzed again, Rupert pressed himself to Callum's side so that he could see the screen.

Appears to be okay. With young woman. Nanny? Have not approached. Cannot take custody. Only you. Do not want to spook kid or nanny or mother.

Rupert clutched Callum's arm, his brain sprinting from one problem to the next. He needed to get to London. He should pack. And buy a plane ticket. Call his solicitors. He needed to make a list of—

"What does he mean about custody?" Jack asked from Callum's other side, snapping Rupert out of his spiraling panic.

"Before my father passed away, he arranged for me to have custody of Oliver, as his mother had never seemed interested in having anything to do with him. But when I arrived in London, she was doting on him, and I foolishly believed she'd changed. I left him with her," he confessed, ashamed, his voice gone hoarse. "It was only a matter of months before she started to be harder to reach, but eventually I would hear back. Would see Oliver on Skype. Then a few months ago—"

Callum started typing. *We're on our way.*

Rupert couldn't seem to hold onto any one thought for long. "We?"

"Jack, can you look into flights?" Callum asked.

Jack practically sprinted from the office.

Callum turned to Rupert. "You shouldn't go alone. You don't know what you're going to be dealing with, and someone might need to be with Oliver while you're handling the fallout. Not to mention, have you ever travelled with a young child?"

"I hadn't really thought..."

"Is there someone who can help you in London? Or someone else you can take? Lamont, maybe?"

Rupert shook his head. There was no one else. And certainly not his best friend, Reese Lamont, who could barely leave his house, let alone the country, without having a paralyzing anxiety attack.

"No, I—" He looked at Callum, utterly overwhelmed. "I have no family."

"You have Oliver," Callum reminded him.

"Yes. Yes, of course," Rupert said. "I just meant—"

"What about friends?"

"None that could get to London in the matter of hours."

"Okay. Then, I'll go." Callum said, looking as incredulous as Rupert felt about that offer. "I mean, if that's—"

"Why would you help me? You don't even like me," Rupert said, bewildered.

"He's a *child*. Barely more than a baby, Rupert."

And oh, god, Rupert knew that. Just hearing someone else say it, hearing the concern in Callum's voice, brought the panic rushing back.

He was so far out of his depth that the water was closing over his head faster than he could begin to swim. Suddenly, the bane of his existence looked like the only life raft he could reach. "Yes. Okay. Thank you. I just—"

"We got this," Callum said with a reassuring amount of confidence.

That made exactly one of them who thought they had any idea what the fuck they were doing.

That night passed in a blur. Jack was a godsend, booking them an early flight through Toronto that would get them into London the following evening. Callum didn't know what he would have done without his help, since Rupert was so overwhelmed, he was useless. Callum had secretly dreamed of seeing the always perfectly put-together Rupert completely out of sorts, but now was really *not the time*.

Callum dragged their asses through packing up laptops and paperwork at the office, then to Callum's hotel for his bag and passport. Once they arrived at Rupert's hotel, another extended-stay set up like Callum's, Callum practically had to shove Rupert in the direction of the bedroom to begin packing.

Callum stayed in the kitchen to call Garrick.

It was getting late and Callum worried that Garrick wouldn't answer. He kind of wished no one had when a sleepy-sounding Rhian Savage picked up the phone.

That was an answer to a question Callum hadn't wanted to ask. Then he heard his sister's voice mumbling in the not-very-distant background and almost hung up the phone.

"I hear you're going to London," Garrick announced by way of greeting once the phone had finally been passed to him.

Callum sighed. "Jack called you, didn't he?"

"Probably no more than two minutes after he left your side."

It wasn't like Callum didn't know Jack was Garrick's oldest friend. Then another thought occurred. "Oh god. And Savannah knows?"

"Of course," Garrick said with a chuckle. "We got to witness the activation of the Morrison phone tree. Pretty impressive."

Callum rested his forehead against a kitchen cabinet. *"Great."* He loved his family, he really did, but they had a compulsive need to be all up in each other's business. Not that he had any right to bitch, since he'd made this trip to Moncton with the express purpose of forcing Garrick and Savannah to sort out their super weird love lives.

But still.

Deciding he'd deal with questions from his family when they arose and not one minute before, he turned the conversation to what needed to be done in the next couple days and secured Garrick's promise to do whatever he could from Boston. Then Callum called Reese, who was far more interested in why Callum was going to London with Rupert than on the business issues the trip might create. At least Reese offered to have his assistant arrange for rooms at Rupert's usual hotel in London, taking one thing off Callum's plate.

It wasn't ideal, but between Reese, Garrick, and Jack, and it almost being the weekend, he thought he and Rupert could disappear for a few days without the whole world, or at least one professional hockey team, falling apart.

He wasn't as sure about Rupert. When Callum hadn't heard any sounds from the bedroom in a while, he ducked his head through the partially open door, expecting Rupert to be passed out or in some kind of catatonic state of anxiety.

Instead, he found Rupert completely naked except for an obscenely tight pair of black briefs that barely stretched across his fucking magnificent ass.

Holy sweet baby Jesus.

With a jerk, Callum stumbled back into the living room, taking deep, even breaths and thanking god Rupert's back had been turned. And not just because of the view, which was— was—*holy fucking shit.* No, it was good that Rupert hadn't seen him and had no idea Callum was standing here, practically hyperventilating, while trying to force his heart rate back to normal.

He reached down and rearranged his dick, absolutely without whimpering, then straightened his shoulders and rapped his knuckles against the door frame. He jumped when the door immediately opened to reveal Rupert in freshly pressed slacks and a tight white undershirt that hugged his biceps and pecs in ways that totally were not sexy.

Liar.

Jesus, how long had Callum been standing there if Rupert had time to get dressed? And how hard did Rupert hit the gym? He was leaner than Callum, but holy cow, he was really *fit.*

Callum shook his head to clear it, then met Rupert's enquiring gaze. "Do you need anything?" he asked inanely, like he was going to be able to do much for Rupert when they were standing in *his* apartment.

"No, I'm accustomed to travel," Rupert returned, possibly even more inanely.

Poor Oliver. His rescuers were a couple of world-class idiots.

"Okay. I suggest you give Reese a call before he pops a major blood vessel."

Rupert rolled his eyes. "He worries."

Which was sweet, really. "And try to get some rest. I'll arrange a taxi and wake you up when it's time to go to the airport."

"You need sleep, too."

"I'll take a nap here," he said, waving at the couch that had to be at least six inches shorter than he was tall.

Miraculously, Rupert agreed without comment and disappeared back into his room. That, more than anything, made Callum worry. Rupert never did *anything* Callum asked without a comment.

A few very short hours later, the first hints of dawn brightened the horizon and Callum knocked on Rupert's door. And again, it opened immediately, revealing a perfectly pressed Rupert. It was pretty obvious he hadn't slept at all.

Worse, he seemed to be even more lost in that fog. Callum actually missed the bitchy, quick-witted, and silver-tongued Rupert. That guy got shit done, which would be really fucking helpful right about now.

Callum juggled their luggage while prodding Rupert out the door, into a taxi, and through the airport. Once they made it to the gate, he settled Rupert into a chair. Callum was sorely tempted to poke at him about being useless, but the slumped shoulders and enormous shadows under his pinched eyes killed the caustic remark on the tip of Callum's tongue. He told himself to be patient.

"You need to eat something. Breakfast is the most important meal of the day," Callum declared, because apparently he was going to deal with this by turning into his mother.

"I'm fine."

"It wasn't a suggestion," he said, his well of patience and compassion running dry in under ten seconds. Possibly a new record.

Rupert frowned, but nodded grudgingly.

Callum considered it a victory of shut-out proportions when he successfully cajoled Rupert into eating a banana and drinking some tea.

As he took the last sip, Rupert made a face.

"What now?"

"Canadians have no idea how to make tea," Rupert said petulantly.

Callum laughed at his pissy expression, relieved to see something other than blank shock on Rupert's face. "We'll get you some more as soon as we reach the motherland, okay, duchess?"

Rupert grimaced. "Are you ever going to stop calling me that?"

Callum pretended to think about it for all of two seconds.

"No."

Chapter Three

Rupert stuffed the stupidly small pillow between his head and the side of the airplane, trying to get comfortable as they reached cruising altitude somewhere above the Atlantic Ocean. He was well and truly exhausted, finally, and thought he might be able to sleep three or four hours before they arrived in London.

Callum was crammed in next to him, his broad shoulders laughably unsuited to the economy-class seat. Rupert's shoulders weren't a lot better, but if he leaned into his little corner, they could make it work. Jack had apologized for not being able to get them business class, but getting to London quickly was far more important than doing so comfortably.

All Rupert cared about at the moment was getting his brain to shut off. He closed his eyes, willing himself asleep and almost succeeding before Callum spoke.

"When was the last time you saw him?"

Rupert considered pretending he hadn't heard, but doubted Callum would buy it. "Almost a year ago."

"Was that for your father's funeral?"

"No, about six months after, but I was back in London to take care of some things to do with the estate," he said, intentionally vague. He wasn't the least bit interested in explaining how he'd assumed his father's mantle and all that went along with that. "In hindsight, I can see how easy I made it for Lydia—Oliver's mom, that is. She had plenty of warning to be in town and to ensure she and Oliver presented a good picture. It was only later I learned that week was the longest she'd been in London in years."

"Even before your father died?"

"Yes, even before. They weren't really..." Rupert sighed. Callum looked at him curiously, not a whiff of judgment on his face. "When my father was diagnosed with cancer, he came to see me. He was, in some regards, very old-fashioned. When he learned he was sick, he was suddenly very concerned with his legacy."

Callum remained silent, not questioning the seemingly random subject change.

"He wanted to talk to me about carrying on the family name and all that nonsense. And, of course, I had to tell him he was out of luck, what with me being gay."

"How old were you?"

"I'm not sure. Thirty, maybe?"

"He didn't know already?"

"No. Not that it was a secret or anything. I've been out to anyone who cared to know or ask for a very long time. My father never fell into either of those categories, I suppose, until he was diagnosed."

"Oh." A complicated series of expressions crossed Callum's face before he managed to get control of it. It was likely hard for someone with a family like Callum's to understand that not everyone had what he and his army of siblings had grown up with.

"Yes, well, I've never lived with him," Rupert continued, not sure why he felt compelled to explain. "Not since I was a small child, and even then not really. He was very supportive once I told him, wished me well and all that. We had a nice visit, actually. Then he left. I never guessed he'd go off and do something stupid."

"Which was?"

"Impregnate the first woman he could find who was willing to marry him in order to serve as his broodmare, I think."

"Oh, wow."

"Oh, yes. And thus we have *Lydia*."

"Can I ask what happened to your mom?"

"Sorry. Yes, of course. She died when I was very young. I don't even remember her, sadly."

46

"I'm sorry."

Rupert gave a stilted nod, always uncomfortable with the condolences people, even strangers, expressed over his mother's passing. He'd never known what it was to have a mother, but their sympathy, their almost tangible sorrow over what he'd lost, made him wonder what they knew and he did not.

"Who did you live with?"

Rupert had lost the thread of their conversation in his wandering thoughts. "What?"

"You said you didn't live with your father. And your mother died. Who raised you?"

Rupert shrugged. "A nanny or two until I was five, then I was old enough for boarding schools."

Callum mouthed the word *five,* clearly struggling to comprehend a child being sent off to school so young, but his tone remained neutral. "That must have been hard."

"It wasn't what I wanted for Oliver. My father showed a remarkable interest in raising Oliver, even while he was sick and getting increasingly weak. I think he hoped to live long enough to see Oliver safely off to school. I had hoped they'd have more time together than that. I'm not sure my father could have shipped Oliver off, when the time came," Rupert admitted, sounding embarrassingly wistful.

"Oliver was three when our father died, having taken a rapid turn for the worse when we'd begun to hope he was getting better. I'd agreed to be Oliver's guardian, should anything happen, and Lydia had been given a lot of money to bugger off. Sadly, my father had not foreseen how quickly she could burn through her severance. Thus, I presume, her charade to keep Oliver so that I would give her additional funds after my father's passing. And I let her get away with it. I thought Oliver had his mother, and the nanny who had been with him for years. That had to be better than coming to live with me. I never thought—"

His voice broke and he turned to stare fixedly at the seat in front of him. There was no reason to air every piece of his familial dirty laundry to Callum Morrison, of all people. Rupert collected himself before continuing.

"Not long after I left London a year ago, I got a call from Jessica, the nanny. Lydia was *never* home, would disappear for weeks or months and sometimes forget to make sure Jessica had access to money to feed and clothe Oliver, let alone be paid herself. When Lydia did reappear, it was for a day or two at most, and she rarely saw, or even spoke to Oliver. There was no one to cover for Jessica, so she'd been working around the clock since my father died, all with the promise there would be more help coming. Jessica wanted to know why I wouldn't let Lydia hire anyone else. I immediately called Lydia, of course, who answered her cell, drunk or high, music blasting in the background. She hung up on me."

The anger returned, as fresh and hot as the day it had happened. It felt good, now. Better than the maudlin fugue he'd been in since Callum had started asking questions.

"It all devolved quickly after that. I flew to London, but by the time I arrived, Jessica had been fired and Lydia and Oliver were nowhere to be found. I spent a week searching for them, then hired Nick to find them. That was almost six months ago."

"We'll get him back, Rupert. By tomorrow night, he'll be with you. Safe. I promise," Callum said with conviction, his deep voice soothing. Rupert knew better than anyone that it wasn't a promise Callum could make, but he appreciated it nonetheless.

Callum's gaze was sincere, if heavy with exhaustion. He hadn't slept the night before either, and he'd been terribly kind to offer to come along at all. Kinder still to herd Rupert through getting ready for the trip.

Rupert smiled when, between one blink and the next, Callum fell asleep, his bright green eyes disappearing, leaving a thick fringe of dark lashes against cheeks that, from this close, Rupert could see still hinted at the freckles that must have once dusted his skin.

He looked younger like this. Rupert could now imagine what he must have looked like before he'd gotten the long scar across his forehead. Or done whatever foolish things he'd done to merit the bump across the bridge of his nose.

They gave him character, those marks. Not that he was short on that, Rupert thought with a wry smile. Loudmouthed, highhanded, and singularly annoying, Callum had more *character* than one man had a right to. How he'd ended up on this plane, haring off to London on no notice with a man he couldn't stand, was a complete mystery to Rupert.

But he was grateful.

Callum blinked gritty eyes against the bright sunset pouring through the window. Sunlight Rupert didn't appear to notice or care about, given that he was still asleep, his face pressed to the Plexiglas square. Callum had managed a brief nap after talking with Rupert, but had been woken by the drink cart banging into his shoulder not long after. He hadn't been able to fall back to sleep, spending most of the flight staring at the map on the screen in front of him or watching Rupert sleep.

Callum could only imagine how heavily the search for Oliver had weighed on Rupert, all while he was moving to Moncton and successfully taking over the management of the Ice Cats. Rupert's mini-meltdown over the past twenty-four hours seemed kind of understandable, given all that.

Callum waited until the landing gear was lowered before nudging Rupert awake. Callum's stomach did a weird twisty thing when Rupert's lashes fluttered, then two sleepy, light blue eyes settled on his face.

He could imagine waking up next to Rupert in bed in another life. A life Callum couldn't have.

Amazing how the anger, the bitterness, could still sneak up and bite him.

"Rise and shine, *duchess*," he said, because he was a jerk.

Rupert sighed and turned away, flipping two fingers in Callum's general direction. Callum knew perfectly well that wasn't a friendly "good morning."

"Now, that's not very nice."

Rupert ignored him, staring at his tray table like it might hold a message from on high. Possibly he wasn't much of a morning person, but it was more likely four hours of sleep wasn't enough to make up for all he'd missed.

And also, Callum *was* an asshole.

The plane bumped down onto the tarmac and they were officially in London. Sort of. Barring any disasters in immigration or customs. Callum silently reviewed everything he'd packed, then looked at Rupert.

"You didn't pack any sex toys or anything, did you?"

Rupert gave him a blank look. "What?"

"Nothing," Callum grumbled, checking his wallet and the pocket in front of him for stuff. He ran a hand over his hair, felt how it stood on end, and hoped he wouldn't frighten the other passengers.

Rupert had somehow spent the night smashed against the fuselage of an airplane and still had not a hair out of place. How the hell was his shirt not even wrinkled, let alone covered in drool?

"You suck," Callum said grumpily.

"Only if he asks nicely."

Callum blinked stupidly, struck dumb by the image that popped into his head, grateful that Rupert was temporarily distracted by dragging his laptop out from under the seat in front of him.

Then Rupert frowned at him. "Are you done insulting me, or do I have more of your scintillating repartee to look forward to?"

"Fuck you."

"You are a terrible human being."

Callum couldn't argue. "Guess you shouldn't have asked me along, then."

"*I didn't.*"

He had a point.

They took a taxi directly from Heathrow to the Marylebone neighborhood of London and the address Rupert had been given, but with the immigration and customs lines, and the always heavy traffic in and around the city, they didn't arrive until after ten o'clock at night.

Callum had decided to take his mother's advice about silence being the better part of valor and left Rupert to his own thoughts for most of that time. But as he chased Rupert through the door of 37 Chiltern Street and up three flights of stairs, he realized they probably should have come up with a plan.

Rupert knocked on the door of apartment 3b. Callum barely had time to pull Rupert's bag from his shoulder and heft it over his own before a gorgeous, miniature Rupert answered the door.

"Rupert!" the boy cried, flinging himself against Rupert's legs.

"Oliver! Oh, thank god."

A muttered "oh shit" issued from the apartment a second before the television cut off. Rupert was trying to peel Oliver from around his legs when a frantic young woman, a girl, really, appeared in the doorway and grabbed Oliver by the collar.

Rupert curled around Oliver, protecting him. Callum wrapped a hand around her wrist until she let go.

"We're coming in," he said, forcing her back into the apartment and nearly toppling Rupert and Oliver in the process. This, at least, convinced Oliver to release his brother long enough for everyone to step into the apartment and close the door behind them.

Callum stopped short, taking in their surroundings. "How much money are you giving her?"

Rupert's face was thunderous as he looked around at the shabby, ancient furniture and inhaled the unmistakable reek of cigarette smoke. It was a nice neighborhood, a nice apartment once, but clearly no love or attention had gone into it in a very long time.

The young woman jerked her hand in Callum's grasp. "Let go!"

"What's your name?"

She seemed surprised he cared. "Grainne. Who are you?"

It would be just Callum's luck if she was one of the exactly fifteen die-hard NHL fans in England. "A friend of Rupert's. How old are you?"

Grainne's chin came up. "Eighteen."

Debatable, at best. More like sixteen, he'd guess.

Rupert, now with Oliver wrapped around only one leg, said, "Call Lydia. Tell her I'm here."

"No fucking way," Grainne said succinctly.

Callum would be the first to admit he had a mouth like a trucker—or, more to the point, a hockey player—but he didn't abide swearing in front of children, his parents, or the clergy. Grainne twisted her wrist and he realized how tightly he was holding on now. He immediately let go.

Rather than go for Oliver again, she spun and disappeared down the hallway without a word.

"What now?" Callum asked Rupert. Because yeah, a plan would have been a good idea.

Grainne returned with a backpack over her shoulder and made a beeline for the door.

"Where are you going?" Callum demanded.

"I'm just the night help," she replied, as if that answered anything. "Mary will be here at eight. I haven't any idea where his mother is, I haven't any way to reach her, and I wouldn't sign up for the abuse even if I did. You can have him."

They could have *him?*

"Oh, and he hasn't had his supper yet," she added helpfully before she darted through the door and shut it in their faces.

Callum and Rupert stared at it, then each other for a long moment.

"Okay," Rupert said at last, "I'll phone Nick. Have him contact Lydia."

Callum nodded, happy one of them had managed to come up

with a next step. He smiled down at the suspicious blue eye peering up at him from behind Rupert's leg and slowly moved closer, pausing when that eye got wider.

He knelt, still a good five feet away. "Oliver, I'm Callum."

Oliver didn't so much as blink.

Rupert stroked a tentative hand over Oliver's head. "He's a friend of mine, Oliver. He came here with me to make sure you're okay."

Rupert tried to take a step but Oliver held on like a burr.

Callum shuffled a little closer on his knees. "Rupert and I are going to keep you safe, Oliver. Okay? You don't have to worry," he promised as he reached out with a hand, running it over Oliver's soft hair and Rupert's fingers.

Oliver watched him, silent and intent, and slowly loosened his hold on Rupert.

"That's it," Callum said softly. "I won't let anything bad happen to you. Not ever. We just want to take care of you. Keep you safe."

Suddenly, Callum's arms were full. Skinny arms and legs clamped around his neck and ribs.

He sat back on his heels, releasing a long breath and burying his face in the soft curls tickling under his chin. "Thank you, Oliver. You've been very brave. It's going to be okay, I promise," he said, rocking gently, pressing one hand across Oliver's back, his other arm wrapped around his tiny waist. He was so thin, shaking silently in Callum's arms. Callum held on as tight as he dared.

None of the tension left Oliver's little frame, his grip never easing. Callum felt helpless as he looked up at Rupert.

He'd seen Rupert angry, frustrated, panicked. But never had he seen this tenderness. Callum's stomach did that weird twisty thing again, and he had to force himself not to look away.

Eventually, Rupert cleared his throat and pulled his phone from his pocket. "I should call."

"Okay, I'll see about some food."

Rupert smiled gratefully. "Thanks."

Rupert stepped into the hallway, but Callum stayed where he was for a while longer, running his hand over Oliver's hair and saying whatever came to mind. Mostly rambling about how much Rupert loved Oliver and how he was going to take good care of him forever.

Oliver clung, unmoving and silent. When Callum stood, Oliver held on, which was fine. Callum didn't want to let go yet, either.

There was almost no food in the kitchen or the tiny fridge, and what there was, Callum could barely identify. He was fairly certain, though, that he didn't want Marmite for supper.

He was standing in the open refrigerator door when Rupert returned and put a hand low on Callum's back. It was the first time Rupert had ever intentionally touched him, and Callum wanted to lean back into it, into Rupert.

"The hotel is less than a mile from here," Rupert said, obviously coming to the same conclusions as Callum about their dinner prospects. "Let's get settled there and order some room service."

Callum tucked his chin to look into Oliver's face. "You okay if we leave here?"

Oliver nodded.

"Great. Let's get you packed up."

It took five minutes and three grocery sacks, Oliver still holding tight to Callum through it all. There was not a single book and almost no toys to bring with them.

When Callum knelt on all fours to retrieve a Matchbox car from under the coffee table, Oliver clinging to his chest, Rupert chuckled.

Callum grinned up at him. "I feel like a monkey."

"What?"

"You know, how the babies hold onto their parent's fur and hitch a ride until they're old enough to go out on their own?"

Rupert laughed. "It's kind of adorable."

Callum actually *blushed.* He quickly turned back to the packing.

Soon they were in a taxi and on their way with Oliver's meager belongings. When they pulled up in front of Claridge's, Oliver looked up with awe and Callum almost whimpered with anticipation. He needed to eat something, and then he was going to fall on his face, dead asleep. If his team's trainers had any idea of how far he'd fallen off the training and nutrition plan wagon in the past twenty-four hours, they'd have a collective seizure.

No one in the swanky hotel's even swankier lobby appeared bothered by Callum's ratty jeans, eau d' airport scent, or four-year-old passenger. The bellmen took their bags without blinking and the front desk seemed delighted to greet them, in spite of the late hour.

It wasn't until they were confirming two rooms and Oliver starting clinging tighter than ever, practically choking Callum, that Callum realized they might have a problem.

"Uh, Rupert?"

Rupert glanced at him, distracted. "Yes?"

"I don't think my little monkey is going to let go. Like, anytime soon."

Rupert stared at him for a moment. "Oh."

The idea of forcefully trying to pry Oliver away made Callum's stomach churn. He turned to the woman behind the counter. "Do you have anything with two beds?"

She pecked at her computer, frowning. "I'm sorry, gentlemen, but you've booked the last rooms we had available. Your suite," she said to Rupert, "has a king bed, a pull-out couch, and a kitchenette, if that helps?"

"We'll just take that, then," Callum answered when Rupert failed to make any sounds the first three times he opened his mouth.

Rupert led the way to the hotel room, their footsteps muffled by the thick hallway carpet. He kept wondering when Oliver would nod off, but he was wide-eyed, watching everything from his relatively high vantage point against Callum's chest.

The room itself was large by London standards, but still way too small by any standard that would allow Rupert to comfortably share a hotel room with Callum.

And the couch was laughable. More of a loveseat, really, and the pullout was certain to include the standard metal bar designed to dig into someone's back all night. Callum collapsed onto the striped cushions, instantly making it look even smaller and fussier.

"Are you okay? Is the monkey thing getting to you?" Rupert asked guiltily, partly because Callum was doing all the heavy lifting, literally, but also because Rupert was shamefully relieved he wasn't the one Oliver had turned to for comfort. Rupert suspected he'd be terrible at it. He'd never spent any time with children. Not even when he'd been one.

"I feel like I've been awake for two days straight," Callum groaned.

"You *have* been awake for two days straight."

Even Callum's smile was tired. "I guess I'm doing okay, then, all things considered. This papa monkey is starving, though."

"Right, I have just the thing," Rupert said, turning toward the kitchen to find the room service menu. His eyes fell on the complimentary fruit basket and he smiled.

He presented the banana to Callum with a flourish.

Callum's laughter was a remarkably warm and engaging sound. "Thanks," he said, taking the proffered fruit. "This can be the first course."

They made quick work of ordering proper meals. The only delay was finding something Oliver would agree to eat besides the half of the banana Callum shared with him. Rupert had no idea what the boy liked, and he still wouldn't speak, so Rupert read off the options and Oliver shook his head or nodded accordingly. Rupert thought children were supposed to be picky about what they ate, but he had no idea if it was normal for a four year old to choose eggs and bacon over macaroni and cheese.

What he did know was that it was far too late for Oliver to be awake. Sitting down next to Callum, Rupert looked into Oliver's little face. Oliver stared back. He really did look a lot like their father. And like himself, he supposed.

"Will you let go of Callum long enough to change into your pajamas?"

Oliver shook his head.

Callum's big hand stilled the motion. "Ollie, I like holding onto you—will all night if you want—but I need to shower, and you need to get ready for bed. Afterwards, we can eat supper in our pajamas, okay?"

Oliver hesitated, his eyes darting across the room. Rupert followed his gaze, then smiled tentatively. "Do you need to use the toilet?"

He nodded quickly, and when Rupert stood, Oliver jumped off Callum like he hadn't spent the past hour acting as if he'd been sewn to Callum's shirt.

Oliver's hand felt tiny in Rupert's. It was a bit frightening, actually.

When they arrived at the bathroom door, Rupert had no idea what to do.

"Do you need help?"

Oliver shot him a deeply offended look and shut the door in his face.

Rupert looked over helplessly at a grinning Callum.

"Do you think he'll be okay in there?" Rupert asked.

"I'm sure he'll be fine. The worst that can happen is we'll have to do some clean up," Callum said with a dismissive wave for what Rupert thought was a fairly horrifying idea. "I'm more concerned about the silence," Callum said quietly.

Rupert swallowed. "I am, too."

"He said your name when he opened the door, at least."

"Yes. I'm sort of clinging to that right now, to be honest."

Callum dragged himself up off the couch and crowded into the tiny hallway with Rupert. "He's going to be okay." It sounded more like a vow than just an observation. "He's scared. We'll get him through it. Find him help if it's needed."

Rupert was appalled to feel his eyes sting. "God, do you think he needs help? I mean, more than I, than we—"

His voice strangled off when Callum pulled him close, long arms wrapping around his ribs until their bodies were flush, Callum's warmth, his strength, seeping into Rupert. The air trapped in his chest rushed from him in a shuddering sigh. Callum held him tighter.

Rupert had never been given a hug like this before, so completely sure and strong. It was bloody marvelous.

"It hasn't even been two hours," Callum pointed out sensibly, obviously trying to be reassuring. And he was.

Rupert wondered if there was something wrong with him that he needed Callum Morrison, of all people, to help him get his head on straight.

He took deep breath to center himself and stepped out of Callum's embrace just as the bathroom door popped opened to reveal Oliver looking up at them curiously. Rupert set to mentally drafting a list of what needed to happen in the next hour, the process alone making him feel more stable.

Having decided on the first steps, he spoke briskly. "Dinner will be here soon. Callum, if you don't mind, I'll just sneak in before you."

"That's fine. Oliver and I will find his PJs," Callum offered, as if he, too, could see Rupert's list.

Callum put out his hand and Oliver climbed right up and settled back against Callum's chest. Rupert understood perfectly, now, why Oliver chose to cling to Callum.

Rupert shut the bathroom door on the picture of Oliver snuggling into Callum and Callum's warm smile in return. He told himself he was not in any way jealous.

By the time he came out again, he'd mentally reviewed every

highhanded, stubborn, or insulting thing Callum had done in the past week and was feeling more sure-footed. Rupert knew how to deal with incredibly annoying Callum. It was easier than tender, gentle Callum, who made Rupert feel confused and unsteady.

He frowned at the mess in the corner of the room where Callum had dropped his open suitcase on the floor and apparently sifted through its entire contents, spilling half of them onto the floor. Meanwhile, Oliver's belongings were missing, except a small pile of clothes by Callum's knee.

Callum looked over his shoulder at Rupert, his eyes tracing thoughtfully over Rupert's chest, causing an entirely inappropriate response that Rupert clamped down on ruthlessly.

"Do you have an undershirt I can borrow?" Callum asked.

"I don't think it will fit," he said, ever the master of understatement.

Callum smiled. "It's not for me," he explained, gesturing at Oliver.

Rupert pulled the luggage rack from the closet—spotting Oliver's bags in the back and noting the smoky stench coming from them—then tucked it into a corner and put his suitcase on top. Ignoring Callum's smirk, he carefully extricated a t-shirt, then watched in awe as Callum made quick work of stripping Oliver down to his underpants and pulling the clean shirt over his head. The sleeves fell to his fingertips, the hem almost to the floor. Callum quickly tied a knot on one side to ensure Oliver wouldn't trip.

Rupert felt incredibly inadequate. "How on earth do you even know how to do that?"

"Six siblings, most of them younger than me," he reminded Rupert. "I can make a nightshirt, an art smock, or a beach cover-up in the blink of an eye."

Rupert looked at Callum, amazed.

Callum rolled his eyes. "They're all the same thing, Rupert. Never underestimate the value of a cheap white t-shirt when you have kids around."

Rupert tried to smile, to share the joke, but instead the truth burst out of him. "I have no idea what I'm doing."

Oliver immediately climbed into Callum's lap and hid his face against Callum's neck. Callum ran a reassuring hand down his back and frowned up at Rupert. "Remember what I told you after the walk-through?"

That seemed like an incredibly random change of topic. Then it clicked.

Never let them see your fear.

Callum nodded. "Same goes for kids. Especially right now."

"But—"

"You're doing fine," Callum said firmly.

Hearing Callum say it was heartening, if not convincing. Callum was so confident. Calm. And bloody good with kids, obviously. Rupert wished *he* could climb into Callum's lap, wrap his arms and legs around Callum's reassuringly solid body, and be the little monkey for a while.

The idea was simultaneously terrifying and hilarious.

Rupert smiled and Callum nodded, apparently pleased with Rupert's effort to buck up. He pulled Rupert down to sit on the couch.

"I'm going to shower," Callum said, then whispered something in Oliver's ear.

Oliver sprang from Callum's arms, bounced off the couch cushion by Rupert's hip, and landed on his chest. The air left Rupert's lungs with an "oof," then Oliver's strong little limbs were curling around him, hugging him tight, and Rupert couldn't breathe at all.

He looked up at Callum as something fierce and hot bloomed in his chest.

Callum smiled. "There you go."

Chapter Four

The water was tepid, the pressure a joke, and the stall clearly designed for someone roughly half his size, but this was possibly the best shower Callum had ever taken in his entire life. He'd just needed these few minutes to *think*.

Rupert was freaking out. He was trying to hide it, but it had been as clear as day to Callum since they'd found Oliver in that dingy apartment. Oliver, unfortunately, sensed it, too, clinging to Callum while his brother got his shit together. Callum didn't mind, of course, but he also wanted to help Rupert. He just had no idea how.

He took a few extra minutes in the bathroom to do some laundry for Oliver, his brain running through ways to bolster Rupert's confidence, but mostly concluding he was too tired to come up with anything useful. Even when fully rested, he had an almost preternatural ability to piss Rupert off, so he probably shouldn't try anything when he was half dead on his feet.

He rinsed out the one outfit and underclothes he'd plucked from Oliver's bags earlier, after discovering everything reeked of smoke, and left them draped over the heated towel bar to dry.

Dinner was waiting when Callum came out of the bathroom in a t-shirt and sweatpants, having not packed pajamas on the assumption he would have his own hotel room. Rupert had also changed while Callum was out of the room, but *his* pajamas were a cliché. Button-up top and long pants in a blue that perfectly matched his eyes, cotton pressed and barely wrinkled after their long journey. It was ridiculous, really, but for some reason it made Callum smile stupidly. They were just so *Rupert.*

Callum had a perverse urge to run over to Rupert and mess up his hair. To do *something* that would ruffle his tidy image, just to see what would happen.

That probably went back to his talent for pissing the man off.

They sat down to dinner and Callum focused on getting

enough food into Oliver before he nodded off. As soon as he took his last bite, Oliver crawled into Callum's lap and fell asleep with his beautiful little face pressed to Callum's sternum.

Rupert and Callum finished their meals at a more civilized pace.

"He trusts you," Rupert said quietly.

Callum smiled down at Oliver, making a mental note that the first order of business tomorrow was a bath to get rid of the lingering smell of smoke. "He's a sweet kid. He trusts you, too."

"He doesn't," Rupert said. "And I don't blame him. I left him alone, with *her*, for months—"

Callum wrapped his hand around Rupert's wrist and squeezed, hoping to stem the tide of self-recrimination. "It's done. It's what you do next that matters."

Rupert frowned, staring at his plate. "I keep wondering what my father would want me to do. Send Oliver away to school? He seems so *young*. I suppose he'd tell me to find a nanny to raise him until he was ready to go. But I don't know." He looked up at Callum beseechingly. "What *do* I do now?"

How was this not completely fucking obvious? *"Love him."*

"But *how*?"

Callum ached to grab Rupert and shake him until he woke the fuck up. The lost look on his face, though, held Callum back. Maybe Callum was finally getting the hang of *not* pissing Rupert off. Or maybe he simply didn't have enough functioning brain cells left to tackle this now.

"Time for bed," Callum announced, standing, his precious cargo still attached.

Rupert took a moment to regroup. "Yes, about that. You should take the bed."

"I plan to."

Rupert grimaced, but nodded before turning away to tidy up the kitchen and their dishes. Callum was completely unsurprised to learn Rupert was a neat freak.

Callum turned off lights and checked the door locks, then

climbed onto the bed, carefully peeling Oliver away enough to lie on his side with Oliver tucked close.

Rupert dithered a little longer in the kitchen. The bathroom. Then began dragging the coffee table out of the way of the couch.

Callum sighed and rolled his eyes.

"Get over here."

"Pardon me?" Rupert said, all snotty and prim.

Callum had no idea why that made him want to smile. "Come *here*, duchess."

Rupert appeared, scowling, on the other side of the bed. Callum waved at the empty half of the mattress. "Just sleep here. We both need some decent rest and I promise you, even without a four year old between us, I would be far too tired to jump your bones tonight."

Which kind of sounded like any other night, it might have happened. *Whoops.*

Rupert cocked his head, studying Callum's hot cheeks, then, thank Christ, turned off the one remaining lamp and lay down. When the bed dipped beneath Rupert's weight, Oliver blinked sleepily, looked over his shoulder briefly, and promptly fell back to sleep.

Rupert scooted closer, curving around Oliver in a mirror image of Callum, their knees an inch apart, a tiny furnace curled up between them.

Callum thought it should be uncomfortable. Too intimate. But he was too tired to worry about that tonight.

He closed his eyes and for some damn reason, pictured Rupert in his tight black briefs.

In a blink, he was asleep.

Rupert woke with a very small foot of questionable cleanliness pressed to his cheek, another digging into his ribs. When he managed to pry his eyes open, he found Callum curled up facing him, and Oliver spread out like a starfish on top of them both.

Rupert chuckled. Who knew a four year old could take up that much room?

Callum's eyes fluttered open and he smiled, the same half smile he'd worn when he'd fallen asleep the night before. Rupert had wondered what he'd been thinking about. How anyone could look so content.

Oliver wiggled and Callum grinned as Rupert carefully moved Oliver's foot before those little toes found their way into Rupert's nose.

"Good morning," Callum murmured, his voice rough and unfairly sexy with sleep.

Rupert barely managed an intelligible response and a reasonably composed retreat to the bathroom. He felt more in control once he'd showered and made himself presentable again. He and Callum even managed to get Oliver up, bathed, and dressed in his one clean outfit without any major disasters.

Rupert judged it a triumph.

When Callum said, "Let's go get some breakfast," Oliver's head popped up off Callum's chest and he looked eager. Almost smiled, even.

Rupert and Callum exchanged a glance, waiting, *hoping* for some sound. Rupert was starting to fear his brother had been through more than Rupert knew. The idea made him frantic. Because he wanted to fix it. And because he didn't feel at all prepared to help a child recover from untold trauma. What if Rupert made it worse? He was doomed to make mistakes. How could he not? He was so utterly *clueless.* Oliver needed someone who could help him. Someone like Callum. Not *Rupert.*

"You two go ahead," Rupert said suddenly. "I need to make a couple phone calls, but I'll meet you downstairs in the lobby in five minutes."

Callum wrapped a protective arm around Oliver's back. "You're not going to—"

"I'm going to do what's right, Callum. What's best for him. I promise."

Callum pointedly ignored the couple in the elevator who stared at Oliver in his arms, their eyes raking over his too-short pants and ratty t-shirt. They could go to hell. He was just a little boy. One who needed a family to care for him. Who needed Rupert to pull his head out of his ass and love him unconditionally.

Callum was pretty sure Rupert needed that kind of love from Oliver as much as he needed to give it. What Callum didn't know was if Rupert knew that, or if he realized what an incredibly lucky son of a bitch he was.

By the time they reached the ground floor, Callum was doing deep breathing exercises to force himself to calm the fuck down. He had to believe Rupert would do the right thing.

He stalked to one of the leather chairs in the middle of the foyer so Oliver could stare at the opulent art deco lobby while Callum kept one eye on the elevators. He spared a polite nod for the two other men seated around the low table, but was too preoccupied to even make an attempt at conversation.

Callum held Oliver close, rubbing one hand between his shoulders, soothing himself as much as Oliver. Callum's own shoulders ached, and knew he had to be careful not to put too much strain on his back, but he couldn't put Oliver down. And, on the bright side, his trainers back in Colorado would be delighted with the impact on his core strength.

The summer seemed too short this year, though he still had months before he was due back. He should be looking forward to training camp. To getting back out on the ice with his team, putting his head down, and focusing on the game. The season should be stretched out before him with endless possibilities.

He was sure he'd get there eventually, but right now, he couldn't see past the next few hours. Days. To getting Oliver settled into his new life with Rupert.

And if Rupert didn't like that plan, Callum would damn well convince him.

As if summoned, the elevator doors parted to reveal Rupert.

Clothes pressed. Hair perfectly coiffed. Expression determined. Callum watched as he veered off to the concierge's desk without seeing them.

"Good lord, David, look at that. His bum should be in a museum."

Callum shot a startled glance at the man to his right, who was staring at Rupert's backside with frank admiration. His friend—David, apparently—nudged him. "Careful, love. Not everyone sees things the way you do," he murmured, nodding at Callum.

The man turned to look at Callum, the quirk of his lips knowing. "He's already noticed, dear. That's why *I* looked."

Callum's cheeks burned. He'd been trying very hard not to notice anything of the sort. Not when Rupert rolled out of bed that morning. Or when he'd come out of the bathroom wearing only a tight t-shirt and those flawlessly tailored slacks that pulled *just so* across his hips. And definitely not when he'd bent over his suitcase to retrieve a pale purple shirt that made his blue eyes glow.

Rupert's eyes, of course, being another thing Callum had absolutely not noticed.

"Oh my god," David groaned as Rupert bent forward to look at something on the concierge's desk. "That *bubble*. How is that even legal? It's a weapon of mass seduction."

Callum grunted, a noise of surprised agreement slipping from him before he could contain it. The men beside him actually tilted their heads to and fro, examining Rupert's ass like a prized piece of art.

Which it sort of was. But it wasn't *their* piece of art, Callum thought irritably, rolling his tight shoulders.

Which was ridiculous. It wasn't like Rupert was his, or that he wanted him to be, or that it was the remotest of possibilities even if he *did* want that. Him. Rupert.

Which he didn't.

Rupert turned, found them across the room, and smiled.

David sucked in an audible breath. "Oh my."

David's friend realized who Rupert was smiling at and shot Callum a look that he was pretty sure meant *lucky bastard.*

Callum smirked, smug when he had no right to be, and stood as Rupert approached.

Rupert had hoped getting out of their room would give Oliver something to talk about. To say. But he remained silent. They had chosen to keep things simple and eat in the hotel's dining room, and Oliver seemed content to sit in his own chair, eat his breakfast, and look around. Rupert worried that the silence would become sullen or turn to anger, but Oliver appeared to be remarkably easy-going, despite all the changes happening around him.

Rupert sincerely hoped that would continue for the foreseeable future.

Thanks to his phone calls upstairs, they only had two hours, and Rupert still didn't know what the right thing to do was. More and more, he knew what he wanted, but he wasn't convinced it was what was best for Oliver.

"After breakfast, we need to go see a friend of mine," Rupert began carefully.

Oliver's eyes narrowed suspiciously. So did Callum's.

"He's actually an old friend of father's, Oliver," Rupert continued. He looked at Callum. "Our attorney," he explained, wishing they would stop staring holes through him. "He's arranged a meeting with—"

Rupert stopped before saying Lydia's name. He wished Oliver didn't have to see her today, not if he didn't want to, but Rupert didn't know how he could possibly prevent it. He had, more or less, taken the child from her custody without warning or notice yesterday, about which he'd already been lectured over the phone by his attorney and harangued via voicemail by Lydia.

He didn't regret it in the slightest, of course, but it meant they had to present themselves for inspection today.

Callum cocked his head, studying Rupert's face, and Rupert stared back, trying to tell him everything silently. He'd read plenty of books with parents who could have entire silent conversations in front of their children. Judging by Callum's blank look, this was either a learned skill, pure fiction, or Rupert and Callum didn't have the necessary magic.

While Oliver watched a waiter glide past with an enormous tray perched on his shoulder, Rupert mouthed *his mother* to Callum.

Already? Callum mouthed back.

Rupert nodded, freezing when Oliver turned back to the table. Rupert made a show of sipping his tea. Oliver gave him a suspicious look regardless.

Callum frowned, then apparently decided the direct approach was best. "Ollie, your mother is back in London, and we're going to see her today. Is that okay with you?"

The clatter of Oliver's fork hitting his plate was loud in the quiet dining room. Callum pushed back his chair, reaching for Oliver, but he flung himself against Rupert's chest instead.

Rupert gathered him close. Callum smirked, and Rupert was pretty sure that was *I told you so* written all over his face.

Maybe Oliver did trust him. Rupert only wished he felt more worthy of it.

"We do have to see your mum today," Rupert began slowly. Oliver's arms tightened around his neck and Rupert stroked his back, rubbing Oliver's spine like he'd seen Callum do. "I don't want to rush you, but I need to know what you want. Can you tell me?"

Oliver shook his head and Rupert silently pleaded with Callum for help.

"Ollie," Callum said, "you know Rupert would never do anything to hurt you, right? That he only wants to do what's best for you?"

Oliver hesitated for a moment and Rupert's heart broke. Then Oliver nodded.

Rupert swallowed hard. How had he ever believed there was more than one possible outcome for this trip? At least as far as he was concerned. But he thought he should ask Oliver what he wanted, even while fearing it was too great a responsibility to put on a boy so young.

He decided to risk it. Callum had been honest with Oliver, and maybe that was the best approach.

"Oliver, if you had a choice, would you rather stay here with your mum, or come live with me?"

Oliver's head popped up and he looked right at Rupert, his blue eyes huge in his too-thin face.

"*You.*"

Callum smiled, almost dizzy with relief to hear that word, *any word*, come from Oliver's mouth. A huge grin spread across Rupert's face, and Callum's stomach did that funny twist.

"Great," Rupert said. He sounded hoarse, but like he really meant it. Rupert's expression dimmed, though, after a moment. "We still have to go see some people. And your mum will be there."

Oliver looked over his shoulder at Callum and frowned.

Callum smiled encouragingly. "Do you want to see her?"

Oliver shrugged, having apparently reverted to silence. Callum strongly suspected the answer was no, but that wasn't something a child could admit to easily. Oliver kept looking at Callum expectantly.

"Would you like me to go with you?" Callum guessed.

Oliver nodded quickly.

"Okay. I'll stay with you the entire time," he promised, silently vowing to keep his cool and do whatever he could to keep Oliver from witnessing the worst of what was likely to come. "And afterwards, we can go shopping. I thought we might buy you some new clothes. Maybe a book or two."

Oliver perked up at that suggestion and, with a little encouragement from Rupert, returned to his seat and started in on his breakfast again. Rupert and Callum shared another smile, but Rupert was quiet for the rest of the meal, mostly looking like he was preparing for battle. Callum let him be and told Oliver all about Moncton and the wonderful things he'd see and do there, searching for interesting stuff on his phone when he ran out of ideas.

By the end of breakfast, Callum thought when his hockey career ended, he could probably apply for a job with the Maritimes tourism board. Rupert, meanwhile, looked calm and resolved.

"Let's get this done with," Rupert said after he'd signed the bill.

They stood and Oliver grabbed Rupert's hand, attempting to climb him as he had Callum. Rupert staggered, obviously unprepared and having no idea how to help. Callum caught his elbow and steadied them against his chest as he boosted Oliver into place.

"Thanks," Rupert said as he shifted Oliver into a more comfortable position. Then he grimaced. "How's your back holding up?"

"Fine," Callum said. "Want me to take him?"

Rupert held on tighter. "No. Not yet."

Callum smiled and ran a hand over Oliver's hair. "Okay."

They caught a cab into the heart of the city, all too soon pulling up to an office building at the address Rupert had given. Oliver crawled from Rupert's lap into Callum's, and they climbed out of the car to stand on the sidewalk. Callum took a moment to collect himself, not unlike what he did to prepare for a big game. He needed to be calm. Focused. Centered.

This would be more complicated than time on the ice. There, he knew what people expected of him. What shots his opponents were likely to try. Here, all he knew was that he needed to be whatever Rupert and Oliver needed him to be.

And he had no idea what that was.

Callum pulled Rupert closer, so that they stared at each

other over the top of Oliver's head. Rupert curled his hands around Callum's biceps.

"I have no idea how this is going to go down," Rupert admitted.

"I know. We'll figure it out as we go. I've got your back."

Rupert smiled gratefully. "Thank you. But I think maybe…"

"What?"

Rupert's grip tightened. "I want you to promise that no matter what happens, you'll do whatever you think is best for him, not me." He looked down at Oliver. "Even if it means leaving with him. Walk right out. Just don't let him hear or see—"

"I got it. I promise." Some of Callum's hard-won equilibrium slipped. "We'll meet you back at the hotel."

Rupert shook his head. "No. If you have to leave, meet me in the Harrods Food Hall."

"I don't know where that is." Callum's nerves jumped he pieced together Rupert's intent. If they had to leave, Rupert didn't want them to be easily found. Not by anyone but him.

"Any taxi in this city will get you there. You can shop while you wait. Eat if you need to. I'll find you. Near the chocolates."

"Do they have kid's stuff? Aside from chocolate, that is."

Rupert laughed. "It's Harrods. You can buy an entire wardrobe, a house, a horse, the saddle, and a trailer. Oh, and lunch."

"I was thinking more along the lines of three outfits in size four," Callum said dryly.

Rupert smiled. "That, too."

"Okay," Callum said, wrapping one hand around Rupert's back and hugging Oliver between them. "Let's do this."

Rupert squeezed back, then they marched into the building like they knew what the fuck they were doing.

The receptionist leapt to her feet when Rupert entered the plush lobby on the top floor. "My lo—"

"Yes. Hello," Rupert said quickly, not even letting her finish.

"I believe we are expected."

"Yes, of course."

They were immediately ushered into a huge office with deep pile carpets and dark wood paneling. The view of St. Paul's out the window was stunning, but Callum hardly spared it a glance. He only had eyes for the incredibly young, beautiful woman leaping to her feet.

"Oliver!"

The boy in his arms turned to look at her, but his grip on Callum never wavered. Callum worried he might be forced to pry Oliver loose so he could say hello to his mother, but after that one maternal outburst, Lydia turned to the other men in the room without even attempting to hug Oliver, let alone check him over.

Callum hung back, hovering close to the door with his hands pressed across Oliver's back, as if he could shield him from the barrage of voices climbing higher in volume with each passing minute. After a particularly loud snipe from his mother, Oliver pressed his face to Callum's neck, and Callum tucked his chin to speak quietly to Oliver. He told him that Rupert would see to everything. That his brother loved him and wouldn't let anything bad happen. That if Oliver wanted to say anything, or tell Rupert something, he could.

Oliver gave no reaction, but Callum kept up the litany of reassurance, hoping to comfort the boy or, if nothing else, drown out the conversation swirling around them.

"Enough!" Rupert barked, slamming his hand down on the desk and bringing the conversation and everyone in the room to a halt. He was mesmerizing. Then Callum recognized the bright spots of pink on Rupert's cheeks, the set of his jaw, and knew shit was about to get real.

Callum started humming his father's favorite folk song into Oliver's ear. It sounded better when it was in tune. And on bagpipes. But Callum knew it backwards and forwards and could keep it going with half a thought.

Rupert looked at them. "You okay?"

Callum arched an eyebrow, but nodded. Rupert seemed to understand.

He turned back to the room. "There's a child in this room. The very boy you all are discussing as if he were so much chattel to be bargained for."

The men Callum didn't know, the ones he assumed were the lawyers, had the grace to appear embarrassed.

Lydia rolled her eyes. "He's just a baby, you idiot. He doesn't understand anything."

Callum's song skipped a beat, then continued. Louder.

It took Rupert a moment to get himself under control. Even Callum had never seen Rupert turn this particular shade of pink.

Callum was now singing loudly enough to be heard across the room. Lydia looked at him as if he were insane and probably very stupid. The attorneys exercised only marginally more restraint.

Rupert turned to the man whose office they appeared to be standing in, his face a mask of fury, his voice wintery. "Charles, is there any way in hell this woman can win custody?"

"It's unlikely," Charles began. He launched into a dissertation on the ins and outs of the law, barely audible over Lydia's screeching, her attorney keeping harmony only an octave lower.

Rupert turned his back on the circus and walked to Callum and Oliver.

"Oliver," Rupert said quietly, ducking his head to look into Oliver's face. "Do you want to say anything to your mum before you go?"

Oliver shook his head. Rupert smiled and ran his hand over Oliver's head, then grabbed Callum's shoulder and squeezed. "I'll find you," he said softly.

Callum didn't move. The weight of his promise battled with the worry of leaving Rupert to deal with this on his own.

Rupert sighed. "I know I've given you cause to think I'm a wimp," he began.

"No, I—"

"They can't touch me. They're not—*they* don't frighten me."

Callum was surprised by Rupert's tacit admission that *somebody* did, but saved his questions for another time. What mattered now was that it wasn't this pack of jackals. "I don't think you're a wimp," he said fiercely. "I just want you to feel safe."

Rupert's expression softened, and the hand on Callum's shoulder slid to his neck and squeezed. "Thank you," Rupert whispered. He glanced back at the rest of the room, then reached behind Callum and opened the door.

"Now run."

Callum did, already halfway down the hallway before the slamming door cut off the cacophony of shouting voices.

Three hours later, Rupert practically fell out of the taxi in front of Harrods. It had taken too damn long to get Lydia to agree to his offer, far longer than he ever would have guessed. She'd threatened lawsuits, kidnapping charges, and everything else she could think of.

But she'd never once asked the name of the man who'd taken Oliver away. Or where they'd gone. Or if Oliver was okay.

Rupert could have resolved their stand-off a lot faster by throwing more money at her. He had it to throw, and there was no worthier cause than making that hateful woman go away, but he couldn't stomach the idea of what felt like nothing more than *buying* Oliver from her.

His phone had rung two hours into their negotiations, and he'd been delighted to take the call from Nick. He'd found Grainne. And Mary. Both had been more than happy to receive their back wages from Rupert and tell Nick, in exacting detail, what Oliver's life had been like for the past months.

Rupert had only heard the highlights, but he considered it a towering achievement not to have flown across the room and wrung Lydia's neck. She wasn't worth it. She wasn't anything. She'd spent the sum total of approximately two weeks in Oliver's company, and now she was, thank god, *gone for good.* With nothing more than whatever she had tucked away in her bank accounts to show for it.

Good riddance.

His only consolation was that after hours of questioning, Nick was confident that neither of Oliver's caretakers—a term used loosely in this case, to be sure—had ever physically harmed him, or allowed anyone else to, either.

Rupert had made one quick stop at his father's—and now his, he supposed—bank to retrieve Oliver's passport and the official custodial documents from the safe deposit box. Even those additional fifteen minutes had been far too long. He should have come straight here.

Rupert ran into the Food Halls, dodging past the pastries and into the candy section, scanning the crowd. He found he desperately wanted to see them, to just lay eyes on Oliver and know that he was safe. Not that he doubted Callum for a moment, but he hated that he might have to wait. They were probably off doing some shopping. He'd only just texted Callum from the bank to say that everything was settled and he was on his way. He hadn't received any message back.

He almost missed Callum's familiar head of brown curls above broad, thick shoulders. He wove through the throngs of people and practically fell on Callum, who was sitting at a small cafe table, his feet stretched out before him, and Oliver passed out on his chest.

Callum looked up and smiled, and Rupert was struck dumb.

"How'd it go?" Callum asked.

Rupert shook his head to clear it and focused on Oliver, amazed the boy could sleep through the racket around them.

He belonged with Rupert now. Forever.

Rupert suddenly needed to sit down. It was good there was a chair behind him, because his legs didn't give him any choice. He landed with a thud.

Callum put a hand over Rupert's. "You okay?"

Rupert nodded slowly. "Yeah." Callum caught his eye, his

steady gaze calming. "Yes," Rupert said more confidently. "It's done. We can take him home."

Callum smiled. "Congratulations."

Rupert swallowed hard. He'd never been so elated. Or so terrified.

Callum tried to give Rupert some space while Callum and Oliver packed up the new clothes, books, and toys they'd picked out into Oliver's brand-new suitcase.

The little boy was still silent, but managed to convey his enthusiasm for the adventure of their trip to Canada. He was smiling more, even sitting and playing on his own, with some encouragement. But there was always one eye on Callum or Rupert. A hand on their knee. And the moment he thought he could get away with it, he was back in one of their laps, tucked up as close as he could get.

Callum didn't mind, and Rupert appeared to be enjoying it, though he still seemed surprised every time Oliver bounded into his lap or took his hand. Callum couldn't decide which was cuter, Rupert's flushed cheeks or Oliver's pleased smile.

Later in the afternoon, Callum left them in the room— Rupert sprawled out on the couch with Oliver sprawled out on top of him, both zoned out to the Octonauts on TV—while he went for a long run, then spent a solid hour in the hotel's gym. It didn't have everything he needed, but it was better than nothing. A half hour in the pool afterwards felt like heaven.

He was coming around the corner to their hotel room door when he heard a child crying, his sobs loud even out in the corridor. Callum broke into a run, fumbling his keycard and swearing as he bent to retrieve it. Goddamn it, he should just knock the damn door down.

He finally burst into the room and almost upended the heavily-laden room service cart holding their dinners. Rupert was on the couch, milk-white and wide-eyed, staring up at Callum. Oliver was in his arms, sobbing.

Callum knelt on the floor at Rupert's feet, his hand going to

Oliver's hair. "What happened?"

"I didn't—I wasn't—" Rupert patted Oliver's back rapidly, awkwardly trying to soothe his brother.

Callum pressed Rupert's trembling hand to Oliver's back. "Please tell me what happened."

"Oliver fell asleep and I needed to use the restroom. I didn't think—" Rupert's unsteady voice cut out. Callum wrapped a hand around the back of Rupert's neck, his thumb rubbing under Rupert's ear, and waited for him to collect himself.

"He didn't wake up when I slid him onto the couch," Rupert continued. "I should have woken him. I just thought after such a late night, he needed his rest."

"Of course."

"No, I didn't think. I shouldn't have closed the door. I'm so bloody stupid," he said furiously.

"You're not, Rupert. It's okay."

"It's not. It's not, Callum. He woke up and he was screaming. Not like this. Like...like you can't... *I've never heard anything like it.*" Something primal clenched deep in Callum's chest when Rupert's eyes filled with tears, his voice wrecked. "I tore out of the bathroom as fast as I could. It was like he didn't see me at first. I didn't know what to do, so I just grabbed him. I think I frightened him, but I'm afraid to let go. I'm trying to hold him the way you always do, but he won't stop. He won't stop crying."

Rupert's eyes pleaded with Callum to tell him he did the right thing. To forgive him.

Callum climbed up on the couch and pulled Rupert and Oliver into his arms. "You're okay," he whispered, again and again, rubbing Rupert's arm and Oliver's back, carding his fingers through their hair, repeating himself until Rupert was sagged against his chest and Oliver's breaths barely hiccupped.

"God, I'm such a mess," Rupert said in a wet voice against Callum's neck.

Callum held back a repeat of his lecture about not letting Oliver see his fear. It was too late for that, this time. Instead, he kept rocking them and let Rupert have a couple more minutes to recover.

Eventually, Rupert sat up a little. "Well, I completely fuu—fudged it up on day one," he said, resigned.

"You tried to take a leak, Rupert. That's allowed, even for parents of young children. You're hardly the first to complain about a lack of privacy, either."

Rupert's laugh sounded genuine, if a little freaked out. "God, what have I signed myself up for?"

The best job on earth.

Callum looked at Oliver and found one glassy blue eye staring back. He smiled and held out his arms. "Come on, let's have our dinner before it goes cold."

It was probably too late, actually, but Oliver climbed off Rupert and let Callum boost him into a chair. From there, it was relatively easy to prod both the Smythe men through their suppers and into their pajamas.

Callum changed too, even though it was only eight o'clock in London, and barely past lunchtime back home. His internal clock was so fucked up at this point that he figured he'd lie awake half the night, but Oliver seemed intent on keeping at least one hand on him at all times again, and what mattered most was that Oliver feel safe.

He left the last of the clean up to Rupert, who wouldn't be able to resist anyway, and turned off all the lights but those Rupert needed. Not surprisingly, within seconds of lying down on the bed, Oliver was out cold. Rupert had been right that the kid needed more sleep. Tonight's crying jag hadn't helped, either.

It was reassuring to watch Oliver's chest rise and fall with each breath. Callum was so mesmerized by it, he was startled when Rupert turned off the last of the lights and lay down on Oliver's other side, facing Callum.

Callum had left the curtains open, letting in enough light from the city to see Rupert's face. He looked sad.

"I never thought I'd have children," Rupert said quietly, out of nowhere.

"Why not?"

"Well, for starters, there was the bit about having sex with a woman."

Callum chuckled, not bothering to suppress his shudder. "Fortunately, that's not the only way to go about it."

Rupert arched an eyebrow. "Fortunately?"

Callum's brain caught up with his mouth and flailed. What the fuck was the matter with him? Rupert didn't know. Couldn't know. Callum's stomach turned, because now he would have to lie *again*. "Oh. I just meant—"

"Do you want a family?" Rupert asked, unwittingly sparing Callum.

"Yes," said Callum without hesitation. He just had to wait for hockey to be over. Then find someone who would love him after all he'd done. "I always wanted a big one, like mine," he admitted, even though with each passing year, that dream seemed farther and farther away.

Rupert smiled at Oliver, curled against Callum's chest, and the protective hand Callum pressed to his back. "You'll be an amazing father."

Callum swallowed hard. "Thanks," he said, his voice rough.

"I'm not like you," said Rupert. "I don't have brothers and sisters. Or didn't growing up, anyway," he said, running a hand over Oliver's shoulder. "But more than that, I didn't have parents, really. Dorm masters, coaches, teachers—even roommates and friends—raised me, and it was fine. I can see from your expression you don't believe me, but I genuinely had a good and happy childhood, for the most part. I never missed having a family. Didn't know any different, did I? And I suppose that translated to not thinking I wanted one, particularly."

"And now?" Callum asked.

"Now I have to figure out what to do. I watch you and I can see I'm not well equipped for this."

"You have everything you need, Rupert."

Rupert sent him an extremely dubious look. "How can I possibly?"

"You love him. That already puts you leagues ahead of his mother. Add in that big old brain of yours and some patience, and he's a lucky kid." *And you're a lucky man.*

"Who are you, and what have you done with Callum Morrison?"

A bark of laughter escaped before Callum could help it. He held his breath when Oliver's eyes fluttered open for a second, then he promptly settled back to sleep.

"That sense of humor won't hurt either," Callum whispered.

Rupert smiled. "Thank you. And not just for saying nice things so that I don't freak out."

"I'm not—"

"You are. And you have been. If it's any consolation, I won't tell anyone."

"Tell them what?" Callum asked, alarmed. Had he been obvious?

"That you're a big softy," Rupert said with a grin.

Oh god, he was. He totally was. No one *ever* saw it. "I do have a reputation to keep up," Callum said, trying for humor.

"Don't worry. Your secret is safe with me."

Callum's smile wavered. "Thanks."

He studied Rupert in the low light, his eyes heavy, his lips curved in a soft smile that made Callum's heart beat a little faster.

He shouldn't let himself be attracted. Should shove it down like he had for his entire adult life, fearing someone might catch him looking, see something they shouldn't, couldn't, on his face. But there was no one else here. And Rupert *did* have his number. Callum had let Rupert see so many things he'd kept hidden for years. Buried, because it was easier. Because he'd told so many lies that he was a stranger to almost everyone he knew. He didn't have friends, except Michaela. What was the point, when he couldn't tell them the truth? When he couldn't be himself?

But now there was Rupert.

"I'm still not convinced Oliver might not be better off away at school than with me."

"You don't believe that."

Rupert hesitated. "Don't I?"

"I get that you're scared, Rupert, but you can do this. You'll get it figured out faster than you think, and in the meantime I'll help you."

Rupert put his hand over Callum's on Oliver's back. "You've already done so much."

"I like kids," he said with a shrug, his voice scratchy. "It will be years before I have any of my own. If ever," he confessed slowly. He *wanted* to tell Rupert the truth, he realized, but he didn't know how. Where to start.

"I don't understand. Why years?"

"I have to wait until after hockey."

"Why can't you start a family before you retire?"

Callum retreated, hating the fear even as he gave into it. "Because I play hockey," he said, scrambling for a way back.

Rupert knew bullshit when he heard it. "*And?*"

Callum swallowed hard, his stomach in knots, and did the unthinkable. He told the truth.

"I'm gay."

Rupert's eyes widened, his mouth dropping open. "*Oh.*"

Callum closed his eyes and pulled Oliver close.

"Yeah. *Oh.*"

Chapter Five

Eight o'clock in the morning, and already Rupert's life was a total shit show. How did that even happen?

He could have guessed it wasn't going to be easy to get them all through that special ring of hell that was the security line at Heathrow. And that traveling with a four year old, even one as easy-going as Oliver, was going to make that especially difficult.

But Callum's total inability to make eye contact with him for longer than five seconds this morning really wasn't helping. *The fucking chicken.*

Callum had clung to Oliver from the moment they'd woken up, probably believing Oliver would provide some protection from the questions practically gagging Rupert after Callum's confession last night.

Seriously, who the fuck came out, then pretended to be asleep?

Rupert had lain awake, trying to make sense of Callum being gay—a concept that from *anyone else on earth* would not have made him bat an eye. And as if Callum's whole bag of issues wasn't enough, Rupert's sleeplessness was *deeply* regrettable, since he had no idea when he would have a chance to sleep again. As it was, he could easily have nodded off while standing in the line to check in. And he didn't think Oliver was going to be able or willing to entertain himself on the plane for seven hours. Or during their layover in Toronto. Or the shorter flight to Moncton. Or once they got back to his hotel room.

Holy shit, was he *ever* going to sleep again?

They finally collapsed into a row of seats on the main concourse, but as much as Rupert just wanted to shut his eyes for a moment, he couldn't. Their flight was in an hour, and they still needed to eat and possibly find some snacks to take on the plane for Oliver in case he didn't want whatever they were serving.

And really, who ever wanted whatever airlines were now serving? Not to mention Rupert still didn't know what Oliver liked. Did he drink anything besides milk? Should he? Rupert had some vague notion that small children shouldn't drink a lot of juice because of all the sugar. Maybe it made them hyper? Or was it that their teeth would rot?

He needed to figure this shit out before he went shopping. The fridge in his hotel room wouldn't hold a lot, so he couldn't just buy one of everything and hope for the best.

Which reminded him—Rupert pulled out his phone and opened the app he used to track his ever-growing lists. He needed to find a place to live in Moncton, an item that had been on one of his pre-Oliver lists, actually, but now was a priority. Oliver needed a home, not a hotel room.

Oliver also needed more clothes. And that food. And schooling. Would it be preschool? Was that public or private in Canada? How should he notify the Canadian government that Oliver was now a resident? He'd have to call his lawyers—he added that to the list. But first there was shopping. He needed books. And toys, and *oh, holy hell,* how were they going to get home from the airport safely—

"Knock it off," Callum said sternly.

Rupert snapped his head up and glared at Callum. "What. I'm fine."

"You're really very obviously not. Are you even aware that you're muttering aloud to yourself?"

"I am not."

Callum snorted. "Tell that to airport security when they're conducting the body cavity search."

Rupert spun to look over his shoulder, searching for approaching uniforms, and noting the stares from the family who had been sitting behind them but was now moving away.

"Dude, I'm *kidding.*"

Rupert settled back into his seat. "You're not funny."

"Actually, I am. Ask anyone."

Rupert gave Callum a look of total disbelief.

Callum was a cranky son of a bitch. Except, well, when he wasn't. Like when he was flying around the world to help a virtual stranger, or coaxing a frightened boy to view him as his personal protection, transportation, and jungle gym, or holding Oliver to his chest and looking at Rupert like he was worried Rupert was going to crack up in the middle of one of the most tightly secured public facilities in the Western world. Because Rupert really was very obviously not *fine*. He was freaking out.

"Okay. You're right," Rupert conceded.

"I'm funny?"

"No."

Callum smiled for the first time that day, actually *looking* at Rupert, and Rupert felt the responding tug on his own face.

"You're a tough audience, duchess. It's not my fault you don't get me."

Truer words had never been spoken.

"You shouldn't call him that," said a small voice from the vicinity of Callum's chest.

Callum and Rupert both froze, then looked down at Oliver.

"What should I call him, then?" Callum asked gently.

"Earl."

Callum cracked up at that suggestion and Rupert felt an almost hysterical urge to laugh right along with him. Instead he leapt to his feet. "Right. Shall I find us some food, then?"

Callum blinked up at him. "Sure?"

"Great!" Rupert said enthusiastically. "Oliver, what would you like? Do you see anything you want to try?"

Oliver peered around at the various storefronts before shrugging, silent once more.

Rupert kept his smile firmly in place as his eyes cut to Callum's. They exchanged a long look and Rupert knew Callum felt the same mixture of hope and frustration he did. The tilt of his chin reminded Rupert to be patient, Rupert's nod in return eliciting a small smile.

It turned out Callum and Rupert *did* have the magic necessary to hold an entirely silent conversation with a look.

Rupert tried to decide if that reassured or alarmed him while he dashed into the snack bar for a ridiculous variety of foods for Oliver to choose from, then to the newsstand to grab something for himself to read on the plane. He always felt vaguely guilty buying the gossip rags, but he couldn't resist the red carpet photos and feel-good stories about celebrities saving the world.

He returned to Callum and Oliver in time for their flight to be called for priority boarding, then it was the stumble along the concourse and up the jetway. Rupert was never so relieved to be on a plane and settled into his seat early.

Oliver was mesmerized by something Callum had loaded onto his phone for him, and Callum had returned to studiously ignoring Rupert, so Rupert sat back and flipped open his magazine. On page seven he realized his mistake.

He stared at the glossy half-page picture.

Longtime partners Callum Morrison and Michaela Price at the Annual Price Foundation Charity Ball, which raised over $4 million for LGBT youth centers and homeless shelters. The question on everyone's mind: When will these two lovebirds finally tie the knot?

Rupert glanced up and found Callum staring at him, his mouth compressed into a thin white line.

"Ask."

Rupert swallowed back the bile rising in his throat. "It's none of my business."

"Ask."

Rupert checked to be sure no one was close enough to hear. "Why did you tell me you're gay?"

"Because I trust you," Callum replied, completely taking the wind from Rupert's sails.

He pointedly looked down at the magazine in his hands

before turning to Callum with his brows raised. "You're bi, then?"

Callum snorted. "No."

"Have you told Michaela?"

"It wasn't necessary. She figured it out within an hour of meeting me," Callum said with a little smile. "Something about how I didn't look at her boobs even once."

Rupert grinned. "She sounds very clever."

"She is. She's the only one who has ever figured it out."

"Did she train you up on proper cleavage ogling or something?"

Callum laughed. "She would, I bet, but no. Her solution was for us to *date,*" he said with sarcastic air quotes, "and women would assume I was too hung up on her to ever notice another pair of breasts."

They both fell silent as a couple were seated in the row in front of them.

Rupert lowered his voice. "And she doesn't mind? That you don't...I mean, I assume that you aren't..." Rupert grimaced, realizing too late that his question was far too intimate and absolutely none of his business.

Callum sighed. "We're just friends. And it suits her, too."

So many questions. Though if asking about Callum was too intimate, poking into Michaela Price's life was well beyond none of his business.

"That sounds...complicated."

Callum scanned the line of people now crowding the aisle, then grimaced. "You have no idea."

He looked like he was begging Rupert to understand, even while his voice sounded as though he didn't expect Rupert to at all. And god's truth, Rupert didn't understand, but after the past couple days, Callum had earned the benefit of the doubt. For now.

Callum couldn't remember the last time he'd felt more out of sorts.

Resolutely ignoring the looks Rupert kept sending his way, he focused on keeping Oliver entertained for the long journey. Rupert finally passed out for a few hours, and as much as Callum was desperate for help, he couldn't bring himself to wake him up.

Callum was absolutely a huge fan of kids. And families. And all that went with that. But by the time they finally stumbled off the last plane at the Moncton Airport, he had to admit that international travel with a small child was maybe not the best part of family life.

Holy crap, it felt good to be home. Or what passed for home for the summer. He couldn't wait to get Oliver settled in so they could start encouraging him to come out of his very thick and stubborn shell.

"Callum! Rupert!" Jack called from the other side of the security barrier.

Callum waved and walked—okay, *staggered*—faster.

"What's Jack doing here?" Rupert asked.

"I asked him to meet us."

"Wonderful. I looked like a warthog's arse before being forced to stand next to *him*," Rupert groused, even as he smiled and waved at Jack.

Callum snorted. Rupert looked as perfectly pressed and handsome as ever. "It was either this, or take Oliver home in a taxi. I asked Jack to buy a car seat and install it in my rental."

Rupert stopped. "You what?"

"I'm sorry I didn't mention it. I thought of it while you were asleep somewhere over Iceland and texted him."

"You're very pushy, you know that?"

Callum smiled faintly. "All part of my charm?"

"God, it really is," Rupert muttered, then fell against his chest and hugged him—awkwardly, thanks to Oliver being in the middle, but like he really, really meant it. "Thank you," he sighed.

Goosebumps rose where Rupert's lips tickled Callum's neck. "You're welcome," he said, his voice gruff. "Let's get the heck out of here."

"Yes, please," came the soft response from Oliver, making Rupert and Callum laugh.

Jack was all smiles and raised eyebrows when they reached him, his eyes on Oliver.

"Oliver, this is our friend, Jack," Rupert said. "He's come to help us get home."

"Hello, Oliver," Jack said warmly, apparently unbothered by Oliver's wide-eyed and silent stare in response. Then he looked at Rupert and wrinkled his nose. "I have bad news on the going home part, though."

"Oh god, what?" Rupert almost whined, which Callum couldn't blame him for at all.

"The contactors didn't show up this morning."

Callum's shoulders slumped. It was Sunday, almost evening, and the contractors had promised to work through the weekend to help put themselves back on schedule. "Did they show yesterday?" he asked wearily.

"Um...no." Jack looked sheepish. "I didn't want to bother you," he offered. "I spoke to Lamont about it and he said he'd come and deal with it. Only, aaah...he never showed either."

"Reese said he'd come to Moncton? Today?" Rupert asked.

"Yesterday, actually."

"By *himself*?" Rupert asked.

"Yeah?" Jack said, clearly as confused as Callum by Rupert's reaction to this news.

Rupert stood with his mouth hanging open, apparently having lost the ability to speak.

"You okay?" Callum asked.

"He's never left Nova Scotia without me," Rupert said weakly.

Callum shook his head, certain he'd misheard. "What?"

Rupert snapped out of his stupor and glared at them. "This goes no further than the three of us, understood?"

Jack and Callum immediately agreed.

"Reese doesn't go out. Not ever."

"What do you mean?" Jack asked.

"He hasn't left his property more than a handful of times in years. And until recently, he hadn't left Nova Scotia in more than five years. I was with him every time he came here. I'm not sure he can do it without me."

Rupert was clearly upset, already pulling out his phone and muttering to himself. For the first time, Callum wondered if Rupert and Reese might be more than friends. The idea rubbed Callum the wrong way, though for no reason he was willing to examine too closely.

"What do you need us to do?" Callum asked Jack.

"We were supposed to have a meeting with the president of the construction company yesterday, which I put off until today, then delayed again when Lamont didn't show." Jack glanced at Rupert, who was leaving a voicemail for Reese to call him immediately. "The guy came all the way down from Quebec City, so I couldn't put it off any longer. The meeting is now scheduled for seven o'clock tonight."

Which was only an hour from now. And would be almost midnight London time, not that Callum's body had really adjusted to there, either. In fact, his body didn't seem to have any idea where the fuck it was anymore. All he knew was it wanted a bed. Now.

He'd been so hopeful when they'd gotten off the damn plane, like the last minute of a long, hard-fought game, with the score on your side, the end in sight. And now the opponent had tied it up.

Overtime *sucked*.

Rupert shoved his phone into his pocket. "Where's the meeting?"

"The arena," Jack answered. "I thought home turf would be

better. And the option of walking the site if needed."

"Smart," Rupert said. "Let's go."

Jack had already installed the car seat and offered to drive, which was great, since Callum didn't think he could safely operate a grocery cart in his current condition.

Rupert climbed in the back with Oliver, and both were asleep before they'd left the airport parking lot. Callum was just plain jealous, though the ten minutes it took to get to the arena probably wasn't going to do Rupert all that much good.

Oliver was asleep in Rupert's arms when they trudged into the arena to find Reese Lamont standing in the hallway, looking a little lost, with a tiny woman hovering behind him.

"Rupert!" Reese said with undisguised relief, charging toward them. When his eyes landed on Oliver, he pulled up short.

Callum reached out for a bleary-eyed Oliver, who promptly pressed his face against Callum's neck and went lax in his arms. Reese watched, fascinated, as Rupert brushed Oliver's hair back from his forehead before turning back to his friend.

"What are you doing here?" Rupert asked. "I texted you last night that we were on our way back."

Callum admired Rupert's judicious avoidance of asking why Reese hadn't shown up before they got here, when he had said he would. Given the look he was getting from Reese, Callum didn't think he was doing a good job keeping this thought off his face.

"Callum," Reese said, sticking out his hand, "it's nice to meet you in person."

"Same," Callum returned, taking his hand from Oliver's back only long enough to shake.

"And this must be Oliver," Reese said, studying his sleeping profile. "God, Rupert, he looks just like you."

Callum smirked. "Yeah. *Poor kid.*"

Reese looked stunned for a moment, then he started to laugh.

Rupert rolled his eyes. "Do *not* encourage him."

Callum wasn't sure which of them he meant.

Reese arched an eyebrow. "Have you been giving Rupert a hard time, Callum?"

"I hope so," Callum said sincerely.

"I assure you, he has," Rupert snapped, but his voice no longer held the heat it once had around Callum.

Reese rubbed his hands together with undisguised glee. "You and I should talk, Callum. The things I could tell you..."

Callum grinned. "Yeah?"

Rupert looked like he was contemplating murder, his cheeks flushing bright pink. "Reese, I shan't ever forgive you if you dare," Rupert said, super primly.

When had that become so adorable?

"Don't worry, duchess," Callum said with an obnoxious wink. "I'll keep your secrets."

Reese's eyes bulged. He looked like he might explode with joy.

Rupert leveled his best death-glare—which was also adorable—on Callum, then turned pointedly toward the silent woman hovering on the edge of their little circle. "Matilda, it's nice to see you. Welcome to Moncton."

"Thank you, Mr. Smythe."

"*Matilda!*" Callum cried, making her and Rupert jump, and Reese scowl furiously. Callum grinned at Reese's assistant, delighted to put a face with the voice he'd heard countless times over the phone in the past few months. He'd pictured her far older and less...*curvy*. Her dark, perfectly demure suit made Callum wonder if she and Rupert used the same tailor.

"Mr. Morrison," she returned politely, a smile hovering on her lips.

"Mati, what do I have to do to get you to call me Callum? We've been over this a thousand times."

Matilda poked her funky little glasses higher on her nose.

"Yes, Mr. Morrison."

Callum laughed. "I'll convince you someday," he promised as Reese inserted himself between them.

"Please do not harass *Matilda*."

There was no mistaking the inflection on her full name. Message received, loud and clear—and doomed to be ignored. He almost cracked up at the shocked look on Rupert's face at Reese's possessive maneuvering.

This evening was turning out to be more fun than he'd expected.

Reese turned to Matilda, solicitous. "Our meeting will begin shortly. I realize it's not in our normal duties, but would you mind keeping an eye on Oliver for a bit?"

Oliver let out a squeak and latched onto Callum's neck. Breathing was suddenly a challenge.

"He stays with us," Callum croaked, pressing a reassuring hand to Oliver's back.

Normal airflow resumed.

Reese looked stricken. "I apologize. I hadn't realized—"

"It's fine," Rupert said gently. "Oliver will stay with me or Callum for a while. Until he asks otherwise, in fact."

Oliver smiled at Rupert.

"I see," Reese said. It was clear he had questions, but they would have to wait, as the group from the contractor's offices chose that moment to arrive for the meeting.

Rupert was impressed. Considering that Callum had to be dead on his feet, he took charge of the meeting with ease.

Rupert had always been able to remember numbers. Big, little, whatever—his brain just liked them. He took the binder from Jack and looked up what was needed when he couldn't recall something from memory. Which wasn't often, since while Rupert had the figures down, Callum was apparently an ace at recalling the details of the project plan—what was supposed to happen when, what the deadlines were for various stages of the project, and, accordingly, when payments were due.

They made a pretty good team, and kept the meeting blessedly short.

Callum and Oliver ducked into the men's room as soon as they were adjourned, while Rupert stood in the hallway and checked in with Matilda and Reese to be sure they'd be all right getting home. Reese's driver was apparently in the parking lot awaiting a phone call, and Matilda was proving surprisingly adept at prodding Reese along. Rupert had never seen her outside her tidy office in Reese's house, but she clearly had a handle on what her boss needed in the outside world as well.

They all jumped when a huge voice boomed out of nowhere.

"*Rupert!*"

Rupert swore silently as he turned to look down the corridor. Sure enough, two of the Ice Cats' core players were exiting the gym just as Callum and Oliver stepped back into the hallway, Oliver's hand tucked in Callum's.

"Hello, Alexei," Rupert said, automatically searching the man for anything that might lead to one of his infamous pranks. Rupert was in no mood to be slathered in lube or Bengay or whatever the hell Alexei might have up his sleeve.

"Alexei Belov?" Callum asked with a childlike excitement.

Alexei's eyes widened. "Callum Morrison!"

Suddenly the two men were doing the manly one-armed bro-hug, pounding each other on the back hard enough to fell mere mortals. It was a wonder the entire arena didn't shake.

Callum grinned as he stepped back. "It's so nice to meet you."

Rupert's mouth dropped open. Callum had managed to insult Rupert's work, his heritage, and possibly his manhood when they'd first met. But Alexei, probably the scariest man on the Ice Cats roster, if not in all of Moncton, Callum practically *humped*?

Mike Erdo, Alexei's best friend and constant companion, caught Rupert's eye. *Goalies*, he mouthed with an eye roll.

"And who is this?" Alexei boomed, looking down at Oliver.

Rupert jumped forward, prepared to grab Oliver if he showed any sign of being frightened by the enormous Russian.

Oliver smiled up at the big man beatifically.

"This is Oliver," Callum said.

As one, Alexei and Mike turned from peering down at Oliver's face to stare at Rupert's.

"You have a son!" Alexei announced, not a trace of question but a whole lot of disbelief in his voice.

"No, I—"

"Rupert! You have so many secrets!"

"I really don't. I—"

"Is he yours, too?" Alexei asked Callum.

Rupert snapped his mouth shut and let Callum be the one to stand there agog for a moment. Reese was giggling now, which was no help to anyone.

Callum finally managed to sputter, "What? No, I—"

"I'm Alexei," he announced, thrusting out his hand to Oliver. Rupert was standing ten feet away and wanted to take a step back, but Oliver just gazed up at the bear of a man thoughtfully, then stuck his little hand into Alexei's huge paw. Alexei gestured with his other hand. "And this is my friend, Mike."

"Hello, Oliver," Mike said, warmly and at a volume that didn't threaten to burst anyone's eardrums. "It's nice to meet you. Alexei and I work for your father."

"No, I—" Rupert tried again, his voice lost under Alexei's.

"Your papa is very sneaky. We didn't know he had a boy," Alexei said while trying to take his hand back. Oliver didn't let go. Alexei appeared quite flummoxed by this.

"He's my brother!" Rupert shouted, cringing in the echoing silence that followed. He cleared his throat. "Erm. Sorry. Yes, well, Oliver is my brother. He's come to live with me. Only just arrived today."

For the life of him, Rupert didn't know why he was

explaining. Or why he sounded like a prig when he got nervous.

Alexei attempted to free himself again, succeeding only in shaking Oliver's entire arm. He tugged Alexei's hand until he crouched down to Oliver's level, his huge thighs as big around as Oliver's torso.

"What is it, little man?" he asked gruffly, for once not sounding like he was competing with a goal horn.

Oliver tilted his head, then reached out and patted one of Alexei's cheeks, leaving his palm pressed there when he was done. Alexei's eyes widened and he almost fell over, Mike's quick reflexes the only thing sparing him the indignity. Oliver just smiled at them both.

He obviously had deplorable taste in men, Rupert thought wryly.

"He's not left mine or Callum's side since we found him in London," Rupert said quietly. "He's had a bit of a rough go and doesn't seem to trust anyone. Doesn't—" Rupert had to clear his throat— "speak, really. Not often, anyway."

Alexei nodded, then looked at Oliver. "Thank you, little man. I will be your friend."

"And him," Oliver said, pointing at Mike.

Mike crouched down, too, his chest to Alexei's back so he could smile at Oliver over Alexei's shoulder. "I'd be honored."

Callum grimaced, trying to give the road his full attention for the short drive from the arena to his hotel. Well, *their* hotel now. It was hard to focus, though, when Rupert was yelling at him from the passenger seat.

"You did *what?*"

"I had Jack pack up your room, check you out of your hotel, and move you to my hotel instead."

"You're such a douchebag." Rupert announced.

"I'm sorry, Rupert. Your hotel didn't have any more rooms. I thought it would be easier this way. My room is just down the hall, so no one will think—no will see..." At Rupert's dark look,

Callum swallowed hard, hating himself a little. "People know me. My name. I can't—"

"I get it, Callum," Rupert said, voice flat.

Callum wasn't sure that he did. He tried to get them back on track. "Jack said he got you settled in, all unpacked and everything."

Rupert slumped into his seat, appearing utterly dejected. "That lovely man has been through my underwear drawer."

What. "What?"

Rupert shook his head. "Nothing."

"I don't think Jack is some kind of pervert, if that's what you mean."

"Of course that's not what I mean," Rupert snapped.

"Oookay. Well, anyway, I'm sure yours isn't the kind of underwear Jack is into. So to speak."

Rupert rolled his head against the seat to look at him. "What do you mean?"

"I mean he's straight."

Rupert laughed. "Your gaydar is terrible."

"What? No. I don't even have—wait. You mean he's gay?"

Rupert shrugged. "He's never said, but I think so, yes."

"Oh."

He knew Rupert was studying him. He kept his eyes fixed on the road.

"I didn't have you figured out, though, so I don't suppose my gaydar is that terrific either," Rupert conceded.

"That's because I'm not, you know..."

"You're not what?"

"You know. Gay, really."

Rupert sat up. "Pardon me?"

"I mean, I'm not really anything. I don't send out a vibe, or whatever. Because I don't...I just don't, okay?"

"You said you were gay."

"*I am.*" Callum sighed, wondering when his life had gone sideways and his sexuality had become something he talked about. "If I had to choose, if I *could* be with someone, it would be a man. I would want that. A guy."

Like you.

Callum packed that thought away, to be taken out and examined never.

Rupert collapsed back against his seat and blew out a deep breath. "Right. Well, what I'd like to know is how on earth Jack managed to check me out of one hotel and into another without my permission."

"I didn't even ask, to be honest. I'm sure you've noticed that between Jack and Garrick, they know just about everyone in this town."

"I had noticed. It's been a bloody boon for the construction project."

"And now it's a bloody boon for us," Callum said, chuckling at how stupid that sounded with his American accent. He snuck a peek at Rupert. "Are you really angry? Or just surprised?"

"I'm not angry. I'm not particularly enamored with your highhandedness, but that's nothing new, is it? I do appreciate you thinking of Oliver. He'll probably want you to stay with us a few more nights, if that's not too much trouble."

"Of course it's not," Callum said quickly. "I didn't mean to imply—"

"Then I'm sure you'll be able to return to your own room at night," Rupert said, sounding depressingly hopeful.

It shouldn't bother Callum, but he felt oddly disappointed.

It wasn't like they were doing anything more than sleeping, and making a scared little boy feel safe. Hell, Callum wasn't convinced it *was* all that safe, since he and Rupert were so exhausted, they'd both probably sleep through Oliver getting up in the middle of the night and doing a tap dance on the mattress.

Callum had only ever slept beside Michaela or a sibling before, and in all those cases, the point of the exercise was to keep as far away from the other person as possible, to turn your back so your breathing didn't bother them or vice versa.

Now, it turned out, Callum *liked* the sound of Rupert's breathing. The soft, rhythmic susurration of his exhale was soothing. Which was stupid, but whatever. He liked it.

A thought suddenly occurred to him. "Do you have a thing for Jack?"

Rupert started to laugh.

"You just—you seemed concerned about him seeing your underwear or something." God knew Callum wasn't going to forget the eyeful he'd gotten. "I wasn't sure if that meant, I mean, you've mentioned that he's attractive."

"Yes, well, I'm not sure you have to be gay to notice that. In fact, I'm pretty sure the only requirement is that you be sighted."

Callum chuckled. "That's true." He paused, waiting for Rupert to answer the question as he pulled up in front of the hotel. When Rupert didn't say anything, Callum caved. "Well, *do* you have a thing for Jack?"

Rupert gave Callum a disconcertingly long, measured look. "No."

"Oh, okay," Callum mumbled, and hey, he'd made things awkward. *Awesome.*

"Do *you* have a thing for Jack?" Rupert asked.

Callum laughed nervously. "What? No. Why would you even ask that?"

"You were at his house the other night. I was preoccupied at the time, but it occurs to me now I might have been interrupting."

"Well, you weren't."

"Why not?"

"Why weren't you interrupting?"

"Yes. Why *not* have a thing for Jack?"

"Because I don't. I mean, I don't have a thing for anyone. Ever. I just don't do that kind of thing."

"What kind of thing? Date?"

"No. I mean, yes, I don't date."

"Why not?"

"Look! We're here!" Callum declared, as if he hadn't been parked in the valet lane for several minutes. He practically fell out his door to escape.

Callum wasn't going to explain his fucked-up life to Rupert. How the hell would he? He could barely explain it to himself.

And anyway, the man was just starting to tolerate him.

Chapter Six

The next two weeks passed quickly, and every day, Rupert gained more confidence. He wasn't always successful—in fact, most days he felt like he fell somewhere between mediocre and absolute crap—but he was doing it. He was a parent. Now he only *rarely* worried that he was going to accidentally maim or dismember Oliver, which was a huge improvement. And, mostly, he felt he could keep the boy alive. So, there was that.

Admittedly, his bar was low.

Rupert had no delusions. He was a parent. He was not, yet, a *single parent*. Callum made dinner, he did "tubby-time", he knew shit like that it was *called* tubby-time. He carried Oliver around for hours every day, took him shopping, made him use his manners, and generally made Rupert look like the child-rearing amateur he was.

What Callum didn't do was make Rupert feel stupid for not knowing half the things Callum did, or one quarter of what he should.

And what neither Rupert nor Callum had been able to do, yet, was to convince Oliver to speak more than the occasional word or two. Each day they heard a little more, and it at least proved he was *capable* of all kinds of speech, but they'd only progressed enough to hear a few short sentences and not a lot else.

So there was hope. Lots of hope. But what Rupert was running out of was time. He'd managed to put off everything and anything that would take him out of town, but his time was up.

Hanging up the phone, Rupert was simultaneously elated and terrorized. They had a chance to sign a new back-up goalie, one that Rupert had kept an eye on for the better part of the last year—long before he had assumed responsibility for the Ice Cats management, in fact.

But that meant he had to go to Montreal, right now, in order to sign him.

Flustered, he ran from his office, already in the corridor and halfway to the gym before realizing he'd forgotten to put on his suit jacket. He stalled, considering going back, dithering in the hallway until he recalled that if he'd learned nothing else these past few weeks, it was that time was now a more precious commodity than ever.

He arrived at the gym to find Alexei spotting Mike at the bench press, and Callum running on the treadmill. Oliver was happily tucked in a corner of the room with his car collection, oblivious to the smell and the absurdly hot men sweating all around him.

Rupert, sadly, was immune to neither.

Rupert was reasonably certain he would have killed any one of his ex-boyfriends within days if they'd spent *nearly* as much time together as he and Callum did. But with Callum, easily one of the most abrasive human beings Rupert had ever met, the only challenge was recalling why it was he'd disliked Callum so much to begin with.

Right now, Callum was lost to the blank stare runners fell into, silent and focused on his training regime. His dedication was admirable.

Rupert stole a few moments to admire a whole lot of things about Callum. His heavily muscled thighs flexed as they pounded out a fast pace, his biceps bulging with the pump of his arms. Sweat gleamed on his skin, his damp curls stuck to his forehead and neck.

It shouldn't be nearly as appealing as it was. All of Rupert's past boyfriends had been slimmer. Smaller than Rupert, mostly. At six foot two inches, he and Callum were actually the same height, but Callum carried a lot more weight in his shoulders. His neck. His chest.

Why had the scars on Callum's eyebrow and upper lip ever put him off? Or the crook in his nose? They added character. Spoke to his history. He was a hockey player and wore it proudly, as much a part of him as his prickly social skills, and the big softy who doted on Oliver without a thought.

Rupert's eyes tracked a drop of sweat from Callum's temple, his hands twitching with the desire to follow that path with his finger, to touch Callum's cheek, pink with exertion. Callum's face would glow like that during sex. His skin hot to the touch.

Rupert dragged his gaze back up and bright green eyes locked with his, bringing his wayward thoughts to a grinding halt. Heat crawled up Rupert's neck and he cursed his pale skin. He spun to look at Mike and Alexei, perhaps hoping to convince Callum that he was in the habit of checking out everyone in the gym. Because seeming like a pervert was somehow better than acknowledging that he was growing increasingly, intensely, attracted to Callum.

Mike and Alexei stared back. Both were trying very hard not to laugh.

"I have to go to Montreal," he said insensibly to the room at large.

Callum had slowed his pace after catching Rupert all but drooling over him, but now he hit stop. Rupert was so busy trying to figure out the look Callum was giving him that he didn't see Oliver coming until he slammed into Rupert's legs, nearly toppling them both to the ground.

"You can't go!" he cried.

Rupert quickly pulled Oliver up into his arms. "It's okay, Ollie. I'll be back. I'll always come back. Remember, we talked about how I sometimes have to travel for my job. That I would have to make some trips this summer." And then they would have to deal with him traveling for fifty percent of the hockey season, since half the team's games were *away*, after all.

Oliver buried his face against Rupert's neck. "You can't go," he pleaded.

"You'll stay here with me," Callum said, coming to rub Oliver's back. "We can go on an adventure. Maybe check out Magnetic Hill."

Oliver held on tighter. "No!" His little body shuddered and he let out a wet sob, absolutely *heartbroken*.

Rupert looked at Callum, stricken, his own breath hitching in his chest. Callum's hand pressed over his on Oliver's back, their fingers threading together. Rupert was so grateful, felt so utterly helpless to ease Oliver's fears, that his own eyes began to sting. Mortified, he buried his face in Oliver's hair.

"It's okay. It's okay," Rupert whispered, not even sure who he was trying to convince anymore.

Mike and Alexei slipped out of the room, closing the door behind them, and Callum wound his arms around Rupert and Oliver. It didn't seem to help Oliver, but Rupert felt like he could breathe again.

"I'm not leaving you. Not ever, Oliver," Rupert promised again as Callum rocked them, his big hand warm on the back of Rupert's neck. Oliver seemed incapable of hearing him, and Rupert didn't know what to say to make him believe.

"We'll go to Montreal," Callum said, his voice raspy and thick. "All of us."

Oliver let out a stuttering sigh and went limp in their arms.

Rupert looked at Callum, their noses almost brushing. "Are you sure?"

"Of course. We'll make it work. Until Oliver is ready."

Which would be, Rupert feared, right about the time Callum would return to Colorado. How was Rupert going to survive without him? Oliver didn't seem to be getting any better and the summer was too short. They wouldn't—

"Rupert," Callum said, his hand cupping Rupert's jaw. Steadying him.

Right. Not panicking. "Montreal. Let's begin there."

"Yes, let's," Callum said, as if Rupert was making any sense. "When do we leave?"

"As soon as possible."

Callum looked down at his shirt plastered to his chest with sweat, and now stuck to Oliver's back as well. He grimaced. "Ollie and I will go back to the hotel, get cleaned up, and pack. You're on logistics."

Rupert nodded, already making a list in his head of what needed to be done.

He could do this. He could get the three of them to Montreal. He could talk to Callum about what to do next. Make a list for that, too.

Would it be totally insane if he had to make a list of his lists?

A week ago, Callum had been ready to swear off air travel with a child for the rest of his life. Now he had to reconsider.

Oliver was a perfect angel for their mad dash to the hotel, through a quick rinse down, dressing, packing—including trying to identify what the fuck Rupert's texts were instructing him to pack in which very particular bag—another mad dash to the airport to find Rupert, the race through security, and, finally, onto the plane.

Now, at thirty-seven thousand feet, Oliver was calmly playing on Callum's phone, and it was *Rupert* that needed a goddamn time out.

Callum slammed his hand down on Rupert's bouncing knee. "Knock it off."

"Sorry," Rupert mumbled, still madly typing on his phone.

"What are you working on?"

Rupert's head came up at last. "A list."

Callum rolled his eyes. At some point, Rupert was probably going to have to accept that he couldn't manage Oliver the way he did the rest of his life. That he didn't want to, even.

Until then, thank god and Air Canada, there was gin.

Callum plucked Rupert's phone from his grasp, and shoved the gin and tonic he'd ordered from the flight attendant into Rupert's hand instead.

Rupert sent him a disgruntled look, but accepted the drink with a nod. "Thank you."

"You're welcome. Now sit back and chill the fu-uh-uh-doodle out."

Rupert's lips twitched. "Fadoodle?"

"You know what I mean," Callum said with a glare.

For once, Rupert didn't fight him when even Callum knew he was being a highhanded prick. It was a quiet and unexpectedly pleasant journey after that.

In typical Rupert style, Hotel Le St-James was the swankiest place in town. Callum didn't really care one way or the other, other than feeling like the proverbial bull in the china shop around all that spindly French furniture.

Rupert was checking them into the suite he'd reserved when the woman behind the counter smiled at Callum with Oliver in his arms. "Your son is adorable."

"Thank you," he and Rupert murmured simultaneously. Callum grinned, figuring it was easier than trying to explain their situation to a stranger.

Rupert was signing the last of the paperwork when a loud voice boomed across the hushed lobby.

"Callum Morrison!"

Every head in the massive, echoing room turned toward that voice, then toward Callum.

Callum's heart stopped dead as Markus Jergeson strode toward him. Callum had been enjoying a certain anonymity, hoping his face was not immediately recognizable, but his fucking name clearly was. Especially when it was being shouted by Montreal's favorite son and power forward.

Rupert stared at Callum wide-eyed, but it was nothing compared to the bug-eyed stares from the team of five people behind the counter who'd just checked him into a hotel room with another man and a boy they'd just acknowledged as *their son.*

Jergeson smiled widely, completely unaware of the shit storm he'd just unleashed. Callum and Jergeson weren't really friends, but after ten years in the league together, they had a lot of shared history, and had even spent a season on the same team. Even with all that, Callum had no reason to trust that

Jergeson, or anyone else bearing witness to this fiasco, wouldn't be emailing Deadspin within minutes.

"Give me Oliver," Rupert hissed and Callum practically dumped the boy into Rupert's arms.

Then he was thrusting out his hand and shaking Jergeson's heartily, with back slaps and shoulder bumps and all the usual manly shit. Callum was transparently awkward through it all. He wanted to run. He wanted to snatch the phones from the growing crowd's hands and stomp them under his heel.

"And who's this?" Jergeson asked, turning to Rupert and Oliver. Rupert looked like he was pinned to the spot, his eyes darting to Callum's for guidance.

"Uh..." Callum stalled, trying to figure out the best way to handle this.

"I'm Rupert Smythe. And this is my brother, Oliver," Rupert said, saving Callum from making this even more awkward.

Jergeson smiled and shook hands and tried to engage Oliver, who smiled shyly. Callum was proud of how well he was doing, which maybe was too obvious on Callum's face, given how Jergeson was now looking back and forth between Callum and Oliver, his expression thoughtful.

"So!" Callum began, winced, then dialed his volume way down. "How have you been?"

Jergeson cocked his head. "Just fine. Enjoying the off-season. How about you?"

"Oh yeah. Me, too. Been up in Moncton. Working with the team."

"The team?"

Oh, right. Not everyone knew everything about his life. "The Ice Cats. The Moncton Ice Cats. EHL team, I'm part owner. Doing construction. Well, I mean, I'm helping manage the project. Not actually doing the construction, of course. And Rupert here is the team's manager."

He glanced over at Rupert and got *exactly* the look that bout of verbal diarrhea warranted.

"How's the season looking?" Jergeson asked Rupert politely, obviously making an effort to keep this conversation on the rails. Callum was oddly grateful and terrified at the same time.

"Good. That's why we're here, actually," Rupert said smoothly. "Going to sign a new goalie."

"That's great. Can I ask who you're going after?"

Rupert smiled benignly. "No."

Jergeson threw back his head and laughed. "Okay. I get it. Well, good luck with that."

They chatted for a few minutes about Montreal. Jergeson suggested a few places they could go for supper that Oliver might like, and Rupert complimented Jergeson on his previous season. It was easy. Rupert *made* it easy by picking up the conversational slack when Callum was too busy worrying over the pictures being taken. Wondering who the front desk clerk was talking to on the phone.

"Callum?"

"What? Oh sorry," he said, guessing he was supposed to have contributed something to the conversation.

"I was just saying," Jergeson said kindly, "that I have to get going. It was good to see you," he said, shaking Callum's hand. "And to meet both of you." He and Rupert shook, then Jergeson held out his hand to Oliver, who studied it for a second before placing his against Jergeson's palm.

"Nice to meet you," Oliver said primly, sounding so much like his brother that Callum grinned.

"And you as well, Oliver," Jergeson returned, then sent Callum one last look. "You all have a good night," he said with a wink, then turned on his heel and left.

Callum couldn't get into the elevator and to their room fast enough. He thought about that stupid wink all the way down the long hallway and while they were getting settled in their absurdly fancy suite. He wanted to pace, but told himself he couldn't. He wanted to sit, but was pretty sure he'd shatter that Louis-something-or-other chair if he tried.

He tried to keep up with Rupert through the phone calls to agents and lawyers, or, at the very least, keep Oliver occupied while the agenda for tomorrow was set, but he felt fairly useless. He was already worried about going back downstairs. Crossing the lobby together. Who else they might bump into.

It shouldn't matter. He wasn't doing anything wrong. Hell, he wouldn't be doing anything fucking wrong even if he and Rupert were lovers.

Except he'd *lied.* Not today, really, but so many times before. His carefully constructed bullshit life was a yoke around his neck—some days choking off his air, others a comforting weight he understood and remembered the reasons for. The latter, though, were increasingly rare. Now, whole weeks passed when he couldn't recall why he'd gone down this road. Why he'd willingly, sensibly—he'd thought at the time—tucked his heart, his whole life, in the very back of the fucking closet.

Because every single damn day, it was lonely. Other than his family, only Michaela, and now Rupert, knew the truth. And that was the same number of people he'd count as his friends.

He looked up at Rupert, standing by the desk while Callum and Oliver played on the floor. He was, as always, *just so.* Shoes polished. Not a hair out of place. His suit impeccable, the jacket a constant presence, Callum suspected, to hide that amazing ass. His cheeks were flushed, eyes focused as he took notes on whatever he was listening to, and, not for the first time, Callum felt helplessly drawn to him.

Rupert was so confident. Honest. *Out.*

Callum knew what courage that took. Rupert made it seem easy. He didn't hesitate. Accepted it as part of who he was, no one's business but his own, even while he didn't care who knew and who didn't. Rupert was afraid of a lot of things, but in spite of that, he was open. He never *lied.*

And he never once, in spite of Callum's admittedly confusing assertions that he was gay and yet wasn't, made Callum feel ashamed. But really, if he wasn't with anyone, ever, he wasn't anything. Straight. Gay. It made no difference.

What he was—what he'd always been—was *alone.*

Callum was uncharacteristically quiet during dinner. They took Markus Jergeson's suggestion and went to a little place around the corner from the hotel. Oliver surprised them by electing to have crepes, once Rupert had explained what they were. Rupert grinned at Callum, only to find him staring back, an unreadable look on his face.

He'd been like this since they'd bumped into Jergeson in the lobby, and Rupert could guess why. It was entirely possible that several people had thought that Rupert and Callum were together. And that, quite clearly, upset Callum. A lot.

Rupert, too, was quieter than usual by the time they returned to the hotel. Oliver seemed to be picking up on their moods, and was particularly good during his bedtime routine, curling up against Callum's chest while he read Oliver a story, patting the big man's arm while his deep voice eased him into sleep.

Rupert would usually be sitting on the end of the bed listening, or doing something nearby as an excuse to be close to them, but tonight he worked at the coffee table in the living room, listening to Callum through the open door.

He heard "the end", then some quiet murmuring as the light went out.

Rupert went into the bedroom as Callum kissed Oliver goodnight. It had taken Rupert aback the first time he'd done it, even more so when Callum had informed Rupert it was his turn to do the same. Now kissing Oliver's cheek was second nature, as was gently running his hand over Oliver's soft hair and wishing him sweet dreams.

Oliver had just begun to allow them to leave the room once he was tucked in, but only if they left the door wide open. One time, Rupert and Callum had fallen silent, the TV off, and Oliver had come running into the living room. Now they made sure there was some noise, some evidence of their presence in the living room, until Oliver was well and truly asleep. Even then, he still came out to check on them if he woke, but was willing to be coaxed back into bed with little fuss once he'd confirmed they were still there.

Tonight, neither of them turned on the television. Rupert tried to get some work done, but Callum couldn't sit still. His book lay discarded on the end table. His laptop on the desk. He fidgeted with the lamps, read the fire escape routes on the back of the door, and generally made a nuisance of himself.

"Do you need to go for a walk or something?" Rupert finally asked, exasperated. It was a risk, of course. If Oliver woke up to find either one of them missing, it might freak him out. But it would probably be better than finding Rupert standing over Callum's dead body, so...

"No, I'm fine," Callum said. He didn't sound angry. Or even tired. Maybe the restlessness had more to do with being cooped up with Rupert and Oliver for days.

"You can go out. There's a nice bar in the lobby, if you want a drink. And, obviously, tons of clubs. Bars."

"I know."

"Rue Sainte-Catherine is only a short walk from here," Rupert said, as innocently as he could.

Callum finally stopped moving to hover in the middle of the room. "What are you suggesting?"

"You seem restless."

"And partying is the cure?"

"No," Rupert said, "but maybe getting out and meeting some nice people would be good for you."

Callum stared at him. Hard. "Rupert, are you trying to get me laid?"

Rupert's stomach soured. He really wasn't. In hindsight, he could admit that what he'd been trying to do was push Callum's buttons.

"Maybe it would help," he managed to choke out.

"No."

"It wouldn't help?"

Callum let out a bitter laugh. "I don't do...that. I can't go to some club and pick up a—" He threw his hands up. "Just *no.*"

Rupert eyed Callum consideringly. "Can I ask you something?"

Callum sighed and slumped against the desk. "Sure," he told his feet.

"How is it that no one knows you're gay?"

Callum looked at him. "What do you mean? You know. And Michaela and my family know."

"And your lovers," Rupert prompted.

"What?"

"Your lovers, Callum. The men you've been with in the past. Lovers. Boyfriends?"

"I don't have any of those."

"Boyfriends, you mean?"

Callum nodded. "Those, too. I've never actually dated anyone."

"*Ever?*" Rupert asked, wishing he'd tried to hide his incredulity when Callum grimaced.

"Ever."

Rupert's mind reeled. "Callum, are you—have you ever...are you a virgin?" Rupert asked, cringing at how bloody juvenile it sounded.

"What? No! I-I've done stuff. In the past." Callum waved his hand vaguely.

"With women?"

Callum almost laughed. "*No.* No, I've known I was gay since I was a kid. Maybe twelve? Maybe younger."

"That's hardly stopped a lot of men from trying to be with a woman."

"I guess," Callum said with a shrug. "I didn't think I'd be able to fake it, and I was worried it would get back to the guys that I'd...you know. Not been able to deliver, or whatever. And I didn't want to do that to some poor woman."

"Get back to the guys?"

"Yeah, well, I moved up here to Quebec when I was sixteen. Juniors. Basically, I moved in with my first team then, even if I actually lived with a very nice, very Catholic family not far from here. Which is how," he continued with a narrowed gaze at Rupert, "I know about Rue Sainte-Catherine and the Village. You're not very subtle."

Rupert grinned. "It seemed like a good idea at the time."

"Well, it wasn't." Callum scowled, but Rupert didn't think his heart was in it.

"Because you don't pick up men in clubs."

Callum looked back down at his feet. "Not anymore," he said.

"Anymore?"

"Yeah, I used to...you know."

Rupert thought he might, so he didn't press. "So there are others that know you're gay."

Callum frowned. "Not really. Those men, they didn't know my name. Who I was. They didn't know *me*."

Rupert felt unaccountably sad. "I'm sorry."

"Yeah, well, I didn't do it that often. A handful of times. Just when the pressure got bad and we'd travel somewhere no one would know me. Recognize me. I never left with them. Not further than some alley out back, maybe. It wasn't great. It was— actually, it was really bad," he said quietly, pausing to swallow and lick his lips. "I'm not making any excuses. But, you know, I'm also not going anywhere. Tonight or any other night. You'll just have to put up with me."

Rupert's imagination filled in some possibilities for "really bad" that made his blood curdle in his veins. And even if it wasn't any of those things, Rupert could guess the sum of Callum's sexual experiences if they'd all happened in some club bathroom or back alley. Quick, furtive servicings. Without affection. Without intimacy. Without love.

Callum didn't offer any more details. He just stared at the

floor, the tips of his ears red.

Callum tried to not to appear as ashamed as he felt. The memories of what he'd done haunted him. Particularly the last time he'd gone out to a club.

He was startled when Rupert's shiny wingtips came into view beside his beat-up sneakers. He dragged his eyes up Rupert's long legs, past dark gray slacks that hung perfectly from his lean hips, a trim waist, and the blue cotton broadcloth shirt that would make Rupert's blue eyes brighter.

At last, he met Rupert's steady gaze.

Callum flinched when Rupert's long fingers cupping his jaw, his fingertips brushing just behind Callum's ear. He searched Callum's face.

Callum forced himself not to squirm. He felt itchy and hot, embarrassed by his confessions even as something he couldn't describe as anything other than *want* grew beneath his skin.

Callum swallowed, his mouth dry. Another lie, one he'd told countless times through omission and deflection, and sometimes spoken outright, hovered on the tip of his tongue. Instead he told Rupert the painful and embarrassing truth, his cheeks burning as hot as his shame.

"I've never kissed anyone before."

Rupert's brows drew in with what might have been sadness. Or disbelief. Though not, thank god, pity. Then his eyes narrowed and he looked...*determined.*

Callum's heart thudded in his chest, his ears. He'd wanted to kiss Rupert since the very first time he'd laid eyes on him in his office, with his flushed cheeks and proper accent and all that fire in his eyes.

Then Rupert *was* kissing him, and Callum couldn't remember to breathe, let alone think.

His eyes slid closed, purely on instinct, leaving him to focus only on their lips brushing, each press a little firmer. Fuller. Each touch almost chaste, but still like a drug, making him crave another and more. He didn't know how to ask for that, though. Didn't know how to tell Rupert what he wanted, *how much* he wanted. How it built in him, alarmingly, until he felt ready to burst at the seams. He felt foolish and frustrated by his lack of experience, knowing that for most people their age, this was nothing.

But not for him.

This. This was what he'd been missing. He'd spent more time than any fully grown man should wondering what this would be like, and it was better and stranger than he'd ever imagined. Almost hypnotic.

Rupert's palm pressed against his jaw and Callum tilted his chin higher, his breath shuddering from him as Rupert's fingertips tickled along his neck, behind his ear, and against his scalp. How could so small a touch, so gentle that he could barely feel it, send shivers down his spine? He should probably be mortified that he was so obvious, so totally incapable of disguising his reaction.

Rupert cupped the back of his head in his warm palm and Callum leaned into that comfort. He clung to Rupert's lips when he drew back, only to be flooded with relief when Rupert ducked in again. Callum put his hands on Rupert's waist, tentative but desperate for something to ground him as the blood rushed in his head, roared in his ears. He felt hot and dizzy, unsteady, as if his feet no longer touched the ground, as if Rupert had turned his world upside down.

Callum gasped when the tip of Rupert's tongue traced the seam of his lips, letting him in without thought. His hands slid to Rupert's hips and pulled him closer, groaning as Rupert's tongue slid over his and his thighs wedged between Callum's.

He shuddered and clutched at blue broadcloth and grey flannel, embarrassed by the sounds slipping from his throat, well outside his control. His cock ached in his snug jeans and he shifted his hips, squirming against its urgent press. Rupert slid closer, forcing Callum to spread his knees until Rupert's thigh jammed against Callum's balls. He groaned, rocking without thought, without plan, against that pressure.

Rupert kissed him thoroughly, carefully, and it didn't take more than a sample of one to know he was really fucking good at it. He cradled Callum's head in both hands, making long, slow sweeps of his tongue, then retreating until just their lips touched. Kissed. Then back again to tangle together once more.

Callum hung from Rupert's grasp, from his lips, and felt safe. Sure. He thought he could spend the whole night like this, even as he was becoming increasingly desperate to do something, anything, to ease the ache in his belly. The tension curling up his spine. He shifted against the desk, pulling Rupert closer, his arms curling around Rupert's back and clutching at his waist, his tongue making its first foray into Rupert's mouth. And another.

He let out a noise horrifyingly like a whine when Rupert broke their kiss.

"Easy," Rupert gasped. "Breathing is still required. Sadly."

Callum wanted to die as he was cast out of heaven to faceplant in whatever version of hell was reserved for really shitty kissers. He leaned back, looking for some escape.

"Hey," Rupert murmured, brushing his lips against Callum's hot cheek, still pinning him to the desk. "Where are you going?"

Callum forced himself to look at Rupert and then tried to make sense of Rupert's flushed cheeks and heavy-lidded eyes. His lips were red, swollen, and curved into a soft smile. He looked really, thoroughly kissed. The realization that Callum had done that, and that Rupert had maybe liked it, hit Callum hard.

He was such a loser. He was ready to come in his pants from a single kiss. Seriously, why would Rupert want anything to do with him?

"I just figured you were done," Callum mumbled, still staring at Rupert's mouth because he was too chicken to meet his eyes.

Callum watched, mesmerized, as Rupert's tongue traced the inside of his lower lip. Not like some cheesy porn come-on, but as if he was tasting their kiss again. Tasting Callum.

Callum barely bit back another whimper. He wanted to run.

116

He wanted to stay and pounce and *try.*

"Do you want to be done?" Rupert asked, his voice rough, intimate.

Callum finally met his eyes. "No."

Rupert smiled. "Good.

Chapter Seven

Watching Callum's eyes dilate, feeling the way his hands clenched against Rupert's back and hip, was dizzying. It wasn't as sweet, as thrilling, as kissing him, though, so Rupert did that instead. Callum, who had clung to him like a limpet, offering up an endless and endlessly erotic litany of small sounds, was now stiff in his arms. Just as he had the first time, Rupert teased at his lips and dipped his tongue between them, coaxing him into reacting. Into responding.

And what a beautiful, beautiful response it was.

He almost smiled at how innocent Callum was. The man had no game. Like, *none*. He'd nearly suffocated Rupert in his enthusiasm, and Rupert had forgotten how thrilling that was in its own right. Not since he'd been a teenager had he, or any man he'd kissed, been so desperate to get closer, so without artifice or grace, that asphyxiation was better than letting go or even easing back an inch.

Kissing Callum wasn't some grand, altruistic gesture to help Callum discover what he'd been missing. Rupert wasn't kissing Callum out of pity. Because maybe he did pity him, pity the choices he'd made that had left him so completely alone for so long, but, honestly, Rupert kissed him *in spite* of that. Rupert kissed him because he wanted to, so much so that Callum's lack of experience and long-standing residence in a closet Rupert had never so much as hung a jockstrap in didn't matter. He kissed him because Callum needed kissing, because Rupert needed to kiss him. Because, somehow, Rupert had actually come to like and admire and respect the man, despite him being a gigantic pain in the ass.

So Rupert's motives were pure, if not exactly chaste. But that didn't mean some not-so-small part of his brain didn't revel in the idea that he was the first. That he could, and would, *gladly* give this to Callum.

In return, he received far more than he expected. The noises Callum made, little moans that communicated his desire as effectively as the clench of his hands in Rupert's clothing or the twitch of his hips, but with a hint of surprise, too. Like Callum couldn't believe they were doing this. How *good* it was.

And that made two of them.

Rupert lost himself in the simple joy of kissing Callum. Their mouths meeting, changing angles, parting for no more time than it took to gasp in air and go back for more. Callum was passive in a way that Rupert never would have imagined possible. He was just beginning to meet him halfway, tentatively, tilting his head the way Rupert would have moved it had Callum not begun to anticipate it first.

First kisses were often ungainly and weird. And this one had certainly had its moments, but now they smoothed out. Found their rhythm. *Rupert's* rhythm, he realized with a zing.

Everyone learned what they liked, and what they didn't, from their earliest lovers. Experimentation, in all its awkward and wonderful moments, was how Rupert had figured out what he wanted from a lover. And what kind of lover he could be.

It was inspiring and more than a little humbling to think that was what this moment might mean to Callum.

With that in mind, Rupert pulled away long enough to relish Callum's soft, disappointed murmur before he bent to drag his lips along Callum's jaw. Callum's head fell back without so much as a suggestion from Rupert, leaving his hands free to coast over Callum's shoulders, his arms. He nuzzled in closer, abrading his lips on Callum's heavy stubble until he reached the smooth, soft skin beneath.

He lavished attention along Callum's neck, slowly working his way back up to trace the shell of Callum's ear with his lips, tasting the lobe with a flick of his tongue. He spread his legs to steady himself against the increasingly powerful and desperate twitch of Callum's hips, touching a hand to Callum's lower back to steady him. Callum jumped, surprised, surging forward until his heavy erection ground against Rupert's hip and Rupert's was smashed against Callum's firm belly.

Rupert groaned, his lips buzzing against Callum's skin as they clutched each other closer, tighter, and took up a slow, dirty grind. Callum's breath stuttered hot and unsteady in Rupert's ear.

Rupert sucked a dark mark into Callum's skin, the idea that he shouldn't discarded in the face of Callum's heartfelt groan and the way he arched his neck against Rupert's lips, pressing into the suction. When Rupert released the abused spot, it was already florid, and he wanted to do it again. And again.

But not before he laid the flat of his tongue against Callum's neck at the point where it met his heavy shoulder, then slowly dragged it up the taut cord of muscle beneath, licking a broad stripe and not stopping until his nose brushed Callum's jawbone.

He leaned back to admire the flush on Callum's cheeks, his heavy-lidded gaze. He looked lost, his breath almost panting from between his soft lips, his mouth slightly open, as if shocked. And impossibly turned on.

Rupert felt the first frisson of unease, only because he was uncertain when this would stop. When it *should* stop. Because he didn't want it to, not even a little, but he was suddenly, acutely aware of Callum's inexperience.

Then Oliver's voice cut like a knife through the fog of arousal surrounding them.

"What are you doing?"

Callum shoved Rupert a good two feet away, plunged into regret the moment his hands dropped away from the warmth and strength of Rupert's body. He gripped the edge of the desk instead of falling to the floor in a puddle of embarrassment and frustration.

"Oliver," he said, clearing his throat when his voice came out as little more than a scratch, "what are you doing up? Are you okay?"

"You weren't making any noise," Oliver said, and Callum

mentally kicked himself for not turning on the television—and thanked all that was holy Oliver hadn't heard what noises they had been making.

Rupert looked at his brother over his shoulder, which struck Callum as weird until his eyes locked on the very obvious erection tenting the front of Rupert's soft flannel slacks. Callum felt branded where it had been pressed against his stomach.

His own dick fucking *ached*, and his breath was still hectic as he tried to come down from wherever the hell Rupert had taken him, but his tight jeans and untucked t-shirt put him at an advantage in this situation.

He stood. "Come on, I'll tuck you back in."

Rupert shot him a grateful look Callum had no idea how to return. He felt awkward and embarrassed, and it had little to do with the four year old and his epic cock block, or even that Callum could barely walk upright.

Based on glint of humor in Rupert's eyes, he was perfectly aware of the latter. Callum's heart clutched at the small smile and the secrets it hinted at. Rupert looked so comfortable with it. With what had just happened. While Callum felt as though his life had gone sideways.

He followed Oliver into the bedroom and boosted him back into the tall bed. By the time he'd tucked him in, Callum's body was back under control, and his mortification was through the fucking roof.

He didn't want to go back out to the living room and face Rupert. He couldn't.

So, like the complete coward he was, he toed off his shoes, changed into his pajama bottoms, and lay down next to Oliver.

Maybe it was the stress of the day, or the comfort of Oliver's hand on his arm, or maybe even his subconscious wanted to run and hide from what had just happened, but Callum was asleep almost instantly.

Rupert spent the next week trying to figure how he'd made

such a huge mistake. He was *supposed* to be working on the Ice Cats travel schedule for next year—organizing the hotels, buses, planes, meals, and equipment was like mobilizing a bloody army for six months straight—but more often than not, he was spacing out, thinking about Callum and that kiss instead.

He'd watched Callum, curled up next to Oliver, for a long time that night. He'd looked peaceful and handsome and really fucking asleep, while Rupert had been anything but. In the end, he'd let Callum have his escape, knowing it was probably for the best.

The days since had been strange. Given Callum's previous sexual experiences, or lack thereof, it was hardly surprising that he might freak out a little. But any time Rupert so much as *hinted* at talking about the kiss, let alone anything else sexual, sexy, or even mildly erotic, Callum turned adorably pink and changed the subject immediately.

It was remarkable, really. Callum Morrison was capable of prudery to rival that of a Victorian maiden.

Which would be fine if he hadn't also taken to touching Rupert, *all the time*. It was a light stroke of fingers down his arm as they passed in the narrow kitchen of their hotel room. Or a hand gently pressed to his back while Callum held the door. Their shoulders constantly brushed when they were seated next to each other, bumping when Callum wanted to give his silent support in a meeting, pressing steadily when they were working together to help Oliver with something. Worse, Rupert was starting to anticipate Callum's touches, hope for them, fleeting though they were.

It was goddamn distracting.

With a sigh, Rupert spun his chair to face his desk and tried to focus on the tasks at hand. Callum and Oliver were off investigating something called Magnetic Hill, but they would return soon, and Rupert didn't want to have to take work back to the hotel tonight.

He and Callum and Oliver had fallen into a nice routine of eating dinner together, then tubby time, stories, and bed for

Oliver. Rupert didn't let anything disrupt that, but once Oliver was asleep, he often had to do more work. Tonight, though, he wanted to sit with Callum and watch some television. Or maybe even talk.

He was contemplating whether he should employ duct tape to prevent Callum's escape, should the kiss come up, when his office door burst open.

Didn't anyone knock?

A pale, wild-eyed Reese staggered through his door. Rupert shot out of his chair and around the desk.

"What the bloody hell are you doing here?" he demanded, searching over Reese's shoulder for Matilda or Hodges or *someone* who might have brought his friend this far. The entire Ice Cats office staff stared back.

Rupert tugged Reese further into his office and shut the door.

Reese stood stock still, a line of sweat-darkened hair along his forehead and smudges on his camel-colored slacks where he had rubbed his damp palms. When it became obvious he wasn't going to speak, possibly wasn't *capable* of saying anything, Rupert did the only thing he could think of.

He did what Callum would do.

Reese went rigid. "What the fuck are you doing?"

"I'm hugging you, you wanker. Enjoy it."

Astonishingly, that didn't help. Reese's arms hung limp at his sides, his shoulders locked up around his ears. Rupert squeezed tighter.

"Why?" Reese asked, as if mildly curious.

"It makes you feel better."

"Does it?"

"Yes. Now shut up and put your arms around me."

After a beat, Reese arms curled around Rupert's waist hesitantly.

"Now, take a deep breath," Rupert instructed, waiting until

Reese complied. "And let it out. Now another. One more."

On his third exhalation, Reese thawed, just a little, his weight shifting against Rupert.

"Go on, give it a go," Rupert encouraged.

Reese took another deep breath and let his chin perch on Rupert's shoulder, his fingers curling into Rupert's shirt.

"Better?"

"Kind of," Reese admitted. "Did you read this in a book or something?"

"This is what Callum does when Oliver or I freak out," Rupert admitted reluctantly.

"Oh, *really*?" Reese asked, dragging the last word out far too long.

Rupert sighed and released his now much more stable friend. "Shut up."

"Is there something you want to tell me?"

"No, there really isn't," Rupert replied primly.

Reese crowed, "I knew it!"

"You knew what?"

"That you had the hots for Callum," Reese said, insufferably smug.

"I do not," Rupert said, mostly because "the hots" was a stupid expression and he didn't need to hear how ill-advised this whole thing was. He was perfectly aware.

"Yes, you do!"

"Bah," Rupert said, fighting the blush he could feel growing by the second.

"Someone's got a crush," Reese sang childishly.

"I do not. I should think I would be aware if that were the case." Rupert cringed at his own stupidity. He sounded exactly like Reese had hit a nerve and Reese very well knew it.

"You're smitten."

"I am not."

"Absolutely twitterpated."

"Do stop this nonsense," Rupert pleaded, knowing it was futile.

"Oh ho, look at you getting all uptight. It's adorable, how you lie, and yet it's so obvious your twitter is well and *truly* pated," Reese said with glee. "That's great."

That brought Rupert up short. "It is?"

"He's certainly a departure from your usual taste in men."

"Is he?"

Reese gave him the look that deserved. "By about four inches and fifty pounds, I'd guess. I think Callum might be able to break that last one...what was his name? Melvin? No, Pointdexter! No..."

"His name was Sheldon, and well you know it."

"Yes! Of course, *Sheldon.* I think Callum could break Sheldon in half without working up a sweat."

Rupert rolled his eyes. "Sheldon was very nice."

"Sheldon was very *boring.*"

Callum certainly wasn't that, but Rupert would sooner stick razor blades in his eyes than admit it to Reese. "Sheldon was a good person. *Is* a good person. I'm sure he's making some nice man very happy right now."

Reese harrumphed. "I think it's far more likely he's slowly forcing some very nice man into a coma, but that, fortunately, is no longer your concern."

"I don't know why you didn't like Sheldon. Or Gavin, for that matter."

"Peas in a pod. A terrible, pale, unassuming pod of boringness. A milquetoast pod, if you will."

"Are you done?"

"No. I want to talk more about this thing you have going with Callum."

"I do not have a thing going with Callum. There is no thing," Rupert said firmly. "Nothing is *going.*"

"Lies."

"It's true," Rupert said, albeit weakly. "And you're right, he's not my type."

"No, he's exactly your type. What he's not is *safe*."

"What the hell does that mean?"

Reese's eyes narrowed. Rupert felt a sudden desire to flee his own office.

"Rupert, I've know you for most of our lives. I know what you like, and for as far back as I can remember, that's been big, athletic men. The same men you shared locker rooms with and who, unfortunately, terrorized you. You didn't used to fear them. You used to *want* them."

"And look where that got me," Rupert snapped, cursing his accelerating pulse. "Terrorized is right."

"Because most of them were assholes. And young. And stupid. And none of that excuses what they did. But did you ever wonder if some of them were looking back at you? They were probably too afraid of their asshole friends and of breaking the mold you were very clearly never going to force yourself to fit into."

Rupert slumped against his desk, resisting the urge to reach down and rub his right knee. "And for that, I paid a price." A steep one, which had come with nightmares of being locked in a utility closet for almost twenty-four hours, or forced out into the snow in nothing but a towel, still wet from the showers.

Reese touched his shoulder gently. "You did. And I'm sorry."

"You were the one to save me, more often than not," Rupert said, his voice flat.

"But not always. Not enough."

Rupert hated this old argument. "Still not your fault."

"No, it wasn't," Reese conceded. "But more importantly, Rupert, it wasn't yours."

Rupert knew that, but he also knew it changed nothing. It certainly had nothing to do with Callum and the thing that *wasn't* happening between them.

He frowned when Reese pulled him to his feet, shocked to be caught up in another hug.

"What are you doing?" Rupert asked, truly stumped.

"You said it made you feel better. I thought I'd give it a try."

Rupert wrapped his arms around his oldest friend, his best friend, and held on. Because, damn it all—and Callum in particular—it *did* help.

Reese's hand came to rest on the back of his neck. "It wasn't your fault," he repeated quietly, tucking him closer.

"I know," Rupert sighed.

"Then take it from me—running from what you fear doesn't make it go away."

Rupert had about twenty things he wanted to say in response to that, but before he had a chance, his office door flew open.

"Seriously," he muttered, "doesn't *anyone* knock anymore?"

"Oh, ah...sorry. I didn't meant to interrupt." Callum, with Oliver riding piggy-back, sort of flailed in place before backpedaling out the door.

Rupert sighed and stepped away from Reese. "It's fine, Callum. Come in."

Callum hovered in the door. "No, that's okay. We can come back later."

"Get your arse in here and close the bloody door," Rupert snapped.

"Okay," he said carefully, doing as Rupert asked while Reese cackled like an idiot.

"Callum! Oliver! It's good to see you both," Reese gasped once he'd gotten himself under control.

"Lamont," Callum said coolly before turning to study Rupert's face.

Reese grinned gleefully at Rupert over Callum's shoulder, waggling his eyebrows like the complete idiot he was. Rupert felt a foolish urge to blurt out that he and Reese were just friends and it wasn't what it had looked like.

This was ridiculous.

"Reese was just about to tell me why he's barged in on me today," Rupert said with a meaningful look at Reese.

It was, of course, a totally wasted effort.

"Oh, yes, I came to look for a place to stay here in Moncton and stopped by to see how you all were getting along," he offered with an emphasis on *getting along* Rupert fervently hoped Callum didn't pick up on.

"We're fine, obviously," Rupert said. "What's this about you getting a place in Moncton?"

"I thought I might need to spend a night or two here, what with you living here now, Rupert."

Had Reese intentionally said Rupert's name with so much warmth? He made it sound like—

"Is that so?" Callum inquired, his cool tone at odds with his ferocious scowl.

Rupert glared at Reese. "How unlike you," he said pointedly.

"Yes, well, I'm trying new things," he said with a grin. "Do you need another hug?"

Callum hitched Oliver higher on his back. "I'm just going to go."

Rupert's office door burst open. *Again.*

Rupert threw his hands in the air. "Honestly. I'm going to put a deadbolt on that bloody thing."

"Oliver!" Alexei shouted as he charged in, uninvited. "Sheila told me you and Callum were back."

Because yes, as if Rupert's life weren't strange enough right now, Alexei and Oliver had become fast friends.

Oliver smiled brilliantly at Alexei and squirmed until he was let down. Alexei promptly swung him up onto his hip. "Michael and I were going to have an adventure and sneak a look at the construction. Do you want to come with us?"

Oliver's enormous smile was clear assent.

Alexei glanced at Callum. "It's okay?"

Reese pursed his lips and raised his eyebrows as Callum gave permission for Oliver to go off on this adventure. Rupert sent him a bland look in return. He and Callum had already discussed that Oliver's interest in spending time with other people was a good thing and should be encouraged, even if one of those people was Alexei Belov.

And as much as Alexei loved to smash all of Rupert's buttons with a big, meaty fist, Rupert trusted him. Alexei's obvious affection for Oliver would melt even the coldest heart, and Rupert certainly wasn't immune.

"I'll join you, if that's all right?"

As one, all eyes swung to Reese.

Alexei smiled, completely unaware of the fact that Reese didn't go on adventures, *ever*. "Sure. It is good to see you again. Reese, right?"

They'd met only a couple times before. To date, Reese had managed to visit Moncton without letting anyone, even team management and the players, know he was one of the team's owners, the one everyone believed to be a recluse. Who *had been* a recluse until very recently.

"Yes. Reese," Reese confirmed awkwardly. Rupert could see Reese screwing up his courage as he closed the door, sealing them all inside like a pack of sardines. "Reese Lamont, actually," Reese said with a wince.

Alexei's expression went blank. "*Edwin* Reese Lamont?"

Reese held his ground admirably in the face of Alexei's dead-eye stare. "Yes. The one."

Alexei looked between Rupert and Reese. Rupert was alarmed by the slow smile crawling across Alexei's face. "You two are so *sneaky*!"

Rupert stood up straighter. "I beg your pardon."

"You make us think that Reese is just your boyfriend, but he's Edwin Lamont! The asshole who nearly sold the Wild Cats to crazy people!"

Reese's mouth dropped open while Rupert's face heated to what he assumed was a ridiculous shade of red. Why did everyone think he was sleeping with Reese?

"Please do watch your language in front of Oliver," Rupert said, woefully snippily. He had hoped the team would have somehow forgotten about that whole bad-deal a few months back. It had, after all, all been a big misunderstanding. And they'd fixed it.

Alexei nodded, somehow managing to look contrite while still grinning. "Yes. I'm sorry. I forgot myself when I learned your *boyfriend* is our *boss.*"

"He is not my boyfriend!" Rupert snapped.

He was probably imagining that Callum looked relieved.

Alexei definitely looked dubious. "No?"

"No. I should think I would know," Rupert replied.

Alexei's smile turned sly. "I suppose you would."

Wow, he'd managed to load that with a lot of innuendo. And why was Reese grinning? Honestly.

"Indeed," Rupert said primly, refusing to rise to the bait. More. "Now, if you'll all excuse me, I have work to do. Enjoy your adventure and do be careful."

Alexei and Oliver led the way out of the room. It wasn't until the door shut behind Reese that Rupert realized Callum had stayed behind.

Callum had never seen anything sexier or more ridiculous than Rupert obviously flustered and wary. Goddamn, there had to be something wrong with Callum that he found it so arousing. So adorable. But Rupert was usually so poised, so *civilized*, and all Callum wanted to do was wreck him.

He wanted to make Rupert look as messy as Callum had felt since they'd kissed.

His hands were on Rupert's face, their hips bumping together, before Rupert could do more than squawk. Then it was all lips and tongues and, holy shit, Callum had no idea what he was doing, but he couldn't stop doing it.

Why had he been avoiding this? He couldn't remember. It must have been because he was a fucking idiot, because this was as good as he remembered. As good as he'd been pretending he'd imagined. Better, maybe, because this time he wasn't just letting it happen. This time, he shoved his fingers into Rupert's hair to learn it *was* as soft as he'd guessed. This time, he traced his fingertips against Rupert's scalp, along his ear and down his neck, delighting in how Rupert shuddered against him. After a week of ignoring how much he wanted this, he let himself wallow in it. Let himself taste and touch and *know*.

It was amazing. And terrible. Because now he was dangerously close to coming in his pants, which wasn't something he'd ever done before, and, as it turned out, wasn't on the embarrassingly long list of things he wanted to try.

He ached for some relief. Some goddamn *friction.* The little noises Rupert made, which Callum swallowed, made his hips jerk, seeking. They stumbled back until Rupert's shoulders hit the door and he gasped into Callum's mouth, the sound strangling off when their bodies met and smashed together from knee to shoulder. It still wasn't enough. Callum cupped one of Rupert's perfectly round ass cheeks in his hand and ground Rupert into the door.

"Callum," Rupert groaned between kisses, the sound firing straight down Callum's spine, his cock jerking in a desperate bid to answer that plea.

He curled his fingers into Rupert's hair, holding fast, and kissed along Rupert's cheek and down his neck, drawing on everything Rupert had done and all the ways Callum had imagined turning that back on Rupert in the days since. He licked behind Rupert's ear, nipped the lobe, then sucked his way down the strong muscles beneath until he reached the edge of a starched collar. He buried his nose there, taking in a deep draught of cologne and shampoo and detergent and *Rupert*, imprinting the scent on his brain.

God, Rupert was totally fucking him up.

Rupert pushed at his shoulder and Callum growled, trying to stay right where he was. A strong grip in his hair yanked him back, but before he could object—or possibly finally succumb to the need to come in his pants because, yeah, turns out hair-pulling was fucking hot—Rupert sealed his lips over Callum's and Callum was lost. Drowning. Chests pressed tight, hips grinding. Seeking. Fucking desperate for *something.*

His heart stopped when someone pounded on the door.

Sheila's muffled voice barely reached them over their panted breaths. "Rupert? Mr. Smythe? Are you okay?"

Rupert tipped his head back against the door with a thunk, still clinging to Callum. Callum buried his face in Rupert's collar once more.

"Yes, Sheila. I'm fine. Is anything the matter?" Rupert called out politely. Callum smiled against the warm skin of Rupert's neck and wondered if everyone in the office could hear the rasp in Rupert's voice.

"Garrick is on the phone," Sheila replied. "He said he couldn't reach you. He sounds a little freaked out, boss."

Callum vaguely recalled the buzz of Rupert's phone on his desk. His own phone had gone off in his back pocket and he'd ignored it completely.

"Shit," he whispered, carefully stepping away from Rupert.

Rupert's hand grasped the doorknob, as if he needed it to hold himself up. "Tell him I'll ring him in a moment, please," Rupert called through the door.

Callum wished everyone could see Rupert's hair standing on end, his lips pink and swollen, the pleat of his trousers utterly ruined by the erection tenting them. He dragged his eyes back up to Rupert's face and met his hot blue gaze.

"We're going to come back to this," Rupert promised softly.

Callum smiled. "Okay."

Rupert looked somewhere between eager and surprised, and Callum felt a pang of guilt. He'd been an asshole, *again*, so worried about what an idiot he'd been, how obviously inexperienced and pitiable, that he hadn't considered that Rupert might have been left wanting, too.

He never wanted Rupert to be wanting. Not for anything Callum was able to give.

Chapter Eight

Rupert's hands would barely cooperate enough to retrieve his phone from his desk and dial Garrick's number. He'd missed three calls.

Garrick answered before the phone had even rung on Rupert's end.

"You have to help me."

"What's wrong?" Rupert asked, alarmed. Garrick wasn't given to hysterics.

Callum came close, his hand brushing Rupert's hip hesitantly. Rupert grabbed hold of it and kept it there.

"I need to find Callum."

Rupert frowned. "Then why are you calling me?"

"He isn't answering his phone, either!" Garrick growled. "Jack says you two are all but inseparable, so I thought you might know where he is."

Rupert wanted to object, but he really couldn't, given Callum was standing right there. "Hold on," he said, then held his phone out. "It's for you."

Rather than take the phone, Callum tapped the screen. "You're on speaker, Garrick. What's up?"

There was a pause, then, "Was he standing right next to you?"

Rupert rolled his eyes. "You got lucky. Jack doesn't know what he's talking about."

Callum shot Rupert a curious look but Rupert refused to explain. He didn't really have any good explanations, and none that he was willing to discuss with Garrick listening in.

"What's up, Garrick?" Rupert asked, diverting attention back to where it belonged.

"I totally fucked up. I just got a reminder that I'm supposed to do a thing with a local scout troop. I completely forgot about it."

"A scout thing?" Callum asked. "What's the problem?"

"The problem is I'm in Boston," Garrick replied and Rupert thought there was little cause for him to speak to them as if they were mentally deficient. "The problem is that I promised to run a skating clinic if they raised enough money for the LGBT Youth program at the Pathways Center. Which they did."

Rupert still didn't get it. "Okay, so?"

"So, the clinic is in *one hour*."

"Oh shit," Callum said, succinctly.

"Yeah, oh shit," Garrick agreed, then perhaps finally realizing now wasn't the time to be a snarky bitch, smoothed out his voice. "Callum, I'm so sorry to spring this on you, but is there any way you could—"

"Yes. Of course," Callum agreed before Garrick could finish asking, and Rupert smiled gratefully, squeezing his hand.

"Thank you so much," Garrick said, his voice tinny over the speaker, but his gratitude coming through clear as day. "When we first started the construction, I had all the summer bookings moved to the University arena. Can you get there in time?"

Callum looked at Rupert blankly. "I have no idea."

Rupert did the calculations quickly. "Yes. The rink is only fifteen minutes from here. We'll need to find Oliver and swing by our hotel room to get your hockey bag, but we should just make it."

Callum was already yanking open the door. "We got this, Garrick. Don't worry!" he called as he ran in the direction Alexei had taken Oliver and Reese.

"*Our* hotel room?" Garrick asked in a slow drawl.

"Uh," Rupert stammered, wondering if he could just hang up and blame it on the wireless company. "Mine and Oliver's, I mean."

"Uh huh."

"Right-o, I do have to run now, Garrick. I've got to get Callum to the arena. Do excuse me," he said, hanging up on the sound of Garrick's laughter.

Callum found Mike, Alexei, and Reese looking at the new ice floor and quickly explained that he and Oliver needed to run and why.

Oliver wrapped his arms around Alexei's neck and would not let go.

"Oliver, please," Callum begged. "We have to go quickly so we're not late."

"But I want to stay with Alexei," Oliver said.

Callum smiled, always happy to hear Oliver's voice, his adorably crisp accent, even if he was being a pain in the butt. Callum looked at Alexei and Mike. "Do you guys mind watching him for a couple hours while Rupert and I go to this thing?"

Oliver's eyes widened. "Rupert is going, too?"

"Yes," Callum said slowly, seeing the dawning panic in Oliver's eyes. He reached out a moment before Oliver dove toward him.

"I'll go with you," he said, clinging to Callum, his lip quivering as he looked back at Alexei longingly.

Mike looked devastated. Alexei folded like a house of fucking cards. "We'll come too," he offered. "If that's all right?"

Oliver's smile lit up his whole face. "You will?"

At some point, Callum thought as they ran toward Rupert and the parking lot, he was going to have to speak with all the adults in Oliver's life about not letting him manipulate them so easily.

"I'll see you all later," Reese said, once he'd found his car and driver out front.

Callum looked over his shoulder. "Dinner tonight?"

Reese smiled, delighted. "Text me where to be and when."

"Will do," Callum agreed, winking at Rupert when he flashed

Callum a grateful smile.

They zipped back to the hotel and grabbed his gear bag, then headed to the rink. He was relieved to see the boys were in street clothes, not all geared up for hockey, and already out on the ice. Callum handed Oliver off to Alexei and Mike, who had taken their own car and were waiting in the bleachers when they arrived, and yanked on his skates. When he stood to go out on the ice, the chatter from the group Callum assumed were the kids' parents abruptly ceased.

"Holy shit," whispered someone.

Callum dove out onto the ice. He was here for the kids, was happy to give up his precious anonymity for them and for the good work they'd done, and he was already late.

He clapped his hands, the sound echoing in the rafters. "Okay, guys, let's get started! Line up on the blue line."

The kids all came toward him, doing as he'd asked. It wasn't until they got closer that they realized something wasn't right.

"That isn't Garrick LeBlanc. He's *way* too short."

Callum stoically didn't wince. It wasn't his fault his presumed future brother-in-law was a freaking giant.

"He looks familiar, though."

"He looks like—"

"Holy shit. Is that—?"

"Hi!" Callum said brightly, hoping he wouldn't have to kick off today's clinic with a lecture on swearing, which, coming from a professional hockey player, seemed like the height of hypocrisy anyway. "Garrick couldn't make it today, so he called and asked me to fill in. My name is Callum Morrison."

The silver-tongued boy's eyes bulged. "Holy fuuu—"

"*Fadoodle!*" Callum supplied.

Fifteen mouths dropped open. Callum refused to acknowledge the laughter coming from the stands, though he would address Rupert's particularly loud giggle later.

"Okay," he said with a big smile. "Let's watch the language, all right?" The boys nodded, still trapped in varying stages of shock and awe. "Right. Good. Then let's get started. Was there a particular drill you wanted to do? A skill to work on? Stick work? Face-offs?"

He wasn't sure what to make of the troop's reaction. A couple of the kids look pissed. A few nervous. At least half of them were looking at a one kid in the center of their group.

"It's a *skating* clinic," said the young man garnering so many looks from his troop. A group of boys on the far end of the line began to snicker, while others shot them furious glares.

"Okay?" Callum said, confused.

"Not a hockey clinic," the spokesman explained, sliding forward.

It was then Callum noticed that the kid was wearing figure skates.

Shit.

"Stupid little faggot, what does he think he's doing?"

The words hung over the bleachers for a pregnant moment, silencing everyone. Rupert turned to see one of the men in the audience scowling at the ice, the parents around him split between amusement and horror.

Rupert kept his face carefully blank and reached to take Oliver from Alexei and Mike, intending to take him as far away as possible.

Mike and Alexei were already standing. Rupert didn't know what he expected their reactions to be, but they both look sickened.

"We're going to move," said Mike, pointing to the visitor's bench, halfway down the ice and separated from the rest of the audience by Plexiglas.

Rupert put a hand on Alexei's arm and smiled gratefully. "Thank you."

Alexei nodded, casting a final look at the arsehole who'd spoken such filth. If the guy had any sense, he would be terrified by Alexei's scowl. Alexei pressed a big hand over Oliver's exposed ear, the other ear pressed to his chest, ensuring he wouldn't hear anything else.

Rupert's shoulders eased, seeing how Alexei kept Oliver safe.

Alexei looked back at Rupert. "You're coming with us, too."

Apparently Alexei's protective instincts reached beyond Oliver. Rupert had never given Alexei any reason to think Rupert could take care of himself. Just the opposite. Instead of being embarrassed, though, Rupert was warmed to know Alexei was looking out for him. Mike, too, judging by the gentle hand against Rupert's back, guiding him to their new seats.

Rupert glanced out on the ice, to Callum smiling at the young man with the figure skates, at the rest of the troop jockeying behind him. It seemed some of the boys had his back. Others not so much.

Rupert felt a rush of empathy for the young man.

"Actually," Rupert said, coming to a halt, "if you don't mind, I'm going to run to my car to get something."

Alexei glared at the bleachers again. "Do you want one of us to go with you?"

Rupert suppressed a sudden desire to hurl himself against Alexei and hug the stuffing out of him.

Honestly, what had Callum done to him? He never used to want to hug anybody.

"No, I'm fine," Rupert promised. "I'll be back in just a minute."

Fortunately, he had what he needed in his trunk from this morning's workout, the one that was only possible because Callum was so generous about getting Oliver up and fed and out the door while Rupert snuck out and let Callum believe he was headed to the gym. Which sometimes he was. More often, though, he was coming here.

When he returned to the arena, Rupert made a point of plunking his gear down on the aluminum bench right in front of the group of parents, catching the eyes of the arsehole and his smirking friends as he yanked his skates out of their bag.

The already subdued group went silent again. The hairs on the back of Rupert's neck prickled, standing to attention as he bent to lace up. He stood, unflinching in the face of their frowns, to shuck his tie and jacket and tuck his shirt in tighter.

He really wanted to tell that horrible man to fuck off. To force him to apologize to the parents of the child he'd just spewed his ignorance and hate about. But Rupert's bravery had limits. Lots of them. So instead, he turned toward the ice.

"Callum!"

Callum's head snapped around as Rupert sailed over the boards, blatantly showing off as he swung his feet through the air then landed on the ice gently. He loved this moment, the sound of his blades cutting through the surface beneath him, the particular smell of the cold air that hovered just above the ice.

He never felt more at home, more surefooted, than when he was wearing his skates.

He stopped short right next to Callum, snowing Callum's pant legs and eliciting giggles from the scout troop, as he had hoped.

He smiled. "I thought you might be able to use my help."

Callum took a moment to stare down at his skates, his *figure skates*, then up at Rupert's face. Rupert arched an eyebrow and waited.

"You said you didn't skate."

"No, I agreed when you accused me of never having played hockey."

A collective gasp went up from the group.

"*Never?*" came from the boy in the figure skates, of all people.

"Never," Rupert said with a firm nod, trying not to laugh at the positively scandalized looks from everyone but Callum.

One boy whispered, "How is that even possible?"

"You heard his accent. He's not Canadian!" deduced another,

and everyone immediately nodded, as if this explained all of Rupert's sad life choices.

Callum bit his lip, his eyes sparkling with laughter. Rupert's heart flipped over in his chest.

"Well, then," Rupert said primly, "Shall we begin?"

One of the bigger boys, who to this point had mostly been left scowling in the back of the group, came forward. "What can you teach me about skating in those things?" He gestured at Rupert's skates with transparent disdain. "I play hockey, and I don't need any of that twinkle-toes gay crap to be good at it."

Rupert felt a compulsion to pull the boy in figure skates closer. To keep him safe. His friends, though, closed ranks faster than Rupert could blink, lining up at his back and glaring at the other boy.

"Let me be perfectly clear here," Callum said, his voice sterner than Rupert had ever heard it. Every boy before them snapped to attention. "There is no room for hate on this ice. Not with me here, not ever, do you understand?" Heads bobbed, particularly the one who'd spoken out. Apparently satisfied, Callum took a deep breath and settled back on his skates. "Now, let's be real. You can learn more about skating from a figure skater than you can from a hockey player any day."

Rupert tried really hard not to look surprised, or to beam at Callum and make his affection blatantly obvious to everyone in the arena. And possibly from space.

"We can?" the hockey player returned with extreme dubiousness, but he was listening.

"Yes. In fact, there are a number of NHL players who were junior champions in figure skating before they decided to focus on hockey alone. Just like your friend here..." Callum paused and looked at the boy in figure skates.

"Christian."

"Christian. I bet you've played hockey some, right?"

"I still do." Christian's sad smile almost broke Rupert's heart. "It's not like I have a choice," he finished with a mutter.

Callum blinked, but didn't break. "And do you think you're a better hockey player because of your figure skating?"

Christian shrugged, but one of his friends clipped him on the shoulder. "Come on, dude. You're an awesome hockey player."

"See!" Callum said with a nod, addressing the whole group again. "If you don't believe me, check out YouTube. There are tons of videos of hockey players figure skating. Even one of a guy doing an axel to avoid getting hit, right on center ice during an NHL game."

Christian grinned up at Callum. Rupert wasn't the only one on the ice with a crush now.

If they hadn't been surrounded by children, Callum would have just given in and stared at Rupert non-stop. Instead he dialed it back to, like, eighty percent. Which was a fucking *achievement.*

Rupert looked so different with his shirt tucked in tight, accentuating his flat belly and his magnificent ass. In hindsight, Callum had no fucking idea how he hadn't taken one look at that butt and known instantly that Rupert skated. *A lot.*

He'd come sailing over the boards like it was nothing, then skimmed across the ice as if he was floating. Spine straight, legs strong, shoulders back, head up.

Honestly, it was super hot. Callum wanted to rip Rupert's clothes off and lick every goddamn inch of his perfect, beautiful body.

Which wasn't really what he should be thinking about in front of a scout troop.

Rupert cleared his throat.

"Right!" Callum shouted enthusiastically, brain scrambling to figure out what the hell kind of skating drill would work for this group. "Let's have everyone go around a couple times, counterclockwise to start, so we can see how you skate."

Everyone took off as instructed, while Callum and Rupert followed. Callum fought the ridiculous urge to take Rupert's hand as they glided along, side by side.

"You *are* sneaky," Callum muttered, fascinated by how Rupert moved.

Rupert smiled. "Maybe a little." His eyes tracked Christian. "And he's quite good, actually."

Even Callum could see as much, and he was decidedly ignorant about all things figure skating related. "I'm glad. I get the impression he gets a lot of shit for his interest."

"Not just from the kids, either," Rupert said darkly, indicating their audience with a tilt of his head.

Callum's good mood soured. "What happened?"

"Let's talk about it later."

They made the kids switch directions a few times, which most handled well. Then Callum called for them to spread out and go around backwards. In under fifteen seconds, two boys were sprawled out on the ice and at least half the troop wasn't far behind, either because of their skill level or because they were laughing too hard at their friends.

"I think we've found something we can work on," Rupert said with a grin.

"Everyone back on the blue line!" Callum called, waiting at center ice with Rupert while the scouts lined up.

"We're going to focus on skating backwards," Rupert announced, taking the lead, which Callum was happy to concede. Rupert launched into an explanation of what he wanted them to do, but was soon interrupted.

"Why should we listen to you? We came here to learn from him," whined their super-rude hockey-playing friend, gesturing at Callum.

"You came here to see Garrick LeBlanc, who was nice enough to send me when he couldn't make it," Callum corrected, his temper on a tight leash.

The boy didn't seem bothered in a slightest. "My father will be pissed if Christian made us do all that work for nothing."

Rupert frowned at the boy. "Is your father in the stands?

Wearing a green shirt, perhaps?"

"No?" the kid replied, confused. "That sounds like Mr. Shaw."

Rupert's expression was grim. Callum was definitely going to ask about whatever that asshole had done.

"Yeah," Christian said with another of his sad smiles, "the guy in the green shirt is *my* dad."

Rupert looked stricken. Callum slid forward, blocking the boys' view of Rupert while he had a chance to regain his composure.

Callum smiled at Christian. "The fundraiser was your idea?"

"Yeah," he said shyly.

"Good for you," Callum said. "You should be proud of yourself."

Christian just shrugged. "I guess."

"No guess about it," Rupert said, returning to stand with Callum. "You've done a very good thing."

"Thanks."

"I'm Rupert," he said, holding out his hand. "Rupert Smythe."

Christian's mouth fell open and he folded his hands high against his chest. He stared up at Rupert like he was witnessing a miracle. "You're Rupert Smythe?" he said in a hushed voice.

Twin pink stains appeared on Rupert's cheeks. "Yes, I am."

"Oh my god."

Callum was definitely missing something. Christian's friends appeared just as lost.

"I don't get it," one of them said. "Is that a big deal?"

Christian gasped, outraged. "A big deal? *A big deal?* Mr. Smythe is *The Earl.*" Callum got the distinct impression that was supposed to mean something to all of them, as far as Christian was concerned. "He was supposed to be the first to win an Olympic gold medal in skating for Great Britain since 1976."

The hockey dickhead frowned. "And he screwed up or something?"

"No," Christian said, suddenly looking for all the world as if he might cry in the midst of his fanboy meltdown, "he didn't compete. He was attacked by a bunch of—"

"Well! Yes, my goodness, what a wonderful trip down memory lane this has been. Thank you, Christian," Rupert said gently, tempering his fairly rude interruption with a smile and a hand on Christian's shoulder. "It's humbling to think there are still those who have heard of me."

"Heard of you?" Christian asked as if the words no longer made sense.

Callum was going to Google the shit out of Rupert the *second* they got home.

"Let's begin the exercise now!" Rupert said quickly, sparing himself from their curious gazes. As soon as the boys took off to begin their first slow turn around the rink backwards, Callum turned to Rupert.

"*Soooo* sneaky."

Rupert huffed in a combination of exasperation and amusement. "I am not."

"You really are."

Rupert spun, skating off backwards and talking to Callum about the boys around them before shouting his suggestions to those who needed help. Callum watched, fascinated, as Rupert seamlessly transitioned to each student, complimenting their form where possible, offering useful suggestions as needed. Callum also offered input, identifying several boys who had probably developed the bad habit of relying on their hockey sticks to keep them balanced and were struggling because of it. Rupert offered new exercises to those boys.

Christian did not have any issues skating backwards. Or forwards. Or sideways. He flew by them, time and again, while weaving in and out of his troopmates. The fifth time he slid past Rupert with a cheeky smile on his face, Rupert took off after him. Once he'd caught the boy, they changed roles, and Callum watched agape as Rupert flew around the rink backwards, dodging children and goal nets with barely a glance. Eventually, Rupert ordered everyone to center ice while he and Christian did another lap backwards, this time with Christian's eyes closed.

He did it perfectly.

"Do a trick!" shouted one of the boys.

Christian grinned, his big, carefree smile transforming his face. "Okay!" His arms floated out and one foot hovered above the ice for a moment, then suddenly he was in the air, launching and spinning and perfectly landing a double axel. A cheer went up from the troop.

"Now you!" another boy shouted.

Rupert grinned, and it was the same carefree smile as Christian's a moment before. Callum's heart did funny things, then stopped altogether when Rupert leapt into the air, his legs spread wide, touching his toes as he flew over the ice and spun a half turn before landing gently and stopping not five inches from Callum.

A cheer went up from the bench where Alexei and Mike sat. He'd also clearly impressed their previously cynical audience, even their disgruntled hockey player. "That was awesome!"

"Thank you," Rupert said, flushing.

Callum just kept staring. At Rupert's hair, still perfectly in place. His long, strong, and apparently, really, really flexible legs. The pink in his cheeks. The sleek black skates on his feet.

"What are you thinking?" Rupert asked quietly after sending their merry troop out on another backward spin.

Callum met his gaze, fairly certain by the deeper reds staining Rupert's cheeks that Rupert could guess well enough.

Rupert was feeling pretty satisfied that their clinic had been a success by the time he sent the boys to the locker room to change out of their skates. Rupert followed Callum toward the seats where they'd left their bags, nodding at Mike and Alexei as they came to meet them.

He hesitated for a moment when he saw the dark scowl on Christian's father's face, then squared his shoulders and calmly walked through the door Callum held for him.

He eyed the people around them as he and Callum changed back into their street shoes. He kept catching Callum watching him, then looking at the parents in the stands with a frown. Alexei, on the other hand, had a sparkle in his eye that Rupert didn't trust at all.

"What did you think?" Rupert asked Oliver, hoping to deflect whatever Alexei was thinking about saying or doing.

"That was fun!" he declared. "Papa used to watch movies of you on his computer sometimes and he'd let me watch, too."

Something tightened painfully in Rupert's chest. "He did?"

Oliver nodded earnestly.

Rupert didn't know what to say to that. Honestly, he hadn't even been sure his father had cared when he'd almost made it to the Olympics. By then, Rupert had been training and living in Canada full-time.

"That's nice," he finally managed, his voice hoarse.

A gentle hand pressed to the small of his back and he smiled at Callum. He was infinitely grateful for the distraction of the troop returning to find their rides home. Rupert stopped Christian as he walked by.

"If there is anything I can do to help you, if you'd like to work together sometime, I'd be honored."

Christian looked up at him with wide eyes. "*Really?*"

"Of course. Let me give you my number."

Rupert had to pluck Christian's cell phone from his hand as the boy stood there, agape and unmoving. He entered his information under R. Smythe and was handing the phone back just as the arsehole in the green shirt came up to them.

"Let's go, Chris, we've wasted enough time on this shit."

Christian blushed, a terrible combination of fury and humiliation crossing his face. "It's Christian," he said defiantly.

His father scoffed. "I named you, I can call you whatever I want. Now let's go. You've got useful shit like homework and hockey practice to get to."

"Sir, might I have a word?" Rupert asked stiffly, battling the strong desire to wring the man's neck.

It was hard to tell who looked more worried—Callum, Alexei, Mike, or Christian.

Christian's father just looked bored. "What do *you* want?"

"Might I ask your name?"

"John. John Shaw," he snapped.

The expected, "*And yours?*" was apparently not forthcoming. Rupert noted Christian's alarmed expression, Oliver's curiosity, and Callum's increasingly stormy scowl. "Might Mr. Shaw and I have a word in private?" he said to their audience.

"No," Alexei said baldly.

Mike stepped forward and plucked Oliver from Alexei's arms. "Christian, right?"

Christian looked up at Mike with wide eyes. "Uh, yeah?"

"I'm Mike Erdo."

"Yeah, I know," Christian replied, star-struck. "And you're Alexei Belov, right?"

"I am," Alexei said with a tight smile.

"Come on, Christian," Mike said cheerfully, his gaze darting between Rupert and Christian's father. "Why don't you come with me and Oliver, and you can introduce me to some of your friends. I'd be curious to learn more about what teams they play on."

Christian grinned. "Okay! They're going to freak the fuuu—"

"Fadoodle," Rupert supplied.

Christian smirked. "Right, they're going to freak the *fadoodle* out."

Mike laughed. "Sounds fun. Come on."

Rupert waited, Alexei and Callum standing guard at his back, until Mike and the children were out of earshot before turning to Christian's father. "Mr. Shaw, my name is Rupert Smythe. I'm the manager of the Moncton Ice Cats, and, as you saw, a figure skater by training."

"So?"

Rupert barely held onto his already brittle smile. "So, your son has a great deal of talent. I'd be happy to work with him some, talk to you about coaching and training programs in the area if he's not already enrolled—"

"No fucking way," John Shaw snapped. "It's bad enough I promised his mother before she died that I wouldn't make him stop all this bullshit, but there's no fucking way I'm going to let you drag him into it any further. The last thing that boy needs is more ways to act like some fucking queer freak."

Rupert was momentarily rendered speechless, his cold disdain turning to hot, hot rage. When Alexei took a step forward, Rupert stayed him with a hand and kept his gaze locked on John Shaw.

"You, sir, have a lovely and talented son. You should be proud of him. You should be *encouraging* him. He clearly loves to skate, and he's bloody marvelous at it, particularly given his age. But beside the fact that you may be too ignorant and bloody-minded to see that, you're also a monster if this is the kind of thing you say to that child at home. There is nothing inherently *queer* about figure skating, but even if there were, it's what Christian wants to do. And if he does happen to be gay, that's not a choice. It's not a decision you can influence. It either is or it isn't, and to try to turn that into something ugly, into something that might make that kind, clever young man turn to self-loathing, puts you among the most despicable creatures I've ever had the misfortune to meet. You don't deserve that boy. And *he* certainly deserves better than you."

Callum caught up with Rupert outside by the car after he'd stormed out of the arena, leaving a red-faced John Shaw stewing rinkside. Callum ignored the curious looks from Mike, Christian, and Oliver as he jogged through the lobby. Alexei could explain as needed.

He was prepared to tease Rupert mightily for his ballsy performance back in the arena, but the words died on his lips when he saw Rupert's pale face.

He grabbed Rupert's hands and felt them tremble. "You okay?"

Rupert nodded jerkily. "I'm fine. I'm so sorry. That really wasn't like me at all."

"Really? You've never been shy about putting me in my place," Callum said wryly. "It seems like that asshole deserved it just as much."

"God, no, you're nothing like that man. I'm sorry, Callum. I never meant to—"

"Easy, duchess." Callum smiled and squeezed Rupert's hands. "Yes, he definitely deserves it more, and for far better reasons. But I deserved it, too. And that was still a brave thing you did in there."

"And thus why it was so unlike me," Rupert said with a grimace.

"What are you talking about?"

"Have you forgotten? This is me, Rupert, the man who cowers in the face of his own hockey team. The one who nearly knocked himself unconscious on a filing cabinet the day we met."

"That's bullshit," Callum spat, furious. Rupert's head jerked up. "You're plenty brave, Rupert. Braver than I could have been. I agreed with everything you said, was thinking the same things. But I'd never have the guts to say it. You weren't afraid to tell that asshole the truth, you didn't worry what he would think. I hide from the truth every day. *All the time*, Rupert. Who's the coward here?"

"You're not a coward, Callum."

"Aren't I? You're out. You own it. Are proud of it in all the ways you should be. It's part of who you are and people see that and it's...you're so..."

"What?"

Callum forced himself to say what he'd been thinking since Rupert had railed against John Shaw.

"Beautiful. Strong."

"Oh," Rupert breathed, the color suddenly returning to his cheeks. "Oh, you—"

"Rupert!" Alexei yelled from the doorway, making Rupert jump. Callum released his hands, happy to have been interrupted before god knew what else came out of his mouth.

Rupert managed a reasonable facsimile of a smile for Oliver. "You ready to go?"

Oliver clung to Alexei's neck. "I want to finish our adventure."

"Sure, little man!" Alexei bellowed with a big smile.

"You don't mind?" Rupert asked.

"Of course not!"

Callum watched, confused, as Rupert pulled Oliver's car seat from the back of his car and thrust it at Mike. "Do you need help installing it?"

Mike only blinked for a second. "Nope. I got it."

Callum considered mentioning Oliver's freak out earlier when he'd tried to leave him with Mike and Alexei, but held his tongue. Oliver didn't seem bothered at all now, leaving Callum to wonder if perhaps *he* should be the one getting lectures about letting small boys manipulate him.

"Great," Rupert said, a tad too enthusiastically. "How about we meet up at six for dinner at Quigley's? Reese will be there, too."

"Sure!" Alexei agreed, mimicking Rupert's enthusiasm. They were both ridiculous. "Maybe then we can learn more of your secrets. You have a lot of them."

"I do not—"

"Ha! Yes, you do!" Alexei called over his shoulder, already walking away, Oliver's giggle trailing behind them.

Rupert glared after him. "That man is annoying on purpose, isn't he?"

Callum chuckled. "I think so, yes."

Rupert harrumphed then turned for the car.

"Where are we going?" Callum asked as he jogged around to the passenger door.

"I thought we might go back to the hotel," Rupert said extremely casually.

Callum paused. "The hotel?"

Chapter Nine

If pressed, Rupert couldn't say how they arrived at the hotel in one piece. This was their first chance since London to be alone, truly alone, for a good long stretch of time. The freedom made Rupert giddy. It was like playing hooky, only better, and, if Rupert got his way, a far more grown-up version then any he'd played in school.

He didn't regret Oliver coming to live with him. Every day, he discovered new reasons he was delighted to have his brother home. Seeing the world through his eyes, having that steady presence and affection in his life was amazing.

But he also now had a keen appreciation for all those times his married friends had talked about the sanctity of Date Night.

He glanced at Callum again. He looked very, very nervous. Rupert thought about telling him it was okay. That they didn't have to do anything. That they could still go to the arena and do a couple hours of work instead of...

Instead of what? Just what the hell *were* they going to do once they got back to the hotel?

Of course, Rupert had a general idea. The semi-erection he'd been sporting since Callum had held his hands and told him he was beautiful sure as hell had ideas. But this was Callum. Who, for all intents and purposes, was a virgin.

Rupert's confidence flagged, even if his erection didn't.

Maybe this wasn't a good idea. Maybe they should go back to work. Maybe Rupert was pulling up to the valet at their hotel and leaping out of the car like it was on fire, a hand shoved in his pocket for decency's sake as he walked around the car to Callum's side.

Rupert couldn't remember ever being so eager to make what was probably a really bad decision. He couldn't remember when it had stopped feeling like a bad decision at all.

Callum was silent, and Rupert might have worried, except Callum had been forced to shove his hands in his pockets upon exiting the car. In spite of his nerves, Callum was still interested. Very interested, if the faint outline Rupert found himself staring at for the length of their elevator ride was any indication.

By some miracle, Rupert got the door to the room open, held it as Callum brushed past him, then let it swing shut with a note of finality. Callum jumped.

Rupert considered again that he should give Callum an out, but then Callum turned to him and Rupert just *couldn't*. He wanted this. Callum wanted this. And even if it was a really stupid idea, it wasn't one he could shake. Not once since Montreal. And, if he were honest, for some time before that.

He stepped up to Callum, their chests almost touching. "Thank you," he said, his lips brushing Callum's.

"For what?" Callum whispered.

Rupert pressed their lips together again. "For saying I'm brave."

"Oh," Callum said, his eyes fluttering shut. "You're welcome."

"And for saying I'm beautiful."

Callum sighed. "You are."

The next kiss lingered, and Callum's arms curled around Rupert's waist.

"Is this okay?" Rupert asked.

"Umm...yeah." Callum kissed him. Still gentle. Nothing like the assault in Rupert's office earlier, but no less keenly felt. "This is better than okay."

Rupert slid his hand along Callum's jaw and into his hair, tilting his head just a little bit.

This kiss was deeper. Rupert brushed his tongue along the seam of Callum's lips, was immediately granted access, and licked into Callum's mouth. Callum's tongue met his, no longer shy, but not bold either. The hint of hesitation, the curiosity, the clench of Callum's hands on Rupert's hips, drew in Rupert more thoroughly than the most experienced lover ever had.

Rupert lost track of time. Place. They stood in the tiny front hallway of their hotel room and made out like a couple of teenagers for what felt like hours. *Days.* Long, drugging kisses with Callum's arms around Rupert, Rupert's curled around Callum's neck. Rupert hadn't kissed anyone so much, for so long, since he'd *been* a teenager. And for the life of him, now he couldn't figure out why. Why hadn't he wanted to do this?

He had a terrible suspicion that it wouldn't have been so sweet, so hypnotic, with anyone else who'd come before. He didn't want think about why, so he rededicated himself to kissing the breath out of Callum as Callum did the same to him.

The urgency hovered, just beneath his skin, eager but willing to simmer close to the surface while Rupert learned everything he could about Callum Morrison. What he liked. What he didn't like as much. It wasn't easy. Nothing broke the flattering and encompassing concentration Callum poured into kissing Rupert. Rupert was fascinated by how Callum's technique changed by the minute. Trying things Rupert had done. Trying things Rupert hadn't even thought of.

Rupert offered all the feedback he could to Callum without ever leaving his lips. He wasn't typically a noisy lover, but he found he couldn't help but moan when Callum's tongue curled around his. Couldn't help but shudder and hum when Callum let him suck on his tongue.

Rupert let his hand roam over Callum's back, drifting over his ribs. Callum shifted against him, pressing into his touch, setting his own hands to coast over Rupert. Callum was not the first lover who couldn't seem to resist Rupert's ass, but never had a man skimmed their hands so gently over every curve. The tips of his fingers traced the line where his butt met his thighs, as if Callum were studying it. He seemed to particularly like the little whimper Rupert couldn't hold in each time his fingers brushed in the middle, dancing over nerve endings that practically screamed for a firmer touch. A lick. *Anything* to ease the ache of his heavy erection and slow the speeding of his heart.

Rupert could see now he'd been overly confident that his experience would leave him a certain amount of control. Of distance. Instead, Callum's curiosity, his hesitation and trust and generosity, were slowly taking Rupert apart. Callum didn't do what Rupert expected. What he had come to expect from his previous lovers. Reese had been unfair to label them all boring, but they hadn't been particularly wild either. Eager in bed, interested, invested even, but they knew what to do. How to do it. In theory. Rupert certainly hadn't had cause to complain in the moment.

But Callum just *guessed* and managed to do it better, more sincerely than anyone before him. Rupert might let the damn man stand there and feel up his ass for hours if he wanted. Because Rupert wanted that. He got a vicarious thrill each time Callum discovered something new, then tried it again and grew more confident, more bold, and then did it again.

Callum's long fingers met again, skimming down over the middle of Rupert's butt, tracing the seam of his trousers before tucking in between his thighs. Rupert broke their kiss with a gasp, holding himself still but paying for the effort. He shut his eyes as tremors ran through his body, begging him to press back and urge Callum to take his exploration in a new direction.

It was only a matter of a second, maybe two, but Rupert knew this hesitation was different. Maybe it was the tension in the arms around him, or that Callum, too, held his breath.

Rupert opened his eyes, blinking against the bright light above them, and drew his head back just far enough to focus on Callum's face.

Callum chewed on his lower lip, and Rupert stared at how red, how swollen, it was. He tasted his own lips, enjoying how they buzzed with beard burn and hard kisses.

A line formed between Callum's brows. "I don't…"

Rupert waited, slowly dragging his thumb across Callum's cheekbone, marveling at the soft skin above where his beard began, at how warm it was. It grew warmer as a blush rose while Callum worked out what he wanted to say.

"I'm not sure…" Callum sighed, then dropped his hands from Rupert's ass. "I don't know what I'm doing."

"Could have fooled me," Rupert said with a smile.

It was, it seemed, the wrong thing to say. Callum stepped away, leaving Rupert to stand alone on decidedly weak knees. "Rupert, I told you—"

"Shhh..." Rupert leaned in and silenced him with a kiss. Then another. "I just meant that what you were doing was good. That it felt good. I wanted you to keep doing it."

Callum studied Rupert with wide, dark eyes, his pupils blown so that only a thin band of emerald green remained. "Yeah?"

"Yes," Rupert said, ready to beg to have Callum's hands on him again. When Callum pressed closer, Rupert held on, trying not to stumble. Callum's hands caught his elbows.

"Are you okay?"

Now Rupert did smile. "I'm feeling a little unsteady on my feet, if you must know."

Callum's slow smile was unpardonably smug. "Sorry?"

Rupert laughed, not bothering to dignify that with a response. He longed to tow Callum down the hall and into the bedroom, but didn't actually consider doing it. He'd finally gotten the worry to leave Callum's face, didn't think Callum was even all that aware that he'd slid his hands down to grasp Rupert's hips, his fingers resting on the top of Rupert's ass again.

"How about the couch?"

"What?" Callum asked, apparently distracted by staring at Rupert's mouth.

"The couch. I'm asking you to make out with me on the couch, as this standing up business is getting difficult."

Rupert wasn't sure what kind of reaction this would get, but he never would have predicted Callum pulling him by the hand to the furniture in question, sitting down and dragging Rupert down over him.

"Like this?" Callum asked, suddenly nervous again as Rupert straddled him, his knees pressed into the cushions next to Callum's hips. Callum's ability to act decisively one moment, then hesitate and question himself the next, should have been annoying. Distracting, at the least. Certainly not so bloody endearing.

"This is good," he assured Callum, resting his weight on Callum's thighs, careful not to spread his legs too far. Yet.

Callum's arms came up to circle Rupert's waist, a hand on his back tipping him forward until their lips met again.

Callum had no idea what the fuck he was doing, but when Rupert's lips were pressed to his, and his gorgeous butt was perched on Callum's thighs, he no longer cared. He just wanted to keep kissing Rupert. Keep touching him. He'd only stopped earlier because he had no idea what the etiquette was here. Was there even etiquette for these things?

Like, really, he had *no idea what he was doing.* He was the ultimate rookie. Worse than a rookie, actually, since this was more like making an NHL debut when all he'd done to prepare was play shinny in the backyard. Callum's sexual experiences had been few, and none of them anything like this. None had been in his home, or even a hotel. Hell, none had allowed for him to sit down, for fuck's sake, let alone for soft furniture and long kisses that made his head spin from lack of oxygen, but felt too fucking good to stop. He'd never done more than groped at a potential partner's ass, the universal sign language for "I want a piece of this". He'd never once been able to take his time, curving his palm over firm muscles and feeling how they shifted as his partner pushed back against his touch.

It was a lot, an embarrassment of riches in the face of his limited history. His fingertips buzzed as they brushed along the soft lines of Rupert's slacks, over his hips, pressing down on the firm, beautiful, and frankly fucking huge swell at the top of Rupert's ass before cresting over that perfect bubble and down to stroke the backs of his thighs.

Callum wanted it all. He wanted to touch and taste and feel and try everything. But he didn't want to rush. Partly he was afraid of humiliating himself, but mostly he couldn't quite ignore the tiny voice in the back of his head, reminding him that this might be his one chance. That he should relish and memorize every touch, every moment, because this might be the only opportunity he had for years to come.

He shoved those thoughts away when he could, but they never left him completely. He wondered if he seemed desperate. Or if he just plain wasn't good at this. He worried that it was weird that he couldn't stop petting Rupert's ass. Though Rupert didn't seem to mind, if the way he squirmed, licking hotter and faster into Callum's mouth, was anything to go by.

Callum was beginning to understand Rupert's signals. The little noises and motions that indicated what he liked. What he loved. With that in mind, Callum curled his fingers around Rupert's hips and held on tight, focusing on their mouths as they clashed together. The kiss went deeper. Hotter. It was wet and messy, and kind of filthy, and Callum loved it.

He tugged Rupert closer, working on instincts that screamed at him to finally do something about the pressure in his balls. The ache of having been hard for so damn long. Rupert's long, lean legs spread around him, his knees digging further into the cushions as he slid his hand into Callum's hair to pull himself closer.

Callum jerked when Rupert's weight settled fully on his lap, tearing an embarrassing grunt from his chest. None of those things stopped him from thrusting up against that warm weight, from gripping Rupert tighter, closer.

He thought he might die when Rupert's hips started to move, making hot, beguiling circles as he ground against him. Callum groaned at the press of Rupert's erection.

He had no idea what to do next. What to do *now*. So he just kept kissing Rupert and holding on tight.

Rupert froze and Callum whined, deep in his throat, only stilling his own motions when Rupert's hand landed on his chest. Rupert gasped against his lips, attempting to start a sentence at least three times before managing, "I refuse to come in my pants. We have to stop."

Callum's heart fell to somewhere around his feet. "We do?"

Rupert leaned back to look at Callum, and Callum bravely stared back. He had a few ideas about what could come next, things he'd done before, but he was oddly loathe to suggest any of them. To *do* any of them.

With a flush of embarrassment, he realized he wasn't ready. God, he was like a fifteen-year-old blushing virgin. It was humiliating.

Rupert touched his cheek. "We can stop," he said, earnestly.

"I don't want to."

"What do you want?"

"I don't know," he confessed. Because he was an idiot. How irritating a lover was he that he couldn't even figure out his own needs, let alone begin to guess at Rupert's?

Rupert, though, just kissed him again, and again, until Callum forgot to worry about what he should be doing, what he was meant to ask for, and could only focus on their tongues dancing together and the grind of their hips. He whined, again— and holy shit, he had to find a way to knock that off—when Rupert slid down his thighs, his ass once more perched closer to Callum's knees and way too fucking far away from his dick.

His fingers dug into the firm muscles of Rupert's ass, his thumbs hooked over his hip bones as he tried to drag him back. His arms went completely lax, though, when Rupert's hand brushed over his erection.

"Oh shit," he breathed, his hips jumping up to meet that pressure.

Rupert smiled, then kissed him again, tracing Callum's shaft while his other hand wrestled with Callum's belt.

Callum wanted to help. He wanted to snap his belt in two and hurl it across the room. But he just lay there, slumped against the back of the couch, and let Rupert have his way. He groaned and gasped and shook as Rupert tore at his clothes, his hips jerking as Rupert's inherent grace was lost to his battle with denim and leather. He only had Callum's belt open and the button freed when he gave up the fight and slid his hand beneath the fabric, pressing his warm fingers along the damp spot on Callum's briefs and directly over his cock.

Callum cried out, the sound muffled by Rupert's lips and tongue as he ground up against Rupert's hand. He wanted to rut against Rupert like this for all of the approximately seven seconds it would take to come, but didn't know if that was right. Or fair. He hadn't even laid a hand on Rupert yet.

Rupert curled his fingers around Callum, cupping his shaft through the cotton, and let out a hum of pleasure.

Every goddamn thought in Callum's head departed for parts south. "Jesus, Rupert, I—"

"Shhh," Rupert whispered against his lips, then kissed his way to Callum's ear. Callum clung to him, his hips twitching in spite of his attempts to hold them still. How was he supposed to do that when Rupert's tongue was tracing the shell of his ear, his teeth nipping at the lobe? He was only fucking human, here.

"I've got you," Rupert said, his lips tickling Callum's skin.

Then strong hands were shoving his shirt up to his armpits, and his pants down over his hips, taking his shorts with them. Callum lifted as best he could with Rupert above him, gasping with relief when his dick finally sprang free of his clothing. He squirmed when his bare ass settled back on the rough upholstery, then Rupert's hand curled around him, fingers hot and tight, and he froze.

"Jesus fuck," he whispered, whimpering when Rupert's other hand fisted in his hair, tilting his face up.

"Is this okay?" Rupert asked as he skimmed his thumb over the head of Callum's cock, sending shivers down his spine.

"Are you joking?" Callum managed to gasp. He couldn't *not* thrust his hips up into that tight grasp. His thighs burned and shook with each frantic contortion. He wanted to shut his eyes and just...fall. Fling himself, even, into the pleasure trying to consume him, but he held Rupert's gaze as they rocked together.

Rupert's smile wobbled, his rhythm faltering, and Callum looked down to see Rupert pressing the heel of his hand to his own erection, as if forcing it to subside.

Callum didn't think, leaving no time to worry about etiquette and roles and the fact that he was operating blind here, he just reached for Rupert's waist and tore at his belt. He felt momentarily victorious when he managed to pry it open, but it was fleeting when he discovered his hands shook too hard for him to get Rupert's fly open in fewer than three tries. Somehow, Rupert's quiet laugh against his ear reassured instead of mocked.

Still, it felt like he was never going get those damn pants open.

At last he succeeded, but his well of determination and confidence had run dry. He stopped, his hands hovering there, but Rupert didn't hesitate, thank fuck, and stood up just long enough to shove his pants to the floor. Callum had no more than two seconds to look at Rupert's thick cock, shaft riddled with veins, head flushed pink, and to think it was all beautiful, before Rupert slid back onto Callum's lap and pressed the full lengths of their erections together.

"Oh, Jesus Christ," Callum cried a moment before Rupert captured his lips and swiveled his hips in a long, delicious, and really fucking amazing grind.

Callum kissed Rupert like his life depended on it, breathing like a bellows through his nose as he held Rupert against him and arched up into his heat. Their shafts, pinned between their bellies and against each other, rolled and rubbed, pre-come and sweat barely easing the too-hot friction. Callum didn't care. Couldn't stop. He could feel his orgasm crawling over his skin and up his spine, poised to tear at him. It was unlike anything he'd ever felt.

He'd had orgasms before, of course. But to this point, they'd been entirely solitary affairs. It hadn't mattered if he'd been jerking off at home alone or leaning against a filthy bathroom stall door, a stranger trapped in there with him and others in the cubicles around them. He'd been, he knew now, in all ways that mattered, completely alone.

Callum clutched Rupert, arms wrapped tight around him,

and pushed harder. Rupert's grip in Callum's hair was painful as he licked into Callum's mouth and rode his bucking hips while circling his own back down. They clung and writhed and somehow created a safe space for each other.

A place where Callum could finally let go.

"Rupert!" he shouted, his back arching off the couch as his climax sank its furious claws into him. He shuddered and held onto Rupert, knowing he was going to leave bruises, but unable to do otherwise.

Rupert moaned against his lips, their kiss now no more than a press of open mouths and shared breaths. Another wash of heat spread between their bodies as Rupert trembled in Callum's arms, the clockwork circles of his hips lost to inarticulate and frantic jerks.

They stayed there, lying in a tangled heap, for a long while. Callum's breathing returned to almost normal, and Rupert no longer shook, but they didn't move to separate or stand up. Instead, they stayed close, pressing their lips to each other wherever they could reach. Callum's hand stroked the length of Rupert's spine, while Rupert's long, elegant fingers traced over Callum's cheek, his ear, soothing his abused scalp where Rupert had yanked his hair.

Callum couldn't really hold onto any thought for long. He felt amazing. Lax and stupid and aware that he finally understood what the huge brouhaha was about "afterglow". This shit was awesome.

It was only when Rupert shifted that Callum realized his brain was still functioning, barely, and the very first real and solid thought that popped into his head promptly came out of his mouth.

"I think we're stuck together."

Rupert chuckled. "Hmmm...and here I was wondering if we could just stay here for another hour."

Something warm and sweet and really fucking scary uncurled in Callum's chest. He ignored it in favor of kissing Rupert slowly, licking past his swollen lips until he hummed with contentment.

Eventually, Rupert eased back, grimacing as their skin peeled apart. He looked down, at god knew what, but Callum kept his eyes pinned to Rupert's face. He was suddenly feeling very shy about his dick hanging out, and what he was pretty sure were the flecks of semen caught in his chest hair.

He forgot to worry about whether he look debauched versus disgusting when he really got a look at Rupert. Hair standing on end, face pink with beard burn, lips puffy and red, and his clothes wrinkled and askew or half torn off.

He was a *mess*. And perfect. Honest to god, Callum had never seen anything or anyone he wanted more.

"You look amazing," he said, then winced, frowning at himself.

"Is that bad?" Rupert asked curiously.

"No!" he said quickly. "I was just noticing that I can't seem to hold a thought for more than ten seconds, and when I do have one, it just comes right out my mouth. It's like you broke my filter or something."

"You had a filter?" Rupert asked, deadpan.

Callum sent him a supremely disgruntled look.

Rupert laughed. "Don't worry. You're just come-dumb."

"Pardon me?"

"I made you stupid, the sex was so good," Rupert said, practically preening.

Honestly, Callum wanted to preen, too. That sex had been *so good*. His dick twitched with interest, but there was no way he was going to recover this fast. He spared a moment to lament his virtuous teens and early twenties, but then let it go. Even that deep well of bitterness couldn't knock him off his contented high.

Rupert was tempted to suggest they shower together. It was probably more than Callum was ready for, but Rupert just...wasn't ready to let go. He'd started this intending to have a good time. To have sex. And they had. So how could it be that once again, it felt as though none of it had gone the way he'd expected?

Rupert could feel the sore spots on his hips and shoulders where Callum had dug in his fingers. There'd been times when Rupert hadn't been able to tell if Callum was in the throes of ecstasy or terror. He wasn't sure Callum had been able to tell, either. One moment Callum would be kissing him, leading the chase of lips and dance of tongues, and the next, he'd hesitate, like when he'd refused to look down at their laps, or his hand had hovered over some spot on Rupert's body that he so obviously had wanted to touch.

Rupert had intended to teach Callum something. To be his happily willing and hopefully able partner through a series of firsts. Now, that was lost to the memory of Callum saying his name, holding him close, kissing him long and hard with every ounce of his considerable focus and sometimes boundless affection honed down to the point where their lips met. Rupert was no longer so arrogant as to think he could or should teach Callum anything. Now, it was Rupert who wanted to learn. To explore what Callum could teach him. To figure out why Callum hesitated, what he really wanted to do, and to tear down the inhibitions that held him in check.

Which, perhaps, would be better left for when they weren't due at a restaurant to see friends and a curious four year old within the hour.

Rupert stood, groaning as his bad knee came unkinked from the back of the sofa. It hadn't occurred to him that it was a bad idea to abuse the already unpredictable joint like that. He stalled for time, tugging his clothes back to where they should be and smiling down at Callum, who didn't seem to know *where* to look.

Maybe this was the result of Callum training himself to not look at other men in the locker room. It was a skill Rupert had never managed to completely master—to his great peril, as it had turned out.

Those memories seemed to make his knee ache more, and put a damper on his mood. A shower, though, would restore his good humor and, hopefully, his knee. He took a step toward the bedroom and wobbled. Badly. Callum shot to his feet, a strong hand hooking around Rupert's elbow.

"Are you all right?" he asked, trying to stuff his junk back in his boxers with his free hand.

Rupert made himself look away from that delightful spectacle and tried to smile. "Yes, it's fine. Or it will be in a moment, I think."

"Did I hurt you?"

Rupert turned, swallowing his pride and allowing Callum to support him. "You didn't hurt me, Callum." He gave Callum a stern look, then smirked. "Not in any ways I didn't enjoy, anyway."

Callum's cheeks turned pink again. Rupert bit back a grin.

"But your knee..."

"My knee hurts, which is par for the course after having been struck by a car, even a decade later."

Callum blanched. "What?" He sounded angry, like he might find that car and exact long-overdue retribution.

"Its fine, Callum. It happened a long time ago. Look, I'm sure it will work now, see?"

Rupert took a step, biting his cheek to keep from whimpering.

Callum arched a dubious eyebrow. "You know I play hockey, right? I've seen a lot of guys pretend they aren't hurt. You kind of suck at it."

Rupert refrained from doing anything childish, like sticking out his tongue.

Callum's grip held firm. "At least let me help you to the bedroom so you don't fall on your face. I don't want to have to explain to Oliver that you're only graceful on skates."

"Generous of you," Rupert murmured, trying to sound put out, but not immune to the compliment buried in there. He started hobbling toward the door to the bedroom and the blessed relief of the shower beyond, Callum at his side, still holding one arm.

Callum released him once they were beside the bed and started backing away. "I'll just, uh..." He gestured over his shoulder toward the living room. "Wait my turn, I guess. You sure you're okay from here?"

Rupert worked hard to keep his expression serious in the face of Callum's maidenly sensibilities. He was tempted to point out they'd just had a rather lovely frottage on the couch, so perhaps Callum need not blush at the idea of seeing Rupert strip down for a shower.

"I'll be just fine," Rupert assured him, letting his smile break free once Callum had turned his back and bolted through the door.

Chapter Ten

"So, Rupert, I heard what happened," Mike said with a laugh as they settled into their booth at Quigley's. "You get that from *How to Make Friends and Influence People?*"

Alexei chuckled as he, Reese, and Mike slid in opposite Rupert, Oliver, and Callum.

Rupert immediately pictured what he and Callum had just been up to at the hotel, his pulse jumping with arousal and fear. "I haven't any idea what you mean," he said, stalling.

That couldn't be what Mike meant, could it?

"With that jerk back at the rink? The kid's father?

"Oh, yes. Right." Rupert said, relieved, then grimaced. "I shouldn't have done that. It was terribly foolish."

"Seemed terribly *necessary* to me," Alexei said.

"Yes, well," Rupert hedged, pleased by the support, "I don't think it will help convince that man to let his son continue to figure skate, let alone work with me."

"That might be true," Callum agreed. "But maybe he'll think before he opens his mouth again."

Reese looked between them all, confused. "What happened?"

Rupert wasn't sure what to expect, but he was abashed to listen to Alexei relay the story of his giant freak out on John Shaw in terms that were, frankly, glowing.

Reese smiled at Rupert, as if he wouldn't expect any less. "Well done, Rupert. You should have punched him in the nose!"

"I hardly think that would have helped," Rupert returned dryly. "And I didn't much feel like getting punched in return."

Alexei scowled. "I would have liked to see him try."

"As would have I," Callum agreed, a wealth of dark promise in his voice.

"I'm sorry I missed it," Reese said as his gaze shifted over their little group. For once, he wasn't the only one backing Rupert up.

It was rather nice. *A lot* nice, really.

"Me, too," Mike agreed. "I had no idea you had it in you," he said, his smile softening the truth.

"Don't be fooled, my friends," Reese said, "Rupert may look like royalty, but he doesn't suffer fools lightly, and shares his opinions without hesitation."

"You don't say," Callum deadpanned.

Rupert ignored that and smiled down at his brother. "Oliver, would you like me to read you the children's menu?"

"Yes, please," he replied, as if he'd never hesitated to speak in his life.

Rupert shared a smile with Callum over Oliver's head. They were hearing that sweet little voice more and more, but usually only when Oliver felt the need to be heard, to demand, or to defend.

Rupert took a moment to help Oliver, trying not to lose hope when Oliver chose to indicate his preferences by nodding or shaking his head silently. Rupert considered prompting Oliver to speak his order to the waiter, but feared putting him on the spot might result in a set-back rather than a breakthrough.

"So, Rupert, I have many questions for you," Alexei said with a smile as he handed over his menu, the last to order.

"You do?" Rupert asked, slightly terrified.

"Yes. You are a man of many secrets, it seems."

Rupert rolled his eyes. "You keep saying that, but it's simply not true."

"Let's review what we've learned," Alexei said with an unmistakable gleam of mischief in his eyes. He held up his hand to tick off the list on his fingers.

"Let's not," Rupert grumbled.

Alexei continued as if Rupert hadn't spoken. "You have a brother, your best friend is a famous recluse parading around

Moncton like he's nobody—"

"Hey!" squawked Reese.

"—you act jumpy around your own hockey team but yell at terrible parents in public."

"I don't usually—"

"Reese is your boyfriend one minute and not the next—"

Callum glowered at Alexei. "Reese is *not* his boyfriend."

"—and now we learn," Alexei continued, undeterred, "that you are a figure skater. A good one, too, from what we saw."

"He was supposed to go to the Olympics," Callum offered helpfully.

Rupert gave him a dirty look. Just ten seconds ago he'd sounded furious about Reese being his boyfriend, and now he was grinning.

"Oh ho!" Alexei boomed. "More secrets revealed!"

"Really, it's not a secret. It's just not relevant anymore."

Mike cocked his head. "Yeah, but it's interesting. Why wouldn't we want to know?"

Mike was talking like they were friends. Like Alexei didn't make it his life's mission to startle and shock Rupert at every bloody opportunity.

Callum, perhaps sensing Rupert didn't know what to say, spoke up. "What I want to know is why they called you The Earl?"

Rupert sent Reese a quelling look.

What Rupert didn't count on was Oliver. "Because he is an earl. We both are."

This pronouncement was met with a startled silence. Rupert could only wish it was because Oliver had spoken two full sentences aloud.

All eyes turned to Rupert, except Reese, who was giggling in the corner like an idiot.

Oliver's confidence flagged in the face of so many strange looks. "Isn't that right, Rupert?" he asked in a small voice.

Rupert could not regret his vow to encourage Oliver to speak about anything and everything he wished. He could, however, lament it for all he was worth.

"Yes, that's right, Oliver. Though, technically I'm an earl, and you're the heir to the earldom."

Oliver nodded, seemingly pleased to have this reaffirmed.

Mike, Alexei, and Callum all just stared at him.

"What?" Rupert asked defensively. He dearly wished someone would say or do something. Reese snorted. Something *useful*.

"You're an *earl?*" Callum asked, dragging out the title like it was foreign on his tongue.

Oliver bounced in his seat, his little legs swinging against the banquette. "Yes!"

Rupert rolled his eyes. "It isn't a big deal."

Now Reese guffawed. Rupert couldn't remember why he was ever friends with that man.

"The earl of what?" Alexei asked.

"Pardon?"

"What are you the earl of? I read books. We have nobility in Russia, too. What is your title?" he asked curiously.

Rupert sighed, having done this particular introduction more times than he cared to count. Before he could give a curt and entirely sufficient answer, Reese spoke up.

"I present to you fine gentlemen Lord Rupert Douglas Macalister Smythe, the tenth Earl of Weckfordham, and The Honourable Oliver Cameron Macalister Smythe, the future eleventh Earl of Weckfordham." Reese gestured at Oliver, who dipped his head regally, like the bloody Queen greeting her subjects.

Rupert shot Reese a baleful look. "*Really?*"

"What? Did I get it wrong?"

Reese knew perfectly well he had not. Rupert was grudgingly impressed that he recalled Oliver's middle name—

not that Rupert would admit anything of the sort.

"Macalister?" Callum asked.

"Yes, my grandmother was Scottish."

"And his cousin is now chieftain of the clan," Reese supplied, proving himself to be a veritable font of unhelpfulness.

Callum grinned. "My father is going to love you, duchess!"

"*Earl*," Oliver corrected sternly.

Rupert had no idea how to deal with this conversation. When did anyone decide Rupert would meet Callum's father? How was *that* ever going to come about?

"So many secrets!" Alexei cried, banging his hand on the table and making everything on it jump. "You are so sneaky!" He turned to Reese. "What else is he not telling us? Does he have a wife he isn't telling us about tucked away somewhere?"

"Hardly," Reese replied dryly.

"Well, then what?" Alexei demanded.

Reese looked up at the ceiling, for all the world appearing to be sorting through his extensive knowledge of Rupert, searching for some new gem. He didn't even notice Rupert glaring at him.

"I think that might actually be the best of it," Reese admitted, sounding terribly disappointed. "Except that he has a thing for black underwear, sucked his thumb until he was eleven, could probably have gone to the Olympics as an equestrian if he'd set his mind to that instead of skating, and his ancestral home is called Woodcock."

"Woodcock?" Alexei asked gleefully. Mike giggled.

Rupert dropped his head into the table. "Ungh." That was the sound of utter defeat.

"That's a good name for a house, Rupert. Very *manly*," Alexei assured him.

"Yes, thank you," Rupert replied as he lifted his head. He didn't bother glaring at Reese. Clearly his powers of telepathy weren't working, or Reese would have self-immolated by now.

Callum's low chuckle and dancing eyes were a better place

to focus.

"I love Woodcock," Oliver announced in a clear, high voice that sliced through the laughter at their table and the hum of conversations from the other patrons around them. The room got noticeably quieter. "Woodcock is so much fun. It's so *big!*"

Reese slumped into the corner, his face buried in his hands. Alexei, Mike, and Callum weren't much better. Oliver, bless him, smiled innocently. He hadn't meant to be funny, of course, but he liked that he had.

"I love it, too," Rupert managed with a straight face, rolling his eyes at the effect this declaration had on his friends.

His friends. It had been a long time since he'd sat round a table with a bunch of friends laughing so hard their ribs would hurt come morning.

Mike was the first to get himself under control. "Why don't you live there? I'm guessing being an earl comes with a bunch of responsibilities. I'm surprised you're over here in the colonies with us."

Rupert shrugged. "It's actually quite easy to do almost anything from here, and I have solicitors in London who handle a lot of what's needed. I came here when I was twelve because I wanted to work with a particular coach, and there happened to be an excellent school nearby that my father approved of. I met Reese and never left."

Alexei glanced between Rupert and Reese. "He was your boyfriend?"

Reese rolled his eyes. Rupert didn't feel even a tiny bit sorry for him.

"You're a little obsessed with this, you know that?" Reese said. "No, I am not now, nor have I ever been, Rupert's boyfriend."

Rupert just smiled. "Not my fault he doesn't have better taste."

Alexei and Mike both studied him, and he knew this particular look. The question. He hesitated only long enough to guess the fallout if they told the whole team, then decided he trusted them, and didn't give much of a damn if the team found out anyway.

"Yes, I'm gay," he said blandly, noticing from the corner of his eye how Callum flinched. He didn't dare look directly at him. Outing himself was fine, and not particularly unusual, but he was aware of how much just the idea of it scared the shit out of Callum.

The man had built a lifetime of lies on that fear. Rupert couldn't fathom what would ever make Callum go about dismantling it.

Mike and Alexei didn't seem particularly fazed by Rupert's revelation. Nor surprised, given the fifty dollar bill Alexei handed Mike—trying and utterly failing to be subtle, to Reese's further amusement.

"That's cool," Mike said with a smile once he'd tucked his winnings away.

All in all, it was a non-event.

Their food arrived and the conversation turned to the upcoming season, who the Ice Cats were scouting, and Mike asking if Callum thought it would be okay to reach out to Savannah about his training regimen, even though Callum's sister was no longer the team's trainer.

The answer was yes, of course. As it turned out, Savannah managed Callum's summer training program and had for years. They laughed about what an ass-kicker she was and started drilling down into the details of their summer workout schedules. Callum was relaxed and happy, and Rupert was struck again that he seemed so different from the man who had barged into his office a month ago.

That was, until Mike and Alexei invited Callum to actively train with them for the rest of the summer and Callum's plans for the coming weeks came up.

"I have to go to Vegas for the awards thing," Callum said, and at first, Rupert thought he was imagining how the light left Callum's eyes. How his shoulders curled in, just a little.

"That's right!" Alexei bellowed, as was his wont when he was excited, or on any day ending in y. "You won last year, right?"

"Uh, yeah," Callum said, staring at his plate. "So, I'm expected in Vegas for a few days, and my agent wants to meet with me while I'm out that way, so I'll be gone for four days."

By the time he finished speaking, Oliver was clutching his arm. The moment he sat back, Oliver climbed into his lap and buried his face against Callum's chest. He curled a hand around the back of Oliver's head, the pressed the other to his back.

"We talked about this, Ollie. It's not for a while and I'll only be gone for a few days. You can hang out with Rupert the whole time I'm away."

"I even cleared out most of my meetings, remember?" Rupert said, sliding closer and brushing a hand over his brother's thin shoulder.

"And we can help," Alexei offered. Mike nodded eagerly. "Will you hang out with us, little man?"

Oliver peered over his shoulder at Mike and Alexei, then blinked up at Rupert.

"Does that sound good?" Rupert asked.

Oliver nodded quickly.

"Okay!" Alexei boomed. "We will have lots of fun. We can come hang out at your house while Rupert has his meetings, if you want."

Rupert smiled at them gratefully.

"We don't have a house," Oliver said quietly.

Alexei cocked his head. "You don't?"

"Woodcock is too far away, so we live in a hotel."

Rupert grimaced. "I promise we'll find a new place to live soon, Oliver." He turned to Alexei and Mike to explain. "We're in an extended-stay hotel until I can find time to look. It's just…" he waved toward Oliver "…it's been busy."

Mike and Alexei exchanged a long look before turning back to Rupert. "We might know a place," Mike offered.

Over the past few weeks, Rupert had become increasingly anxious about the idea of moving. It wasn't that he didn't want more space—bloody hell, did he want more space—but he was worried that leaving the hotel would mean losing Callum. Oliver clearly wasn't ready. And neither was Rupert. Especially after this afternoon.

Rupert hedged. "I'll probably need at least three bedrooms. And I'd like to stay close to the arena."

Mike smiled. "There's a four-bedroom unit available in our building."

Rupert definitely hadn't considered living in close proximity to members of the Ice Cats organization. Though at least these two knew him and wouldn't be idiots about Rupert having a man in his life. The thing was, currently that role was filled by Callum, which might be more problematic.

"I like my privacy," Rupert admitted, "so I wasn't thinking of an apartment."

"The floor is accessed by private elevator, and we're the only others on that floor."

"Oh," Rupert said. It did sound private, and like it would stay that way, even if Mike or Alexei moved out. "So, there are only three apartments?"

Mike and Alexei shared another look, and it was only then that Rupert's gaydar pinged, *loudly*.

"There are only two apartments on the floor, actually," Alexei said, the quietest Rupert had ever heard him speak.

"*Oh*," Rupert said with a growing smile.

Alexei slipped his hand over Mike's, resting on the table between their plates, and threaded their fingers together. He tilted his chin up, proud, daring anyone to say something. Rupert snuck a glance at Callum just as his mouth fell open.

Alexei looked between all of them, arching one eyebrow. "Is this going to be a problem, boss?" he asked coolly.

Rupert wasn't sure who he's asking, since in one capacity or another they were *all* his bosses, but he was happy to be the one to answer.

Rupert grinned. "No problem at all, *neighbor*."

Callum stared at Alexei and Mike's hands for a long time. Alexei's big and wide and battle-scarred from years in the net, his pinky obviously having been broken at least once and unable to lie as flat as the others. Mike's long, thin fingers, the sinews stretching and flexing as he tightened his hold, gave Alexei's a little squeeze.

Callum didn't know what to say. How to say what he was thinking. So he stayed silent, aware of the looks he was getting, and held onto Oliver a little tighter. Mike and Alexei's expressions grew suspicious, and Callum knew he'd have to find a way to make it clear to these two incredibly brave men that he wasn't a bigot.

The weight of the life he'd carefully constructed was heavier than ever. He thought about the voicemail waiting on his phone. Michaela, calling to see if she was needed as his plus-one in Vegas. His beard. His big fat lie.

The push of Rupert's shoulder against his pulled him out of his own head. He wanted to drag Rupert closer, to press his face to Rupert's chest and hold onto him as tightly as Oliver clung to Callum. That he couldn't, that he didn't dare so much as reach out and brush his hand over Rupert's on the seat between them, only made him feel worse.

Reese broke the awkward silence. "You two make a handsome couple. May I ask if you've been together long?"

Alexei cast a wary eye on Reese. "Are you asking out of curiosity, or as the guy that's been writing my paychecks for the past five years?"

Reese didn't bat an eye. "I'm asking as your friend."

"Three years," Mike answered, his soft smile making something in Callum's gut clutch tight with envy. "We just celebrated three years."

The warmth in Alexei's eyes as he gazed at Mike was

beautiful. It hurt Callum to see it, even while he was happy this was something they got to have. That they got have each other.

"That's great," he managed, his voice little more than a rasp, his smile wobbling but sincere. "It can't be easy."

Mike nodded, his gaze still suspicious, but Alexei just shrugged. "It's not so bad."

"But you play hockey," Callum said, quick to point out the obvious.

Alexei laughed. "Mike had this problem, too. It's not like we're the only two gay men in hockey. Mike's not even the first hockey player I've dated. Or the second." Alexei grinned at Reese's raised eyebrow. "Don't worry boss, I have not made a second job of debauching Ice Cats."

Mike's cheeks turned a warm rosy color, making it pretty clear *he* had been thoroughly debouched. Callum normally would have laughed, but he was too fixated on what Alexei had said.

"You know other gay players?"

Alexei cocked his head. "Yes. A few."

"All in this league?"

"In *every* league," Alexei replied seriously.

Callum's heart sped up. He wanted to ask. He wanted to *know* so he could look at someone's career and see how they did it. How they lived and if they thrived. So he could go out and find them and beg them to tell him how they shut it off. Kept it hidden.

Only it wasn't hidden if Alexei knew.

"I'm not going to tell you names," Alexei said with a hint of anger, as if he could read Callum's mind.

"No!" Callum said quickly. "Of course not. I would never ask you to betray—"

"Alexei," Mike said gently, his grip changing to hold Alexei's hand, and his attention, more firmly. "I think Callum was just surprised."

He cast Callum a sly glance, as if he could see all his secrets.

Callum wanted to object, to make a loud comment about the hot waitress or how if he'd been in a locker room with any gay guys he sure hadn't noticed—at least that was true, anyway— but he didn't have the heart, or the will, to put another lie together. Instead, he glanced at Rupert helplessly, who took mercy and started asking questions about the new apartment. Apparently, it was huge, available immediately, and it was inordinately important to Mike and Alexei that Oliver be given a particular bedroom.

What was up with that?

Callum was too lost in his own thoughts to poke at their weird conditions for Rupert moving in. Among other things, Callum had to call Michaela back. And set up that meeting with his agent. And figure out if he could get in and out of Vegas in fewer than four days. He tried to remember who from his team would be there and realized he'd been ignoring those emails for too long. He'd been ignoring everything for too long. Pretending he could just come to Moncton and be someone else. Be himself.

He was quiet for the ride back to the hotel, silently shadowing Rupert and Oliver to the elevator and down the hallway, casting a bleak look at his door. He hadn't spent more than ten minutes at a shot in there. He tried to run in once a day to mess up the bed and throw a towel on the back of the toilet, but he'd skipped even that a few times in the last week. It was just more lies.

"Are you okay?" Rupert asked quietly as he opened their door.

Callum looked past Rupert to the entryway where they'd made out just a couple hours ago. His chest ached at the memory. At how simple and easy it had felt, in spite of his nerves and indecision.

Rupert touched his arm, bringing him back to the present.

"Yeah, I'm okay," he said gruffly, then waved a hand over his shoulder. "I just need to run to my room for a few minutes. To make a phone call."

Rupert frowned, aware that Callum could make any calls he

needed to from Rupert's place, as he had been for weeks already.

"Okay, I'll get Oliver ready for bed," he murmured, ushering his brother inside with a hand on his shoulder.

Oliver spun out of his grasp and marched back to Callum, taking his hand where it hung useless at his side. "You're coming back, aren't you?"

Callum swallowed, but his voice still came out thick. "Yeah, yes, of course."

Oliver tugged at his hand until he crouched down to his level. Oliver wrapped his sturdy little arms around Callum's neck and squeezed, and Callum was helpless to do anything but hug him back. They stayed like that long enough for Callum to feel the tension leave Oliver's body, for him to sag against Callum as the fatigue of a day filled with adventures caught up to him. Callum ran a hand over his back and rubbed his cheek against the mop of dark silk hair.

Oliver pressed a sweet kiss to Callum's cheek. "Goodnight. I love you."

"I love you, too," Callum whispered.

Satisfied, Oliver marched past Rupert, who looked at Callum for a long moment before letting the door swing shut.

Callum staggered down the hall and through the door to his room on wooden legs. He dialed without thinking, determined to tell Michaela that he was willing to brave the awards red carpet on his own.

"What's wrong?" she asked as soon as he'd said hello.

His best friend was way too perceptive. "Nothing's wrong," he said, feigning innocence.

"You are incapable of hiding shit from me, Callum William Morrison. Give it up. What's wrong?"

Honestly, he'd never admit it, since he wanted to live to see forty, but sometimes he loved Michaela so much because she was *exactly* like his mom.

"It's nothing. Just shit going on with a couple players on the team," he said, sticking as close to the truth as possible in case that long-distance lie detector thing wasn't just Michaela's wishful thinking.

"Uh huh," she said dubiously, "is that what you're going with?"

"What? It's true!"

"Okay, Callum, I'll let it go, but only until we get to Vegas. Then I'll get the truth out of you."

Which, actually, was why he was calling. "About that—"

"It's no trouble. I already made plans to meet up with some friends, and I bumped into Abby the other day. She and Mitch are going, so I suggested we get drinks."

Callum deflated against the pristine kitchen counter. "Right, Mitch is going."

"Of course, he's up for the Masterton Trophy, you goof."

"Right," Callum repeated, the reality of it sinking in. There were going to be a ton of the guys there, drinks and meals and photographers and TV cameras...it was going to be a total clusterfuck, just like it always was. And he could do it alone. He could. But it would be so much easier with Michaela there. She was used to the press. The constant attention. And while she found it as exhausting as he did, she'd been doing it since she'd hit puberty and the world had discovered the heiress daughter of one of America's wealthiest families was also a knock-out. His agent had commented more than once that she'd stopped worrying about Callum's press once he'd started dating Michaela. She was better at training him on how to behave in front of a camera than any publicist could have been. Hell, Anna, his agent, had even invited Michaela along to their lunch meeting.

"Callum?"

"Oh, yeah. So I'm going to book my tickets. Do you want me to book yours?"

"No, I can do it. Just send me your itinerary," Michaela said. They'd done this a million times in the past few years. "Callum, what's up—?"

"It's nothing. Really,"

He heard her frustrated growl but didn't say anything more, instead asking after her parents and what she'd been doing since they'd last spoken. She let him get away with it, because she was a good friend and she knew him well. She also was sharing a hotel suite with him in Vegas, and he knew he better have his answers ready when he got there.

Rupert lay stretched out on the king bed he'd been sharing with Oliver and Callum for the last month. Oliver was sprawled across his chest, the covers pulled up over them both. It was dark and warm and quiet in the still room, the curtain drawn and hum of the air handler in the corner blanketing them from the sounds of the city and the rooms around theirs. There was something deeply comforting about the Oliver's rhythmic breaths, his chest rising and falling against Rupert's, and the steady beat of his heart against Rupert's ribs. Rupert rubbed gently with the hand on Oliver's back, careful not to wake him, but unable to resist soothing them both, even now, when Oliver was none the wiser.

Rupert supposed it was an accomplishment that he'd gotten Oliver ready for and into bed without any trouble. Mostly, though, he just felt disappointed. He'd been telling himself that this was what he needed Callum for. That Callum was the magical four-year-old-child whisperer and that Rupert would be lost without him.

But that wasn't true. Rupert could do it himself. And yet, he still felt lost.

Occasional bouts of panic that Callum wouldn't come back struck Rupert, but were quashed when he recalled Callum's promise to Oliver. Callum had a lot on his mind, but he wouldn't lie to Oliver. He wouldn't lie to either of them.

Rupert let out another deep breath.

Oliver shifted against him, wriggling to make himself more comfortable while using his big brother as a mattress, pillow, and safety blanket all rolled into one. These were roles Rupert had never in his life thought to play for anyone, and certainly not for a child, but he liked it. No, he loved it. He loved how Oliver needed his care, needed to be held and how he held Rupert back. No one had ever done these things for Rupert, but it felt like he was making up for that loss by doing this now with Oliver.

He had Callum to thank for that. For showing him what simple physical affection with family was. It was pathetic, really, that he hadn't known, but now he wouldn't have it any other way. Oliver had hugged him goodnight and told Rupert he loved him, and Rupert had said the words back so easily. The momentary flinch he'd experienced the first few times was not only gone, but something Rupert was ashamed to have felt at all.

Of course he loved Oliver. And he was so grateful that Oliver loved him in return. He smiled down at the boy sleeping on his chest and knew he was lucky in a lot of ways.

He didn't move when he heard the door open, just lay there in the dark and listened to Callum move around the living room. It was early yet, far earlier than Rupert would normally be in bed, but he had no intention of going anywhere else tonight. Not even as far as the couch in the next room. He had everything he needed right here, if not everything he wanted.

Callum appeared in the bedroom door, his shoulders curled in, his hands fisted at his sides. His face, lit from the muted sconces in the hallway, was blank, but Rupert knew whatever was going on inside that man's head was nothing like the calm, bored façade he liked to present. Just like the arsehole Callum tried to be was so very far from who he really was, in his heart.

"Come here," Rupert said quietly, holding his hand out.

Callum hesitated by the door, then again beside the bed when Rupert asked, "Are you going to sleep in your clothes?"

Callum stared down at them for a long moment, then stripped down to his boxer briefs and a t-shirt and tugged on the pajama bottoms he'd purchased as soon as they'd returned from London.

Rupert stopped Callum with a hand on his chest when he climbed in the far side of the bed. "Hold on one second," he whispered.

Moving carefully, Rupert slid Oliver off his chest and laid him on the side of the bed, then scooted toward the middle of the mattress, tugging Callum closer until he hovered beside Rupert on his hands and knees.

"Come here," Rupert said again, and pulled at Callum until he took Oliver's place, his head tucked beneath Rupert's chin, his face pressed to Rupert's chest, their legs tangling.

They'd never slept like this. They'd never even touched like this, if he didn't count this afternoon. Oliver had always been in the middle, but not tonight. Rupert wrapped his arms around Callum's ribs and held on, resuming his comforting rub, just on a different back.

Callum needed this, the tension bleeding out of him and his arms curling around Rupert, his breath warm and damp on Rupert's skin as they settled against one another.

"Thanks," Callum said quietly, well after Rupert was convinced he'd fallen asleep.

Rupert kissed the top of Callum's head and left it at that.

Chapter Eleven

Callum woke up slowly, still totally relaxed. Something was different, but he was too groggy to piece it together until the warm presence plastered to his back took a deep breath.

Blinking, he noted the bright light fighting to get around the edge of the blackout curtains of their hotel bedroom, and remembered coming to bed the night before. He'd been unsure of the reception he would get. Rupert had surprised him by pulling him into the bed, hours before they would normally go to sleep, and just holding him.

Another first. One Callum hadn't even known to miss in all the years of being alone. He'd miss it now, though. While he was in Vegas. And back in Denver.

Rupert's hand, resting on his chest, petted him gently. Callum reached up and pressed it over his heart, their fingers naturally threading together. It probably meant little, if anything, to Rupert. Just something you did with the man you woke up next to, but Callum could close his eyes and picture Mike and Alexei's hands doing the same, the looks they'd shared. The three years they'd had, so far, together.

That was what he wanted, he thought as he slid his fingers along Rupert's, over and over.

What he couldn't have.

Rupert pressed at his shoulder, rolling him over so they lay facing each other on their sides. Callum lifted his head enough to see Oliver sprawled across half the bed, starfished on his back with one foot hooked over Rupert's hip. Callum grinned, shaking his head with silent laughter. Rupert rolled his eyes.

Callum opened his mouth to say something. What? *Thank you for giving me the best orgasm of my life yesterday? For tolerating my freak out? For cuddling me all night?* But Rupert spared him any of the possible indignities by pressing their mouths together.

189

The kiss was slow, languid. Callum gave a passing thought to stale morning breath, but it was lost to the taste of Rupert. The arm that had held him while he was sleeping hooked around his back, towing him closer.

It didn't erase the worry of Las Vegas, and only made it even more obvious what Callum was going to miss most when the end of the summer rolled around, but it was still good. Worth it.

Rupert pulled back, a gentle smile on his face, a moment before Oliver popped up on his knees behind Rupert's back, throwing the covers to the foot of the bed.

"Good morning!" he chirped brightly as he dove between them.

Callum closed his eyes and thanked Christ he and Rupert hadn't taken it any further when Oliver's ridiculously pointy elbow nailed his lower belly.

"Oof."

Rupert chuckled at the near miss and dragged his squirming brother off Callum, tickling him until he screamed with joy. Callum was trying to laugh while still attempting to get the muscles in his stomach and groin to unclench. The results were breathless and hoarse, and only made Rupert laugh harder until Callum dove on him, encouraging Oliver to tickle Rupert until he was thrashing around and screaming almost as loudly as Oliver had.

The three of them landed in a heap on the floor, Callum barely twisting in time to ensure he fell beside Rupert and Oliver landed on top of them both.

Unfortunately, Oliver's left heel didn't miss this time, glancing right off Callum's nuts.

Callum rolled on this side and gurgled, while Rupert cackled maniacally, which Callum thought was awfully cruel. Rupert finally took mercy and pulled himself and Oliver off Callum and to their feet.

"That's what you get," Rupert, the vengeful bastard, said with a smirk before nudging Oliver in the direction of the bathroom. As soon as the boy was out of sight, Rupert knelt and pressed his lips to Callum's.

"Are you okay?"

When Callum nodded, Rupert kissed him once more, smiling softly, and left him to suffer in peace.

Callum thought about waking up next to Rupert and their good morning kiss for the rest of the day. He almost broke his leg, he was so distracted on the treadmill. After the third time he'd tripped over his own feet, he left Oliver with Mike and Alexei in the gym and snuck into Rupert's office. Rupert looked up from his desk, the phone pressed to his ear, and arched a brow as Callum shut the door behind him.

Callum skirted the edge of the desk, coming to hover in Rupert's space while someone rambled on the other end of the line. Callum didn't care. He cupped his hands around Rupert's jaw, tilted up his chin, and kissed him, tracing the seam of Rupert's lips immediately, demanding entrance. Rupert leaned into him, kissing him back, until Callum could hear a tinny voice calling Rupert's name.

Callum stepped away, grinned, and left Rupert scrambling to explain himself to whoever was on the phone.

It became a game, Callum always on the lookout for a time and place he could sneak a kiss with Rupert. It wasn't as often as he would have liked, since between their work, his training schedule, and Oliver, they were almost never alone. Mike and Alexei unwittingly aided him more often than not, but even then, usually all Callum could manage was one quick peck.

Any kind of kiss was great, but even better was the often amused, sometimes wary expression on Rupert's face whenever they were alone together. Callum could tell Rupert was now as constantly aware of their surroundings, and their audience, as Callum had become.

The less-great aspect, though, was that after a lifetime of limited sexual contact and years of celibacy, Callum was suddenly obsessed. Seriously, he was horny *all the time*. And he didn't think he was alone. Yesterday he'd come into Rupert's office and closed the door, a now-favorite part of his afternoon, and by the time he'd turned around, Rupert was on him, slamming his back to the wall, his cock rock hard and pressed to Callum's hip.

Callum had been prepared to do something wildly inappropriate, right then and there. His knees had shaken as Rupert sucked on his lower lip, grinding their hips together, their hands grappling at each other.

Then a sharp rap at the door had sent them reeling apart, barely managing to look sane, let alone decent, by the time Sheila swung the door open to tell Rupert his two o'clock meeting was waiting for him.

"Jesus," Rupert had whispered after Sheila departed, "I have *got* to put a lock on that bloody door."

Now, only one day later and less than a week into his campaign, Callum was filled with woe and regret. And hormones. He stood by Jack's side, listening to a subcontractor reel off all the reasons something was behind schedule, and had to force himself not to think about how fast he'd gone off in the shower that morning. It hadn't even taken the edge off. He *needed* more than five consecutive minutes alone with Rupert.

"Callum?"

Callum blinked. "I'm sorry, what was that?"

"I asked if you had any other questions. I'm going to guess no," he said dryly, nodding at the subcontractor who promptly went scurrying back to his work.

"Sorry," Callum said with a half laugh, half sigh. "I've been distracted this morning. I apologize if I'm making your work harder."

"Not at all," Jack assured him with a warm smile. "You've been a flake for days, so it's not like I'm not used to it."

"Hey!" Callum said, trying for indignant and failing miserably, because it was true, and because Jack was grinning at him.

There wasn't a straight woman or gay man alive that could

work up a temper in the face of that...*face.* Goddamn, Jack was gorgeous.

They walked around the concourse, stopping here and there to check on progress, speaking with workers and foremen about their schedules, missing supplies, extra crew, and anything else that came up. Normally, this was one of Callum's favorite parts of the project. He and Oliver had taken to meeting Jack in the conference room in the mornings so they could wait for Rupert to get there from the gym or rink and take Oliver with him into his office. Then Callum and Jack would spend an hour or two on the project. Today, though, he had the attention span of a gnat.

Jack sighed. "Earth to Callum?"

"What? Sorry," Callum groaned, rubbing a hand over his face after realizing he'd been staring at a hot dog vendor sign for god only knew how long.

"Dude, what is *up* with you?"

Before Callum could come up with some bullshit answer, because he was pretty sure Jack didn't want to hear that he'd been walking around with a hard-on all day, he heard Rupert call his name.

The last time Rupert had been on the construction site, all hell had broken loose. Callum spun in the direction of Rupert's shout and saw him hurrying along the fresh tile floor in his wingtips. Callum's heart nearly stopped when Rupert skidded for a moment, his arms flailing, before he regained his footing and plowed on.

Callum ran to meet him. "What? What is it? Is Oliver okay?"

That brought Rupert up short. "Oh, yes. I'm sorry, I didn't mean to alarm you."

Callum slumped. "It's okay." God knew he was a little high strung today.

Jack smiled at Rupert. "What's up? What brings you up here?"

Rupert glanced around them, as if only just remembering his reception last time, but the smile that had been hovering broke through again when he met Callum's eyes. "I've just received a text from Christian. You remember the boy from the skating clinic?"

"Yes, of course."

"Well, he's asked if I can meet him at the rink after school. He'd like to introduce me to his coach, who has expressed an interest in having me join them for some training."

"You coach hockey?" Jack asked, commendably keeping almost all incredulity from his voice.

"God, no," Rupert said with a laugh. "I'm a figure skater."

Jack's "oohh" sounded a lot like "of course".

"Anyway," Rupert said with a bright smile that made Callum's heart beat a little harder, "I know it wasn't in the plans for today, and that you still have a lot you need to do, and that meeting with the contractor and Oliver—"

"You can go!" Callum said with a laugh.

"Thank you so much," Rupert said, flinging himself against Callum's chest.

Callum caught him, laughing until he realized the site had gone silent around them.

His arms dropped to his side. "Uh..."

Rupert stepped back, confusion on his face, his smile fading as Callum darted his eyes pointedly at the men staring at them. It broke something inside Callum to see the light leave Rupert's eyes. Worse, Callum suspected it may have broken something between them.

Rupert tidied his already perfectly tidy suit and offered an awkward goodbye, not looking at anyone before walking away in the direction he'd come. Callum wanted to chase after him. To hug him close and apologize. Most of all, he wanted to be someone who could do that and not give a shit who saw and what they thought.

Instead he was left standing alone as the sounds around them returned to normal. He studiously ignored the expression on Jack's face, unable to decipher if it was surprise or disappointment.

He and Jack finished their walkthrough quietly, only discussing things as they came up, their easygoing banter from earlier gone. When Callum spaced out again, Jack snapped at him and Callum made a point to pay close attention from then on.

He felt like he should apologize to Jack, but he didn't know why. More importantly, there was someone else he needed to apologize to first.

"I need to go," he blurted when Jack was pulling out his binder to review a few more things.

Jack stared at him for a long moment while Callum shifted on his feet, itching to go. Jack's lips twitched, the first sign of humor Callum had seen since Rupert had come to find them. "Okay."

Callum spun to leave, but Jack's hand on his arm stopped him.

"He really likes you, Callum," Jack said gently.

It took everything Callum had not to blurt out that he liked Rupert, too. He wanted so much to tell Jack the truth, his mouth opening as if he might be able to actually do it, but he didn't know how to start.

He swallowed hard. "I know. I didn't mean to..." He didn't know how to finish that either.

Jack nodded, as if maybe he understood. "There's nothing wrong with hugging him. He's your friend. No one is going to think you're gay, even if they know he is. Which, really, they probably don't, and it's none of their fucking business anyway."

Callum died a little, knowing he deserved this lecture. Knowing that he was an even worse person than Jack thought. "I know," he said again, his voice little more than a whisper. "I know that. I do."

"You embarrassed him," Jack said quietly.

Callum couldn't hold in the hurt noise that escaped.

Jack searched his face, then nodded, as if he'd found whatever it was he was looking for. Callum turned and bolted down the concourse.

Rupert plowed through the paperwork on his desk, determined to clear off everything he could before taking the afternoon off. He'd felt guilty about being so excited to, essentially, goof off—right up until that debacle with Callum. Now he would do anything he could to get the fuck out of this building for a while.

He seriously considered taking Oliver with him, just so he wouldn't have to face Callum again, but he didn't know what to expect at the rink. He didn't want his brother there if he had another run-in with John Shaw.

Callum would take good care of Oliver. Which was more than Rupert could say about how Callum took care with him, sadly.

He didn't bother to glance up when he caught a movement out of the corner of his eye, assuming it was someone coming to drop yet more work on his desk. Then the door shut and he closed his eyes, taking a deep breath to calm his suddenly racing heart.

If Callum tried to kiss him, he swore to god he would punch him in the nose.

He finally lifted his head when strange noises got the better of his curiosity, and watched Callum jam one of Rupert's guest chairs beneath the doorknob.

"Need a fucking lock on this door," Callum muttered.

Rupert could hardly argue, though he didn't appreciate Callum sealing them in without his permission. He didn't really feel any appreciation for Callum at all, at this point.

Callum spun and charged around the desk like a man on a mission. Rupert acted without thought, leaping from his chair and taking a hasty step back. It wasn't until his back slammed into the file cabinet that he realized he'd unwittingly reenacted the day they had met.

Callum froze and his face blanched white. "Rupert," he

breathed, his voice rough and low, "I would never hurt you. You can't think that I—"

Rupert could withstand the horror in Callum's voice, but the sheen building in his eyes was, apparently, kryptonite to Rupert's temper. He grabbed Callum's arm. "I know that, Callum. That's not why I stood up."

"Then *why*?"

Rupert twisted his lips wryly. "I thought you were going to kiss me."

"Oh," Callum said, and he still looked miserable. "I guess I didn't think. I just wanted to be close to you when I said..." he trailed off, uncertain.

"What?"

"Sorry. I was going to say I'm sorry. But I don't know, it doesn't seem adequate."

Rupert sighed. "It's a good place to start."

Callum used Rupert's grip on his arm to tow him closer. "I never meant to embarrass you. I was happy to see you so excited. I *wanted* to hug you. But I just...reacted. It's instinct, I guess. A terrible instinct, but after all these years I can't shut it off. I don't even know if I should. But not because I'm ashamed of you," he added quickly. "Or even of me. I just..."

"Don't want anyone to know."

"I don't even know if that's true anymore," Callum admitted quietly.

Rupert was stunned. "Pardon?"

"I almost told Jack. He's barely spoken to me for the last hour and I wanted to tell him the truth. About me."

"*You did?*" Rupert asked, genuinely shocked.

"Yeah, well, don't be too impressed. I chickened out."

Rupert thought there was a victory in there anyway. He smiled tentatively. "You can trust Jack. He would never tell anyone."

"I know. I should have. But I've never done it. You're the only person I've ever told." Callum grimaced, a sour twist of his lips that reminded Rupert of the man he'd first met. "I'm so used to the lies, I can spout them in an instant. But actually speaking the truth scares the shit out of me. What does that say about me?"

Rupert brushed the backs of his fingers down Callum's cheek. "You don't have to tell anyone, Callum."

"I don't? I mean, I guess I'm surprised you think so."

"I'm sorry if I somehow gave you the impression that I think you should out yourself to anyone."

"But..."

"Callum, coming out is a deeply personal and sometimes terrifying thing, particularly at first. For everyone. No one can or should tell you that you must do it. If and when you're ready, though, I'll support you. As would your family and Michaela, I bet."

Callum almost smiled. Rupert stepped a little closer.

"If there's anything I've been hard on you about, that I don't understand, it is that you've forced yourself to live alone. That you've been celibate for god knows how long—"

"I haven't so much as touched anybody in four years."

Rupert's jaw practically fell to the floor. "You've been totally celibate for the past *four years*?"

"Well, if you don't count the last two weeks," Callum said with a quick smile. "And nothing I did before, ever, came close to what it's like just to kiss you."

Rupert was speechless, his heart aching for Callum, and yet so full. He rewarded Callum for his sweet words the only way he knew how. He kissed him again.

A lot.

He didn't mean to get carried away. They were in his unlocked office with a guest chair under the doorknob as their only protection from being walked in on by anyone from Oliver to the cleaning crew. None of that mattered, though, when Callum opened up beneath his lips, meeting Rupert's tongue with his own, his hands curling into Rupert's shirt to pull him closer.

Rupert was starving for time alone with Callum. Truly alone. And the chances of that happening before Callum left for Las Vegas were slim to none. Callum was determined to get the project ahead of schedule before he left, and Rupert was booked solid with the draft, trade negotiations, and team logistics. This was their one and only chance to be alone for *days.*

With that in mind, Rupert forced Callum backwards around the desk while they kissed. He put his hands on Callum's hips to guide him, desperate to get closer, to get Callum pressed up against something hard so that Rupert could, in turn, press up against Callum.

At last, Callum's shoulders thumped against the door, the chair tipped under the knob almost taking out their legs.

Now, at least, no one could walk in on them easily.

There was still a huge risk, sending adrenaline pumping through Rupert's veins, making him both needier and more reckless. He yanked at Callum's shirt, his belt and button and zipper, shifting back only so that Callum could do the same to him. He sealed their lips together, because he wanted to kiss Callum, because he loved kissing him, and because he really needed to muffle the hums and groans and other wonderful little noises coming up from Callum's chest.

All right, and his own, too.

God, they were both way too noisy for clandestine office nookie. Which was too bad, really, since there was no way in hell Rupert was going to stop. He managed to shimmy Callum's jeans and boxers down over his hips, far enough that Rupert could grab fistfuls of fabric on both sides and yank it all down as he dropped to his knees.

He spared his bad knee a passing thought, knowing that this was definitely not on his orthopedist's list of approved activities. Callum's cock stood firm, the tension Rupert could see rippling through Callum's belly making his thick shaft sway temptingly in front of Rupert's face. The plump, dark pink head looked as soft as it had felt, the ridge wide and smooth and absolutely begging to be traced by the tip of Rupert's tongue. His mouth watered, but when he braced one hand on Callum's thigh, the other intent on wrapping around that thick shaft, Callum's hand stopped him.

"No."

Rupert looked up past Callum's tight belly, expecting to find Callum blushing, flustered at the least. Instead, Callum had gone white as a sheet.

Rupert sat back on his heels. "I'm sorry. I didn't mean to rush you."

"No, it's not that. I mean, I want you to…" Callum began, his frown deepening.

"But?" Rupert prompted, not willing to guess or do anything until he understood better.

"It's too much like what I've done before," Callum confessed in a rush. "With those other men."

Rupert rubbed his thumb over Callum's bare thigh. "Was that wrong?" he asked carefully.

"What? No. I mean, yes. I mean, those men—they were *servicing* me, Rupert. They didn't know or care who I was, and they probably wouldn't have if I'd told them. But I didn't. I didn't hesitate to use them like this."

Rupert rose to his feet slowly, his head spinning. He'd gone from zero to sixty then thrown it in reverse, all in the last three minutes. In deference to Callum's sometimes-delicate sensibilities, Rupert gently tugged some of his clothes back into place.

"Callum, they were all adults, were they not?"

"Yes, of course," Callum said, appalled.

"And you didn't pay them or coerce them? To the best of your knowledge, they were reasonably sober and not high?"

"I thought so, yes. I mean, I definitely avoided people who didn't seem to be in control or whatever," Callum said earnestly, but also like an apology for having been there at all. Rupert wanted to hug him. And then maybe shake him until he came to his senses.

The man was so fucking confusing.

"Callum, those men knew what they were doing. And more so, I'd guess that they enjoyed it as much as you did."

"No way."

Callum succinct and dead-sure answer gave Rupert pause. "Why not?"

The color returned to Callum's cheeks with a vengeance. He looked away from Rupert. "I didn't touch them. I didn't *do* anything. They just knelt and, um,"—he swallowed hard, his face going redder—"did it. And I let them."

"So? Wasn't that what they were offering? What they wanted, too?"

"Yes. I mean, I guess it's what they wanted? But I don't get it. They didn't get anything out of it."

Rupert couldn't help but smile.

"It's not funny," Callum muttered.

"Callum, some people like it."

"Like what?"

"Giving head," Rupert said bluntly, no longer surprised by Callum's blush. Honestly, it made Rupert feel helplessly fond.

"They do?"

"Yes. More so, some people like to...what did you call it? Service someone? Others even like the feeling of being used."

Callum looked desperate to believe that. "How do I know if that was true for the men I was with?"

"You don't," Rupert said with a shrug. "But they consented, and they presumably had their reasons. If they didn't tell you what those were, then that's their business. And their right."

"But what if that wasn't it," Callum said hoarsely, pulling Rupert closer until he was clinging to him. "What if I—"

The thought was apparently too painful for Callum to finish. Rupert pressed close, their foreheads touching, their disheveled clothes tangling together.

"It would never be that way for me," Rupert said softly. "I didn't offer for any reason other than I want to taste you. And I want you to feel good."

A shudder worked through Callum, his hands tightening until Rupert feared for the future of his shirt.

"And I don't have to kneel. You don't have to stand, even. You could sit in a chair. On the couch. Or I could spread you out across the bed and lie between your legs." Rupert's legs felt rubbery just thinking about it, so lying down would probably be a great idea.

"And it would feel good? For you, too?" Callum asked, his voice deep.

"Yes," Rupert promised, his body coming back to life at the way Callum was staring at him. He leaned forward the mere inches it took to press their lips together again. Callum kissed him back, but only for a second.

"Do you touch yourself? While you do it?" Callum asked brazenly. Rupert could feel the heat coming off his cheeks.

"Sometimes. Sometimes not."

Callum frowned, clearly dissatisfied with that answer. "But it wouldn't be considered, like *rude*, right?"

"To jack off while you're giving a blow job?" Rupert asked with a chuckle, trying to figure out where the hell Callum was going with this. "Uh, no. I don't think that would be considered rude."

"Okay," Callum said with a nod, as if something had been decided. His smile was uncertain, but it made it all the way to his lovely eyes.

Rupert smiled back. "What?"

Rupert's feet almost left the floor when Callum grabbed his arms and spun him around, so that their positions were reversed. Rupert's mouth fell open to protest, but the words got stuck in his throat when Callum dropped to his knees.

Callum went to work stripping away Rupert's clothes from the waist down. Rupert yanked his shirt up so he could see Callum's face clearly.

"Callum, you don't have to do this."

Callum smiled. "Now you sound like me."

Rupert huffed out a laugh, but couldn't say anything else as his pants slid to mid-thigh and Callum stared at Rupert's cock like it was something wild and mysterious. It should have been funny, but it made Rupert's chest ache instead. He tentatively stroked his fingers through Callum's hair. Callum leaned into his touch as he ran his warm, calloused palms up Rupert's thighs.

"You don't have to do this," Rupert said again.

"Stop saying that," Callum said without taking his eyes off Rupert's cock.

Rupert swallowed and pressed harder against the door, his legs barely holding him up.

Callum looked up. "I have no idea what I'm doing."

Rupert cupped his jaw. "You don't—"

Callum's hands gripped his hips punishingly. "I dare you to say it again." He was so fucking close, his breath brushed across Rupert's shaft. Rupert wanted to die. He wanted to come all over Callum's face.

He remained resolutely mute, and watched Callum stare at his tackle from not two inches away, for possibly the longest minutes of his life. It was fairly disconcerting.

Rupert hated to risk irritating the man breathing directly onto his penis, but he had to hazard a question. "Is something the matter?"

"What?" Callum asked, glancing up at him. At *his eyes*, to be specific. "No, I was just…"

"Looking?"

"No. Well, yes. And, uh, trying to figure out where to start."

"Oh," Rupert said stupidly. "Perhaps if you let me—"

Rupert's offer to demonstrate was interrupted by an undignified gurgle when Callum's hand encircled his shaft, lifting until it the head was poised a hair's breadth from Callum's lips.

Callum's pink tongue slipped out and brushed across the excruciatingly sensitive nerve endings trembling for his attention. Seemingly emboldened by that success, Callum did it again. And again. Rupert couldn't breathe, every muscle in his body tightening to the point he was forced to hunch over. He planted one hand on Callum's broad shoulder, the other on Callum's head, very carefully not grabbing the great fistful of hair his twitching fingers begged for.

Callum's tongue continued its agonizing explorations, sometimes curling around the head, sometimes testing at the ridge, or poking into the slit, before returning to the long, lathing licks. The broad flat of Callum's tongue was soft, warm, and slightly rough.

Rupert had never, in his life, been so acutely aware of the mechanics of a blow job—given or received. He understood, with the four functioning brain cells remaining to him, that Callum was just trying different things. The look on his face was almost clinical, if not exactly detached. It should not have been that hot.

So why did it feel like Callum was taking him apart, breaking down his every wall, one brick at a time? Soon, he would be little more than rubble at Callum's feet.

Callum's hand slid a few inches along his shaft, and Rupert groaned, trying to keep his hips still. What would have been a thrust became more of a squirm, which would have been embarrassing, had it not been so intriguing to Callum. He moved his hand again. Farther this time. Then again, holding tighter.

"God, please. Keep doing that."

Callum's focus remained on his hand. "You didn't like my tongue?"

"Are you joking?" Rupert gasped as Callum's palm passed over the head, fingers squeezing until Rupert popped free and bounced up against his belly.

He wasn't sure if he'd *ever* been this hard, or had every muscle in his body wound so tight.

Callum pulled his cock down again, then let go, watching in fascination as it bounced against Rupert's belly. Rupert flinched, but not in a bad way.

The next time Callum pulled his shaft down, he leaned

forward, sucking the head into the hot cavern of his mouth.

"Oh, sweet baby Jesus," Rupert moaned.

Callum snorted, laughing with his mouth full, then he met Rupert's eyes and began to suck.

"Oh, Christ, that's lovely," Rupert breathed, running his fingers through Callum's hair. "Yes, please, keep doing that," he babbled, letting out a stream of inarticulate nonsense and pleas, petting Callum wherever he could reach.

Callum responded to every touch. Every word. Sucking harder, then moving, just a little, to slide the head of Rupert's cock along his tongue.

Rupert groaned, and praised Callum more. He felt like Callum's teacher, sex toy, and cheerleader all at once, but it was really working for him. And apparently for Callum. After a particularly detailed description of how fucking magical Callum's mouth was, Callum reached down and shoved his pants back down to his thighs.

Rupert could feel the furious pace of Callum's arm in the way he rocked against Rupert, in the brush of biceps against his thigh, in the clench of Callum's other hand around Rupert's cock. Rupert panted, the tension coiling in his belly and along his spine. His fingers curled into fists, grabbing great hanks of Callum's hair, but doing no more than hanging on.

Callum spread his knees on the floor, groaning, and Rupert whimpered as the vibrations hummed up his shaft. He gasped around Rupert's cock, his eyes sightless, his expression so, so eager. And that was enough.

More than enough.

"Callum," Rupert gasped, trying to warn him. He shoved at Callum's shoulder.

Callum hummed again and sucked harder. Rupert's balls grew heavy and tight, the hand in Callum's hair shaking as he tried to push Callum away.

"*Callum*," Rupert cried, shoving with all his might as the tension gathering in his gut finally found its release. Callum's lips left his cock with an audible and perfectly obscene pop a moment before Rupert's come struck his lips, his chin, and his cheek.

Callum gasped, his eyes slamming closed, and groaned, long and low. Rhythmic shudders racked him as he came into his own fist. On the last pull of his hand, he fell forward, his face planting against Rupert's hip, smearing Rupert's come all over both of them.

It was utterly artless. All of it. The blow job, the mess they'd made, the way they leaned against Rupert's *goddamn office door*, but nothing had ever felt more perfect.

Rupert's knees finally gave out and he slid down the door until he landed on his ass, his legs spread around Callum. When he didn't look at Rupert, Rupert tucked a finger under his chin and tilted his face up.

Callum blushed, but met his gaze. Rupert tried to smile, but it was wobbly at best.

"Now do you believe me when I say some people like giving almost as much as receiving?"

Callum nodded, wiping trembling fingers across his chin, then stared at the mess on his fingers. His smile was almost sweet.

It occurred to Rupert, several weeks and one blow job too late, that he was in big trouble.

Chapter Twelve

Rupert swung around the ice, arms out, back straight, head up. He didn't turn to check if Christian was paying attention, both because it would have thrown off his lines, and because he was certain the young man was giving him the same laser-focus he put into all their training sessions.

Christian's coach, Mark, stood just inside the Zamboni door, calling out suggestions and observations. They were working on a new short program for Christian, in spite of the fact his father was resisting—to put it mildly—signing him up for any more competitions.

Rupert executed a complicated diagonal pass, his feet dancing as he spun across the ice, his balance and form still excellent—*thank you very much*. Footwork was an area he could help Christian with quite a lot. And the choreography. He could also offer his input on the more challenging and athletic requirements, but at this point, if Rupert attempted to do a triple-anything, he'd probably put himself in traction.

Callum had teased him about this, but his smile had been understanding. It wasn't like Callum didn't limp on his way to the bathroom in the morning. His knees hurt—his hips, too, sometimes.

Callum had come to several of Christian's practices over the past couple weeks and had gotten to know Christian. It had been Callum's idea to sneak into one of Christian's summer-league games, where it had been immediately obvious Christian was a gifted hockey player. His skating, unsurprisingly, was phenomenal. But his stick handling and shooting were well ahead of the average twelve year old, as well.

Rupert had expected Callum to lament, at least a little, that Christian was willing to walk away from so much hockey potential. Callum hadn't, though, instead pointing out that Murdoch was one of the best skaters in the Morrison family, and no one had ever questioned his desire to be a doctor. Fair point. And, far more irritatingly, it was another example of how Callum was somehow *still* becoming more and more likeable. There should be a limit to such things.

Rupert completed his turn around the ice and stopped next to Christian.

Christian grinned. "Pretty fancy for an old man."

Rupert scoffed, pretending great offense and like his knee wasn't going to hate him tonight if he sat still for longer than ten minutes. No way was he giving his impudent protégé any more material.

"I *am* fancy," Rupert said with as much dignity as he could muster, which obviously wasn't much. "Now you do it."

Christian gave him a sharp and entirely sarcastic salute. "Aye, aye, Captain!" He took off down the boards, his laughter trailing after him.

Rupert rolled his eyes. He had been delighted to learn that Christian a very cheeky young man. His wit was quick, razor sharp, and rarely contained. Rupert vowed, for the sake of all of Canada, to never, ever let him meet Reese.

But more than being smart and gifted, Christian was unfailingly upbeat during their time together. Just *happy*. In a way Rupert couldn't remember being at that age, with the onset of puberty and the challenges of trying to do the sport he loved in spite of what everyone else thought of it.

For the most part, that didn't seem to faze Christian. He clearly loved to skate. He loved the choreography, the music, the tricks. He tackled the sometimes excruciatingly repetitive drills with a smile, even while Rupert and Mark were trying not to let their eyes glaze over.

Rupert wished he'd had a chance to meet Christian's mother, as she had to be the one responsible for this joyful, confident young man. Who was a stark contrast to the person he became the moment his father came around. Simply mentioning his father made Christian go quiet and lose his smile. In those moments, Rupert struggled just to get Christian to make eye contact, let alone turn his full attention to what they were working on.

So Rupert had learned not to bring up John Shaw, and made it a point to be away from the rink before he would arrive. He'd made the mistake of staying out on the ice after their first session together, working on something by himself while Christian changed into his street shoes.

John had taken one look out on the ice and spat, "What's *he* doing here?"

"It's public ice time, Dad. Anyone can be here," Christian answered.

Mark, for whatever reason, hadn't contradicted him. And Rupert had pretended he'd not heard any of it, not acknowledging John's presence at all.

After that, it was Mark who texted Rupert about the schedule, and he always chose public-skate hours. They rarely had a lot of company on the ice, given it was almost full summer. Private ice time cost a fortune, and would be worth it if Christian's training continued to bear fruit as quickly as the past weeks had done, but for now it was far simpler this way.

Rupert had given up his own morning training regimen in order to arrive at work earlier and be available for Christian in the afternoons. This was now *his* ice time as well as Christian's. And god knew it was more than enough time on the ice. Rupert's knee was sore and his arse was killing him. Another week or two of this, and he'd have to see his tailor about adjusting his trousers. As it was, he suspected the difference was beginning to show, given how frequently he caught Callum staring these days.

Rupert watched Christian make another pass through the footwork and wondered idly if he could ask Callum to rub his sore bum. Just to make it feel better, of course.

"What's so funny?" Christian shouted from the middle of the ice.

Rupert wiped the smile off his face. "Nothing!"

Callum parked next to Rupert's car and unbuckled Oliver from his car seat, taking his hand so Oliver could tow him through the lot and lobby and to the side of the rink. Callum nodded hello to Mark.

"Rupert!" Oliver cried, his voice ringing above the ice and the music playing. Other than a couple young girls working their way around the rink under the watchful eye of their mother, the ice belonged to Christian and Rupert.

Callum's heart skipped a beat when Rupert turned a bright, happy smile on them and immediately skated over. He wondered if he could drag Rupert somewhere private, eying the storage closet across the hall speculatively. Because seriously, Rupert's pants were just so *well-tailored.* It should be illegal.

Oliver tugged on Callum, and he boosted the boy up to perch on top of the boards so he could hug his brother.

Rupert pressed a kiss to the top of his head while giving him a big squeeze. Not that long ago, Callum had needed to demonstrate how to kiss the boy goodnight and instruct Rupert to tell Oliver he loved him.

Rupert had looked alarmed, Callum remembered with a smile as Rupert closed his eyes and pressed his smiling face to Oliver's hair.

"Oliver!" Christian called, coming to join them.

"A ride?" Oliver asked Christian, then turned pleading eyes on his brother and Callum. Callum tried to scowl, as if he might say no, then pulled a helmet from the bag over his shoulder. He knew better than to set foot in this building without it.

"Yay!" Oliver cried, tipping his face up while Rupert plunked the helmet on his head and attached the chin strap. The moment it was secure, Callum let go and Oliver fell forward into Christian's arms.

The boys took off, flying around the rink, the sound of Oliver's laughter echoing across the ice.

Rupert turned to Mark with an apologetic smile. "Sorry. We'll get back to training soon."

"Don't worry about it. It's good to see him so happy doing something that isn't work."

Which wasn't something that anyone should have to say about a twelve-year-old boy, in Callum's opinion. He knew Rupert was also increasingly concerned about Christian. The better they got to know him, the more they wanted to find a way to help. Callum liked to dream up ways to force John Shaw to see the light and support his son in his skating, while Rupert sanely pointed out which of those ways would land Callum in prison.

At least, for now, Christian was thriving under Rupert's attention. Mark spoke constantly of how much Christian had improved. How grateful Mark was to have Rupert's help.

"Hey," Callum said, brushing his hand over Rupert's hip to get his attention, and as an excuse to touch him, no matter how briefly. "Alexei and Mike called. They said we could stop by and see the apartment today."

Rupert spun to look at him. "Today? Now?"

"Well, once you're done here. Unless you have to go back to the office or something?"

Callum could practically see the wheels spinning in Rupert's head as he stared blindly over the ice. He barely acknowledged the boys returning as he reached for his phone, balanced on the boards nearby.

Callum was about to tease Rupert about checking one of his infamous lists, sure that "Check Out New Apartment" had to be on at least *one* of them, when Rupert drew his hand back.

"Fadoodle it. Let's just go."

Callum was pretty wildly fucking impressed. Rupert didn't even look back at the phone, and he wasn't scaling through the mountains of data he kept in his head—Callum knew the abstracted and, honestly, constipated expression Rupert wore when he did that.

"That's not a real word, you know," Christian said with a giggle.

Callum grinned. "It is now."

Christian rolled his eyes. "You guys are such dorks."

Callum might have taken exception to that if Christian hadn't said it with so much affection. As it was, he reached out and ruffled Christian's hair, hoping the kid had some idea of how much Callum and Rupert cared. This kid, more than most, needed to know there were grown-ups who genuinely liked him.

Another thing that no one should have to say about a twelve-year-old boy.

Mark cleared his throat. "I have one more thing I want to work on today, Christian, before you dad gets here in five minutes."

Mark was subtle like a brick to the face.

Rupert plucked Oliver from Christian's arms. "What do you say, Oliver?"

"Thank you, Christian."

Christian held up his fist and Oliver bumped it, then they both made an explosion with their fingers. "It's cool, little dude. We'll do it again next time, okay? If you come earlier, we can spend more time on the ice. Maybe even find you a pair of skates to try."

"Figure skates?" asked Oliver enthusiastically.

Callum was about to agree, but Christian shook his head. "No, I think we should start you in hockey skates. They're much easier to learn in. I'm sure your—er, Callum, will be able to find you some that fit."

Oliver looked up at him with big eyes. Who the hell was capable of saying no to that?

"Sure, Ollie. We'll get you some tomorrow, okay? Right now we have to go visit Mike and Alexei." As a consolation prize, Callum knew it would be a winner.

"Okay!" Oliver agreed, tucking his head under Rupert's chin and smiling serenely, like everything in his world was perfect.

"Right, back to work now, Christian," Mark said briskly. "Your father will be here any minute."

The reminder had two immediate effects: The light and

laughter drained from Christian's eyes, and Rupert plunked down on the bench and practically tore his skates off.

Or maybe three immediate effects, because now Callum really wanted to punch something.

Callum held Oliver's hand in his and threw Rupert's bag over his shoulder while Rupert pulled on his shoes. In the blink of an eye, perfectly pressed Rupert was back.

"Looking good, duchess."

"Thank you," Rupert said dryly, leading the way out of the rink and to Callum's car.

The trip to the address Alexei had given Callum was quick, but once they arrived, he stopped the car so all three of them could stare up at the huge ugly warehouse.

"Ummm, so, this is unexpected," Rupert said slowly.

Callum checked his phone again. "This is the right place," he said with a frown. He held up a garage door opener. "Alexei gave me this and said it would get us in."

He pressed the button and the massive cargo doors parted before them.

"This is so cool!" Oliver declared.

Callum and Rupert shared a long look before they pulled inside and parked next to Alexei's truck, its presence somehow reassuring and yet *not*.

What the hell was this place?

Rupert eyed the cavernous space, keenly aware of the door trundling shut behind them, sealing out a lot of the light. There were a few dim bulbs lighting a path to what looked to be a freight elevator in one corner. The only other things in the space, which would have easily fit a dozen eighteen wheelers with their trailers attached, were Mike and Alexei's vehicles.

"Okay, seriously, do you think Alexei is pranking us?" Callum asked.

Rupert huffed out a weak laugh and climbed from the car,

feeling decidedly wrong-footed. He hated unexpected changes to his plans, and Callum turning up at the rink and bringing them here was a double whammy. Rupert took a deep breath, distracted for a moment by a growing concern that he stank to high heaven after a long training session with Christian. He took a moment to dig through his bag in the back seat and apply a copious amount of deodorant.

"What?" he groused when Callum smirked at him.

"Nothing."

Rupert threw his deodorant back in his bag and took another deep breath to make sure he smelled better. He should have gone back to the hotel for a quick shower after leaving the rink, but that would have taken more time, and the quicker solution simply wasn't possible.

Rupert didn't shower at the rink. Any rink. Ever.

Shaking off those grim thoughts, Rupert looked around while Callum released Oliver from his car seat.

The floor was concrete, in good condition but covered in a film of dirt, as one would expect in a garage, even a super bizarre one like this. There were high windows, too grimy to let in much light, and more massive doors along the far wall, though if Rupert wasn't mistaken, those would lead almost directly into the river. A single man-sized door with a light above was to the side, presumably exiting onto another street or alleyway.

"I have no idea what this place is," Rupert admitted, "but I'm not overly excited at the prospect of living here."

Callum hitched Oliver higher on his hip. "And you were worried about what you smell like."

"Shut up," Rupert said, "Nobody wants to rent to someone who's going to contaminate their space with body odor."

Callum laughed. "Alexei and Mike are hockey players. Body odor is probably a comfort to them. I promise you, if Yankee Candle had a *Soothing Scent for Hockey Players,* it would smell like old, used socks and sweaty jock straps. Seriously, have you *been* in the locker room?"

Rupert tried to smile, but he could feel the heat working its way into his cheeks, his shame burning him from the inside out.

Because the answer was no.

The manager of the Ice Cats was afraid of setting foot in his own team's changing space, even when the team wasn't in it.

Callum put a hand on his arm. "Hey, I was just kidding."

"I know," Rupert said, then made the terrible mistake of looking into Callum's concerned eyes as his arm curled protectively around Rupert. "But you know I'm not...I hate the locker room. Any locker room. That's where they—"

"*Rupert,*" Callum whispered, pulling him closer.

"Sorry."

"Don't apologize. I need to learn to shut my mouth. I didn't know."

"It's not unreasonable to expect, given my current position, that I would be well acquainted with the locker room. It's my own fault. Perhaps tomorrow I'll go check it out. See if I, too, find the smell of sweat and feet as calming as you apparently do."

Callum smiled. "I'll come with you."

Oliver's hand landed on Rupert's cheek. "Me, too."

"That would be nice, thank you," Rupert said.

Callum's smile faltered, but he didn't look away. "You're welcome."

"Can we see Alexei now?" asked Oliver, his patience with old people acting weird having dried up.

"Yeah, kiddo," Callum said, looking around with a frown. "And I'm telling you both right now, I will kill Alexei if this was all some joke."

Rupert shook his head. He'd lived in constant fear of Alexei Belov's infamous pranks when he'd first come to Moncton, but the man he'd come to know, the friend who doted on Oliver and made a point of harassing Rupert, wasn't cruel.

"Are we supposed to wait here, do you suppose?" Rupert asked.

"Oh. No, his email said we should to take the elevator to the fourth floor." Callum cast a dubious look at the lift in question. "Do you think we're supposed to bring the car with us?"

Because it *would* possibly fit.

It took them a few moments to figure out how to close the doors and get the thing moving, but eventually they were headed upwards at a slow rattle and sway. Callum got paler with every floor, smiling weakly when Rupert threaded their fingers together and gave his hand a squeeze. Rupert wondered if he had a thing about small spaces, but then again, this elevator was only a few square feet smaller than Rupert's office, and was at least twice the size of the janitorial closet Callum had dragged him into just yesterday to steal a kiss.

They came to a juddering stop, and Callum practically threw Oliver into Rupert's arms. Years of being forced to train with a partner for potential pairs skating *finally* came in handy. Callum had the doors open in three seconds flat, revealing a hallway so luxurious, Rupert felt like they'd gone down the rabbit hole.

The walls were dark teal, the crown molding, baseboards, trim, and chair rail a pleasantly contrasting cream, the carpet a dark pattern of colors with just a hint of the teal picked out within it.

Mike and Alexei stood proudly before a dark wood door with a discrete brass *2* on it. At the other end of the hall was a second door with a *1.*

"The garage definitely sells the place short," Rupert observed.

"You should see the other floors," Alexei said. "They're just a mess of demolished materials and bare bulbs right now, but we have addressed anything dangerous, and the rats are definitely gone for good."

Mike gave his boyfriend a bone-dry look. "You're no longer in charge of marketing."

Alexei grinned and sent Rupert a wink. "Well, we don't want just anyone to move in here, do we?"

"I should hope not," Rupert agreed with a grin.

"Ready to see it?" Mike asked, and received three ardent nods in return. He threw open the door and stepped inside, running his hands over the glossy wood. "We just installed this for you. We'd been putting it off until the very end."

"Congratulations, then, on the project being done. I'm sure I will—"

Whatever Rupert had been about to say flew out of his mind when he stepped into the apartment. He tried to look at everything at once. The dark cherry cabinets and warm brown granite in the kitchen, the rich red walls and mahogany floors in the open living and dining rooms beyond. From the door, you could see out the massive windows to the river and the countryside beyond, and down a long hallway lined with doors to another window and the city below.

"Holy shit," muttered Callum behind him.

Oliver giggled, but no one bothered to correct Callum's language.

"Do you like it?" Mike asked with a hint of insecurity.

"I love it," Rupert assured him. "It's gorgeous."

Mike looked pleased, smiling at Alexei, who threw his arm around Mike's shoulder.

"The bedrooms and full bath are down there," Alexei said, gesturing at the hallway. "The half bath is here." He opened the door off the foyer. "The ceilings in the bedrooms are a more standard ten feet, with a large crawl-space above for storage, all of which will keep noise from traveling out here and between bedrooms."

Rupert didn't think anything of that factoid until Mike blushed. Rupert smirked. "Very considerate. Thank you."

Alexei went on with the tour, opening doors and pointing out features. Oliver was utterly delighted with his new, bright yellow room, as was Rupert with his dark blue office and warm gray master bedroom.

"The colors are lovely," Rupert said.

Mike shrugged, almost shy. "I chose them with you in mind.

If you don't like any of them, we can change them this week."

Rupert hardly knew what to say. "No, I—they're perfect. Thank you."

Mike shrugged again, but now he looked pleased, and Alexei was beaming at Rupert. Was it only a month ago Rupert had been prepared at all times for Alexei to drown him in muscle cream or shave off his eyebrows?

"So, when can we move in? And what do you need from me?"

From there it was fairly simple. A check, some paperwork, their detailed list of ways they had made sure the property was safe for Oliver—including finishing the fire stairs and replacing the emergency exit doors so that he could open them easily. Rupert was honestly touched by the amount of care they'd put into making this place a good home for them.

"So, it's ready any time," Mike said.

"Great," Callum said. "How about we move in as soon as I get back from my trip?"

We? Rupert kept his face carefully neutral. Obviously, he'd hoped Callum would move out of the hotel with them, but he hadn't known how to broach the subject. He also didn't think Callum realized just how *obvious* he was being, given the expressions on Mike and Alexei's faces. But then, maybe Callum thought they could set up a guest room for him. Rupert cataloged his belongings and decided he could buy what was needed if that was the case.

"That sounds great," Rupert said.

And so it was settled. Which was all well and good in theory, but left Rupert little more than five days to get all his belongings from a storage unit in Nova Scotia to Moncton. He reached for his phone without thinking, pulling up his list application and starting a new one.

He paused halfway through to laugh at himself.

He was getting better at being flexible, but he wasn't cured yet. If Callum's fond smile was any indication, his obsessive list-making wasn't entirely a bad thing. At least it gave Callum something else to tease him about.

Chapter Thirteen

Callum stared blindly at the in-flight magazine and counted down the minutes until his arrival in Las Vegas. The return to his "real" life made him think, a lot, about the last couple months.

Kissing had been a revelation. The way it made his heart speed up, how good it felt to hold Rupert close, to press their bodies together and hold on for the ride. In his weaker moments, when he'd lain awake at night alone in his bed in Denver, pining like a teenage girl, he'd hoped it would be like that. The real thing was better than the imagined, by far, but he'd *hoped*, anyway.

The blow job, on the other hand, had changed everything. Changed Callum.

He'd been nervous, and objectively terrible at it, but he'd wanted to do it. Like, *a lot*. And he wanted to do it again. Callum had been sure that giving oral sex was something he'd do because it was his turn or he had some favor to repay. He'd been even more certain that he'd never want someone to come on his face, and, *wow*, he had been wrong about that.

How had he never figured out how hot *filthy* could be?

He'd had men ask for that, kneeling beneath him on some probably disgusting bathroom floor, and when he'd done it, he'd always felt worse after. All his sexual encounters before Rupert had left him feeling hollow, the release of tension gratifying, but also leaving a hole in him he couldn't fill. He'd gone longer and farther between those nights, sneaking out of a hotel in a city where he was sure no one would recognize him. Tampa Bay, Phoenix, Dallas. Hell, most of Dallas didn't know they had a hockey team, let alone what anyone else's looked like.

He'd waited almost a year before he went out that last time. And now it had been four years since then.

Callum shut his eyes and shuddered, forcing himself not to go back to that club. To remember anything that happened that night. Not that he could forget, but nothing good came of dwelling on it.

He shoved the magazine back into the seat pocket in front of him. The stranger in the seat next to him glanced over but clearly had no idea who he was, except for some nut that couldn't decide whether or not he wanted to read about the miracle of Antigua's beaches.

Callum relaxed and tried to clear his mind. They were about to begin their decent into McCarran, where he would be greeted by whatever driver the league had sent, the one-hundred-and-two degree weather—who cared that it was a dry heat when it was that freaking hot?—and possibly some fans hanging around the airport hoping to catch the arriving players without the big crowds of the award show.

He should be looking forward to it, but he'd gladly ditch the tuxedo and the red carpet and the television cameras to stand by the Université rink, holding Oliver's hand, and watching Rupert and Christian.

Rupert stood in the middle of the perfectly clean, just-Zambonied sheet of ice and took deep, measured breaths. He was waiting for Christian, who'd asked to meet him for an extra training session today since school was finally out for the summer. Five minutes ago, Christian had run into the arena and straight to the locker room. A moment later, his father had charged in after him.

There were several other people in the locker room with them, Rupert knew, having watched the charming and aromatic Université intermural summer hockey team leave the ice. A few of those men had looked at him askance, but most were perfectly pleasant, one even joking that he'd tried figure skates once and had toe-picked himself into a broken nose. His buddies had cracked up at that, but none had given him a hard time about anything other than his clumsiness.

John would be forced to behave in their presence. Wouldn't he?

Rupert hesitated a moment longer, furious with himself, then took off for the door to the tunnel. He was just stepping off the ice when several of the hockey players came out of the locker room, grim expressions on their faces.

The man with the toe-pick issues caught Rupert's eye. "Do you know the kid in there?"

Rupert's stomach knotted. "Yes."

"You should go help him out. His old man is a piece of work," another of the men said.

Rupert froze. He wanted to run for help. To beg these strangers to go back in there with him. He yanked his cell phone from his pocket and dialed.

"Da?" Alexei barked almost immediately. He, Mike, and Oliver were off getting ice cream at a creamery they'd heard about outside of town.

Rupert hadn't really thought this through. What the hell was he going to say to Alexei?

"Rupert?" Alexei said. "Are you okay?"

"Christian's father is here," he said stupidly, as if that explained his bizarre behavior. Or excused him delaying going into the locker room.

"Shit," Alexei said vehemently. "Do you need us to come?"

"No," Rupert said firmly as he started toward the locker room. He'd like to think he was charging right in, but with his skates on, it was more of a tromp. "I'm sorry. I shouldn't have called. I'll let you know when we're done here," he said, confirming their original plan, then hung up.

His phone rang the moment he shoved it into his pocket, but by then he was pushing open the door and being assailed by John's furious shouting.

"You will *respect* me, Christian Michael Shaw! I said no, and I meant it. You will not sneak off alone to meet up with some faggot. God knows what he wants to do to you."

Rupert very nearly threw up, swaying as the blood left his head in a rush. A hand gripped his arm and he turned to see a stranger looking at him with alarm. Several others around them had expression of horror and disgust. One man slung his bag over his shoulder and charged out of the room, his complexion gone white.

"Don't say shit like that, Dad!" Christian yelled, his twelve-year-old voice cracking painfully. "Rupert is just being nice. He just wants to help me."

"What, you call him Rupert now? What happened to *Mr. Smythe*?"

"That's his name, Dad. What's wrong with that?"

"You have no idea what he could do to you."

"Why do you think like that?" Christian cried, and Rupert ached at the grief in his voice. "He's not a pervert! *You're* the pervert, Dad, thinking all that awful stuff."

"We're leaving," John snapped a moment before Christian let out a pained squeak.

"No!" Christian shouted.

Rupert flew down the row of lockers and around the corner. John immediately released Christian and the boy stumbled away from his father. Rupert caught him and set him on his skates again, then curled his hands into fists to keep them from encircling John's neck.

"Mr. Shaw," he said furiously, refusing to quail in the face of such blazing bigotry and hatred, "how dare you accuse me of— of—*you are disgusting*. Do you honestly believe that I'm some kind of monster because I...what? Figure skate? What the bloody hell is the matter with you?" Rupert shouted, his own voice echoing back to him.

Christian was looking between his father and Rupert with wide, terrified eyes.

"No," John sneered, "I think you're *gay*."

"Which means what, exactly, in your feeble little brain? Because last I checked, that means I am attracted to men. Not boys, not *children,* for the love of god. What the fuck is wrong with you? Do you live under a rock?"

224

Christian made a choking sound, then tried to insert himself between his father and Rupert. Rupert gently pushed him back, stepping forward to ensure Christian stayed safely behind him.

"You are not going to lead my son astray."

"You're right. I'm not. I'm going to teach him to bloody figure skate, which is what he wants to do. There is nothing nefarious about any of it, you fucking idiot."

The rational part of Rupert's brain, which clearly was not in control at the moment, reminded him that continuously insulting the man was probably counterproductive. Damned if Rupert could give a shit.

"We're going, Christian," John snarled, reaching for the boy.

Rupert shoved his hand away. "No, you are not. I already saw you mishandling him. I'm not going to let you forcibly drag him out of here."

"He's my son!" John roared.

"Yes, he is. And, sadly, I cannot change that. But until you calm down, so that I can be certain you will not harm him, I think he should stay here."

"You have no right!" he bellowed, and Rupert feared he was right, legally speaking. "I'm his father!"

"*You*," Rupert said very clearly, "are a *monster*."

Rupert didn't know what he expected, but the punch to his face was hardly surprising, in hindsight. He staggered back until he bounced off the lockers, blinking against the pain searing through his nose to his entire face.

"*Dad*!" Christian shouted. He tried to put himself in front of Rupert, but Rupert stayed him with an arm across his chest.

From there, things devolved quickly into chaos.

John lunged toward Rupert again, but was stopped by the arrival of the remaining members of the intermural hockey team. It took two of them to hold him back. He howled horrible curses and slurs, the hockey players cursing back, begging him to shut his mouth as they attempted to drag him away. Rupert could hardly breathe, his courage deserting him as collapsed against the lockers and held onto Christian, who was curled in on himself and pressed into Rupert's side.

Shouting came from the corridor, then the man who'd fled the room earlier charged into the room with a man Rupert recognized as the rink manager. *"Get out!"*

John tore himself free of the men holding him and Christian attempted to wedge himself behind Rupert, shuddering while his father stormed out of the room.

For a good minute, no one spoke. Rupert couldn't stop blinking, tears flowing down his face, the taste of blood strong in his mouth and throat.

He gently pried Christian out from behind him. "He's gone," Rupert whispered, appalled when bright red flecks appeared on Christian's white shirt.

"Jesus," one of the men muttered, passing Rupert a towel from his own bag. Rupert accepted it gratefully, stoically refusing to wonder where, exactly, it had been rubbed in order to acquire its distinct odor. He pressed it to his nose, and it immediately turned bright red.

Rupert looked down at his shirt and the even larger stain there, and swayed on his skates. That was *a lot* of blood.

Someone, and he worried it might have been poor Christian, helped him to sit on a bench. Someone else offered some ice, in a brand-new bag, which was heavenly against his poor face. It was cool and it didn't smell at all of testicle sweat.

He sat and tried to stem the bleeding. He startled when door to the locker room burst open.

"Rupert!"

"Jack?"

Jack flew around the corner and stuttered to a halt. "Holy smokes!"

"It's not as bad as it looks," Rupert said, wincing at his nasally voice.

"Really?" Jack asked with extreme dubiousness.

Rupert shrugged. Then winced. Perhaps he could save that

argument for another time. "How on earth did you find me?" Rupert asked instead.

"Are you kidding? They were talking about you in the parking lot!"

"I mean," Rupert said patiently, sort of, "what are you *doing* here?"

"Alexei called me and told me to come. He sounded freaked out, shouting about rushing and how I was closer." Jack eyed Rupert's face. "I accused him of over-reacting. My bad. Guess I owe him a beer."

"I could use one, too," Rupert muttered.

A great sigh from beside him on the bench made him wince. He turned to Christian. "Jack, this is Christian Shaw. I've been coaching him a little. Christian, this is my friend, Jack Chevalier."

Jack thrust out his hand. "Nice to meet you, Christian."

Christian kept his hands and his gaze buried in his lap. "Nice to meet you," he mumbled.

Rupert prodded Christian with his elbow. "Come on, now. Manners," he scolded gently.

Christian straightened, lifting his gaze to see Jack. Rupert almost felt sorry for the boy when all he could do was gape for a moment. Jack smiled encouragingly and held out his hand once more.

Christian shook it. "It's a pleasure to meet you, Mr. Chevalier."

"Jack, please. Call me Jack," he offered.

Christian smiled widely, then looked over at Rupert and his face fell. "Oh god. I'm really sorry, Rupert."

"Bah, Christian. It wasn't your fault."

"But it was my dad!"

Jack's eyebrows, which had already been steadily climbing, shot way up. Before he could comment, though, the locker room door burst open again.

"Rupert!" Alexei bellowed loud enough to be heard for

twenty miles. Honestly.

"I'm here," Rupert called back. "Be warned though—" Alexei and Mike barreled around the corner with Oliver in Mike's arms "—I look a little rough," Rupert finished lamely. So much for warning Oliver.

"Rupert!" Oliver dove forward, but Mike caught him before he landed on Rupert, holding him mid-air. "Easy, Oliver. You don't want Rupert to get hit in the face."

"Again," Jack added helpfully.

"What happened?" Alexei asked.

Christian shot to his feet. "I should go."

Four men shouted "No!" at once. Christian sat again, his shoulders slumped.

Rupert put the ice pack down on the bench and shot a quelling frown at Jack when he hissed upon seeing Rupert's face. "Christian, let's get started. Once we're done, perhaps it would be best if Mike and Alexei took you home. I don't think your father wants to see me again today."

Christian looked sick with worry as he studied Rupert's face. "Are you sure we should practice today?"

"Yes, yes," Rupert said bracingly. "I'll be fine. Go along."

When Rupert nudged him, he hesitated before letting out another long sigh and going toward the door.

"Go ahead and get warmed up. I'll be right behind you!"

Callum stepped out of the elevator and into the lobby of the Bellagio hotel, craning his neck to catch sight of Michaela. He knew she was somewhere nearby, since her bags were already in her bedroom of the suite and they were meant to meet for lunch. Often she liked to go unnoticed, dressing down and wearing the huge sunglasses that he joked made her look like Jackie O. Other times, like today, apparently, she need only stand still and smile, and the world would slowly shift to rotate around her.

She was wearing heels, based on the way Callum could see

her above the heads of the swarming crowd. She had her public smile on, polite, gracious, and nothing at all like the toothy grin Callum loved to coax from her when it was just the two of them. She spoke with someone to her left, the crowd growing steadily, including several members of the Bellagio security staff. Callum felt better when their dark, broad-shouldered blazers took up position on either side of her.

It never ceased to amaze him how many people wanted a piece of Michaela. A word, a smile, a signature, and far too often, a touch. They'd reach out to brush their hand over some part of her, as if it were their right. Normal, good people would lose their minds, forget that she was a person whose rights and space should be respected like any other's. As if, by being a public figure, she were theirs to have.

Callum waited by the elevators until Michaela looked up and saw him. For a moment, the grin was there, then she was wading through the crowd, which parted for her until she could pick up speed and launch herself into Callum's arms. He laughed, happy to have her there again. She was the only part of his life in Denver he'd genuinely missed.

He'd learned to keep his eyes open in spite of the firestorm of flashes going off around them, tired of turning up in magazines looking like he was asleep, bored, or had suffered brain trauma. It was mostly phones pointed toward them today, but there were a few more professional-looking devices trying to get lost in the crowd.

"I've missed you," Michaela said, leaning back to plant a smacking kiss on his lips.

"Ditto."

He dropped her back onto her feet, glad he hadn't told her not to come, but eager to end the show for the people and press around them.

"Shall we get lunch?" he asked.

Michaela agreed, her look understanding, her hand in his as she led them through the lobby and out to the waiting car.

The moment the doors were closed, the tinted windows

sealing them off from prying eyes, they both slumped back against the seat.

"We should have just met up in our room," Callum muttered.

Michaela chuckled. "I figured you'd want to put on at least one or two performances in addition to the show tomorrow night."

Performances. Shows. He sank deeper into the upholstery and stared out the window. This was his life. The one he'd chosen.

"Callum?"

He sighed and turned his head to face her. She was beautiful, and his best friend, and he would rather stick a hot poker in his eye than have sex with her, let alone marry her. Fortunately, she knew all that.

"You're right, of course," he said. "I'm sorry if I'm grumpy. I've just been thinking a lot this summer, I guess."

"You're always grumpy. What have you been thinking about?"

He gave her a self-deprecating smile. "Life."

"Did it hurt?"

"Shut up."

"You shut up," she said. "I want to hear more about this existential crisis."

"Ugh. It's not...I don't know. I guess I'm just tired. And old."

"You are not old," Michaela said firmly, always a staunch friend, even if it required lying.

"I am for hockey."

"Not really." Because Michaela also wouldn't let him get away with feeling sorry for himself. "What's really the problem?"

Callum thought of Rupert. "It's not a problem," he began, wincing when Michaela's eyebrows lifted. "There is no problem, I swear. I just—"

Callum was saved from answering by his phone buzzing. He scrambled to pull it out of his pocket, reminding himself that he hadn't outright lied, it was just that for the last five years, she'd been the only one who'd known the truth. The whole truth. Omitting what was going on with Rupert just *felt* like lying.

He was both relieved and alarmed to see Jack's Facetime request. "I have to take this," he said to Michaela, who waved off the implied apology. He accepted the call. "Hey, Jack. Everything okay?"

"Ummm..."

The long note of hesitation drew Michaela's attention. She leaned closer and got a good look at Jack's face. "Oh my."

Callum studied Jack and his surroundings, confused. He appeared to be in a locker room. When the camera tilted, Callum recognized the crest painted on the wall.

"Are you at the Université rink?" Callum checked his watch and did the time-zone math. Rupert was supposed to be coaching Christian right now.

"Uh, yeah," Jack said. "About that..."

"Jack, what the fuck is—" The screen blurred and now, instead of Jack's handsome visage, Callum was faced with one he barely recognized. "*Rupert?*"

Rupert frowned furiously, which looked like it hurt. A lot. His nose was several shades of red and purple, and it was obvious he was working his way toward two really impressive black eyes.

Rupert glared just above the phone. "Really, Jack? Tattling on me now, are you?"

"Sorry," said Jack with zero sincerity.

"Rupert!" Callum snapped, wincing when Rupert winced, then winced again when that obviously hurt. It was a regular wince-a-thon until Rupert forced his poor face to settle into a neutral expression. Callum's heart hammered against his ribs. More than ever, he felt an overwhelming need to *not be in fucking Las Vegas.* "What happened?"

Rupert sighed. "John Shaw happened, I'm sorry to report."

Callum growled, long and low and deep in his throat. He was

going to fucking kill that man.

Michaela stared at him, her mouth fallen open. He may have said that last part aloud.

"Honestly, Callum, you should be doing whatever it is you're meant to be doing," Rupert said primly, his eyes cutting left, where he was no doubt noticing Michaela hovering over his shoulder. "Everything is fine here. Oliver is over the initial shock of seeing me like this, and Christian is on his way home with Mike and Alexei."

"You let him go home to that asshole?"

Rupert frowned. "And what would you have me do? Kidnap him?"

It wasn't such a bad idea, when compared to whatever Christian faced at home.

"Callum," Rupert said gently, his eyes pleading for him to understand. "I don't like it any more than you do, but I didn't have a choice. You know that, right?"

"Of course," Callum said with a sigh. "I'm sorry."

Rupert smiled as much as his face allowed. They just looked at each other for a moment, until Callum realized Michaela was staring at him again, once more agape.

"So, what'd you do to piss him off this time?" Callum asked.

Rupert grimaced. "More yelling, I'm afraid. He was trying to drag Christian out of the locker room, declaring that it was for Christian's own good, since as a *fag* I was obviously only interested in molesting the boy."

Callum went cold inside.

Michaela sank her claws into Callum's arm. "That fucking prick!"

Rupert blinked, then smiled shyly at Michaela. "Hello. It doesn't seem Callum is inclined to introduce us. I'm Rupert Smythe. It's a pleasure, and not just because you've defended me, a complete stranger."

Michaela's laugh was warm, her smile genuine. "The pleasure is all mine, Mr. Smythe. I'm Michaela Price."

"Please call me Rupert."

"Michaela."

Callum rolled his eyes. "Are you two done? Because I'd still like to know what the fuck happened!"

"What happened," Rupert said patiently, "is that I defended myself, loudly, and when I informed him that he was a monster, he took exception and popped me right in the nose."

"Did Alexei kill him? Tell me where he hid the body. I swear I'll never tell."

Rupert tried to grin. "Alexei wasn't here, sadly. I doubt John would have done it had he been. But Jack did come to my rescue," he said with a look above the phone.

"I got here five minutes too late!"

"He did miss the best parts," Rupert conceded.

"I got to hear about them, though." Jack's face appeared over Rupert's shoulder. "Apparently Rupert here has quite a pair of lungs on him. The whole rink heard him."

"Yes, well, it seems I can't help but be rather foolish around that man."

"Rather brave, you mean," Callum said.

Rupert dismissed that with one eloquent shrug. "And look where that got me."

Punched in the face while Callum was a couple thousand miles too far away to do anything about it.

"Do you need me to come home?"

Michaela's grip tightened around his arm, but Callum only had eyes for Rupert. He knew what Rupert was going to say, but he would decide for himself whether he would listen.

"No, no. We're fine. *I'm* fine, Callum, I promise."

Jack grinned at the camera and Michaela made a humming sound. "I'll take good care of him until you get back, Cal. Don't worry."

Rupert rolled his eyes. "I'm perfectly capable of taking care of myself."

"Then stop getting punched in the face," Callum suggested.

"I promise to work on that," Rupert replied dryly. He looked at Jack. "Now that you've discharged your duties as keeper and tattle-tale, can we hang up?"

"I had no idea you could be so bitchy. Now I know what Callum was talking about." Jack replied before the call went dead.

It was silent in the back of the car, but the look Michaela leveled on him spoke volumes. It didn't waver as she reached out and pressed the button to ensure the privacy panel was fully in place.

"Callum," she said. "Is there something you want to tell me?"

And god, she sounded *just* like his mom. And just as if he were sitting at his mother's table, safe in childhood home instead of the back of a livery service car, he folded like a house of cards in a wind storm.

Chapter Fourteen

Rupert watched the award show partly out of solidarity, but also out of morbid fascination to see Callum and Michaela take the red carpet by storm.

Callum was invited to the awards this year ostensibly because he'd won last year. In reality, Rupert suspected the league would be happy to have him come every year, provided he brought his "ever beautiful and devoted girlfriend."

She positively lit up the entire party. Hell, she lit up the back of a car over Facetime—how could she not glow in the face of all those lights and cameras and fans? She was willow slim, tall—taller than Callum in those heels—and poised. Her gown, the diamond earrings she told the press Callum had bought for her, hell, even her smile, *glittered*.

And she'd leapt to Rupert's defense without knowing a thing about him. Indeed, if he had any read at all of her expressions, Callum had kept Michaela in the dark about Rupert until that moment. Rupert tried not to be stung by that. If nothing else, he knew now that she wasn't jealous. Indeed, she'd looked delighted.

Rupert watched enough to see them woo the crowd, and for the press to do a bit about their joyful reunion the day before in the hotel lobby. They showed a clip of Michaela throwing herself into Callum's arms and his bright smile in response. Rupert recalled how he'd done the same not long ago, and it hadn't gone nearly so well.

He sighed. He was being foolish. Micheala was Callum's fake girlfriend and real best friend. Rupert was Callum's...

What?

Summer fling, he supposed.

On that note, Rupert switched off the TV and turned his undivided attention to his work.

Michaela was driving Callum *nuts*. Everything they saw or did, there was a comment. Would Rupert like that? Maybe you should buy that for him? Or for Oliver? Do you think Rupert likes Las Vegas? What about Denver?

That was when Callum drew the line.

"He's not going to be in Denver," he said flatly.

Michaela looked at Callum, somehow managing to make it appear romantic and coy and not, as anyone who knew and loved her would know, like she wanted to kick him in the shins. They were at an after-party for the awards, surrounded by colleagues and teammates, the people who should have been Callum's closest friends.

Michaela was careful to restrict her comments to when she would not be overheard, which was relatively easy, given the distance Callum liked to keep from everyone. That being said, there was no way she could launch into the lecture, or campaign, or *whatever* Callum could see brewing in her eyes.

"It's just sex," Callum said quietly before throwing back the rest of his scotch in one go. He'd just had it refilled, but searched for a waiter to order another.

"Bullshit," Michaela muttered while looking down at her gown under the guise of rearranging the drape of her already perfectly draped drapey-ness.

Thank god for tuxedos, was all he was saying.

"Callum!"

Callum turned with a bright smile, probably shocking his teammate, Mitch, and Mitch's wife, Abby, by encouraging them to join them. Her back to the room, Michaela sent him a sour look.

He wasn't a fool. He'd bought himself a respite, at best. And another lecture, at worst.

He tried to focus on the conversation, but if he flaked out occasionally, he knew it would be excused simply because he was a goalie. Goalies were universally viewed and accepted as odd. Callum didn't really get that. So he volunteered to have hard rubber projectiles shot at his head at over a hundred miles per hour. So what?

Seriously, it was *fun*.

By the time the night was over, it was almost morning and even Michaela was dead on her feet. He walked her to her bedroom in the suite and pecked an affectionate kiss on the cheek before nudging her through the door.

He'd almost gotten away when her hand shot out and stopped him.

"We're going to talk about it. Tomorrow."

He sighed. "We have lunch with Anna at noon. We can talk on the way, okay?"

"Fine," she said through a huge yawn, then let the door swing closed in his face.

Callum chuckled, went to his own bedroom, and passed out two seconds after he'd stripped off most of his tux.

He wasn't surprised in the slightest the next morning when Michaela started in the moment the car pulled away from the hotel to take them to lunch.

"It's not just sex."

"Oh, really? How would you know? You haven't even met Rupert, let alone seen us together."

"Neither of those things are true either."

"It was one phone call! For, like, five minutes!"

She patted his hand consolingly. "I know it's hard to understand with your limited social skills."

Callum rolled his eyes. "Yes, thank you. But that doesn't change the fact that I live in Denver, he lives in Moncton, and even if we were to reside less than two thousand miles apart, I'm a professional hockey player."

"So?"

Callum never lost his temper with Michaela, but he was getting damn close now. "*So*, I can't have a boyfriend, or whatever the hell you're suggesting,"

Michaela planted a finger against his chest. "That's the worst bullshit you've spouted out yet."

"No, it's not!" Callum barked, feeling more and more off-balance. Michaela was the one who knew. Who *got* it. *She* was the one who suggested she could be his fake girlfriend.

She dropped her hand to grab hold of one of his. "Callum, you're allowed to have a boyfriend. You're allowed to have a *life*."

"No, I'm not."

"Yes, you are," she gritted out.

"What am I going to do? Force some poor bastard to live in the closet with me? Pretend he's my buddy? And what if we get caught? What if someone figures it out? You're my girlfriend, at least as far as anyone out there is concerned," he said, gesturing to the strangers lining the Strip as they flew past. "If they thought I was cheating on you, you'd be humiliated, and I'd be eaten alive. I'd deserve no less. That was never how this was going to work. I thought you understood."

Maybe that last part came out more desperate, more broken, than he'd intended. Michaela looked devastated.

"I do understand, Callum. Of course I get how hard it is to live under the microscope. But I never meant for you to think this was it. That our fake relationship was the only relationship you could have. I only meant to take the pressure off both of us. So that you could take a deep breath before you snapped. And maybe as cover, so you could have a real relationship without worrying everyone was watching and wondering."

"They'll never stop watching. Not as long as I'm playing."

"No," she agreed sadly. "To some extent, that's true, but—"

"And I can't do it. Not another lie. Not another dozen lies. Hundreds of *lies*. I'm just...I'm too tired, Mic. I can't do it." He slumped back against the seat, utterly defeated.

Michaela tucked herself close to his side, her head on his chest. His arms went around her automatically. Maybe even clinging a little.

"You don't have to lie. Not to everyone," Michaela said softly.

"I know. I have you. And my family. And now Rupert." Just saying his name made Callum's chest ache. He missed Rupert. He wished he was here.

"No," Michaela said, "I mean, you could tell people."

Callum's body went rigid. "What?"

"Easy there." She patted his chest, soothing him. "I don't mean the public. I just mean—I don't know. Some friends."

His kneejerk reaction was to tell her he didn't have any. But...that wasn't really true. Jack was his friend. And so were Mike and Alexei. Reese, even. But telling them would also mean them knowing about him and Rupert. Because even he could see they weren't doing a very good job hiding it, relying on Callum's aggressively heterosexual image to let people assume what they would.

"What about Mitch?" Michaela asked, drawing Callum back to Las Vegas from his longing for Moncton.

"What about him?"

"You could tell him. And Abby?"

The tension that had been steadily ebbing came roaring back. "No, I couldn't."

"Why not?"

Why not? The list, actually, was horrifyingly long. "Because I've been on the same team with him for *seven years*. Because he and Abby know and adore you and think we're perfect together. And because we've both let them believe that. What if he wasn't comfortable with me in the locker room anymore? Or he told someone? What if he told management?"

Callum was working up to a really spectacular hypertensive event, maybe even a stroke, when Michaela's voice cut through his panicked ramblings.

"His brother is gay, Callum. And his brother's husband is one of his best friends."

"Oh." Because that was...well, interesting. Callum deflated a little.

They rode in silence for a while, Michaela against his chest while he stared out the window.

"I didn't know that," he admitted, trying to wrap his head around what it would be like to tell Mitch. And to be *accepted*. He honestly couldn't imagine it. "I don't know that he should forgive me, though."

"I think if you apologize, if you try to explain, he might understand. Abby, too. She volunteers with kids in crisis. She sees a lot of the shit all kinds of kids go through, including LGBT kids. Maybe you can explain it to her."

"Yeah, maybe," he agreed, but it all seemed so *unlikely*. Not unlikely that they'd understand, but that he'd ever actually do it.

The town car pulled up to the Ritz Carlton, the doorman immediately present to open their door.

"Just think about it," Michaela said, kissing his cheek before climbing from the car.

Lunch with Anna Fernandez was always a raucous affair. She had a big voice that suited her even bigger personality. She often seemed fearless to Callum. In the ten years they'd been working together, she'd built her agency into an empire, and was still one of the only women in the field. She understood adversity. Discrimination. And anyone would know, just by looking at her, that she'd just as soon punch you in the face than make nice if you crossed her lines.

Honestly, she would be terrifying if she wasn't on his side.

Today, she sat at a quiet table in the back of the equally quiet restaurant, her back to the corner so that she could see the entire room. She caught the eye of a man on the other side of the room and nodded imperiously, but another man, just seconds later and a few tables over, got a sly smile. Her suit had probably cost about as much as a mid-size Japanese car, and it showed off her long legs, tiny waist, and curvy front-bits—if one was into those sorts of things—perfectly. She exuded power and femininity in equal measure. Callum thought if he looked up the word "coy" in any dictionary at Anna's house, the entry would have been redacted.

She kissed their cheeks and swapped designer details with

Michaela in a swirl of information that made Callum thank Christ that his toughest fashion decision was usually if the jeans on his bedroom floor could be worn again before doing the laundry.

He thought Rupert would love to be here for this. He'd know what the hell they were talking about, and could probably tell them where they could find a better tailor or whatever. And god help them all if these two ever got to take Rupert shopping. No one would be safe.

"What are you smiling at, young man?" Anna asked, as if she weren't just a few years older than him.

"Nothing," he said, trying to erase his grin. Anna and Michaela's matching arch stares made it impossible.

"My," Anna said mildly, "you're in an awfully good mood. Anything you two want to tell me?"

And just like that, Callum couldn't do it anymore. Not with this fierce woman who had done so much for him. It helped that she was contractually obliged to look out for his best interests, and that he'd thought he should tell her before now. But in the end, what mattered most was that the lie wouldn't come. Not anymore.

Goddamn Michaela. He totally blamed her for this.

"I do have something I want to tell you," he said, sounding surprised and foolish and plowing on anyway.

Michaela took his hand, squeezing tight, and Anna smiled as she took it in. He could see how well they'd played this. How years of letting people believe what they wanted had made the outright lies unnecessary.

Callum was absolutely terrified.

"I'm gay."

Michaela's smile was blinding, her grip on his hand downright painful. He needed both.

"Pardon?" Anna said.

"I'm gay," Callum said again, and he could swear it was getting marginally easier each time he did this. This was the second time this summer, and it was only like ripping off a limb, not the full-scale evisceration it had been just weeks ago when he'd told Rupert.

Anna sat back in her chair and looked at Michaela, who looked steadily back, eyebrows raised, as if daring Anna to say one wrong word. Callum couldn't breathe.

"Okay," Anna said at last.

"Okay?" Callum asked weakly.

Anna sighed. "What did you think I was going to say, Callum? I mean, I'm surprised. But the only reason I'd be pissed was if you'd hurt Michaela, and she seems like she's pretty okay with this development."

"It's not exactly a development," he admitted.

Anna rolled her eyes. "You're so stupid. You should have told me. I could have helped you if the shit hit the fan."

"Umm...really?"

Anna gave him a stern glare. A lesser man would have shaken in his shoes way harder than he was. "Of course. Look, it's not like you're the only one, okay? I've had this conversation plenty of times."

"You have?"

Anna frowned. "Callum, you do know ten percent of the population is gay, right?"

Michaela snickered. He shot her a dirty look.

"Look," Anna continued, "you don't have to tell me anything, but maybe if you get serious with someone or you think it might hit the press, you could give me a heads up? So I can help you any way I can. I want to help, okay?" she said, pressing her hand over his and Michaela's.

"Okay," he said, his voice embarrassingly hoarse.

Anna nodded once, then asked Michaela about the gala the previous month. Callum sat and listened, well aware they were giving him a moment to collect himself before they got down to the real business he and Anna had come to discuss.

He slipped his phone from his pocket and smiled down at

the good morning text still waiting for him. He thought he should send back a greeting. Ask after Oliver. Tell Rupert what he'd just done. Instead, he unlocked his phone and typed in what he really wanted to say.

I miss you.

Rupert stared at his phone. Every time he deluded himself into believing he'd got the hang of this thing with Callum, Callum went and yanked the rug right out from under him.

"Rupert!"

"Reese!" cried Oliver, pulling on Rupert's hand. Rupert held firm, but grinned at the happy and increasingly vocal little boy.

Reese climbed from the back of his car in front of the hotel as if it were an everyday thing, no hint of anxiety in his expression or body language. It seemed there were several people in Rupert's life who were determined to surprise him these days.

Reese smiled as he let someone pass him on the sidewalk before he jogged over to them. Two months ago, this man could barely leave his estate. Rupert hugged him the minute he was close enough.

Reese hesitated, then hugged Rupert back. "So, this is a thing we do now?"

"Yes," Rupert said, giving one more squeeze before letting go.

Reese studied him. "Does your face hurt?"

"No," Rupert lied.

"Really? Because it's killing me," Reese said jokingly.

Rupert rolled his admittedly very black eyes. He'd trained himself in the last twenty-four hours not to scrunch up his nose, because even though it wasn't broken, it still hurt like a son of a bitch.

Reese turned to Oliver. "Hello, young man," he said very formally. "How are you this evening?"

Oliver giggled. "You sound like Rupert when he's cross."

This, of course, set Reese off cackling.

"Come on, you two, we have a lot to get done tonight."

Rupert led the way into the hotel, curious when Oliver pulled his hand free. He immediately reached for Reese, who took it without hesitation. Something painful and sweet twisted in Rupert's chest. He even understood what it was, now.

Family. It was new and fragile, and Rupert cherished it.

"So, what's the plan?" Reese asked.

"Pizza!" bellowed Oliver. Alexei's influence was becoming clearer every day.

"Yes, pizza," Rupert promised at a more reasonable volume. "It should be here later."

"And now," Oliver said in an excited, high voice, "we can pack up. First our room. Then Callum's."

"Oh really?" Reese asked, missing innocent by a mile. "Callum is moving, too?"

"Yes!" Oliver continued. "His room will be easy, since he never sleeps there."

Rupert could not get them into the elevator fast enough, hitting the door close button repeatedly.

"Is that so?" Reese drawled.

Oliver turned serious. "Yes. I was very afraid when Rupert first found me. Callum and Rupert wouldn't let me sleep alone."

Reese's humor faded. "Of course not."

"I used to sleep in the middle," Oliver continued blithely, "but now Rupert uses Callum as his pillow, and I get the other half of the bed."

It was remarkable, really, how Rupert had gone from rejoicing at every word Oliver spoke to longing for his silence again.

"Well, that's fascinating, Oliver," Reese said, a gleam of unholy glee in his eyes. "I'd think Callum was too big to be a pillow."

"Oh no," Oliver replied. "Callum is very strong. He gives the best hugs. And his pajamas are really soft. Sometimes I fall asleep on top of him when he puts me to bed. Like a really big pillow."

"I see," Reese said with a sage nod. "That does sound nice. Perhaps I will ask if Callum will be *my* pillow some night."

Oliver giggled.

Rupert cast Reese a dark look. "You wouldn't dare."

"Would I not?" Reese murmured as he brushed past Rupert and into the hallway. "Come, Oliver! Show me the way to Callum's room. Do you have a key?"

"We keep it on the counter in our room. Come on, I'll show you!"

Rupert followed them as Oliver bounded to their door. It would be a long evening if Reese was going to harass him about his relationship with Callum. Rupert wasn't even certain there *was* a relationship, so how was he supposed to answer questions about it?

He pulled his phone from his pocket and flicked his thumb to see the text message still up on his screen. He smiled and enjoyed the swoop of his stomach in anticipation of Callum's return.

If Rupert had his way, tomorrow they would begin the process of moving Oliver into his own room. Rupert was very much looking forward to having a bed to himself.

Well, not *all* to himself, of course.

"How'd it go with ordering new furniture for Oliver?" Reese asked, as if reading Rupert's mind.

Oliver beamed and wriggled with excitement. Reese looked at him expectantly, but when Oliver remained silent, he glanced at Rupert. Apparently, Oliver was done speaking.

"Oliver picked out some very nice things," Rupert supplied. "The salesman was very helpful, but I think that was a function of his desire to get me out of the store before I frightened more customers away."

"I can't blame him. You are a fright to see."

"Thank you," Rupert said dryly.

They set to packing up Oliver's belongings first, which took little time even with all the stuff he'd accumulated since London. Rupert worried his brother thought almost daily shopping sprees were the norm.

Rupert's packing was not quite as quick, but that was mostly due to all the shit Reese gave him about his six suitcases, three garment bags, and the box of what Reese insisted on referring to as "beauty supplies." At least Reese's antics distracted him enough that Rupert could tuck his and Callum's clothes for tomorrow aside without an audience. Reese would have a field day over Rupert poking through Callum's underwear drawer, which Rupert absolutely didn't linger over, even if there *were* some interesting options.

They took a break for Oliver's coveted pizza, the grown-ups enjoying a beer and a few minutes to put their feet up.

"What's next?" Reese asked once they'd finished.

"We go get the rest of Callum's belongings," Rupert said, leading the way down the hall. Once inside, he hauled out Callum's empty suitcases and packed away the token amount of clothing he found in one drawer. It didn't fill a tenth of the bag.

Reese lifted his eyebrow, but before he could say anything, Rupert handed him Callum's enormous, and rather pungent, hockey duffle, and led the way back to their real hotel room. Reese stood watch, pulling a terribly amused face, while Rupert drew open the drawers of the second dresser in his bedroom and carefully packed the rest of Callum's clothes.

"You know, they say if you do it too much, your face will get stuck like that," Rupert said.

Reese snorted, glancing to confirm Oliver was still in front of the TV before saying, "You know, for a man who doesn't have a thing with Callum, you two seem pretty cozy."

Rupert sighed and sat back on his heels, careful not to put too much weight on his bad knee. It wasn't Rupert's place to out Callum to anyone, even Reese, who had a better view of things than he probably should. Rupert had considered asking Callum if he could be honest with Reese, but it raised the twin issues of Callum's likely panic at the very idea, and Rupert more or less acknowledging that there was something between them to talk about.

"I can't talk...can you give me some time?" Rupert asked, looking over his shoulder at Reese.

Reese nodded. "I didn't intend to pry into—"

"No, it's not that," Rupert said. "You can ask me anything. You're the only family—well, *adult* family—I have. Of course you can ask."

"Oh," Reese said, apparently nonplussed. "I—ah, thank you."

It wasn't something they'd ever talked about, but today it felt like it had needed to be said. It deserved to be acknowledged.

Rupert went back to packing. "Thank *you*."

Reese left it at that, for which Rupert was grateful. Honestly, between the hugging and the talking about their emotions, he was operating so far outside his comfort zone it was now in another province.

Soon it was time for Oliver's bedtime routine, which Rupert had learned was not to be trifled with. Ever. Reese called Hodges to come pick him up, and promised he'd be there in the morning to help load up for the drive over to the warehouse.

Callum was due back the following evening, and by then Rupert hoped to have at least what was coming from the hotel settled into their new space, and the bedrooms ready for occupancy. It would take a while to get everything from Rupert's old apartment unpacked, and even then he would guess the new apartment would look empty. It was a truly enormous space, and at a price so low, Rupert had actually argued with Alexei to charge him more.

By the time Oliver was ready for bed, Rupert wasn't far behind. He lay dozing beneath his brother, thinking vaguely about getting up and getting some work done, but just couldn't be fussed.

He was deeply asleep, in the dead middle of the night, when something tugged him back to consciousness. He tried to sit up, but realized Oliver was still on top of him. He slid the boy to one side of the bed as Callum came through the door, already stripping off his shirt.

He'd come home early.

Rupert closed his eyes and smiled. Callum slipped into the bed, his arms curling around Rupert's shoulders and waist, pulling him closer, until they were pressed together from chest to toes. Rupert tucked his head under Callum's chin, his face to Callum's throat, and sucked in a deep breath, letting it out with a contented sigh as their legs tangled together and they settled into the bed.

Callum's big hand spread across his back, and Rupert dropped off into sleep, still smiling.

Chapter Fifteen

Callum stood in the middle of Rupert's massive new living room and looked around in wonder. The twenty-foot ceilings soared above them, dwarfing the chocolate leather couches and mahogany dining room set the movers had placed on the dark wood floors. The public rooms were all open to one another, separated by the suggestion of breaks in the space, changes in lighting, and now Rupert's colorful rugs.

The windows reminded Callum of his apartment in Denver, each pane easily ten feet high and six feet wide. The view of the river and the New Brunswick countryside beyond was as breathtaking as his view of the Rockies, maybe better.

Shaking that off, he turned his attention back to the massive wall of floor-to-ceiling bookcases and the pyramid of boxes beneath. He knew Rupert would end up rearranging it all to whatever exacting system he desired, but for now, the goal was to get as many empty boxes back out the door as possible.

Mike and Alexei were in the kitchen, feeding Oliver his snack while Alexei put away various kitchen supplies. The copper pots hanging above the island gleamed in the bright lights. They'd all made good progress when a howl of frustration came from Oliver's bedroom.

"*Callum!*"

"What's wrong?" Callum shouted.

"I can't put this bloody bed together. I hate this fu...fadoodling thing!"

Snorts of laughter issued from the kitchen, as well as the office, where Reese was supposed to be hard at work. Callum tried really hard to wipe his grin off his face as he walked down the hallway and entered Oliver's new room.

The dresser, desk, and bookcases were already in place. All that remained was the bed. The mattress and footboard leaned against one wall, the headboard was against another, and the frame teetered haphazardly between. Rupert stood to one side with his hands planted on his hips.

He look, frankly, adorable—even with his matching shiners and poor bruised nose. He'd stunned Callum this morning by coming out of the hotel bedroom wearing honest-to-god blue jeans. They were slim and dark, painfully new, and probably hand-sewn by Calvin Klein himself, but they were the real deal. Callum had spent the entire morning staring at the way they stretched across Rupert's butt, having obviously been tailored to accommodate that bubble. Later, Callum would think to admire the way the tight t-shirt clung to Rupert in all the best ways, but most of that was because it served to emphasize *that ass.*

Callum couldn't resist a quick peck to Rupert's cheek, letting his hand skim over the bubble in question before going to the far side of the bed. He enjoyed the half-smile that replaced Rupert's furious scowl. Callum would have been tempted to go back around and do it again, but now everyone else piled into the room.

"What is wrong, Rupert?" Alexei asked, loudly enough that even Callum winced.

Rupert rolled his eyes and gestured emphatically. "I give up."

"It's okay, Rupert," Oliver said. "I'll just keep sleeping in your room."

Callum tensed and hoped like hell that his and Rupert's chat with the little boy about not discussing who *else* was sleeping in Rupert's room had stuck.

"What?" Mike asked. He and Alexei exchanged a long look.

"I sleep with Rupert. And—" Oliver cut himself off, but not before Callum's heart had stopped.

Callum steadfastly ignored Reese's pathetic attempts to not appear amused.

"You sleep there every night?" Alexei asked.

Oliver shrugged.

Rupert put a hand on his shoulder. "Oliver, we talked about this. Once we get your new room set up, you can try sleeping in here. I'll stay with you if you need me to," he promised, and Callum smiled encouragingly, hoping Oliver understood Callum would stay, too, if Oliver wanted. Not being able to say it, to just admit he was going to be here, chafed.

"Yes," Oliver agreed, "but now the bed doesn't work, so I can definitely stay with you tonight."

"Now, now," Alexei soothed, shooing the Smythe brothers out of the way and kneeling by the bed.

Mike practically dove to the side by Callum. "We can do this."

Two minutes later, the bed was set up and sturdy as an oak.

Callum was impressed. "I had no idea you two were so handy."

Alexei chuckled. "Who do you think built this apartment?"

"What?" Rupert asked, his mouth dropping open. "I thought Belvedoro Construction and Property Management built it."

Mike smirked. "Rupert, you're one of the smartest people I know. Think about that for a moment."

Rupert looked both pleased by the compliment and deeply confused. "Golden beasts?"

Mike laughed. "That *is* what it means in Italian, but not what I meant." He shot Alexei a look. "I told you people would think that was a little weird."

Reese clapped his hands together, startling everyone. "Ha! Belov and Erdo. Belvedoro is all the letters mixed up."

Mike grinned at Rupert. "He's making you look bad, boss."

"He considers it a calling," Rupert said.

Alexei turned to Oliver. "So, little man, you will sleep in here tonight?" he asked with an unwarranted amount of hopefulness.

"I'll try," Oliver promised solemnly.

Alexei grinned and ruffled his hair. "Good boy!" he said, then winked at Mike, who blushed furiously.

Callum was missing something. He thought Rupert might get it, based on his mildly horrified, completely amused expression, but then he jumped, distracted, and pulled his phone from his pocket.

"I don't know this number," he muttered to himself, hesitating for a moment before swiping his thumb across the screen. "Hello? ...I'm sorry, *who* is this?"

Callum had been about to return to his project in the living room, but now he went to Rupert's side.

"Yes, I know Christian...What? *What?*" Rupert cried. Callum surreptitiously put a supportive hand low on Rupert's back. "Of course, I'll be right there. I'll be right there!"

Rupert tried to hang up the phone three times before succeeding.

"What is it?" Alexei demanded.

"That was the Pathways Center. Christian turned up there after hockey practice today."

"Does he volunteer there? I remember that was who the troop did all that fundraising for." Callum said, rubbing his thumb along Rupert's waist.

"Yes, that's right. But he's not there for that. He says he doesn't want to go home." Rupert swallowed, his voice hoarse when he said, "He says he doesn't feel safe."

This was met with a charged silence.

"He gave them my name, apparently, and they called the office, who in turn gave them my cell number since I wasn't in today," Rupert explained. "They're hoping I'll come down there to speak with him, and them, about what to do next."

Rupert was more than a little freaked out. So was Callum—he was twitching with the need to *get there now.* He wasn't the only one, apparently.

Alexei swooped Oliver up into his arms. "We go. Now."

Everyone charged for the door, Christian's personal army coming to the rescue, when Rupert pulled up short. "Wait!"

"What is it?" Callum asked, checking his pockets for his wallet and keys.

"We can't all go. I don't want to overwhelm Christian or the center. And perhaps Oliver should stay here."

Callum turned to Alexei and Mike expectantly, surprised to find them looking back at him the same way.

"You stay here with Oliver," Alexei told him. "We'll go with Rupert."

"But—"

"We volunteer there," Mike explained.

"Yeah, but—"

"It's an LGBT youth center, Callum," Alexei said, as if Callum were missing the point. "That might be why Christian chose it."

"I'm aware of that."

"So," Alexei said, drawing out the word, "Maybe that's not so much your area of expertise."

Callum was struck by the curious amusement on Reese's face. In a flash, Callum realized Reese already knew, or strongly suspected. And Callum could tell Rupert was about to jump in and try to save his ass.

Which did not need saving, even if he *was* totally having a panic attack meltdown on the inside.

"If you're done patronizing me," he said to Alexei, "*and* finished implying all straight people are out of touch, then I'll take this moment to tell you I'm gay, too."

And, wow, in just two short months he'd gone from this feeling like a full-out evisceration to going all out for the three-for-one coming-out special and it only making him mildly nauseous.

Rupert looked more stunned than anyone else.

Alexei turned to Mike and dug out his wallet, muttering under his breath. Mike held out his hand for the fifty-dollar bill Alexei smacked against his palm, a shit-eating grin on his face.

So Mike, like Reese, had suspected. Callum felt kind of itchy and hot thinking about that, so he focused on the more pressing issue at hand.

"So, who's going with Rupert?" he asked.

"I can stay here," Reese offered with a bland smile. "Since apparently I'm underqualified."

Oliver clung a little closer to Alexei, who cast a judgmental eye over Callum before nodding grudgingly. "We can stay."

Callum bit back twin urges to thank him and smack him in the back of the head. He turned to Rupert.

"Let's go."

Rupert jumped into Callum's car and buckled up, silently screaming for Callum to go faster. He wasn't dragging his feet or anything, but the shocked look hadn't left his eyes since he'd come out to Mike, Alexei, and Reese, all in one shot.

Rupert was so proud of him.

He threaded his fingers through Callum's where they rested on his thigh as he drove.

"You okay?" Callum asked.

"Me? Yes, I'm fine. Worried about Christian, of course." He paused, wondering if being honest was a good idea. "And you."

"I'm fine." Callum said, not particularly believably.

"It would be understandable if you wanted to have a bit of a freak out."

"Nope."

"Nope?"

"We have shit to get done right now. But I'm totally going to lose my shit later, if that's okay with you."

Rupert smiled and squeezed his fingers. "That's fine. Perhaps after Oliver is in bed."

"Great. It's a plan," Callum said.

Rupert had been making far grander plans for their first night without Oliver sleeping next to them, but perhaps this would be better. It had occurred to Rupert this morning as they'd been dumping Callum's bags in the master bedroom closet that he'd never actually asked Callum if he *wanted* to move into the apartment with them. He'd just assumed. And Callum hadn't said otherwise.

Perhaps more than tacit agreement was warranted before they went any further.

"Um, speaking of tonight..."

Callum sighed. "I can't wait to crawl into that big bed with you."

Oh. Well then.

Before Rupert could sort through the barrage of images and ideas Callum's quiet wish invoked, they were turning into the Pathways Center parking lot.

Rupert leaped from the car the moment it stopped moving, Callum right behind him as he burst into the lobby.

The woman behind the desk shot to her feet. "Sir, I have to ask you to stop right there!"

Rupert skidded to a halt, surprised until he remembered where he was and what his face looked like. He glanced at Callum, who seemed far more familiar with the concept of appearing threatening. Before Rupert's eyes, he seemed to shrink a little, his hands where they could be seen, his eyes direct. Rupert wondered how many foolish opponents had been lured closer and regretted it.

"I'm terribly sorry," Rupert said to the receptionist, reaching calmly for his wallet. "I'm Rupert Smythe. One of your directors, a Mr. Gabriel Santangelo, called me a few minutes ago and asked that I come." He offered the woman his license, Callum following suit a moment later.

The woman stared down at Callum's license, then up at Callum. "Oh."

Uh oh. Hockey fan.

"If we could speak with Mr. Santangelo, please?" Rupert said.

"Yes, of course," she said, still gawping at Callum.

Callum smiled back and nodded, as if encouraging her. When she still didn't move, his smile slipped and his cheeks warmed. "Is Mr. Santangelo still in?"

"What? Oh, yes! I'm sorry," she said with a breathless giggle. "I'll go get him."

The moment she disappeared, Rupert started laughing.

"Shut up," Callum muttered.

The door burst back open and the woman fell into the room, even more breathless than when she'd left. "Gabriel asked me to bring you back."

They followed her silently, Rupert watching in fascination as their escort attempted to walk forward and look over her shoulder at the same time. The second time she almost slammed directly into a doorframe, Callum stopped her with a hand on her arm.

Rupert had never seen a fifty-something year old woman blush like a school girl. Callum looked like he rather wished the floor would open up and swallow him whole.

"Thank you, Janet," came a nice, deep voice through the door to their right.

Janet stood staring at Callum, blocking their way. Rupert was starting to feel torn about who he felt sorrier for. God knew he'd had moments like this, staring at Callum.

"Janet, is there a problem?" came the voice again.

"Oh, right." Janet stepped aside, tittering nervously as she edged around Callum, then turned and bolted for the front office.

Her boss stared after her, confused.

"This visit will probably be in the papers tomorrow," Callum muttered darkly. When Rupert looked at him with alarm, Callum waved it off. "Not important. We've got bigger fish to fry."

The first of those was Director Santangelo. Rupert quickly did the introductions and Gabriel, as he suggested they call him, asked if they'd like to sit down as he returned to his desk.

Rupert remained on his feet, Callum standing silent sentry at his shoulder.

"I'd really like to see Christian, if I may," Rupert said, hoping he wasn't being rude, but increasingly desperate to see the boy.

"Of course. Of course." Gabriel eyed him, still not moving.

Rupert felt oddly exposed in his jeans and t-shirt. He hadn't gone out so casually dressed in...well, possibly ever. He had been enjoying it back at the apartment, but now he felt naked under Gabriel's suspicious scrutiny.

Rupert sighed and explained quickly how he knew Christian, and all that had happened in that relatively brief a period of time. Gabriel looked appropriately alarmed that Christian's father was responsible for the damage to Rupert's face. Rupert finished by saying, "As you can imagine, I didn't want to send Christian home that evening, but I didn't feel I had much choice."

Gabriel frowned. "You didn't."

"Then I'm sure you can understand that I'd like to see Christian and be sure he's okay."

"Please," Callum added sincerely, and it was a testament to how frazzled Rupert was that Callum Morrison was the one with good manners.

"Come with me," Gabriel said, leading the way further into the building, including through another set of locked doors. He explained how the center helped families in crisis and the homeless, including children whose families no longer wanted them at home.

"Are there many?" Callum asked.

Gabriel sighed. "One is too many, but yes, we often have as many as a dozen minors here with us, just from the immediate area. Christian is younger than most we see, but it's not unheard of."

Callum had the same mixture of horror and rage on his face as was brewing in Rupert's gut. The boy was *twelve*. He packed it all away, though, when they entered a lounge and found Christian slumped on one of the ratty old couches.

"Christian."

He jumped to his feet and faced them, eyes red and fingers white where they clenched each other.

Rupert rushed to his side, then hesitated. He didn't know

this boy well. He knew what he wanted to do, but—

Callum saved Rupert the effort of figuring out what was right by grabbing hold of Christian, and Rupert, and smashing them together in his arms and against his chest.

"We got you, kid," Callum said.

Christian wrapped his arms around Rupert and collapsed into tears.

Callum held Rupert while Rupert held poor Christian. The boy's sobs broke Callum's fucking heart, but his rage was also still burning bright. Callum would never forget how broken Christian had looked.

Callum glanced up at Gabriel, who was watching them closely and yet trying to give them some space. The other people in the room, mostly children, weren't as discrete.

"Is there somewhere private we can go?" Callum asked.

"I'm sorry," Gabriel said, "but I can't let you be alone with him. There's a room down the hall where we can all sit down together, if you'd like."

"That's fine," Callum said, herding everyone in that direction as best he could, respecting that the center was careful with their charges' safety. As soon as they were all inside, Callum planted Rupert and Christian on a couch together and sat on the coffee table facing them. Gabriel shut the door and remained standing there, watchful.

Christian still had his face buried against Rupert's shoulder, his chest hitching with every breath, but he was calmer.

"Christian," Callum said, "Can you tell us what happened?"

Christian squeezed his eyes shut. Callum shared a helpless look with Rupert as a tickle of fear worked its way up Callum's spine.

Rupert ran a hand over Christian's head. "Please, Christian. We want to help."

"He was really mad," Christian said, his voice hoarse.

"Your dad?" Callum asked.

Christian nodded.

"You mean the day before yesterday? When he came to the rink?" Rupert asked.

"No," Christian said, then paused and looked up at Rupert's face. "I mean, yes. That started it."

Started it? Callum pressed his damp palms to his knees. "What happened after that?"

"When Mr. Belov and Mr. Erdo dropped me off at home, he wouldn't look at me. They brought me to the door and I could tell he'd been drinking, but he was nice to them. When they left, he made me give him my phone and told me to go to my room, so I did. I didn't come out."

Okay, that didn't sound too bad. Not great, by any stretch, but not terrible.

"At all?" Rupert asked. "Did you have supper?"

Christian shook his head.

"To use the facilities?" Rupert asked gently.

Christian hesitated, then shook his head again.

Gabriel stood straighter. Rupert pressed his lips to the top of Christian's head and sighed. "I had nights like that," he confessed quietly. "When I was about your age, too."

Callum tried to imagine it. Rupert trapped in his room, terrified to go out and face his dorm mates just to use the bathroom. Where had the teachers been?

"I was always glad to be a boy, those nights. And that I could keep an empty pop bottle handy."

Christian twitched, then made a sound that almost sounded like laughter. Callum met Rupert's eyes and thought everything he was feeling must have been right there on his face.

"What happened in the morning?" Rupert asked Christian, still looking at Callum.

"He told me I couldn't go out. Not even to hockey practice. That I had to stay."

"Home for the day?" Callum asked.

"In my room."

Rupert's eyes closed and he took a deep breath before asking, "How long?"

Christian shrugged, as if it was nothing. "He stayed home, too. Called out sick to work. When he cooked himself dinner, I could tell he was drinking again, so I waited until I was sure he was asleep. Then I left."

"What time was that?" Callum asked, trying not to picture Christian, hungry in his room, smelling his father cook dinner for himself, waiting for him to pass out drunk.

"Four o'clock this morning. I've just kind of walked around for a while, then I thought I should come here."

Gabriel spoke up. "I know you already spoke with Kelly, but can you tell me why you don't want to go home, Christian?" He raised his hands to fend off Callum and Rupert's glares. "Not that I think you should, I just want to make sure I understand, too."

"I don't feel safe," Christian said automatically, and Callum understood, in that moment, that someone had taught Christian what to say in circumstances like these. Not that this made it any less true or important, but Callum could see why Gabriel was trying to get another answer.

Callum put a hand on Christian's knee. "How so?" He was expecting Christian to be worried about being trapped in his room for days again, or that his father might hit him.

He wasn't expecting Christian to say, "I think I'm gay."

Callum blinked, otherwise frozen. Twelve years old, and already braver than Callum ever was. Rupert put his hand over Callum's and squeezed.

"And your father?" Rupert asked hesitantly.

"I think he's guessed. I mean—" Christian looked up at Rupert's bruised face. "I think that's why he was so mad at you. Why he doesn't want me to skate with you."

Christian was a very perceptive kid.

"But you haven't told him?" Rupert asked.

"No. I can't. He'll..." Christian swallowed. *"He'll hate me."*

The very worst part was that neither Rupert nor Callum could deny it. Or maybe the worst part was how Christian looked between them, clearly hoping for that denial, and then seemed to fold in on himself.

Callum would have liked to drive directly to the Christian's house and beat John Shaw within an inch of his life.

"What can we do?" Rupert asked Gabriel, sounding determined. Callum hoped Christian found that as reassuring as Callum did.

Gabriel sighed, studying Rupert's face. Callum hoped it served as a reminder of what John Shaw was capable of. "I need to notify Christian's father that he's here." He looked at Christian. "Do you want to spend the night with us?"

He shrugged. Then looked up at Rupert. "Can I come home with you?"

Rupert opened his mouth, but Gabriel cut him off. "I can't let you go home with Rupert just yet, Christian."

Christian looked like he was ready to burst into tears again. "Why not?"

"I'm sorry. I have rules I have to follow, and they exist to make sure you're safe. Once either Child Services or your father says it's okay, you can stay with Rupert." Gabriel ducked his head to force Christian to meet his eyes. "Do you want me to call your father?"

Christian pinned Callum with wide, wet eyes. "What do you think I should do?"

Answers crowded Callum's brain, jockeying for position between the simmering rage and the burning desire to call his parents and tell them how much he loved them. He settled on the one that would keep Christian the safest and not result in a life sentence in Canadian prison for either kidnapping or murder.

"I think if you don't feel safe at home, Christian, then you should stay here with Mr. Santangelo."

Christian nodded, his shoulders slumped. "Okay." He looked

at Gabriel. "I'll stay, if that's okay."

"Of course it's okay, Christian. What do you want me to tell your father if he asks to speak with you, or wants to come see you?"

Christian's eyes widened, a hunted expression taking over his face. "I don't want to."

Gabriel raised a placating hand. "You don't have to. You don't have to do anything you don't want to." He paused, cocking his head toward the door when a faint ringing reached them. "Christian, dinner is ready. Why don't you go get something to eat while I talk to Rupert and Callum some more."

Christian hesitated until Rupert nudged him along. "We'll be here when you're done. Go on."

Christian nodded and left the room. Gabriel closed the door behind him and turned to Rupert. "Would you have taken him home?"

"Yes," Rupert said without hesitation.

"For the night?"

Rupert glanced at Callum, then sat up straighter. "For as long as he needs me."

Gabriel nodded. Callum pressed his hand over Rupert's on his thigh. He was so fucking brave. Not that long ago, he'd been afraid to take in his own brother, and now...

Gabriel cleared his throat, dragging their attention back to him.

"I'm not going to lie, it's a long shot. But you have two options, if you're serious."

Chapter Sixteen

Rupert sat on the edge of Oliver's new bed and gently stroked his hand over his brother's dark, silky hair. It had taken the better part of an hour, but Oliver was asleep, curled up on his side and blissfully unaware of the massive panic attack that was slowly turning his big brother inside out.

For a while it had been easy to put it aside and focus on getting Oliver settled in their new home. Rupert was pleased with how everything had turned out. There were things Rupert would still need to buy or have shipped over from Woodcock, but Oliver's room was already cozy with its new rug and furniture. So much so that Oliver had not put up nearly as much resistance to sleeping in here as expected.

Callum had stayed with them until Oliver was tucked in. Rupert had watched Callum kneel by the bed and brush Oliver's hair off his forehead before kissing him there and saying goodnight. Oliver had kissed Callum's cheek and told him he loved him, and Rupert had been so proud of all of them at that moment. The scared and silent child they'd brought home was almost gone now, and in his place was a sweet and affectionate boy who knew he was safe. And loved.

Every child should be able to expect that much from any adult, but most of all from his parents. Rupert *should* have had that, and would make sure Oliver did from now on. He considered himself infinitely fortunate to be able to do it.

He only wished he could do the same for Christian. Tomorrow he and Christian were going to speak with his father, and Rupert was going to do everything in his power to see that someone, somewhere, loved Christian exactly as much as he needed and deserved to be loved.

With a last kiss to the top of Oliver's head, Rupert slipped out into the hallway and pulled the door almost closed.

"Hey," Callum said from close behind him.

It was the most natural thing in the world to step into Callum's arms and bury his face against his neck. Callum held him close.

"You okay?" he asked quietly.

Rupert nodded, but didn't let go.

"You sure about that?"

He was. He was fine. Better than most, luckier by far, to have Oliver home, to have Callum here. His silent and constant support today—hell, for the past two months—was a debt Rupert could never repay. A gift he could never properly or sufficiently thank him for. And yet it didn't feel like either of those things, exactly. It just felt like...

Well. Rupert understood perfectly why it was so easy for Oliver to love Callum. Rupert felt the same. He only wished the words would come so easily, or be so well received, if they were to come from him.

Rupert pressed his lips just behind Callum's ear, trying to communicate maybe one small part of what he was feeling.

Callum shivered in reaction, his hands flexing against Rupert's back.

Oh. Rupert did it again, delighted when he got the same reaction and Callum shifted closer, their hips brushing.

And then, in a deep voice that belonged in the bedroom, Callum said the sexiest thing Rupert could possible imagine. "I already did the dishes."

It was sad testament to the state of Rupert's life that this was the sweetest of sweet nothings Callum could have whispered. He checked over Callum's shoulder and saw most of the lights in the kitchen and living room were out, the door to the master bedroom wide open, the soft light of the bedside lamp spilling into the hallway.

Rupert pressed his lips to that spot again, an open-mouthed kiss this time, his tongue tasting the salt of Callum's skin. Callum shuddered against him and tilted his head to the side.

"Is this what you wanted?" Rupert asked, smiling against

Callum's warm skin.

"What? No, I—" Callum words became garbled when Rupert sucked the delicate skin, letting Callum feel his teeth. His hips twitched and Rupert slid a thigh between Callum's, a shudder shaking his own spine when Callum pressed into him, against him, his hands scrabbling at Rupert's back to pull him closer and keep them on their feet.

The moment Rupert released the abused skin with a gentle pop, Callum dove in for a kiss. Rupert groaned into his mouth, hitching his leg higher. They staggered and almost crashed into the wall.

"Come on," Rupert said, taking Callum's hand. He towed him into the bedroom and locked the door behind them, smiling when he saw his big bed, made with fresh linens and piled high with pillows. It looked decadent and welcoming, particularly after weeks in the hotel. But none of it looked at good as Callum, standing in front of one of the tall posts, staring at Rupert like he wanted to tackle him and yet rooted to that spot.

Callum's eyes widened, tracking Rupert's hands when he untucked his shirt. Rupert wasn't going to attempt a strip tease, since he was fairly certain he'd look like a complete idiot, but he went slowly, watching Callum's face as he pulled the shirt up and off, exposing his belly and shoulders. Callum's eyes followed his every move. Rupert toed off his trainers, managing to remove his socks without falling to the floor, then fingered the button of his jean thoughtfully.

Callum stood stock still, mouth hanging open, utterly fixated on Rupert's fingers, nerves conquered by curiosity, perhaps. Or need. Or, even, the loss of blood flow to his brain, given the impressive bulge outlined by his old jeans.

Rupert knew what he wanted. He was desperate to finally have the time and space to explore Callum fully. To learn everything he could about his body and what he liked. But before he could do that, he wanted to know what, exactly, Callum wanted.

"May I?" Rupert asked seriously, mindful that to date, Callum had only ever seen him with his trousers around his thighs and his shirt shoved up. This would be different.

"Take them off?" Callum asked, voice hoarse.

"Yes."

"I've seen it all before."

"Pardon?" Because honestly, Rupert was aware that Callum had spent enough time in locker rooms to see all manner of man without his clothes on, but Rupert would be damned if this was *anything* like those times.

"I mean," Callum said, "I saw you. Once. By accident, before London."

Rupert arched a brow. "Did you, now?"

"You were wearing briefs. Black ones," he confessed, his voice little more than a scratch. "Made my heart stop."

Rupert smiled, warmed by Callum's confession. Charmed by the genuine apology in his voice. "Would you like to see it again?"

Callum licked his lips. "Yes, please."

Rupert popped the button, then slowly slid down the zipper, pressing his other hand to his erection, more out of the necessity to protect himself than to tease. He peeked down. "Black again today, I'm afraid."

Callum took a step toward him. "Can I—"

Rupert let his hands fall away. "Whatever you want."

Rupert made a sound that he would forever deny was a whimper when Callum fell to his knees at Rupert's feet. And again when his hands hooked in the waist of Rupert's jeans and tugged them down.

Callum left the briefs in place, and Rupert didn't push, lifting his feet when Callum's hands pressed his ankles, using Callum's shoulder for balance as he carefully peeled the jeans off and threw them to the side.

His hands returned to Rupert's waist, then spanned his hips, his thumbs rubbing over bone. Rupert stumbled then caught himself when those hands pressed gently, turning him in place until he faced away from Callum.

"Your ass is ridiculous."

Rupert let out a startled laugh. "In a good way, I hope."

Callum's only answer was to slide his hands over the bum in question, shaping its every curve in his palms. Rupert groaned, then groaned again, louder, when Callum pressed hot, open-mouthed kisses above the waistband of his briefs, his tongue dipping into the dimples there, his nose burrowing into the trench of Rupert's spine.

Rupert's legs shook with the effort of keeping himself upright, his knees weakened by how Callum worshiped every inch of exposed skin he could reach. His hands coasted over Rupert's thighs, his knuckles tickling the backs of Rupert's knees, his calves. Shins. Palms flat against the front of his thighs until they separated and held Rupert's hips still. He'd unconsciously begun to shift, pressing back against Callum's lips.

"Please, Callum," he said, not even sure what he was asking for but ready to beg. Because once again, his carefully constructed plans to thoughtfully introduce himself to anything and everything there was to learn about Callum were burnt to ashes by Callum's innocent explorations.

Callum seemed to revel in every touch. In every taste. And Rupert would do nothing to change their course if it risked losing that.

Callum might be buried in the back of a closely guarded closet when he was in Denver, or even Las Vegas, but here in Moncton, in Rupert's bedroom, he didn't have to hide. He could be himself. He could be gay—and not just for selfish reasons did Rupert want that for Callum.

Rupert reached back and ran his fingers through Callum's hair, his hum of pleasure transmitted directly through Rupert's skin, like electricity along his nerves. He wanted to tell Callum how proud he was of him for coming out to Mike and Alexei and Reese. For holding Rupert's hand in the Pathways Center's little meeting room and not caring what Gabriel thought. For trusting that regardless of what Gabriel thought, he would be discrete.

For letting any worry he had about any of these things be trumped by his desire to support Rupert while they sat and listened to Christian's options, most of which were grim, the rest so unlikely it was impossible to hold much hope.

But there was *some* hope. With Callum here, Rupert could be brave enough to do anything. He loved all the crazy twists and turns his life was taking. He thought he might even give up making lists for his personal life, because they would change in a matter of minutes. And that was fine. Good, even. Truly, the only twist he didn't want, the one he knew was coming, was Callum's return to Denver.

Rupert turned, cupping Callum's face in both hands and bending to kiss him. Callum rose on his knees, the meeting of their lips quick and desperate. Rupert could not put into words all the things he poured into that kiss.

They tore apart with a gasp, their foreheads still pressed together.

"If we don't get on that bed in the next thirty seconds, I'm going to fall to the floor and beg you to ravish me," Rupert said between breaths.

Callum's eyes creased up with a smile. "Isn't that what I was already doing?"

Rupert laughed. "Fair point. How about, then, we move this ravishment to the bed? I promise, it will be worth your while."

He'd meant only that the bed was wonderful and soft, but the look Callum gave him as he climbed to his feet said that he had interpreted it to mean something else entirely.

He wasn't wrong about that, either.

Callum stood by the bed and watched Rupert carefully peel his obscenely tight, extremely *brief* briefs down his legs. When he stood again, all long limbs and smooth pale skin, Callum's breath caught in his chest.

Rupert crawled onto the high bed, and Callum had to press a hand over his pounding heart. All the air in his lungs left in a rush, like he'd been punched in the solar plexus by the sight of Rupert's perfect, round, firm butt. Rupert pushed aside a pile of pillows, until he was left kneeling in the center of the mattress, knees spread. He settled back on his heels and dropped his hands between his legs, a passing attempt at modesty when he was still fully, gloriously, on display for Callum.

Callum had been surrounded by naked men his entire adult life. Hockey locker rooms weren't built for modesty, and they certainly weren't built with the wandering eye of a lonely gay man in mind. But they were also a sacred space, to him. A place for team and work. A place where he wasn't gay, and the men around him, his teammates, weren't sexual beings so much as a bunch of stupid braggarts and liars and merciless pranksters. Of course they joked about sex, but it wasn't about the bodies in the room, even when they were the ones bragging or being called out for their bullshit.

Sure, he'd looked. They all had. To see how colorful a particular bruise had become. To study the healed incisions of surgical repairs, or judge the trainer's ability to put in a decent, straight stitch. Any team could tell you who among them had the strongest thighs, heaviest shoulders, most brute strength. Every team had at least one player who was ruthlessly teased about the size of their ass—it was a hazard of the business. Just as any team could say who among them was deceptively lean, able to hide the power coiled in their smaller frames until you felt them run you into the boards like a fucking Mack truck.

Rupert was like that. They might be the same height, but Rupert was lean, while Callum tended toward brawn. Smooth where Callum had coarse hair and a tracery of veins over his muscles. But Rupert was also achingly pale, his fair skin glowing in the warmth of the bedside lamp. Soft, even over places Callum knew to be all firm muscle beneath. Aside from his blackened eyes, the only color was the hint of pink in his cheeks, his sharp blue gaze, and the thatch of dark hair hidden behind his hands.

Callum knew Rupert was trying not to freak him out too much, to let him get used to this. He probably ought to be embarrassed by it, but mostly he was just grateful that Rupert had guessed this was something he needed. That being here, doing this, might freak him out a little.

Though Callum wasn't really *freaked out* so much as painfully out of his element. It was a lot to take in. A lot to learn. The guys in the locker room liked to talk about a woman's curves, how they drew men to touch and learn each dip and swell. Callum hadn't really understood that. He'd heard men practically lose their minds over women who looked the same, to Callum, as the girlfriend before. Bigger chests, smaller butts, longer legs. It was still all mostly the same, he'd thought.

But now he knew differently.

Rupert had curves. Lots of them. And not just the swell of his skater's ass, tucked between his heels. His quads arced from hip to knee where his calves pressed from below. His biceps and triceps swelled gently beneath his ivory skin. His shoulders, as wide as Callum's own, led to the strong column of his neck, the shallow divot between his collar bones, and the smooth expanse of soft, hairless skin over his pectorals. He didn't have a six-pack, just the hint of tone beneath milky skin, above the twist of his belly button, and on to the flat plane of his stomach, framed by the line where his thighs met his hips, the twin ridges that pointed down, in an utterly enticing vee, to...

Callum lifted his gaze back to Rupert's face and found him patiently watching. Waiting.

"You're beautiful," Callum croaked.

"Thank you," he said graciously, having been taught to accept a compliment, Callum would bet, even when it embarrassed him a little.

Callum stepped closer to the bed, the press of the mattress to his blue jeans reminding him that he was still fully clothed.

Right. About that...

Callum took in Rupert again, *all* of him, sitting calmly, proudly naked in the light and under his inspection, and stripped off his clothing as quickly as he could. Rupert's eyes remained on his face the entire time—an admirable effort, and another kindness. By the time Callum dropped his boxer briefs to the floor, he felt a childish desire to leap onto the bed and yank the covers up over himself.

He didn't, instead following Rupert's lead and climbing up on the huge, high bed, steadying himself with a hand on one of the four posts that had to reach seven feet in the air, at least.

Just as he'd never really looked at another body, another human being, the way he'd just seen Rupert, Callum had never felt more exposed. His cock, still more than half hard, swung between his legs as he crawled closer to Rupert. He was achingly aware of his many scars, the chest hair his brother Kieran was always scolding him to tame and which he had spent his entire life ignoring, the cracks and pops issuing from his beat-up knees as he shifted his weight on the mattress, which felt as though it might be stuffed with feathers and good taste.

Rupert looked refined. And beautiful.

Callum felt coarse. And…well….

"Look at you," Rupert whispered when Callum settled on to the bed within arm's reach, not sure what to do next.

"Yeah, sorry," Callum mumbled, looking at Rupert's knees, studying the web of scars across the right one. The pinks and purples were faded, but still jarring in contrast to Rupert's fair skin.

He was totally unprepared for Rupert to tackle him to the mattress. There were a few awkwardly placed knees and elbows, and a shove to his shoulder that forced him onto his back. He blinked up at Rupert, his eyes crossing at the unbearably good slide of skin against skin as Rupert's weight settled on top of him.

Callum groaned, loud and needy.

"You're sorry?" Rupert demanded.

Callum had completely lost hold of any thoughts that had existed before he discovered what *this* felt like. Rupert's cock was trapped against Callum's hip, while his was wedged into the trench between Rupert's thighs. Callum released his death grip on the sheets to wrap his arms around Rupert's ribs, his palms flat to Rupert's broad back.

Softer, even, than he'd guessed.

Rupert captured his fractured focus with a firm hand cupping his cheek.

"Uh—What?" he asked.

"What on earth were you just apologizing for?" Rupert asked.

"Um, me?"

"You?" Rupert echoed back with utter disbelief. Callum's lips twitched. "What part of you are you apologizing for, do you suppose?"

"I'm just, you know, not as pretty as you, duchess."

Rupert rolled his eyes. "Thank god for that." He paused to think about what he'd just said. "Also, I'm not *pretty*. Nor am I a duchess, as well you know."

Rupert rolled his hips forward, just a little, reminding Callum quite vividly.

Callum grinned. "Close enough."

"I'm sure the entire British aristocracy has just shivered with a chill, you bloody American heathen."

Callum laughed, shifting Rupert against him in the process, the sound almost hysterical by the end.

Rupert shut him up soundly with a kiss. It started out gently enough, but soon Rupert was licking into his mouth, tipping his chin so they fit together better and Rupert could deepen the kiss.

Callum's laughter died, if not the smile. Or the happiness, really, at all.

His hands wandered over Rupert's warm skin, testing the feel of muscle and bone, finding spots that made Rupert wriggle a little, learning how hard to press to make his touch a caress instead of a tickle. Every minute brush of skin, the growing warmth between them, the little sounds Rupert made in the back of his throat, set Callum's heart racing faster. His breaths heaved in and out of his chest, lifting Rupert, who slipped one knee, then the other, between Callum's.

Callum didn't want Rupert to pull away. His weight, pressing Callum into the bed, felt like the only thing that kept Callum tethered here. That prevented him from floating away.

He spread his legs wider, moaning into their kiss as Rupert slid against him. He lifted his knees until his thighs cradled Rupert's hips.

Rupert rolled his hips, once, slowly. Callum gasped, his head falling back to the bed with a silent thunk.

"You like that?" Rupert asked with a smile and another slow grind that just about killed Callum.

"Nnnhg," Callum responded articulately, smashing the back of his head against the mattress when his cock rolled and settled against Rupert's.

Holy Jesus fuck, that felt good.

Then Rupert moved away.

Callum jerked, his eyes snapping open. "No, please."

Rupert's smile was a little smug, but Callum couldn't argue when Rupert's long fingers reached between their bodies and curled around Callum's cock, his thumb circling over the wet tip.

"I'm not going anywhere," Rupert promised. He stroked his fist down Callum's shaft and back up again. "What do you want?"

"This. Anything. I don't know," Callum gasped, electric shocks zipping up his spine. He wished he knew what to ask for. How to ask for it. He wanted everything. Anything. *Right now.* And however Rupert wanted to give it, that was how Callum would gladly take it.

Rupert's chuckle told him he hadn't managed to keep all that inside. Rupert knelt on the mattress again, knees spread as before, only now Callum lay sprawled out between his knees, Callum's thighs draped over Rupert's, bracketing his hips.

And he'd thought he'd felt exposed before.

The slow burn of embarrassment mingled with the heat of arousal, an overwhelming combination.

"Easy," Rupert murmured, letting go of Callum's cock to run his palms up Callum's inner thighs. "I like it when you tell me what you're thinking."

Callum stared at Rupert. "Okay?" He wasn't convinced there was anything sexy about him being totally clueless, though.

Rupert studied him. "There's so much I want to do."

Callum's dick twitched where it lay against his belly, a little whine slipping from his throat. "Please."

Rupert arched one brow. "Can you reach the nightstand behind you?"

It took Callum a few seconds to clear his fogged brain enough to reach up the bed and feel that he could. He pulled open the drawer carefully.

"I tucked something in there as soon as the movers left," Rupert said, resuming his slow strokes up Callum's thighs. "Can you grab it?"

Callum plunged his hand blindly into the drawer and wrapped his fingers around the first thing he found. Rupert looked as stunned as Callum felt when he held the big purple dildo aloft between them.

Rupert stared at the sex toy balefully.

"How in the hell did that get in there?"

Callum frowned. "You don't know?" Because, seriously, this seemed like something Rupert should know.

"No. That was tucked away with several other...er...*things* in a box very carefully labeled *Bedroom: Do Not Unpack.*"

Callum snickered. "Mike and Alexei were working in here."

Rupert's shoulders slumped. "Oh my god."

"Bedroom: Do not unpack? That's like waiving a red flag in front of a bull."

"*Oh my god.*"

Callum reached up again, suddenly very curious what else he might find in the mystery drawer. He'd almost grabbed another promising hard plastic cylinder when Rupert threw himself on top of Callum, wrestling his arm away and reaching into the drawer himself. He came out with a tube of something and snapped the drawer firmly shut.

He had, perhaps, forgotten that Callum was still holding the frankly enormous purple dong in his other hand.

He wriggled it back and forth in front of Rupert's wide eyes, grinning. Rupert snatched it from his hand and tucked it behind him on the bed.

"That's for another night, I think."

Callum's heart stumbled, a pulse of blood going straight into his dick. "Uh..."

"I just mean, that's a bit advanced for us right now."

"Advanced?" Callum asked with a laugh.

"Yes," Rupert said firmly, resettling between Callum's legs and drawing his thighs back Rupert's.

As distractions went, it was a good one. "So, this is like school?"

Rupert arched a brow. "I don't know. Are you learning anything?"

"Yes," Callum gasped as Rupert's palms slid all the way up his thighs, his thumbs brushing Callum's balls gently before retreating.

"Is there more you'd like to learn?" he teased, lifting Callum's leg and brushing his lips against the inside of his knee.

"*Yes.*"

Callum was caught in Rupert's unexpectedly serious gaze. "What would you *like* to learn?"

"Everything," Callum confessed, shamelessly.

Rupert's grin was absurdly sexy. He stared down at Callum thoughtfully while he tucked the tube of what Callum assumed was lubricant under Callum's hip.

"To warm it up," Rupert explained.

For what?

"Oh no, not tonight for that either," Rupert said, reading his mind, or perhaps just his expression.

Callum was at once soothed and annoyed. "Why not?"

Rupert laughed. "Impatient, are we?"

"I have a lot to learn." And not very much time to learn it. Callum pushed that thought, and the ache in his chest that came with it, aside.

"I don't know about that," Rupert said with a sly smile. "It seems to me you've a good command of oral sex already."

Callum frowned. "Really? I thought I was terrible."

Rupert's hands froze mid-sweep up his thighs. "What on earth are you talking about?"

"Just, you know." Callum waved his hand. Was this conversation more or less awkward to have when he was sprawled out and on display in Rupert's lap? "I didn't know what I was doing. I just guessed."

"I assure you, you guessed well," Rupert said dryly.

"But there's more stuff I could do. Better. Like…"

Rupert arched a brow, resuming his petting. "Like?"

Callum blurted out the truth. "Taking you deeper. Into my throat, even." Because he'd had men do that for him before, and while he didn't like to remember those times, he couldn't pretend it hadn't been super fucking hot. "Or—I don't know. Other…stuff."

"You mean, like this?" Rupert asked innocently, then bent and fluttered his tongue just under the head of Callum's cock.

"*Holy shit*," Callum groaned, his back arching.

Rupert's hands clamped around his hips. "Or this?" His lips sealed around the head and tugged, again and again, while he sucked every last thought out of Callum's brains until he was released with an obscene pop.

"Oh god, *yes*."

"Or we could work on this," Rupert continued, opening wide, taking Callum into the hot cavern of his mouth, the wildly sensitive head of Callum's cock pressing over his tongue until it bumped the back of Rupert's throat.

Callum gurgled. There was no other word for it, and it only

got worse when Rupert gagged around him, swallowing and then pulling back.

Callum lay limp on the bed, staring up at Rupert. "Yeah, that was...that's something to work on, I guess," he managed. "It might be a little advanced for me, though."

Rupert grinned. "We'll just call this the Master Class, and you can take notes when we're done."

A huff escaped Callum, the beginnings of laughter ruthlessly cut off when Rupert wrapped his hand around Callum's shaft and pressed it to his belly, then bent low and licked a long, hot, dirty stripe right across Callum's balls.

Callum honestly wondered if he could die from this alone, his body twitching like a live wire as Rupert mercilessly teased and licked and sucked a thousand previously unimaginable sensations from his body.

Callum tried to be silent. To be still. But Rupert wouldn't have it. He hummed against the fragile skin of Callum's sac, then sucked one ball, then the other, between his lips, rolling each over his tongue until Callum was wet with spit and crying out his name.

Rupert was obviously determined to teach him everything, and Callum faithfully recorded a long, long list of things he wanted to try himself someday. Rupert stroked Callum's cock, sucking and biting the insides of his thighs, around the base of his shaft, making Callum's hands flail in the air, searching for somewhere to land that wasn't pushy or useless.

Rupert grasped them and put them on his head. "Don't force, just encourage. And I rather like having my hair pulled," he informed Callum before licking another long hot stripe up the underside of Callum's shaft.

"God, Rupert. You just...you're..."

He could feel Rupert's grin against his skin and he smiled helplessly as his fingers curled into Rupert's hair and tugged.

The blush staining Rupert's cheeks spread further, down his neck, across his shoulders. Callum yanked again, just to test. Rupert moaned, the vibrations going right up Callum's shaft and to the top of his head. Even his fucking toes tingled.

"Fuck, Rupert. Fuck me, that's. Just."

Rupert hummed again, obviously learning Callum as quickly and as well as Callum was learning himself.

"If you ever don't like anything—" Rupert began, pausing while Callum gave a gasping laugh of disbelief.

"I'll tell you, I swear," Callum said between panted breaths.

"Good," Rupert murmured, then sealed his lips around the crown and did that tugging, sucking, fucking mind-blowing thing again. Callum barely registered the hard press of the lube bottle disappearing from his hip, the click of the cap opening. He wondered if Rupert was going to use it to jerk himself off and tried to protest, managing nothing more than an inarticulate grunt. That was Callum's job. He wanted to turn the tables and try all these wonderful lessons on Rupert, and he would, just as soon as he was able to pull his shit back together enough to reach for the lube.

His wandering thoughts were interrupted by the press of a cold, slick finger behind his balls. He shivered all over, eagerly pushing down against that pressure.

"Is this okay?" Rupert asked in the space of a breath between torturous sucks.

"Yeah. Yes. Please, don't stop."

The cool finger drew downward, tracing the seam of skin there, until it pressed gently against his hole. Then it circled, not pushing, never retreating.

Callum whined deep in his throat. "*Please.*"

The tip of one finger eased into him and Callum jerked in reaction, trying to anchor himself to the bed with his feet. A cool hand on his ankle stayed his frantic thrashing, pulling until his foot was planted on one of Rupert's widespread thighs. The other foot did the same without assistance. His knees fell open shamelessly.

A lifetime of butterfly stretches paid off tenfold.

He stopped wondering how he'd felt exposed before, and

what might take it to the next level. The possibilities seemed infinite now. There was no room for modesty, or any hesitation, as it all would have been bullshit.

This was what he wanted. This was what he'd wanted for such a long time, he'd stopped letting himself think about it. He hadn't even let himself do this alone, forcing himself to stick to a specific regimen of hand-on-dick and a mental spank bank filled with images that didn't include dreams of being laid open, laid bare, and fucked properly.

He arched his back to shove his ass down on Rupert's slick, narrow finger.

Rupert's mouth left his cock with a gasp. "Callum," he groaned.

Callum whimpered, trying to memorize the feeling of being penetrated, at last, the gentle stretch, the tug on his rim as Rupert's knuckle passed through him. His hips kicked in a circle, the press of Rupert's finger along his walls amazing and not enough. He slid up the sheets and grunted in frustration, throwing one hand above his head as an anchor against the headboard.

Better. He thrust himself back down, shoving Rupert's finger deeper. "More," he pleaded. "Please, Rupert, I need…"

"Jesus Christ," Rupert gasped, his lips brushing against Callum's thigh.

The lube bottle made a rude noise and then a second fingertip tested his rim, pressing here and there. It felt delicious and wild, and it was not what he wanted. He shoved at the headboard again, his other hand tight in Rupert's hair, and pushed down, slowly, counting on Rupert to hold still as he forced himself onto two fingers.

"Jesus Christ," Rupert whispered again.

Callum was ruined, panting, teasing himself with the tug of Rupert's knuckles popping in and out of his body as his hips moved in tiny circles. The tension in his belly, his balls, was crawling slowly up his spine.

"Yes, that's…shit, that's amazing. God, *Rupert*, please.

What...how do I...oh god, I'm going to come. I *need* to come."

"Shhh..." Rupert soothed, murmuring against his thigh, nuzzling at his balls and the base of his shaft. "I've got you."

Callum tried to take a deep breath, but all he could think or feel or know was the stretch of Rupert's fingers in his ass, the hot gusts of Rupert's breath across his balls. Rupert's soft hair tickled his thigh, then was gone, the protest hovering on Callum's lips cut off when Rupert's perfect, beautiful mouth sealed around his cock and sucked until his cheeks hollowed out.

Callum groaned, the sound torn from deep in his gut, then choked off when Rupert's fingers thrust deep. He took up a rhythm, one Callum couldn't hope to follow or work around or with or whatever the hell he was supposed to do. His head spun, each push of Rupert's hand punching another sound from his chest.

Rupert's other hand wrapped around Callum's cock, so that Rupert's lips met his hand on every downward suck, and preventing Callum's thrashing hips from forcing himself too far down Rupert's throat.

Then Rupert did something, something that even the Master Class would never have prepared Callum for. On the next thrust in, Rupert's fingertips hit something fucking magical deep inside Callum, and his whole world fell apart.

"Rupert, oh god, oh god, fuck, fuck *fuck!*"

Rupert did it again.

Callum's orgasm tore through him. It was like his first NHL shut-out, winning an Olympic medal, and having his heart broken, all at once. Then his mind went white.

He returned to consciousness slowly, wondering how long he'd been out. When he pried his eyes open, he found Rupert propped above him on one arm, staring down at him with concern, and something Callum couldn't place until he followed the line of Rupert's arm down to where he had a hand clamped around his own cock, the shiny head so red it looked painful.

Callum really wanted to do something about that, but when he went to move, all he could manage was to weakly flap one hand against the bed.

"Jesus Christ, I think you broke me," he said weakly, his voice hoarse.

Rupert's chuckle was pained. "Sorry?" he said without an ounce of sincerity. He was panting, his cheeks red, eyes bright as they looked down at Callum. His eyes fluttered shut when he ran his hand up his shaft.

"What do you want me to do?" Callum croaked, looking down at Rupert's cock.

Rupert curled in on himself and gasped, his hand moving faster. "I can't...wait. I have to..."

"Yeah, do it," Callum groaned, finally finding enough strength to press a hand to Rupert's side, pulling him higher. "Come on me. Ruin me properly."

Rupert whimpered above him, trying to crawl up the bed at Callum's urging.

Callum didn't have nearly enough brain power left to apply a filter, and he didn't think he needed one anyway. "I liked it when you came on my face."

Rupert jerked, his whole body shuddering as he spilled into his fist and onto Callum's chest and collar bones. Rupert's hand kept going, milking himself through it brutally, until a high whine was forced up from his chest.

"Jesus, Rupert," Callum said as Rupert collapsed down on the bed and against Callum's side. Callum wrapped an arm around him, pulling him closer, and waited while Rupert slowly came back to himself.

"For future reference," Rupert mumbled against his chest some time later, "if you want me to come on your face, don't tell me until I'm in range."

Callum, still high and fucked out and utterly content, chuckled. "I'll put that in my class notes."

Rupert hummed, nuzzling in closer to Callum's chest. "You do that."

Chapter Seventeen

Rupert stood in his kitchen and scowled at Callum. And Jack. And Alexei and Mike and Reese. Hell, even Oliver.

They all scowled back.

"You're not going alone," Callum said for at least the tenth time.

Everyone except Rupert nodded in agreement.

"I must," Rupert insisted. "I told Christian I would go with him to speak with his father. I'm sure this will not be made any easier for him, or his idiot father, if I bring a throng of protectors along with me."

Even if it kind of made Rupert want to hug everyone present.

"Rupert," Reese began in his most diplomatic, ergo most irritating, voice. "The man punched you in the face. You still look like shit!"

"Yes, thank you for that," Rupert said.

"Rupert, listen to your pretend boyfriend," Alexei cajoled, because he was a total douchebag, even if Rupert did love him a little for trying to protect him. "You're going to see that Christian is safe. The first and best way you can do that is if you're also safe."

And top marks to Alexei for hitting on an argument Rupert couldn't defeat. *Shit.*

"I don't know why I should listen to you," Rupert said to Alexei, stalling. "I was having a perfectly lovely evening last night until I realized you had short-sheeted my bed."

Alexei grinned, utterly unrepentant. Mike rolled his eyes.

Rupert sighed. "Fine. What do you propose, then? I'm not bringing you lot. Not all of you, anyway."

"I'll go," Callum said firmly. Rupert knew that expression. There would be little use in arguing.

Reese nodded, but didn't volunteer, which was a relief. He was already the one on stand-by with a battalion of lawyers, should they be needed.

"John Shaw likes hockey. Maybe Alexei and I should go. He might be willing to listen to us?" Mike suggested.

Rupert frowned. That might work, actually.

"I have a better idea," declared Jack, who'd been dragged into this fiasco just this morning when Callum had called to tell him he wouldn't be able to do their walk-through and why.

Jack had arrived twenty minutes later.

"I have a friend, Grady," Jack continued. "He's a Mountie. I'm pretty sure he has the day off. I could ask him if he'd be willing to go?"

"I'm not sure how I feel about bringing a complete stranger," Rupert said, trying to weigh the options.

"Think about it," Jack said. "John Shaw isn't going to assault you, or Christian, with a member of the RCMP standing right there. And if, god forbid, he does, you can't ask for a better witness, right? And he's dealt with a bunch of stuff like this. He'll know what to do. And say. And worse comes to worse, he can always arrest John on the spot."

"Will he have any issues with the fact that I'm gay? That Christian wishes to come out to his father?"

"None," Jack said confidently.

"How can you be sure?"

Jack hesitated, looking around as if to assess his audience. His lips quirked. "He's friends with me, isn't he?"

Mike sighed dramatically and pulled out his wallet to slap a fifty-dollar bill into Alexei's hand.

"*Really*, you two?" Rupert asked.

Jack ignored them, to his credit. "So, should I call Grady?"

Rupert looked to Callum, who lifted his eyebrows, as if to say, "It's your call."

Which was how, two hours later, Rupert ended up in the

back seat of Callum's rental car with Christian, while Callum and Grady, whose legs were approximately two miles long, sat up front.

"Thank you again for this, Officer McDonnough," Rupert said.

The tall, lanky man—he rather reminded Rupert of a cowboy—looked over his shoulder and smiled. "It's Grady, and I'm happy to help."

Indeed, he'd agreed immediately when Jack had asked. And based on the smile he'd bestowed on Jack, and the way his eyes had tracked Jack around Rupert's apartment, it wasn't that hard to work out why he was so willing.

"That's my house," Christian said quietly. "The yellow one on the left."

Callum pulled up in front of a modest two-story on a quiet street in a development of similar homes, though in this case, the faded paint and unruly lawn made the Shaw house stand out amongst its neighbors. Rupert wasn't surprised, so much as sad. He and Callum had spoken to Christian last night, and again this morning, about his home. His father. Christian had nothing but happy memories of the time his mother was still alive, even though she had been battling cancer for as long as he could remember. Ultimately she had managed ten years with her son. After that, though, nothing had been quite right in Christian's world, and it had only gotten worse over time.

Rupert turned to Christian. "Are you still okay with this?"

"Yeah," Christian said. Rupert wished Christian sounded more confident, looked less frightened and pale. But then again, he was only twelve.

God's truth, Rupert was terrified, and he had a few more years than that under his belt.

"You're to stay in the car, right?" Rupert reminded Christian and Callum.

They both nodded, Callum more reluctantly, while Rupert and Grady climbed from the car.

Gabriel had spoken to Christian's father just this morning,

confirming Rupert and Christian would be here at this hour.

Rupert knocked. For a long time, nothing happened. A good two minutes later the door shook violently, then swung open to reveal John.

"*You did this!*" he growled, reaching for Rupert.

Rupert stumbled back, almost tumbling down the stairs. Every instinct he had screamed at him to run away, to go back the safety of the car and Callum.

Grady stopped John cold, a long hand clamped around his arm, holding him still. The easy-going cowboy was gone, replaced by a fiercely intimidating cop.

"Sir, I'm officer Grady McDonnough of the Royal Canadian Mounted Police. If you assault this man, I will have you arrested and charged, do you understand?"

John appeared to consider his options. The sound of a car door opening reached Rupert, but he didn't move, his eyes locked on John. Grady, however, looked over his shoulder and shook his head once. The car door closed again.

John yanked his arm from Grady's grasp and Rupert twitched, almost giving in and making a break for it.

"Come in, then," John muttered, stomping back into his house and leaving the door wide open for them to follow. Rupert's heart was pounding so hard, he thought Grady might be able to hear it, but he walked calmly into the house.

"Where's my son?" John demanded as soon as they entered the living room, his face red, eyes bright. Rupert couldn't tell if he was inebriated, or so hung over from the night before that the smell had lingered.

"He's in the car, sir," Grady said.

"I want to see him."

"Not until I know it will be safe," Grady returned.

John threw up his hands and hurled himself into his recliner. "What the hell do you want me to say? I've never laid a hand on the boy."

And that, thank god, was mostly true. Christian had said the same, but that didn't actually make it safe. "I'd like to talk to you about Christian," Rupert said, going for professional and collected even though inside he was a slowly devolving mess. He sat gingerly on the couch.

"I don't have anything to say to you."

"Yes, well, Christian asked me to speak with you. On his behalf," Rupert explained.

"I don't know why he can't just tell me whatever he needs to himself. I didn't raise him to be a coward."

Rupert had to work his jaw a few times before he could speak. Rupert's job, his primary goal, was to try to reconcile the Shaw men, even if it left a bitter taste in his mouth, and no matter how unlikely it seemed.

"He'd like to come home," Rupert said, though that wasn't entirely true. Not as home stood now. "He is worried, though, that you will force him to remain in his room for days, again. And that you might become violent."

Rupert had hoped this would be the point John would gasp with horror and express his extreme disgust at the very notion.

No such luck.

"And why does he think that?" John asked instead, his mouth settling into a cruel twist.

"Because he believes he might be gay," Rupert said evenly, his stomach churning. Christian had asked him to be the one to tell his father. Had specifically requested Rupert, above Gabriel, or Callum, or even the far-more-intimidating Grady.

John stood slowly. "Is that so?"

Rupert rose as well. Grady remained leaning against the doorframe, for all the world appearing unconcerned, except that he'd gone unnaturally still.

"Yes, that is so," Rupert replied. "He'd like to know that's something you can accept. That he won't be punished for it, should it prove to be true."

"You did this. You did this to him. Made him think there's something wrong with him."

"I did nothing of the sort. I think you know that very little has actually changed about your son in the few weeks since we met. And he does not believe there is anything *wrong* with him. He thinks he may be gay."

"Same thing," John snapped.

"It is not the same thing," Rupert said as calmly as he could manage, but the frustration, his growing ire, was translated in the shake of his voice and his hands. "There is nothing wrong with being gay, John."

"You would say that, the way you prance around, surrounding yourself with perfectly respectable hockey players for your own entertainment and filthy imagination."

Rupert laughed, shocked by the sound. "Is that what you think? How bizarre."

John's face darkened. "I want to see my son. I want to hear him tell me himself that he thinks...that he would dare..."

"Be gay?" Rupert asked.

"Yes!"

Rupert looked at Grady, not sure of the right thing to do. He didn't want Christian exposed to his own father's bigotry, but it was unavoidable. If they couldn't find a way to make this house safe for him, then they'd need as much proof as possible that it wasn't.

Grady frowned, but nodded once. Rupert pulled out his phone.

Callum answered immediately. "You okay?"

Since no honest answer to that question was likely to help, Rupert stuck to the script. If John had proven open to hearing Christian out, to supporting him, Rupert was to have said, "Christian's father wants to see him." Instead, he said, "Please bring Christian inside."

"Oh no," Callum sighed.

Rupert ached at the disbelief in Callum's voice. Even after all they'd heard and seen, Callum couldn't fathom a world where a parent wouldn't love their child unconditionally. How odd that

Callum had never believed a friend or team mate might offer the same support if he told them the truth about his sexuality. How could a man be so sure of his family's love, and so completely distrusting of anyone else's?

The front door opened, and Christian, followed by Callum, entered the room. Callum's eyes immediately went to Rupert, searching him from head to foot as if looking for damage.

"*You?*" John said incredulously.

Rupert turned, prepared to defend himself again. His heart sank when he realized John was focused entirely on Callum.

"Mr. Shaw," Callum said, his voice clipped, his game face on. He stood at Christian's back, a hand on his shoulder, his support unwavering.

"Are you a faggot, too, then?" John asked.

Callum flinched, his hand clenching briefly on Christian's shoulder, and Rupert realized too late that he'd put Callum in a terrible position. He opened his mouth to issue the denial, to take one lie off Callum's already bent shoulders, but it was too late.

"I am not," Callum said woodenly.

"This is hardly the point of this meeting. Nor relevant," Rupert said severely. "We're here to make sure you won't hurt your son."

John's focus swung back to Rupert. "How dare you!"

"I dare because I care about your son. I need to know he'll be safe and properly cared for. That is why we are all here."

John pinned poor Christian with a glare. "Is it true? Did you tell these people some bullshit about you being one of *them*?"

Christian stared, eyes wide and unblinking, at his father. "It's not bullshit, Dad. I think…"

He swallowed hard, and Rupert's chest tightened to the point he could hardly breathe. Callum looked sick, his complexion waxy. Coming out could be hard, even to people you trusted. Even when you were an adult. This—this wasn't something anyone should have to endure. Rupert would do anything to spare Christian from this moment if he could.

"You think? You think what?" John demanded. "Can't lie to my face, is that it?"

Christian swallowed again, but his chin came up. "I think I might be gay."

"You *think?* You *might?*" John echoed in disbelief.

Christian edged back, until his shoulders touched Callum's chest. "I'm twelve," he said in a small voice.

They'd talked about this, about how Christian was young and didn't have to decide anything right now. Or ever, for that matter. It was enough that he was asking the question. That he thought he knew the answer.

It was patently obvious that wasn't enough for John. "I want you out of my house. All of you!"

Rupert edged toward the door, toward Callum and Christian, eager to comply.

John lunged for Christian, clutching his arm until the skin went white beneath his fingers. "Not you. You can go to your room," he hissed furiously, dragging the boy from Callum's grasp.

"Dad, no!" Christian shouted, trying to free himself. Grady rushed forward but John jerked to the side, forcing Christian to stumble with him. The panic on Christian face, his frightened cry, broke something in Rupert. He flung between Christian and his father, uncaring if John hurt him. He hardly felt the blows to his shoulder and ribs as he fought John's grip on Christian. Finally, Rupert pried John's little finger loose and bent it back viciously.

John yowled with pain and let go. Rupert shoved Christian behind him and walked backwards until Christian was safely pressed between Rupert's back and Callum's chest.

Grady wrenched John's arm behind his back. John fought to come at them anyway, but Grady held firm.

"Mr. Shaw," Grady said in a voice so cold it should have frozen John's blood in his veins. "You were warned. I've now witnessed multiple assaults and am certain that this child, if left in your custody, would be in danger." He pulled out his cell phone.

"Wait! Wait!" John cried desperately. He turned to Rupert, his face a mask of disgust. "What do you want?"

Grady looked at Rupert and waited.

"It's not what I want, John, it's what Christian wants. What he needs. *A father.*"

Rupert thanked god that Christian couldn't see his father's face, though maybe he could guess. He didn't plead with his father to love him. To be a good person. To understand.

"I want to live with Rupert," Christian said, his voice quavering but clear.

"And you want that, too, don't you?" John asked.

"I would be honored to have Christian be part of my family."

Two hands, one big, one smaller but with a grip no less fierce, curled into the back of his shirt. For the first time since they'd pulled up in front of this house, Rupert felt calm. All doubt was gone.

John glared at Rupert and sneered. "Fine, you can keep him. What do I have to do?"

Callum walked out to the car on legs made of rubber, his hand on Christian's shoulder as they waded together through the tall grass.

As soon as they reached the sidewalk, Christian turned and wrapped his arms around Callum, hot tears immediately soaking through his shirt. Callum held on tight as Christian shook apart in his arms.

Callum had never felt less *worthy*.

"I'm sorry," he whispered, rocking them in place and rubbing Christian's back, all if it so fucking inadequate. "I'm so sorry."

Sobs racked his slender frame and he held Callum tighter. Callum wished desperately Christian was still Oliver-sized, small enough to carry around for as long as he needed.

He looked back at the house and worried. He wouldn't be

able to relax until Rupert was out of there. Wished he could go back in and stand by Rupert's side and support him.

But then, Callum had already been given the chance once, and all he'd done was lie. It made him feel sick. Furious. He *despised* the man he'd become, who would put his career and his privacy before the truth and supporting the boy who clung to him.

Christian thought Callum was strong, when in truth he was a complete fraud. Thank god Christian had Rupert, who was brave and honest and worthy to be Christian's legal guardian.

A dark sedan with tinted windows pulled up to the curb a few feet away and Reese and two other men Callum didn't recognize climbed from the back seat.

The lawyers had arrived. Thank Christ.

Reese stood on the sidewalk and watched Callum slowly rock a still-distraught Christian. The lawyers went up the driveway and through the front door without knocking.

Reese kept his distance, perhaps sensing this wasn't the time for him to be introduced to Christian. Callum didn't think the boy was even aware of his audience. When it became clear Christian wasn't going to be able to pull himself together anytime soon, Reese tipped his head toward Callum's rental and mouthed, *go on.*

Callum nodded. "Let's go home," he said to Christian, gently urging him around the car and into the passenger seat.

"What about Rupert? And Grady?"

"They're all set," he assured Christian. "They have another ride."

Christian nodded and slumped back into his seat, silent for the short drive to the warehouse. He perked up a bit when Callum triggered the massive doors and drove right into the first floor of the building to park next to Alexei's truck.

Christian looked around with wide eyes. Callum was still trying to get used to it, too, vaguely nauseous every time he rode in this stupid wobbly elevator.

"What is this place?" Christian asked.

Callum chuckled. "Your new home."

"Does Rupert live in a storage unit?"

Callum was pleased to see Christian crack a smile at last. "You'll see."

They came to a stop, and Callum quickly opened the elevator doors, revealing the luxurious hallway that always seemed wildly incongruous compared to the rest of the building.

"We're in Unit 2," he said, pointing at Rupert's door. "Mike and Alexei live in Unit 1."

Christian looked up at him. "Do you live here, too?"

Callum frowned, stopping in the middle of the hallway. It occurred to him, here in the eleventh hour, that he hadn't given this a whole lot of thought, beyond *must get Christian safe.*

"I'm visiting for the summer," he hedged.

"Oh. I kinda wondered if you were Rupert's boyfriend," Christian said, "But then you told my dad you aren't gay."

Callum's rubbed a hand over the back of his neck. "Yeah, um...I lied."

"Oh," Christian said again, looking at his feet. "That's okay."

"Actually, it isn't."

Christian shrugged. "It isn't really any of my dad's business. You didn't have to tell him." He sighed, deflating a little. "I think maybe I should have just lied, too," he said quietly.

"No!" Callum bent down until their faces were level and Christian stared back. "Don't say that. You did a very brave thing today, Christian. Don't let the fact that I'm an idiot make you question your decision."

Christian appeared ready to argue, but their apartment door opened and Jack popped his head out. "Callum! Christian! Come on in. Alexei is making lunch."

Christian's eyes went wide. "Alexei...*Belov*?"

Callum smiled. "Yeah. He promised to make us omelets. I guess it's a specialty of his."

Mike stepped into the hallway. If possible, Christian's eyes went wider.

"You're just in time," Mike said enthusiastically. "If you hurry, you can still tell Alexei what you want in yours."

Christian stood still, mouth hanging open. "Am I dreaming, or are the Ice Cats making me lunch?"

Callum pushed him along with a hand between his shoulders. "Well, not *all* of them."

"Oh, okay, that makes this totally normal, then."

Rupert arrived back at his apartment hours later to find utter pandemonium had been let loose.

He stopped in the entryway with Reese and Grady at his back, each carrying at least two grocery sacks filled with Christian's clothes and other belongings, and took it all in.

Christian and Jack were on the couch, trying to teach Oliver how to play MarioKart on a game system Rupert didn't even own. This, from what Rupert could gather, required a lot of shouting at the television.

Mike and Alexei were moving in and out of what was to have been Rupert's office, apparently assembling furniture that Rupert hadn't yet purchased. Bags from Target lay piled beside the door, overflowing with sheets and pillows, and even some books and posters.

And Callum was in the kitchen. He was peeling potatoes onto a cutting board already overflowing with chopped vegetables, a steaming pot at his elbow. He looked up, apparently surprised to see them, and promptly attempted to peel off the top of his thumb.

"Fadoodle!" he yelped, dropping the peeler and jogging off toward the bathroom with his hand elevated over his head.

Rupert was sure this was his new house. He recognized the furniture, and the copper pots hanging above the island in the kitchen, and the books lining the wall. Not to mention the contents of his office haphazardly stacked in the hallway.

The rest of it, though.

"What the bloody hell has happened to my life?" he asked no one in particular.

Reese started to laugh behind him. Alexei turned and spotted them first.

"Rupert!" he bellowed, loudly enough to part Rupert's hair. "Welcome home!"

Oliver leaped off the couch and bounded toward him, not bothered by the indignant shouts of his opponents as one of the little go-karts on the screen flew off into space. "Rupert!" he cried, leaping into the air.

Rupert caught him easily. "Hello, Ollie," he said as he swung the boy around and then hugged him close.

Oliver giggled. "You called me Ollie! You've never called me that before."

"Haven't I?" Rupert asked.

"No! That's what Callum calls me."

"Oh, well, should I stop then?"

"No! I quite like it." He shoved at Rupert's shoulder, squirming. "Now, put me down, please. I have to finish my game."

Rupert did as commanded, trying not to wince when Oliver took a short cut over the back of the couch and landed with a bounce.

Callum came out of the bathroom with a bandaged thumb, bypassing his work in the kitchen to come to the entryway. He was wearing an apron Rupert didn't recognize, but could guess where it had come from by the "Caution: Goalie" symbol emblazoned across Callum's broad chest. Callum's t-shirt was just a shade too small, emphasizing his shoulders and biceps. He should have looked ridiculous, but mostly Rupert wanted to climb him like a tree.

"Definitely a step up from Sheldon," Reese muttered.

Rupert was about to tell his dear friend to shut up when Christian arrived at their side.

"How'd it go?" he asked anxiously.

Bloody awful was the truth. All that really mattered, though, was the outcome. "I'm happy to report," he said to the young man worrying his lip with his teeth and fidgeting before him, "you're allowed to stay here as long as you like."

"Yeah?" he asked with a hesitant smile.

"Yes. We have your things," he said, gesturing at the bags stacked beside him, "and we can talk about anything that's missing. I also have your health card, passport, birth certificate, and the phone number for your guidance counselor at school."

Christian gave a wholly unimpressed eye roll at that last item.

Rupert was just happy to see the anxiety from earlier gone from his face. He put his hands on Christian's shoulders. "Are you sure you're okay with this?"

"I'm okay," he said, too quickly. Because, of course, he wasn't. But they'd tackle that, a day at a time, and figure out what was best. Christian wrapped his arms around Rupert's waist and hugged him so hard it hurt. "Thank you."

"No, Christian, thank you," Rupert said gently, running a hand over tousled hair. "Thank you for trusting me to look after you. I promise to try very hard not to screw it up."

Callum smiled at Rupert over Christian's head. "You're amazing," he said, then pressed a quick kiss to Rupert's lips in front of god and country and at least two people who hadn't known he was gay.

He pulled away quickly and went back into the kitchen, his cheeks bright red. He returned to his potato preparations as if the fate of the nation lay upon his getting it right.

A great whoop went up from the couch. "I win!" cried Oliver.

Christian gasped with outrage and spun around. "You little sneak! It was supposed to be paused." He launched himself at the couch to defend his honor and demand a rematch.

A gentle hand landed on Rupert's shoulder. He shuffled to the side to let Grady into the house properly. "Sorry."

Grady's grip tightened, and he smiled. "You've got a nice family here, Rupert."

Rupert looked out at the chaos overflowing from every room. Once, this would have been so foreign as to be unrecognizable to him. Now, though, he understood.

He'd made a home.

"Thank you," he said to Grady, for at least the thousandth time that day.

Grady went to join the group on the couch, tucking himself in right next to Jack.

Reese leaned in, bumping his shoulder against Rupert's. "Congratulations," he said over the din.

"For what? Or which?" It was fairly amazing that Rupert had so many good things happening to him that summer, he couldn't know for certain.

"You've just become a father for the second time in as many months."

The word *father* sort of scared him witless, but Rupert couldn't disagree. Not if he was going to do this right. "I have."

"And you have a lovely new home."

Which, thankfully, had another small bedroom at the end of the hall. He'd have to start moving the office in there. "I do."

"And you're in love."

Rupert gave Reese a long look, his heart aching and full. "I am."

Reese hugged Rupert. "Does this help?" Reese asked.

"Help what?" Rupert mumbled into his shoulder.

"The panic."

"Maybe a little."

Reese squeezed tighter. "I'm kind of digging it, actually. I almost hugged Hodges the other day, but worried the shock would kill him and then I'd have to remember how to drive."

"Perhaps it's better that you didn't, then," Rupert agreed. "I'm sure you could practice with Matilda, instead, if you wanted."

Rupert was abruptly released. "I have no idea what you're talking about."

Rupert laughed, even more delighted when Reese pointedly ignored him and went to join the MarioKart competition. Rupert had Reese's number now, but he'd let that stew for a while before poking at it again.

Turning to the kitchen, Rupert approached the still-blushing Callum carefully.

"I didn't know you could cook," he said, watching Callum pile ingredients in a bowl.

"My mother, and apparently your new neighbors, would tell you that I can't. But I'm well-trained enough to do the prep work while Alexei tackles the new furniture."

"Yes, speaking of, where did that come from?"

Callum shrugged, focusing down at the counter instead of up at Rupert. "I figured you'd want Christian to settle in quickly."

Rupert sidled closer and put a hand on Callum's back. "Thank you. You're very good to me. To all of us."

Callum frowned and pressed his hands flat to the cutting board. "No, I'm not."

Rupert sighed. He'd suspected Callum wasn't going to just shake off this morning. "Come along," he said, nudging Callum toward the hallway. Callum put up a token protest before walking, his head down, into the bedroom. Rupert closed the door quietly behind them, counting on the battalion of adults invading his home to keep the kids entertained, safe, and away from this room for a few minutes.

Callum jerked with surprise when Rupert pulled him in for a kiss. Rupert didn't let it discourage him, rubbing their lips together until Callum opened for him, then taking the kiss deeper.

It felt like gentling a wild animal, if self-loathing professional hockey players could be counted as such. Which, actually, they probably could.

When Callum's arm curled around Rupert's waist, he pulled back and pressed their foreheads together.

"I'm sorry," Callum said, his voice rough.

"For what?" he asked, though he thought he knew.

"For being a chicken. For not telling the truth when it was important."

Rupert sighed. "Callum, you're too hard on yourself. It would have been foolhardy at best, disastrous at worse, for you to come out to John Shaw, of all fucking people."

"But I lied in front of Christian. He was trying to come out to that asshole, and I didn't back him up. I should have backed him up." Callum's voice cracked, and Rupert squeezed him tighter, trying to press warmth and comfort and love into Callum.

"You were there, Callum. You stood up for him. Made sure he was safe. You would have carried him out of there before you let his father hurt him further. You were everything he needed you to be today."

"Except out."

"Except, possibly, out. But given that the kiss you snuck out there didn't raise any eyebrows, I'm guessing you spoke to him afterwards."

"Yeah, I told him once we got home."

"That was very brave of you, Callum."

Callum's huff was pure frustration. "I don't know why you would say that. I'm not brave. Christian is brave. *You're* brave."

Rupert wanted to crawl into his bed and pull the covers over his head. "I am not."

Callum forced him back with his hands banded around Rupert's arms. "You were Christian's knight in shining armor today."

Rupert frowned, staring at Callum's shoulder. "I was scared witless," he admitted.

"So?"

"So, I'm afraid *all the time*," Rupert said, his hands flailing at his sides. "Callum, the entire team, the *team I manage*, can see that I'm afraid of them. Today I almost jumped off the porch and ran back to the car. To you. Because I knew you'd keep me safe, too."

"I would have," Callum agreed.

"So! You see my point."

"No, actually, I don't. Because you *didn't* run back to the car. And you *did* take a job that clearly freaks you out. Courage isn't about not being afraid. It's about being scared witless and doing it anyway."

Rupert frowned. "Shakespeare?"

"Nelson Mandela, actually. And do not try to distract me, because my point is valid. More than that, it's *important,* and you need to get it through your thick head. Look, I was dumb enough to confuse how nervous you get around some people with a lack of courage. But I was wrong. Everyone who thinks that is fucking *wrong*."

Rupert swallowed past the thick lump in his throat. "Do you know why I didn't make it to the Olympics?"

"What?" he asked, clearly confused. "What are you talking about?"

"Do you know why I didn't make it? Why I didn't compete?"

"Uh, yeah. I sort of Googled you," Callum admitted. "You got hit by a car outside your training facility."

"No," Rupert said softly, hardly able to believe he was going to talk about this.

"What?"

"I mean, yes, I was struck by a car. I ran right in front of the poor woman who hit me—didn't even see her until she was on top of me. I was too terrified, so fucking afraid and focused on trying to escape that stupid rink that I couldn't think. Couldn't *see*."

Callum's grip on his arms tightened. "Why? Why were you running?"

Rupert swallowed again, tried to clear his scratch from his

voice. "There was a hockey team. In the locker room that day..."

"No," Callum whispered.

"No," Rupert agreed. "They didn't do anything. Not really. But the ones before, the kids at school who locked me in closets and stole my gear. Who cornered me in the shower until I promised myself I'd always wait until I got home to wash up. The ones who tried on my performance clothes and tore them while they pranced around the locker room like great, hairy, talentless drag queens, mocking me and everything I loved. Each one of them alone was nothing, but together, *as a team*, they were powerful. Infinitely more clever and effective in their torture as a group than as individuals. So they taught me to never be alone in a locker room. To shower at home. To keep my distance. And to be afraid. So that when that other team, the one that laughed and threw me dark looks and stood as a unit to stare me down...I ran. Straight into a car, as it turned out."

He was afraid to look up, to see what was on Callum's face, so he wasn't expecting the kiss. Rupert kissed back, briefly, because it was a relief. Because it made him feel better, and if he let it go on long enough, it would help him forget. But he didn't understand what Callum was getting out of it. Why he would do it at all.

Rupert ended the kiss with a gasp. "What are you doing?"

"Kissing you?"

"Yes, well, I noticed that bit. But I don't know why."

"Because you are brave. And you're beautiful. And I wanted to kiss it and make it better." His lips twitched and he shrugged. "Or something like that."

Rupert's heart clenched, and the words were there, right on the tip of his tongue, begging to come out.

He was saved by a loud knock on the door.

"Callum! I need those potatoes!"

Chapter Eighteen

Callum spent the rest of the evening trying to wrap his head around what Rupert had told him. But there was dinner to prepare, and a bedroom to set up, and a four year old to put to bed, and a twelve year old to settle into his new room before his first night in his new home.

Callum was exhausted. It had been a long day, and it hadn't helped at all that Rupert had only become more subdued as the day had gone on.

It was sweet relief to crawl into bed once they'd sent everyone home. Reese had left immediately after dinner, as had Jack and Grady, but Mike and Alexei had lingered. They'd seemed inordinately concerned that everyone was settled in and ready to sleep in their new bedrooms. Callum was grateful, if confused. It was one thing, as landlords and the designers of the space, to be interested in how well it was all coming together, but that didn't really translate to Alexei telling Oliver that he would be so proud of him if he spent the entire night in his room again.

They'd watched television for a while after Oliver was asleep, Christian trying hard to stay awake but fading fast. After a particularly huge yawn, he'd confessed he hadn't been able to sleep well at the shelter the night before. Callum could only imagine what had been going on in the poor kid's head. He'd thrown his arm around Christian and, within minutes, he'd been asleep against Callum's shoulder, Rupert smiling over at them in a way that made Callum feel a little tight through the chest.

At last, though, Christian had gone to his room and Mike and Alexei had left. The apartment was quiet and Callum was quick to change into his pajama pants. He was almost used to wearing them at this point. That Oliver was likely to come see them at any point in the night was a compelling reason to adjust, obviously, but now he thought he might keep wearing them in Denver, even if there was no hope of late night visitors who made them a requirement. He thought they might be a comfort he could hold onto.

The moment Rupert climbed in the other side of the bed, Callum mustered the last of his energy and rolled over Rupert, pinning him to the bed.

"Hello," Rupert drawled, almost managing to smile.

Callum wasn't necessarily looking to start anything, but he wanted to be closer to Rupert. To break through whatever was quietly running through that gigantic brain.

He started with a kiss, not stopping until Rupert began to respond.

"Better?"

Rupert shrugged. Callum kissed him again, tracing his tongue along the seam of Rupert's lips until he let Callum in. Callum indulged in several long, slow sweeps of his tongue before pulling away. Rupert squirmed a little beneath him, aligning their hips and bringing his knees up to cage Callum.

Callum refused to be distracted. "You understand," he began, holding Rupert's stare, "now, all these years later, that what you did wasn't cowardly, right? That it was the perfectly natural instinct to protect yourself."

"I ran into a *car,* Callum. I ruined my chance to go to the Olympics. You went—you know what I missed. You can imagine what losing that was like for me."

"You were bullied. Mercilessly. For years. I cannot be the first person to tell you that wasn't your fault."

Rupert's frown was downright petulant. "Reese and I have this argument on an almost weekly basis, actually."

"Well, there you go!" Callum declared.

"But he doesn't know...he doesn't know I ran. He, and everyone else, assumed those boys chased me."

"I don't understand."

"Callum, I never looked back. Or forward, sadly. I just panicked." He paused, his face pale and his eyes pleading with Callum to understand. "I was such a monumental idiot I ruined my career, my *knee,* possibly for no better reason than I was an utter coward."

"You're *not* a coward."

Rupert sighed with utter exasperation. "You are very stubborn. I have no idea why I like you at all."

"Easy there, duchess," Callum murmured, smirking.

Rupert rolled his eyes and opened his mouth, no doubt to demand Callum stop calling him that, when a loud thump issued from Mike and Alexei's apartment through one of the bedroom walls.

Callum took advantage of the distraction to kiss Rupert again. This time it only took seconds to gain Rupert's complete cooperation. Callum hummed when Rupert's hands skimmed over Callum's ribs and in, pressing against his lower back while his hips rolled up.

Callum trailed kisses over Rupert's cheek. His neck, and behind his ear. He was busy worrying the soft lobe between his teeth when they heard another, louder thump, followed by a faint cry.

Callum lifted his head. "What was that?"

Rupert pulled him back down. "I'm sure it's nothing."

This kiss was deeper, and there was no mistaking the intent. Callum planted his knees on the mattress and thrust his growing erection against Rupert's.

Thump. Thump.

"Do you think they're okay over there?" he asked as nibbled his way under Rupert's jaw and toward his ear. He was intent on the texture of Rupert's nighttime stubble against his tongue. He hardly heard the next muffled cry.

Rupert cocked his head to listen. "Do you recall what room is on the other side of that wall?"

Callum had to think about it, mapping Mike and Alexei's apartment in his mind even as he mapped the shell of Rupert's ear with his mouth. "The master bedroom, I think."

No sooner had the words come from his lips, and those lips

has sealed around Rupert's ear lobe, than a long, desperate wail could be heard faintly.

Callum sat up on his knees between Rupert's wide-spread thighs. "I think that was Mike," he said, genuinely concerned now.

Thump. Thump. Another cry, this one sharper, followed by a lower sound.

Rupert clapped a hand over his mouth and actually *giggled.*

Callum looked down at Rupert curiously. "Do you think he's okay?"

Rupert grinned, silent while another long cry reached them. "Oh, yes," Rupert said in a deep voice, his cheeks pink, "I think Mike is, in fact, very happy right now."

The next cry was the loudest yet, accompanied by the entire wall giving a hard shudder.

Callum finally caught up. His cheeks burned. "Oh. *Oh.* Ha! I guess we know why they were so bent out of shape about Oliver sleeping in his own room, huh?"

Rupert laughed, loud and bright. Callum grinned down at him. Both their eyes widened when something that could only be Mike bellowing, possibly in Russian, came through the wall.

"Wow, that's..." Callum wasn't sure what words to use.

"Kind of hot?" Rupert suggested.

Callum swallowed. He traced his eyes down Rupert's long, lean torso to linger where Rupert's erection tented his pajama pants. That was so hot Callum's brain fried, taking his filter with it, and the truth just fell out of his mouth.

"I want you to fuck me." Callum could feel a hot blush making its way over his face and down his neck. Even his chest felt warm.

"Okay," Rupert said at last, his voice hoarse.

"I mean," Callum said, suddenly realizing he'd made all kind of assumptions, "only if you want to."

Rupert's scorching look went completely blank. He arched

one brow. "Oh, gee, let me think."

Callum laughed, though he was having a hard time looking too long at Rupert's face. He couldn't honestly believe he'd just blurted that out.

"Are *you* sure?" Rupert asked.

Callum nodded, staring somewhere in the vicinity of Rupert's sternum. "Yeah, I really...I really want that. I've never done it. I mean, you know, where I was the one, umm...on the receiving end?"

And he really didn't want to think about the times he was on the giving end either. Because this...wasn't that. At all. The differences were so vast, so startling, that Callum could hardly bear to think about what he'd done. How wrong it felt now.

"Callum," Rupert said, pushing up on his elbows and ducking his head so that Callum had no choice but to look at him. "Are you okay?"

Callum swallowed. "Yeah," he said, trying to sound less like a dithering idiot and more like a man who knew what he wanted. "Why?"

"Because you went rather alarmingly pale in the space of a few seconds."

Callum huffed out a breath that almost sounded like a laugh, only it wasn't. "Yeah, I was just thinking about stuff. From before."

"The men you've had sex with, you mean?" Rupert asked.

Callum winced at how direct Rupert was, how *simple* Rupert made it seem. "Yeah, I guess."

Rupert studied him, obviously picking his words carefully. "I know you are no longer interested in pursuing company that way, but you seem more upset than just the memory would seem to warrant."

Or maybe he was appropriately upset and Rupert just didn't know the truth.

Earlier, Rupert had trusted him with something he'd kept from almost everyone. Callum trusted Rupert as much. Rupert wouldn't judge, but Callum still ached at the thought of saying anything. He'd worked hard at packing it away for a lot of years.

"It wasn't good," he blurted.

"The sex?"

"Yes. No." Callum sighed. "The sex was usually fine? But it was...er...fast. And mostly, kind of alone. If that makes sense? The men, they would be prepared. And we didn't really talk. Or kiss," he added, though Rupert was aware of that already. "I think maybe...I worry that I didn't do what they wanted. That I might have assumed stuff and then..."

"Callum, we've talked about this. These men were consenting adults there for their own reasons, maybe even the same reasons you were. You didn't force them, did you?"

"No!"

"And if they asked you to stop, did you?"

Callum swallowed heavily, swaying where he knelt on the bed. He planted a hand in the mattress to steady himself. "I...yes. I think so?" He looked at Rupert and said aloud what had haunted him. "I don't know."

Rupert sat up slowly, his knees pressing into Callum's sides, his hands curling around his elbow and his jaw. Callum thought Rupert should to be moving away, not closer.

"What do you mean?" Rupert asked calmly.

Callum shook his head. "I mean, I would have stopped if I'd heard him say no. If I'd known he didn't want me to...to keep going," he said, his voice growing hoarser. He blinked hard against the sting in his eyes.

"Are we talking about a particular he, here?"

"Yes. I don't know his name," Callum confessed in a whisper.

"Why do you think he wanted to stop if you didn't hear him say so?"

"It was loud. In the club. They had...they had speakers, in the bathroom?" Callum shook his head again, trying to clear the song from where it had been stuck on repeat for four years. "We were in a stall. And his back was to me." He felt the first tear roll down

308

his cheek and watched it land on Rupert's shoulder. "I tried to ummm...reach around. Help him out? But he shoved my hand away. Kept moving. I thought he was trying to get me to hurry up. But then I...I was done, you know? And he shoved me away, like, way too fast, and he wouldn't look at me. He, um, he had been saying *something* the whole time, kind of chanting it, and I'd just thought it was him making noise, you know? Into it, I guess. But then he turned, and he still wouldn't look at me, and he was saying, *fuck you*. Over and over. *Fuck you fuck you fuck you.*"

Callum swallowed and gave up any pretense at composure. His face was streaked with tears, and he couldn't hold in a wet sob. He'd been here before, and it never helped.

Rupert held him, pulling himself closer until he was practically in Callum's lap. Callum pressed his forehead into Rupert's strong shoulder as he waited, aching and raw, for Rupert to tell him he'd made a terrible mistake. That he should find a way to make amends. He could tell Rupert about the hours he'd put in on Michaela's family foundation, how he'd made huge anonymous donations to LGBT centers that needed help, that he'd attended as many events as possible with Michaela, just in case that meant one more person, one more fan of his might show up and donate. And he could tell him how it may have made a difference to the bottom line, to a lot of kids, but it had never once eased the ache of knowing he might have hurt that man.

"You're very stupid, you know," Rupert said quietly.

He was. So stupid. He never should have gone to those clubs. He buried his face into Rupert's warm neck and took a deep, shuddering breath.

"Is this why you've been living like a monk for four years?"

Callum nodded.

"Did you go back to that club and look for that man?"

Callum's hands curled into fists against Rupert's back. *How did he know that?* He nodded again more hesitantly.

"Was he there?"

"Yes," he said, his voice little more than a scratch in his

throat.

"And what did he say?"

"He saw me and turned away. Left before I could get to him."

"Was it the next night?"

Callum couldn't understand why Rupert was asking these questions. "No, it was months later. The next time the team was in town."

Rupert sighed and put a gentle hand on Callum's cheek, forcing him to lift his head. "Callum, did he shove you away while you were having sex?"

"No?" He didn't think so.

Rupert arched a brow, so Callum really thought about it.

"No. Definitely not."

"Were you holding him down? Restricting his movements? Covering his mouth or being rough?"

"No! I mean, we were standing. My hands were on his hips, and maybe the wall for balance. I mean, it was maybe rough, I like it rough," he said, his words rushed, his face flaming hot. "But I thought he liked it too. I would never...I wouldn't..."

"I know. And so should you."

"But he was cursing me, Rupert. He looked miserable."

"He probably was."

It was like a punch to the chest. Callum tried to look away, but Rupert's hand on his cheek wouldn't let him.

"Callum, other than you being bloody gorgeous, I don't know why that man let you fuck him in the men's room. I don't. And neither do you. But he had his reasons and he *did* consent. That's what matters here. Yes, it would have been nice to know he was such a mess before you agreed, and I imagine you would have said no if you'd known—"

"Yes. I mean, *no.* I would never have touched him if I'd known that he would...that it would make him so..."

"Broken?"

Callum nodded miserably.

"I'm sorry that happened, Callum. To you. To him. But that man was probably quite broken before he set foot in that club, not by anything you did that night."

"How can you be sure?"

"Because your instinct is to protect. You would never hurt someone."

"You haven't known me that long."

"That's true, I suppose, but I think I know you well. And more than that, I know *me*." Rupert said, his voice rough and soft. "I could never fall in love with a man who would hurt me."

Callum squeezed his eyes shut, fresh tears rolling down his cheeks. Because that...that was nothing he deserved and everything he wanted. He was humbled and honored and so, so grateful that someone as beautiful and kind and smart as Rupert could feel that about *him*.

He kissed Rupert, his tears making it messier and better and worse than it should have been. He just couldn't let go. He wanted to hold Rupert like this, close and warm, all night.

Rupert drew them down onto the bed, kissing him back. They weren't going anywhere with it, mostly because they were right where they should be. *This* was right where he should be.

At some point they dozed, and a little after that, they made enough effort to climb from the bed and open the door in case the boys needed them, then to settle into the bed properly.

Callum couldn't stop touching Rupert, a hand on him at all times. Rupert didn't seem to mind, his smile soft, if a little rueful. Callum was totally out of his depth, but he could guess Rupert hadn't come to bed that night intending to tell Callum he loved him.

Callum understood. Denver loomed closer every day, regardless of what Callum harbored in his own heart.

Rupert woke up the next morning feeling a bit like he'd been rolled under a truck—and not just because he'd spent the night with Callum sleeping half on top of him. Not that he was complaining. He'd needed that closeness. As had Callum, he'd venture.

Perhaps laying his heart out for Callum hadn't been wise, but Callum had needed to know. Even if it wasn't reciprocated, he'd needed to understand what he meant to Rupert—despite his horrific story and his sad history and the so-called life waiting for him in Denver, closet and all.

Rupert had no regrets. Not even that it made Callum cry. He found that oddly flattering, actually. If nothing else, it was evidence that Callum understood the importance of what Rupert had told him. And that the words had mattered, at some level.

A warm hand slid under his t-shirt, and he rolled his head to smile at Callum.

"Good morning," Callum said with a shy smile. "You want the first shower?"

God, that sounded like heaven. Rupert leaned in and pressed his lips to Callum's, saying good morning back with a long, sweet kiss.

"Eeww, are you guys always this cute together?"

Rupert laughed against Callum's lips, then looked over his shoulder. "Good morning, Christian."

Christian hovered by the door. "Is it okay? If I come in, I mean?"

Callum sat up against the headboard and shoved a few pillows behind him. "Sure. But just to warn you, sometimes we're downright adorable."

Christian padded over to the bed, then hesitated.

"Come on up," Callum said, patting the bed. Then he threw a couple pillows at the footboard. "You can have that end, just so I can keep an eye on you."

Christian rolled his eyes, failing to hide his smile as he fussed with his pillows and untucked the comforter so he could climb beneath.

A flash of movement in the corner of his eye was all Rupert's warning before Oliver was airborne and crashing into him.

"Good morning!" Oliver barely spared Rupert's cheek a kiss then studied Christian for all of three seconds before grabbing his own pile of pillows and setting up his own spot across from Rupert. "This is nice. Can we eat breakfast in here?"

Rupert laughed. "Breakfast in bed?"

"Why not? It's Saturday and we don't have a single plan," Callum said with a grin. "I'll make you a deal. You go get your tablet so you can read the paper, and these two can go get a couple books, and I'll get breakfast." He looked around to see everyone nod, then clapped his hands once, loudly. "Ready, break!"

They all leaped from the bed and took off, Rupert laughing when Christian hip checked him out of the way to get through the door first.

"No fair! No hockey moves!"

"I can't help it if I'm good," came the retort from inside Christian's bedroom.

In ten minutes, all four of them were back in bed, munching on bowls of fruit and dry cereal. Callum had made the grown-ups really excellent coffee with which Rupert was quietly communing while he watched the boys tussle for pieces of strawberry from each other's bowls.

Christian caught him watching. "When can I have coffee?"

Rupert had no bloody idea. He looked at Callum, who shrugged then looked at Christian. "How about when you're twenty?"

"Gah! Twenty? I should have guessed you two would be hard-ass dads!"

Rupert choked on his coffee, sputtering into his napkin and trying to catch his breath.

Callum calmly patted Rupert on the back with one hand and picked up his tablet with the other. "I take that as a compliment. And no swearing."

Christian rolled his eyes, predictably.

Callum's iPad chimed. He looked down at the screen and

cringed.

"Uh, I have to take this. It'll just be a sec," Callum said in an apologetic tone, then he tapped the screen. "Hi, Mom."

"Callum, sweetheart, how are you?"

Rupert opened his mouth before his brain fully engaged. "Holy smokes, she sounds exactly like Savannah."

There was a pregnant pause, then Callum's mother asked, "Darling, who was that?"

Callum turned a baleful eye on Rupert, which he could admit he probably deserved.

"That's Rupert, Mom. He manages the Ice Cats, remember?"

"And he does this from your bed, while you're in your pajamas?"

Callum groaned "*Mom!*" just as Christian burst into giggles.

"And who is *that*?" she asked, her voice climbing higher.

Callum was casting baleful looks in every direction, now. "*That* is Christian." He turned the tablet so Christian could wave to Mrs. Morrison with a cheeky grin.

"Nice to meet you, Christian. And who are you, young man?"

"I'm Oliver. Rupert's brother."

"I see. Is Christian your brother, too?"

Christian's smile waivered and Oliver looked at Rupert, unsure. Rupert held out his hand and pulled Oliver into his lap.

Callum leaned forward and grabbed Christian by the ankle. "Come on."

Christian clamored across the bed and landed between Rupert and Callum with a flounce that made the whole bed bounce, tucking himself in under Callum's arm. Callum turned the camera on all of them.

"Mom, this is Rupert Smythe."

Rupert ran a self-conscious hand over his hair. "Very nice to meet you, Mrs. Morrison."

"Oh, you should call me Mary. After all, it seems you're quite, uh, close to my son."

Rupert didn't envy Callum for being on the receiving end of *that* look.

"Oliver and Christian live with Rupert, Mom. As he mentioned, Oliver is his younger brother, and Christian is his…"

"Ward," Rupert supplied, the word springing to mind after signing a thousand documents the day before to that effect. "Though, really, he's family, which is what's important."

Rupert was warmed by the matching smiles from Mary and Christian.

"Oh, you're in good with her now," Callum muttered.

His mother and Rupert both ignored him.

"Well," Mary said gamely, "I had no idea you were keeping such splendid company up there in Moncton, Callum." Which clearly was an oversight for which he would pay dearly. "I'm delighted to meet you all. You must come visit! Callum, I expect to see everyone at the end of summer weekend."

"Oh, I—" Rupert began, desperately trying to gauge Callum's expression.

"That would be so cool!" Christian said enthusiastically. "Are you in Denver, Mrs. Morrison?"

"No, dear," Mary replied. "And you must call me…well, I don't know. Mrs. Morrison doesn't seem right, does it?"

Callum's mouth was just kind of hanging open now. It would have been funny if Rupert hadn't felt like things were rapidly spinning out of control.

"How about Mimi? Would that work?"

"Okay," Oliver agreed readily.

Christian's smile had faded to something softer and sweeter than his usual grin. "I'd like that. Thank you."

"You're very welcome, dear. I can't wait to meet you in person. We're in Connecticut." She looked at Oliver. "Do you know where that it?"

The next ten minutes were spent listening to Mary extoll the apparently endless virtues of New England, northwest

Connecticut in particular, the Morrison end of summer weekend, and the Morrisons themselves. This somehow turned into Mary telling them how very very much she was looking forward to having them all come to stay. Apparently they were all to bring their skates, and hockey equipment if they had it, and could expect to be plied with an endless supply of chocolate chip cookies.

Callum looked resigned. Rupert couldn't help but smile. Mary Morrison had a gentle and warm way about her, but Rupert had no doubt where Callum got his stubborn streak.

He ran his hand over Callum's, twining their fingers together out of view of the camera.

Callum cast him an apologetic look. "Is this okay?" he asked softly.

Rupert wasn't really sure. He probably should ask Callum the same thing.

"Rupert, I'm terribly sorry," Mary said, concerned, and apparently having ears like a bat. "I should have made sure it was okay with you before I asked your children to come stay."

Twin looks of abject longing were turned on him, Oliver's hand clutching his shirt. Honestly, no man could withstand that, least of all Rupert.

"No, it's fine, Mary. Thank you for inviting us. It sounds lovely."

"So do you have any questions? Anything I can do to help you?"

Rupert thought he could probably find his way to the Morrison house by landmarks alone at this point. There was, though, something he could use her help with.

"Actually, I do have one question."

"What's that, dear?"

"At what age did you allow your children to drink coffee?"

Callum slumped back against the headboard with Christian leaning against his chest and Oliver half on top of everyone, and listened to his mother's detailed explanation on the merits and dangers of caffeine consumption.

He was well familiar with this particular subject and his mother's opinions around it, of course. As was he familiar with his mother's tricks. He never should have answered her call, and in bed with Rupert and the boys, no less. He was such an idiot.

He'd done, in his opinion, a clever job of avoiding his siblings and parents for most of the summer. He'd spoken to them, of course— in particular Savannah, with whom he checked in three times a week for his training. But he'd done it in the gym or after his morning walk-through or when Mike and Alexei had taken Oliver out on some adventure.

It wasn't that he didn't want them to meet Oliver and Rupert and now Christian. It was that he wanted it too much. He wanted what he couldn't have, far too much.

Obviously, his mother was going to adore the children. She had seven of her own and hadn't killed one of them yet, so she clearly had a capacity for patience and love that far exceeded normal limits. And he could have predicted that his mother would take to Rupert. The reverse, though, he might not have foreseen. Rupert was hanging on his mother's every word.

Christian, on the other hand, was trying hard not to object when talk turned to limits on sodas. Oliver looked bored.

"Go get your book," Callum whispered in Oliver's ear under his mother's watchful gaze, impressed she never once paused in her dissertation on the perils of red dye.

Oliver slid out from under the iPad for just a second, then returned with *Curious George* to settle on Callum's lap. Christian took the tablet so that Callum could hold the book for Oliver and Mimi—*really, Mom?*—could still see everyone.

The looks his mother was sending him while she continued to answer questions and he quietly read to Oliver were kind of hilarious. Eventually, though, even Rupert had learned enough for one day and the call began to wrap up. Callum was well-aware there'd be a phone call later and a whole new lecture delivered then, just for Callum.

Could he get away with "accidentally" flushing his phone down the toilet? Doubtful, since his mother looked close to starting in on him then and there.

"Okay, Mom, it was great to talk to you. We have to run, though. Lots to do today!" Callum announced cheerfully, ignoring the looks from the boys and Rupert at that blatant lie.

His mother took a few minutes to reiterate how excited she was to meet everyone, but at last Callum ended the call.

"How much trouble are you in?" Rupert asked as they both stared at the blank screen.

"There is no way to measure it with currently available technology."

Chapter Nineteen

Callum survived the phone call with his mother later mostly by making sure she could hear the kids shouting in the background as they played on the ice at the rink. Oliver wore his brand-spanking-new first pair of skates—hockey skates, no less—and was having a ball holding on to the pant legs of anyone who would let him tag along for a ride.

For the next two weeks, though, Callum paid a heavy price for his familial avoidance strategy. All six of his siblings took an opportunity to reach out and tell him all about the fascinating story they'd heard from their mother. Callum listened and harrumphed and generally remained tight-lipped, to the consternation of all. Eventually he started to let Oliver answer his phone, which was dirty pool, but he didn't care. He was done being interrogated by that pack of hyenas.

The only one he couldn't avoid was Savannah, since she was, technically, his trainer. She was also the only one who didn't give him a lot of shit. She'd called the day after his Skype disaster with their mom, acknowledged she'd heard a pretty interesting tale of bed snuggles and happy children, then asked only, "Are you okay?"

He'd promised he was, and she'd let it go. Maybe because as the only girl in that pack of hyenas she was more sensitive, but more likely because he hadn't called her and asked, "Are you seriously in love with two men and are the three of you getting freaky together in bed?"

So, maybe it was sisterly love and maybe it was détente. Either way, Callum appreciated it. Especially because he really, really didn't ever want to ask her that question, let alone hear the answer. He supported her, he loved her, he even cared about the two men in question and looked forward to them joining the family, but she was still his *sister*. As far as he was concerned, she didn't even know what sex was, let alone have it.

319

Actually, maybe *that* was why she didn't ask about him—she was afraid of hearing the details. Which was probably wise, since he and Rupert couldn't keep their hands off each other. They held hands on the couch, watching movies with the boys. And under the table at restaurants when they were out with their friends. They stood closer than they should in public, and spent far more time than was probably professional in Rupert's office with the door closed.

Every night they climbed into Rupert's ridiculously large, soft bed, pajama pants at the ready over the footboard, and spent the first hour, or three, exploring each other. Callum hadn't gone to bed this early on a regular basis since he'd been ten years old. But Christian liked to read in bed at night, and Oliver was asleep before sunset, and, well, once the house was quiet, all Callum wanted was to curl up with Rupert.

Rupert didn't seem to mind. After a particularly handsy morning teasing each other, Callum met Rupert for his now daily visit to the locker room, expecting to continue helping him with his anxiety about the space. Instead, Callum was immediately dragged into the trainer's office, the door shut firmly behind them. A few minutes later, Callum was pretty sure he heard Jack calling his name, but he didn't answer. His mouth was full, in any case.

So he had sex. A lot of sex, over the next couple weeks. But they didn't actually *have sex*. Callum had told Rupert he wanted Rupert to fuck him and he'd meant it. Rupert had seemed more than willing, but now the damn man was taking forever. It wasn't from lack of *very clearly expressed* interest. Rupert had just gotten it into his head this was something Callum needed to prepare for.

Now, as training regimes went, this one was way more fun than anything else Callum had done. Too bad this wasn't an Olympic event, because he would totally have brought home the gold. Every night Rupert would roll him onto his back and kiss him, long and slow and deep. It started with one finger, then two. Callum had progressed to the point he could take three of Rupert's long, slender fingers in almost no time, and he'd had some of the most shattering orgasms of his life.

So why, he asked himself for the hundredth time that day alone, was he still the oldest virgin in fucking North America?

He *wanted* this, but Rupert stilled seemed vaguely disbelieving, in spite of the fact that Callum came, shouting against Rupert's mouth, at least once a day, begging for it.

"Earth to Callum?"

Callum's head snapped up. Holy shit, he'd just totally spaced out in the middle of the conference room, daydreaming about his sex life.

"You okay there, buddy?" Jack asked with a smirk.

"Shut up."

"Because you were staring at Rupert's office door all kind of moony-eyed and I thought maybe I'd lost you for a second there."

Callum rolled his eyes. "No, I'm still here. Totally engaged in this super-interesting shit you've been talking about. Tell me more about the exciting world of durable, no-slip, commercial grade bathroom floor tile, *please*."

"There is no call for being snide just because you're horny," Jack said.

Callum's head hit the table with a thunk. "Oh my god, I can't even argue with you. That's exactly my fucking problem. No pun intended."

Jack cracked up, then pulled out his cell phone. "Don't say I never did anything for you."

"What?"

Jack just smiled and spoke into his phone. "Mike! Where are you? ...Perfect. Can you keep Oliver busy and away from home for, say, the next three hours? ...Yes, well, it will take that long if they do it right." Callum could hear Mike laughing from across the room. "Okay, I'll let them know."

Jack hung up. "You're cleared for go."

"Really? I'm cleared for go?" Callum asked, his bland voice

belying his speeding pulse.

"Are you going to stand there and take issue with my word choices, or are you going to go find Rupert, drag him home—*not* into the trainer's office, I thank you very much on behalf of the entire staff, particularly the cleaning crew—and do whatever it was you were thinking about doing a few minutes ago?"

Callum didn't bother to answer. Hell, he didn't even bother to clean up his mess on the conference table. He'd be back in three hours, and not one minute less if he had anything to say about it.

He knocked on Rupert's door once and walked right in.

"Still no lock on that door, I see," Reese said mildly.

"Hi, Reese. Bye, Reese. Come on, Rupert, let's go."

Rupert stood. "Is anything the matter?"

"No, no, nothing is wrong. We just have to go. Come on."

"But Callum—"

"Do you have meetings? Besides with him." He dismissed Reese with a wave.

"I beg your pardon?" Reese said.

"No," Rupert said slowly. "Not until later this afternoon."

"In like, more than three hours?" Callum asked hopefully.

Rupert checked his watch. "In about four hours. What is this about?"

"We have to go," Callum said again.

"What's wrong?" Rupert demanded.

"Nothing! It's just that Oliver is occupied with Mike and Alexei for the next three hours, Christian is at camp and then at the rink, and I don't have any meetings either, so I wanted to…" Callum glanced at Reese, whose eyes absolutely danced with delight, before looking back at Rupert. "Be alone with you," he finished lamely.

"Oh," Rupert said, his face flaming.

"Well, I can see I'm not needed here," Reese said as he stood, his voice shaking with laughter. "I will return in three hours, perhaps three and a half. Don't hesitate to prolong your absence in order to properly bathe before returning. And do try not to make it obvious to all the nice people out in that office that you're having a nooner while they have to stay at their desks, will you?"

"Oh, I ah…" Callum suddenly felt guilty. Not in the least bit dissuaded, but guilty.

Reese sent Rupert a meaningful look. "*Definitely* not Sheldon."

Rupert grinned. "Thank god."

Callum had no idea what the hell they were talking about, nor who the hell Sheldon was, but right now he didn't care. They had a schedule to keep. Or something.

The moment Reese left the office, Rupert grabbed his iPad and shoved Callum out the door. They blew past Jack grinning at them from the conference room door.

"Does everyone know what you're up to?" Rupert hissed in a low voice as they charged toward the parking lot.

"It was Jack's idea," he explained.

Rupert drew up short. "Going home for a matinee was *Jack's* idea?"

Callum put a hand on Rupert's back and urged him along. "Yes, and it was a good one. He was tired of me staring into space and trying to walk around upright while I'm constantly walking around erect, if you get my drift."

Rupert laughed, somewhat hysterically, almost jogging by the time they got the car.

Callum was putting on his seatbelt when Rupert asked, "Wait. Has Jack been looking at your pants?"

"What?" Callum started the car and tore out of the lot. "No!"

He broke all land speed records and at least three traffic laws to get them to the warehouse. The freight doors had barely begun to close by the time Callum and Rupert were in the elevator, and they were kissing before the elevator doors were fully shut.

For the first time since they'd moved in, Callum didn't give a shit about the creaky elevator. He thrust his fingers into Rupert's hair, pressing him back against the swaying walls as they rose to the fourth floor. He couldn't get enough.

Rupert turned his head, gasping for breath. Callum skimmed his lips over Rupert's smooth cheek, tucking his nose behind Rupert's ear and inhaling deeply before biting down.

Rupert's legs gave a little, his weight shifting against Callum's. They were pressed too tightly together for Rupert to actually go anywhere, but Callum curved a hand around one of Rupert's perfectly round butt cheeks and shifted him up, closer. Their growing erections rubbed against each other.

"Please, Rupert," Callum groaned against the soft skin of Rupert's neck, his tongue swiping over the little bites he left behind.

"Yes," Rupert gasped again. "Yes, come on."

Callum ignored Rupert's hands pushing at him until he realized he was working against himself here. They weren't going to have sex in the elevator, if for no other reason than they needed lubricant. Really, that was about the only reason. Callum was so primed he felt lightheaded.

Rupert shoved the doors open and they spilled out into the hallway, stumbling in their haste to reach their door. Rupert dashed for the bedroom the moment they were inside, tossing his suit jacket on a kitchen stool, his fingers working his shirt buttons. Callum's t-shirt hit the floor of the hallway, his shoes flying into a corner of the bedroom. His pants hit the floor with a dull thud, heavy with wallet and cellphone and keys. He left it all there in a heap and reached for Rupert.

Rupert stopped him with an outstretched hand.

"What?" Callum asked, desperate.

"You're gorgeous. And sexy. And I honestly want to eat you alive. But I'm not getting in bed with you if you're still wearing your socks. A man has his limits."

Callum burst into laughter, hopping around on one foot, then the other, to strip himself of the offending footwear. As soon as he done, he figured *what the hell* and dropped his boxer briefs to the rug, too.

Rupert's hand immediately wrapped around his cock, pulling him closer to the bed and tearing a grunt from his throat. He was easily led, but it wasn't about Rupert's hold on his dick. The draw was entirely about Rupert.

He kissed Rupert, cupping his jaw, thumbs tracing his high cheekbones. Rupert hummed into his mouth, his eyes fluttering shut as he submitted to Callum's touch. His kiss.

Callum loved these moments. Loved how careful he could be with Rupert. How the sizzle of arousal still burned in his blood, his need demanding, but there was still room for this. It felt vital, and urgent, but he could take his time. There was no reason to be quick or quiet. There was no reason to hide who or what he was, what he wanted, how much he *needed.*

Rupert's hands skimmed down his back and over his hips, touching him everywhere he could reach in long, slow strokes. The frantic kiss in the elevator had gotten them this far, but now it was like they'd dropped it down a gear. Or three. These were the kisses that often started their nights, when they'd crawl under the covers and reach for each other.

Callum had mostly gotten over his self-consciousness about being naked and intimate with Rupert. He hadn't gotten over how much he loved to look at Rupert like this. Or with his clothes *on*, to be honest. But like this, their warm skin brushing, made Callum groan against his lips, and arch against his curious hands.

Rupert's skin was smooth and pale as milk except the wonderfully tempting pink parts—his cheeks, neck, and chest when he was aroused, his belly and thighs where Callum had sucked up marks, hidden from public view but always there. Callum had taken to marking one particular spot on the inside of Rupert's thigh, just low enough that Callum could brush his fingers over it under the table at a restaurant, or even beneath the conference room table. Rupert would twitch, sometimes a small smile hovering on his lips as he continued speaking to someone else, sometimes turning to give Callum a dark look, full of promise.

Callum was a slave to those looks. They drove him to take risks, to pull Rupert into storage closets and empty offices and on top of Rupert's desk, so desperate for a touch, for even one kiss, he was willing to risk discovery.

Moncton had begun to feel safe. Foolishly so, he knew, but it just made him feel so...*whole,* for once in his life. Like he was living instead of hiding. And it would all be over soon. This life, stolen from his reality, and yet still so exquisitely real.

Callum tucked his lips up under Rupert's jaw, nosing the soft skin there until he was behind Rupert's ear, inhaling deeply once more. Sometimes this was all he needed to escape his thoughts about the future, and the accompanying dread that congealed in a cold lump in his gut. Rupert smelled like sex. And love. And home.

Rupert ran a gentle hand down his neck and smiled as he stepped back and drew Callum to the bed.

Callum was helpless to resist. He climbed onto the mattress with Rupert, meeting in the middle on their knees for another long kiss, their chests touching, cocks bumping. Callum slid his hands down Rupert's back and over the firm, high curve of his ass. He knew its shape and strength. Knew Rupert's body almost as well as he knew his own.

And that worked both ways. Rupert's lips slid along his jaw and down the cord of muscle to his shoulder, sending shivers through his body. Callum hadn't known his neck was so sensitive. Or the insides of his elbows, or, oddly, his hips. They were sore a lot these days, twenty-plus years in the goal having taken its toll. But when Rupert's hands rubbed over them, or held on, fingers digging in, it felt as good as any massage. Better, because instead of sending the message that they were broken, something to be overcome or ignored, the pain Rupert soothed or exacerbated told Callum he was alive. That it didn't matter how much he'd beat the shit out of himself over the years, his body still worked and stretched and felt good in Rupert's hands.

Rupert barely had to push for Callum to fall back on the bed, pulling Rupert down with him, surprised when Rupert used that grip on Callum's hips to roll him onto his stomach.

Rupert's lips tickled along the tiny hairs beneath his hairline. Then the broad flat of his tongue warmed Callum's spine down to his shoulders.

He was steeped in the pleasure of Rupert's undivided attention, utterly accepting. Ready and content. Rupert laid down on top of him and pressed his knees between Callum's, spreading Callum's thighs wide. Rupert's erection moving against his skin was a tease. Callum's lips curved up in direct response to the feeling of Rupert's smile pressed between his shoulders and his shaft sliding between Callum's cheeks and along his perineum, the blood-hot head nestling against his balls.

Callum buried his face in a pillow and groaned. Hands rubbed down over his sides to his hips, Rupert's full weight on his back.

"I love it when you're like this," he murmured against Callum's ear.

"Muffled by the pillow?"

Rupert's laugh was less an auditory thing and more a tactile one, shaking Callum with each huff.

"Smartarse," he whispered affectionately, working his lips over Callum's shoulders and down his spine. Callum missed the warm weight on his back, but let Rupert do as he wished without comment or request. At least verbally. He couldn't keep his hips still. His cock rubbed against the bedding, the gentle friction not nearly enough, building more tension rather than easing it.

Twin licks over the dimples at the base of his spine tickled and he squirmed until Rupert's tongue slid lower. Every muscle locked up tight, poised, as Rupert drew a cool, wet stripe into the valley of his ass, until the clenched muscles prevented Rupert from going any further.

"This okay?" he asked in a low voice.

Whatever Rupert did was okay. Even Callum's addled brain could remember that.

"Yes," he gasped, holding himself perfectly still as he waited to see what would come next.

Rupert stared down at Callum's long back, round arse, and wide-spread thighs and felt spoiled for choice.

"You know," he said, running his hands thoughtfully over the expanse of smooth skin at his fingertips, "your bum is just as big and round as mine. I don't know why everyone insists on teasing me and not you."

Callum gasped the words "smaller waist," just as Rupert's thumb brushed over his hole.

Rupert paused. "Pardon?"

Callum groaned, shooting a dirty look over his shoulder. Apparently, he didn't feel now was the time for this discussion. Rupert just looked back, one eyebrow arched, fingers digging into the meat of Callum's bum.

Callum growled in frustration. "You have a smaller waist. Leaner legs. That's what makes your ass such a perfect bubble."

Rupert rolled his eyes. He hated that term. The expression on Callum's face, though, told him Callum felt differently about it.

He traced a finger down the valley of Callum's arse, circling the tight pucker of muscle until Callum's mouth hung open, gasping.

"I rather like yours better," he told Callum.

"It's yours. Do what you want with it."

Rupert chuckled at Callum's ready surrender. He didn't think he'd ever get used to this. To how pliable and sweet and generous Callum could be in bed. He hardly seemed the same man as the irascible, cranky lunatic who had first barged into Rupert's office.

"I rather think I will," he said slowly.

"You will what?" Callum groaned into the pillow he hugged against his chest.

Rupert slid down on the bed, using his hands to spread

Callum's knees until his thighs could go no further.

"Do what I want," he murmured. He licked Callum's perineum, his tongue hot and firm, starting at the soft skin over his balls and ending at the tightly clenched entrance to Callum's body.

"Oh fuck," Callum cried, writhing against the bed.

Rupert licked again. And again, his arms straining to hold Callum still as he panted and wriggled beneath him. Rupert worked at the muscles beneath his lips, prodding one moment, soothing the next, with long, wide laps of his tongue.

Callum hugged the pillow tighter, his face buried in it. It wasn't an effective muffle, every grunt and whimper like music to Rupert's ears. Callum's ass lifted in the air after one particularly deep stab of Rupert's tongue, and he finally managed to get his knees planted under him. He immediately canted his ass up to Rupert's face, begging for more.

Rupert circled his spit-slick hole with one finger, then pushed in.

"Oh god. That's...that's so good. Please, Rupert. *Please.*"

Rupert thrust deeper, his knuckle catching on the rim and tugging gently when he withdrew. Callum jerked, the sensation rocking through his entire body.

Rupert had worked Callum up to being able to take three fingers with grand plans of toys and torture, but each time they'd had time alone, he hadn't needed or wanted to bother with anything more elaborate than the two of them.

That was more than enough. Sometimes almost more than Rupert could handle, his heart full to bursting, his body thrumming. It was a lot to process. A lot to feel and love and do, all without the anchor of a future to plan or even think about.

He was foolish, rushing toward his own heartbreak, exacerbating it with every touch, escalating how much it would hurt every day they spent raising their little family and building something new and better for their team. They were carefully crafting a future they could not have. It was the most singularly stupid thing Rupert had ever done.

He slid his tongue around his finger hooked against Callum's rim, tugging so that he could push in beside it. Callum let out a garbled moan, and Rupert smiled.

He wouldn't change anything about the past two months. He would change the future, if he could, but he refused to delude himself into thinking that he might.

There was only this. This summer. This bed. This night and however many more he could steal before Callum went away. Then he'd face working with him from a distance, and trying to separate Callum's presence from the home he'd helped Rupert build.

He kept working with his finger, his mouth, fascinated by the sounds he could draw from Callum. By the way he opened up beneath his touch. When he was sure Callum was ready, and Rupert couldn't stand to wait any longer, he leaned over to grab the lube and a condom from the bedside table.

"No," Callum panted.

"No?" Rupert asked, tucking the lube under Callum's thigh to warm it, but still holding the condom, unsure.

Callum slowly turned his head and peeled open his eyes. "I meant don't stop," he said, voice hoarse, his words less certain toward the end. His eyes caught on the foil square in Rupert's hand,

Rupert carefully pulled his finger from the hot clench of Callum's body and laid down over him again, his lips brushing the shell of Callum's ear.

"What do you want?"

Callum sighed as Rupert's weight settled. "You."

Rupert's stomach swooped. He ran his hands down Callum's sides and slid forward, dragging his cock over Callum, feeling the slick of his own spit along his shaft.

"You have that," Rupert agreed. "Now, what do you want me to *do*?"

"God, you know what I want. I want you to fadoodle me," Callum growled. "I want you to fadoodle me right through the mattress."

And that. That shouldn't have been sexy. At all. Not when it forced Rupert to bury his face against Callum's neck and muffle uncontrollable snorts of laughter.

Callum's smile was slow, obviously pleased with himself.

"You are ridiculous," Rupert said, smiling down at Callum.

"You love me anyway," Callum murmured, his eyes popping open the moment the words left his mouth.

"I do," he agreed quietly, still kissing Callum's shoulders. Down the trench of his spine.

"Rupert, I—"

Rupert grabbed a globe of Callum's ass in each hand and spread him open, cutting off his words with a strangled whimper.

Callum persevered. "Rupert, you—I—I want to—"

Rupert thrust his tongue against Callum's hole, cutting off Callum's incoherent mutters and relishing the low moan he got instead. They could talk later. Or tomorrow. Or never.

Nothing Callum could say could turn Rupert away. Or keep Callum here forever.

Callum writhed beneath him, beautifully responsive as he cried Rupert's name. Sighed and breathed and moaned it. Rupert worked his tongue in and around the tight muscles, waiting for them to loosen again, then he retrieved the lube from under Callum's leg.

He slicked his fingers and eased one into Callum.

He kissed the smooth skin stretched over each cheek, the crease where thigh met arse, the thin skin along Callum's inner thighs. Rupert worked his finger deeper, until Callum's legs shook and his hip canted to meet each thrust.

He eased his finger free and Callum made a weak, broken sound of protest. Rupert teased with the tips of two fingers, testing muscles. Callum growled and pushed back, taking both easily and burying his face in the pillow to muffle his shout of pleasure.

Rupert added more lube, his other hand soothing over Callum's hip and back. He would not be rushed, no matter how Callum gasped and growled. He kept his pace steady, unrelenting, until the third finger hardly met any resistance.

"Please, Rupert," Callum groaned. "Please. Do it. Don't make me wait any longer," he implored.

Rupert felt a drop of guilt somewhere in the tsunami of desire cresting over him. He'd meant to tease Callum, to build up to this moment for the sake of anticipation, and to ensure Callum was truly able to enjoy every aspect of it. Perhaps two weeks had been too long.

Given how Rupert's hand trembled as he rubbed Callum's spine, it had been far too long.

"Shhh...I've got you," he promised.

Callum nodded, as if he believed it completely. Rupert groped frantically for the condom.

He kept his fingers moving, stretching Callum, adding more lube, tearing into the foil packet with his teeth. Callum's hips worked in counterpoint, his hair damp along his forehead and neck, cheeks pink beneath his thick black lashes and above his open, panting mouth.

Rupert turned his wrist, slowly, dragging another long moan out of Callum, until his fingertips brushed over the hard knot of Callum's prostate and he sobbed.

"You're fucking gorgeous."

Callum's almost managed a laugh between huffs of breath. "Should we call a doctor?"

Rupert didn't think he could wait another second to finally be inside Callum, but he paused in the act of slowly extricating his fingers from Callum's ass. "What?"

"I think you've gone blind," Callum explained.

And that wasn't funny. Rupert freed his hand and curled around Callum, unintentionally forcing his cock against Callum's open, waiting body, making them both moan.

When Rupert could see straight again, he pressed his face to

Callum's cheek. "You need to learn to take a compliment."

Callum wriggled against him. "Thank you," he said completely insincerely.

Rupert was inordinately grateful that Callum couldn't see his hands shaking so hard it took three attempts to get the condom on. He was supposed to be the experienced one here, for Christ's sake, and he was close to falling apart. He swallowed a hysterical giggle when the bottle of lubricant shot out of his slippery hand and across the bed. He had enough already—more than enough to necessitate changing the sheets later—but that was good. He needed to be sure this was as close to perfect for Callum as Rupert could make it.

He was so bloody nervous. He hadn't wanted anything as much as this, as *Callum*, in his life. Hadn't been as giddy or jittery since he was a teenager.

The memory of himself in that cheap hotel room just on the other side of the parking lot from the rink where he'd been competing, and the beautiful young man with him that day, settled his nerves now. That boy, another competitor, had been as overwhelmed and fumbling as Rupert, but he'd taught Rupert everything he'd needed to know, once and for all, about who he was. And who he liked.

Rupert looked down the long, strong arch of Callum's spine and smiled.

Rupert still knew.

Sliding forward, he pressed up against Callum's spread thighs and drew his cock down between Callum's cheeks and over his hole. Callum lay limp beneath him, his cheek to the mattress, shivering at the touch. Still open. Ready.

Rupert sucked in a deep breath and pressed the head against those twitching muscles and eased forward.

"Oh, Jesus," Callum whispered.

Rupert froze.

The eye Rupert could see popped open and glared at him. "Don't stop," he growled.

Rupert tried to smile, but it wobbled as the pressure built, flattening his sensitive head, good and yet so, so terrible, because he needed…he wanted…

The head popped in. Rupert froze again, panting, as Callum clamped down around him, unbearably hot and tight and perfect.

"Rupert," he groaned, and just the tiny vibrations of his voice were enough to make Rupert whimper.

He ran both hands over Callum's back, his hips, trying to soothe himself as much as Callum. He would do this slowly, he reminded himself sternly, or he wouldn't do it at all.

Callum, however, had other ideas. He took deep breaths, each one let out longer and slower than the last, his spine melting into a deep bow before he nudged back, just a little, and gasped.

Rupert's hand clenched his hip, his fingers settling over the bruises he'd already left there, and held Callum still.

"You're not ready," he told him in a hoarse voice.

"I am," Callum vowed, nudging back again.

And, well, Rupert was only human. He met Callum's press with a gentle thrust, staring down, wide-eyed, as his shaft slipped further into Callum's body, unable to tear his eyes from where Callum was stretched around him.

"Oh god," he muttered, meeting Callum again. And again.

The sight never became less entrancing. He forced himself to look away, only to see Callum staring into the distance sightlessly with one wide eye, his open mouth hanging open.

Rupert's hips snapped forward, his hands clenched tight, and he sank in to the hilt. Callum's legs gave out beneath him until he lay pressed fully to the bed, his knees by his ribs.

Goddamn flexible goalies.

His ran his hands up Callum's ribs and under, to hook over Callum's clavicles, his face pressed to Callum's back.

He wished desperately he were taller, so that he could kiss Callum, get as lost in his mouth and tongue as he was in every other way lost in Callum right then.

Callum sighed beneath him. "That would be nice," he murmured.

Rupert wasn't certain which parts he actually said out loud. He rolled his hips forward, reveling in the noises spilling from Callum's lips.

"Maybe next time," Rupert promised.

"Next time?" Callum gasped, his head spinning. "Please, Rupert. You have to finish *this* time. Soon.*"

Callum sounded as desperate as he felt, but he didn't care. The stretch, the feeling of being full, of being *filled*, was exquisite. Every single one of his nerve endings was dancing with joy, but none more than in his ass, the heavy presence of Rupert inside him, the burn of his rim around Rupert's shaft.

He couldn't remember anymore what he thought this would be like, but this is definitely, definitely, better.

Except for the part where Rupert was *not moving*.

Callum shoved the pillow he'd been clinging to away, shoved all the pillows away, and pressed his chest to the cool cotton beneath, his arms spread, his hands on either side of his head gathering up great fistfuls of the sheets. He used those anchors, and his knees, to grind up against Rupert, his cock dragging against the bed at the same time.

Rupert's mouth latched onto the base of his neck and sucked, hard, the pain a perfect point to focus on as a host of other sensations stormed through his body. Callum continued the relentless swivel of his hips until Rupert's cock brushed his prostate. He jerked and cried out.

"Rupert, *please*."

Rupert nodded against his back, apparently beyond words, and shifted against him. Callum hummed and twitched and tried to figure out what the fuck Rupert was doing, until Rupert planted his knees and slowly pulled his hips back.

"Oh, Jesus," Callum groaned. "Oh fuck. Oh oh oh oh..."

Whatever other nonsense was about to escape his mouth

was cut off when Rupert thrust forward, their hips hitting with enough force to send a shockwave through Callum. All the air left his lungs with a fierce grunt.

"Do that again," he begged.

And Rupert did. God, did he ever. Callum let go a stream of stupid noises and pleas and god knew what else. Every slow drag out made him shudder, every grunt-inducing thrust perfect. He rolled his hips, meeting Rupert's harder, faster, until they slammed together. Rupert's hands slid from around Callum's shoulders to rub down over his arms, their fingers threading as they moved together, against one another, rolling and gasping. The weight on Callum's back anchored him, pressing his cock against the mattress, the friction just on the right side of too much. And yet not enough.

Callum wasn't the only one making noise. Rupert chanted his name, telling him he was bloody beautiful and that he loved him and so many things Callum wanted to hear. *Needed* to hear, though he could hardly process them, let alone *believe* them.

He was dizzy with need and overwhelmed with gratitude. *Thank god* this was happening. That *this* was how he learned what it meant to be intimate. To make love. He hadn't let some stranger take this from him in a bathroom stall, and now he knew why. He'd pretended it was because guys saw a man his size and figured he'd only top, but that was more of the bullshit he'd been telling himself, protecting himself with, for years. Some part of Callum's fucked-up, lonely, stupid brain had held this back. For this. For now.

For Rupert.

Rupert hitched just a little higher, and the next thrust bounced over Callum's prostate. He let out a wild, uncontrollable, and hopefully very manly squeak.

Rupert hit it again.

Callum groaned. "Yes, yes, just that, just th—"

His orgasm wasn't so much a trip and fall as being slammed into the boards, blind-sided, without pads on. Suddenly, it was just *there*.

He roared, his voice breaking as Rupert thrust again, his movement jerky, his hands gripping Callum's until the feeling was cut off from his fingers. Callum shook with the force of his release, full-body shudders that rattled him to the core. Each time Rupert hit his prostate, he let loose another jet of hot and wet against his belly, another cry, another shudder, until he was wrung out, empty, his body still tightening in almost painful pulses with nothing left to give.

He held onto Rupert's hands through it all, held on tighter as he opened his mouth to beg Rupert to stop, but then Rupert thrust deep and ground against him, burying his face between Callum's shoulders.

Callum released one of Rupert's hands to reach over his shoulder and curl his fingers into Rupert's hair, hoping to offer some kind of anchor for Rupert as he'd done for Callum.

Rupert collapsed on top of him, his full weight pressing Callum down into the bed. He was actually really heavy, Callum realized, and had been holding a lot of his weight on his knees and elbows after all. Now he was motionless, draped over Callum and trying to catch his breath. Callum's ass was going from turned-on pleasure-center to well-fucked and sore, but he would have happily lain here, like this, forever.

He couldn't begin to guess how long they stayed like that. He felt Rupert softening inside him and thought nothing of it until Rupert suddenly jerked to life against his back, his hand jamming between their bodies.

"Sorry," Rupert warned, before slowly pulling out.

And okay, *ow*. But also, *wow*. Callum was a hockey player. He'd always had a hard time separating what hurt from what felt good, and now, more than ever, it *all* felt good.

Rupert flopped onto the bed beside Callum, less graceful than Callum had ever seen him. His hair stood on end, his cheeks red with beard burn and shiny with exertion, and his lips swollen. Perfect, prim Rupert, was a big, sexy *mess.*

"I like you like this," Callum confessed, running a hand through Rupert's hair.

Rupert blinked at him, bemused.

Callum grinned. "You okay, duchess?"

Rupert's only answer was to lean in and kiss Callum.

They lay like that, making out, until the alarm on Callum's phone went off and it was time to return to the arena.

Chapter Twenty

As much as Rupert wanted to have his hands all over Callum at any given moment, he at least still tried to be mindful of who was around and might see them. Callum either wasn't paying any attention to that, or simply didn't care.

It felt good to hold his hand. To sit close. To smile at him and know that whatever look on his face was probably embarrassing, if the constant eye rolls coming from Christian were any indication. But it also felt terribly dangerous. Both for Rupert's heart, and for Callum's reputation.

There were no out players in hockey. Not openly, publicly out, though Alexei assured Callum often that there were degrees of knowledge and secrets. Callum seemed fascinated by these stories, but Rupert wasn't sure how much of it he was considering applying to himself. He spoke of Denver as if it were another planet, and threaded his fingers through Rupert's while they ate with the boys as if he hadn't a care in the world. As if his name wasn't known in millions of households across at least two countries. Or his face familiar to many people around him, even if they couldn't quite place him.

Some of Rupert's most out-and-proud ex-boyfriends hadn't felt the need to touch him as much. At home, at the office, at the grocery store. And not all of those touches necessarily would tip someone off, but if someone saw them together enough, could put all those touches together, well...it was safe to say Callum wasn't putting the 'b' in subtle.

And if Callum was being obvious in public, he was downright shameless amongst their friends. They returned to the arena after their *nooner*, as Reese had called it, and Callum couldn't stop grinning. Not that Rupert was much better, but honestly, anyone who saw Callum would know he'd just had really fantastic sex, even if he hadn't marched into the conference room, yanked out his chair, and proceeded to sit ever-so-gingerly. His wince when his bum had touched the chair was so blatant, *Jack* fucking blushed.

Rupert darted out of the room and to his office, cheeks hot, smile unrepentant.

Later that night, Callum flopped down on the couch and again winced mightily, setting Alexei into hysterics while Mike smiled sympathetically and Rupert practically dove over the back of said couch to distract Christian. The boy was young, not stupid, and with the internet at his disposal, Rupert couldn't be sure what he knew or understood. Likely things most of them hadn't had a clue about until much later in their lives.

They got into a routine after that. Every night, they put Oliver to bed, then sat with Christian to watch television. Or play a game. Or just talk. Christian was a bright and articulate young man, far too old for his age, and getting increasingly more comfortable in his new family. He still looked sad sometimes, but he was talking about it, even talking about his father sometimes, and getting stronger every day.

Then Christian came home from his skating lesson one afternoon, storming through the door ahead of Callum and Oliver and blowing past Rupert without a word.

Rupert looked to Callum, who shrugged. "He was like that when we got there to pick him up."

Rupert bided his time until Oliver was in bed, and the three of them were slouched on the couch together, Callum's arm around Christian's shoulders, his other hand laced with Rupert's as they watched television. Christian often sought to be close to Callum, in particular, though he would lean into Rupert, or throw his arm around Oliver, too. He was a tactile boy, in need of physical reassurance of their presence, Rupert suspected. Tonight that seemed especially so, as he practically burrowed into Callum's side.

Rupert turned off the television at the end of the episode. Christian looked at him warily. Normally they would watch for a bit longer before calling it a night.

"What happened today to upset you?" Rupert asked.

"Nothing." Christian studiously examined his hands where they lay clenched in his lap.

Callum frowned at the top of Christian's head. "Come on, bud. Maybe we can help."

Christian's huff of laughter was an achingly jaded scoff. "Yeah, I don't think so." He took a deep breath and tried to give them a reassuring smile. "It's fine. No big deal."

"Then tell us what it is," Rupert cajoled.

Christian appeared to do some internal battle, while Callum rubbed his arm encouragingly. Finally, he sighed.

"It's nothing. Really. A bunch of my friends saw you drop me off this morning, and they wanted to know who you were," he said, looking at Rupert. "I didn't really think about it and I told them how I'm living with you, and, of course, they wanted to know why."

Rupert's heart sank. "Okay. What did you tell them?"

Christian shrugged. "I lied. I said my dad was having some issues and I was just staying with you for a little while."

"Well, that's mostly true," Rupert offered.

Christian's eyes shot to Rupert's. "But I can stay, right? I mean, it's not just going to be for a little while, is it?"

Rupert grabbed Christian's hands in one of his. "Yes. Yes, of course. As long as you want or need, okay? We'll always be here—this will always be your home."

Callum's hand squeezed Rupert's painfully when he said "we", but Rupert pushed on. He and Oliver *would* always be there, and there was little any of them could do about the fact that Callum would not. Christian was aware Callum was due back in Denver at the end of the summer.

"Okay," Christian said, settling against Callum again.

"So what had you so upset?" Rupert asked.

"I kind of wanted to tell them the truth."

"But you didn't?"

Christian frowned. "I don't want to lose my friends."

Rupert rubbed his thumb over the back of Christian's hand. "Are you sure that's what would happen?"

"I don't know. What if the whole school finds out? Even if my friends are cool, that doesn't mean everyone else will be. I figure most people are like my dad."

"I sincerely hope not," Rupert said honestly. "But there will be some people who are jerks."

"Yeah, there will," Christian said, and Rupert despaired at how very certain he sounded.

"And how will you handle that?"

"Ignore them, I guess."

"Right," Rupert agreed. "You should be proud of who you are. You're a great student, a brilliant skater, and a good friend. It shouldn't matter to anyone if you're gay."

"But it will."

"Sadly, yes, but those people aren't worth your time."

"It just seems easier, you know? If I don't tell anyone, if they don't know, they can't hurt me." Christian looked up at Callum with wide, trusting eyes. "That's what you do, right?"

Callum swallowed and stared down at Christian's open, earnest expression, hearing Rupert's sharply indrawn breath.

"No, I—"

"You said I could never tell anyone about you and Rupert. I heard you tell Alexei that no one could ever know, except your close friends here. Your family."

Callum couldn't breathe past the boulder lodged in his chest. God, he wanted to deny it. With all his heart, he wanted to lie. Again. A bigger, more horrible lie than all the ones before it, just to hide the terrible truth.

"Yeah, kiddo. I said that. And you're right," he admitted, surprised his voice came out evenly. Flat, even. His heart broke a little at the look of complete understanding and faith on Christian's face. Such a smart goddamn kid, so full of potential and hope, and looking to Callum to learn how to make good decisions. And boy, he'd come to the wrong place. "But I do it wrong."

The words hung in the air around them.

Christian's face fell. "What? Why?"

Rupert squeezed his hand. "Callum, that's not—"

"No," he said, cutting off Rupert. "Christian's right. I don't tell anyone. Worse, I lie about it."

Christian looked at Callum like he'd run over his dog.

"I made a bad choice. A series of bad choices a long time ago that I didn't even have the sense to regret until much later. Then it was too late to change them. Or I thought it was."

He shook his head. He didn't know how to explain that fifteen years ago, the world had been different. That *he'd* been different. But he'd also been years older than Christian was now, and far less brave.

"Don't look at me for a model of what to do, Christian. I'm the last person you should consider. Look at Rupert. See how he lives, what choices he makes. That's what I do," he admitted with a small smile. "He's the brave one."

"But, I don't understand," Christian said. "Why aren't you brave?"

"I don't know," Callum confessed. "I wish I was," he finished lamely.

"That's bollocks," Rupert snapped. "Christian," Rupert said firmly, turning to the boy, "Callum did what he felt was right at the time. That's what's important. And in many ways, what he did *was* brave. How many men, do you suppose, give up their dreams of playing hockey because they are gay?"

Christian cocked his head. "Lots, I guess."

"Yes, lots. Probably most, back when Callum was coming up through the ranks."

"No need to make it sound like the Stone Age," Callum muttered, his chest aching at Rupert's defense.

"It *was* the Stone Age, Callum. A lot has changed in the years since. Now Christian can count on his school and many of his friends to stand behind him. To protect him. When I was in school, the teachers were often as cruel as the kids. The coaches even worse. If not for Reese...well, it's the past. That's what matters. Things are different now." He ducked his head to meet Christian's gaze. "You can tell anyone whatever you want. Or you can wait and see what you think a year from now. But don't *not* tell your friends because you think it's easier. Don't lie to them about where you live and who you live with because you're afraid. You have nothing to be ashamed of, and your real friends will stand by you."

Callum nodded, so fucking grateful Rupert could help Christian and that he didn't condemn Callum as most would. He had to swallow before he could speak. "That's what I never figured out. Not until too late. I could have told people. And trusted them. But instead I lied, and that may have protected me on some level, but it also forced me to keep a distance, to push people away."

"So it's better to tell the truth?" Christian asked, clearly not convinced.

"Yes," Callum stated firmly. "Yes, it's better to tell the truth. To have *real* friends and to be yourself. You're lucky, like I was, though I didn't have the good sense to see it at the time. I had my family, and you have us to back you up no matter what. That's a great place to start."

Christian buried his face against Callum's chest and hugged him tight. "Thanks," he said, his voice scratchy. "You guys are the best family ever."

Callum closed his eyes, wrapped his arms around Rupert and Christian, and wished like hell it could be true. That this could really be his family. He didn't kid himself, though. There was only so much he could do from thousands of miles away.

Callum wasn't sure how long he held them, his eyes screwed shut while he wished for something he couldn't have.

"Callum, darling," Rupert said quietly, his voice muffled

against Callum's neck. "Your bum is vibrating."

"They can call back."

Christian sat up, then quickly stood with his back to them, surreptitiously wiping his eyes. "Go ahead and answer it. I'm going to change into my pajamas."

Callum and Rupert shared a look while Callum dug his phone from his pocket. There were so many things he needed to say to Rupert, none of which he could articulate, but he would be damned if he didn't try.

"Hello?"

"Callum? It's Bob. We need you back in Denver."

Rupert was alarmed by how the color drain from Callum's face. He squeezed Callum's hand, his heart lodging in his throat when instead of squeezing back, Callum let go and stood.

"What's up, Bob? It's only July."

Rupert slumped back on the couch. Bob was Callum's coach. He didn't have to listen to the rest of the conversation to know that their time was coming to an end, weeks earlier than planned.

As he'd anticipated, known, ignored, and denied would happen—Rupert felt very stupid. How had he let himself get so attached? Why had he let Oliver and Christian become so attached?

Callum paced around the living room, negotiating when he'd have to get on a plane—within a matter of days, it seemed—and Rupert realized he was a greater fool than he'd ever imagined.

He wouldn't change a thing.

Were it not for Callum, there was a very real possibility that Rupert wouldn't have Oliver and Christian here at all. Oliver might be shipped off to some boarding school or tucked away with a nanny somewhere, and Christian he never would have met.

Thanks to Callum, Rupert had fallen irrevocably in love three times this summer. How could he ever want to change a thing about that?

Callum looked physically ill as he stood staring out the window at the river beyond. His shoulders locked up around his ears, his fingertips white where they clenched his phone. Rupert wanted to be angry, wanted to tear the phone from his hand and yell at him that he couldn't leave, he couldn't break Rupert's heart like this, but that would be hideously unfair to both of them.

Callum had always had to return to Denver. He'd never lied about that. He'd been more honest with Rupert than he'd been with anyone else, including possibly himself, in a very long time. Rupert wouldn't punish him for that, or for the fact that his real life, his home, his job, were thousands of miles away.

Callum jumped when Rupert came up behind him and wrapped his arms around Callum's waist. Rupert thought Callum would remain standing there, rigid, perhaps hoping Rupert would give up. Then a hand clamped over one of his, their fingers lacing, and Callum wilted, pressing into Rupert as his head fell, chin to chest, and he sagged in defeat.

Now Rupert did cry, but not for himself.

"Yeah. Okay. Tuesday. I'll be in the training room by eight," Callum said in a monotone and hung up.

He was silent for a long time.

"I have to go back," he said, his voice hoarse, his body still curled in on itself.

Rupert swallowed hard. "I know."

"I'm sorry."

"Don't be. We knew you'd have to go back soon."

Callum turned to look at Rupert. "Yeah, but I didn't, I don't—
"

Rupert shushed Callum with a brush of their lips. "I know."

"But the boys. They won't understand."

"They'll understand fine, because we will explain it to them. You still want to be in their lives, don't you?" Rupert thought he knew the answer, had been so sure, but he still held his breath for the second it took Callum to swallow and answer, his voice a raspy whisper.

"Yes. Of course. But only if you—"

"Do not insult either of us by finishing that sentence."

"Okay," Callum agreed, as meek as Rupert had ever seen him. "Thank you."

Rupert brushed their lips again. "We'll figure it out."

Callum deflated in his arms. "I can't—we can't keep doing this. It wouldn't be fair to you. And in Denver, the press…it's not just my reputation at stake." He scrubbed an angry hand through his hair. "God, I'm so stupid. The press would go nuts if they ever found out. And then you, the boys, Michaela would all get dragged through—god, I don't even know what. I can't—"

"Shhh…" Rupert murmured. He quashed the anger, a perfectly reasonable attempt to protect himself from what the coming, and focused on the tiny ember of joy that Callum so clearly wanted more, wanted Rupert beyond the intransigent deadline of the end of summer. That was more than Rupert had ever allowed himself to hope for, even if it was of little comfort now.

"I'm so sorry," Callum said again, his voice thick with the tears.

Rupert brushed their lips together again and gave Callum the only thing he had left to give. Acceptance.

"I understand."

All the air left Rupert's lungs with the force of Callum's embrace, and he held on just as tightly, running a hand through Callum's hair, over and over, unable to soothe either of them.

"I'm going to bed," Christian announced from the hallway, his voice soft. Rupert turned his head to look at his newest charge and smiled gratefully. He wasn't sure what Christian had overheard, or that Callum had heard Christian at all. He'd sort that out in the morning. He'd have to talk to both boys about Callum going away.

Once the door to Christian's room clicked shut, Rupert

towed Callum toward their bedroom, shutting off lights as they went. It was too early for bed, normally, but every minute was suddenly precious. More so than ever, and Rupert had come to treasure the last two months more than any others. Time spent with the boys had been some of the very best of his life, but right now, he only wanted time with Callum.

Callum would still be in their lives, of course. He owned the Ice Cats. He loved the boys. There was the phone and Skype and Facetime and email and all the other wonders of technology to allow him to be part of their lives. To love and support them.

But this, Rupert thought as he carefully tugged the clothes from Callum's body, was only now. Just a few more achingly short days and it would be done. Then they could go on as friends. As family, even. But Rupert would not ask for Callum's love. Or his fidelity. Callum had only just figured out who he was, who he *really* was, and Rupert would not try to keep that all for himself. Not from two thousand miles away.

Rupert wouldn't ask, but he knew, in his heart, he would accept it if it was offered. It hadn't been, though, and that was okay. Somehow, he'd make it okay. For everyone.

He guided a docile Callum onto the bed and spread him out across the soft linens. He took his time, looked his fill, touched every inch of a body that had become as familiar to him as his own, and even more beloved. He kissed all the spots he knew made Callum sigh. When the tension vibrating from Callum's muscles finally eased, Rupert moved on to kissing the parts that made him twitch. That made him groan and grasp and writhe against the bed.

Rupert tasted salt, musk, and sweat. Licked smooth skin and scars. Rolled Callum across the bed, until there wasn't a spot on Callum left untouched. Then Rupert made love to Callum like he'd ached to do since he'd answered that damn call. Since Callum had protected Christian from that horrible bully in his troop. Since they'd gone to London and Callum had coaxed Oliver into his arms.

Callum stared up at him as they moved together, his eyes

open, a wealth of emotions Rupert couldn't sort out, there for him to see. Except the sadness. That he could pick out just fine, so he leaned forward and urged Callum up, sealing their lips together as their rhythm shifted, heartrates quickening. Callum's hands dug into Rupert's scalp, his hip. His huge goalie thighs around Rupert's ribs squeezing him tight, pulling him closer as he went over the edge, gasping into Rupert's mouth.

Rupert jumped with him, his heart and head soaring, even knowing that perhaps not this time, maybe not even the next time, but *soon* it would be his last trip to these particular heights, and there was no way in hell he was going to stick the landing.

Callum stood in the Moncton Airport, his carry-on bag on his shoulder, his gear bag and suitcases already being loaded on the plane. His brain screaming at him to turn around. To walk back out the door and get a new rental car, or just walk and walk and walk until he was home.

No. Not home. Home was Denver. He *knew* that. He'd always known that, since the moment he'd shown up in Moncton with no notice and less of a plan for how he was going to spend his summer.

He'd known it when he'd kissed Rupert. When he'd given his first blow job and lost his virginity in any way that mattered. And he'd known it would suck to leave.

So that was where he was. The suckage. A little early, but just as expected.

Shaking his head, he forced himself through security and to the gate.

Saying goodbye to Jack and Mike and Alexei had been hard. They'd swapped numbers and emails and promised to be in touch, but it hadn't made hugging them goodbye any easier. It hadn't made letting go any less painful.

The kids had actually been less traumatic, but, then, he'd see them again in two weeks. Mary Morrison wasn't about to rescind her invitation to the end of summer Morrison gathering, and neither was Callum—and not just because he was terrified of his mother's wrath. Which he was.

Rupert had offered to back out, to call Callum's mother and explain they couldn't make it, but Callum had stopped him with a kiss and little in the way of explanation. He didn't really have one. He just knew he wanted them there. He selfishly wanted, no, *needed* a couple more days with the boys.

With Rupert.

He'd been saying goodbye to Rupert since he'd gotten the call that his coaches wanted him back early, pulling him away from…

Well, everything.

Callum didn't have words for Rupert. He wished he did, but every time he'd opened his mouth, he'd been left mute. Dumb, in more ways than one. So, he'd tried to say goodbye with actions. There wasn't a moment they'd been together over the past few days when Callum hadn't been touching Rupert in some way. His hand. His back. Spooned around him in bed all night, pressing as close as he could get. He thought Rupert might have understood. Anyone else in their right mind would have told Callum to fuck off. To leave him alone, or at the very least give him some space.

Instead, Rupert had kissed him any time they were alone. Stripped them both behind any closed doors. Held him close and fucked him thoroughly, repeatedly. Hard and fast or slow and gentle, he had told Callum goodbye all the ways Callum tried to say it back. Without the words. Not even the one Callum promised himself he wasn't dying a little to hear again.

Rupert said a lot of things, but he didn't say *that* word again.

Which was fair, even if it ate at him not to hear it.

The flight was uneventful, the change of planes in Toronto the same. Callum barely remembered any of it, somehow surprised to find himself standing in the middle of his living room in Denver, staring out the massive floor-to-ceiling windows and over the entire city.

His bags were piled around his feet, the faint stench of his gear reaching him over the astringent smell left by his cleaning service working for two months with no one to make a mess between visits. His massive entertainment center was exactly as he'd left it, framed jerseys still on the wall, a shelf of pucks and pictures of his family prominently placed.

This had been his home for a long time. His safe haven when everyone outside these walls made demands and set expectations that he worked so fucking hard to meet.

It wasn't, he realized with a sinking heart, his home any longer. He had no idea how to fix that. How to fix any of it.

Sometime later, he heard the door lock snap open and blinked against the setting sun coming in through the windows.

Only one person had a key to his place, aside from the cleaning crew that wouldn't be here at this hour, so he didn't worry about his guest. Or mind the intrusion.

He kept watching the sun set, glancing over when Michaela stepped up next him. He smiled, briefly, then looked out the window again, perfectly aware that she had the identical view three floors down and wasn't here to brood with him.

Michaela didn't watch the sunset, in any case. She watched Callum.

He stoutly refused to ask *"what?"* like a brat. He knew, anyway.

It was almost full dark when Michaela threaded her fingers through his and sighed. "How long have you been standing here?"

He looked at the clock. "Three hours," he answered, which explained his aching hips and knees.

"Three hours," Michaela repeated with a slow nod, as if confirming what she'd already known. Her hand stroked the back of his.

He wished, now, that he'd called her. That he'd spent more time this summer telling her what the fuck he'd been up to and less trying to hoard it all to himself, creating a perfect fantasy of everything he wanted and couldn't have.

Maybe she could have helped him figure out what he was doing. What he'd done wrong. Because none of it had felt wrong at the time, even if he'd known it wasn't something he could keep. But now. Now *everything* felt wrong.

"Callum?" Michaela said gently, and he could hear the worry in her voice. Feel it in the way she soothed and petted him gently. "What exactly did you *do* this summer?"

Callum sighed, because he'd known going in what he was supposed to be doing. And when things had changed, when Oliver had clung to him, and Rupert had kissed him, and Christian had challenged everything he'd told himself he'd had to do over the past decade, he'd thought he'd known what was happening. He'd been sure he'd understood what his role was, where his limitations lay. And maybe those hadn't changed.

But it wasn't until he'd stood in his own living room in the wrong damn city, state, *country*, that he actually figured out the answer to the question of what he'd done that summer.

"I fell in love."

Chapter Twenty One

Rupert was getting mightily sick of everyone around him treating him like he was fragile. He was *not* fragile. He was tough. Fierce. He was completely capable of containing himself in all the ways necessary so that should he feel the need to cry, he did so in the privacy of the master bathroom after the children had gone to bed.

And he felt fucking manful about that, thank you very much.

He stood by as Alexei and Mike took over his kitchen for the third time in as many nights, insisting that they wanted to try another new recipe on Rupert and the boys. Interestingly, this need for culinary guinea pigs had only sprung up the day Callum had left for Denver. And Rupert couldn't imagine why two men were in the habit of making three times more food than needed and filling Rupert's fridge with it. What did they think would happen? Rupert would have a nervous breakdown and be unable to care for his own children?

The thought was infuriating. And Rupert would have been really pissed off about it, if only he could get over the desire to hug them and thank them and beg them to keep coming around as much and as often as they wished.

Rupert didn't do that, though, because then he might not be manful enough to hold out for his bathroom later.

A knock on the door distracted him from that lowering thought and he went to answer it. He wasn't surprised to find Jack standing in the hall with a six-pack of beer, another of cream soda, a massive binder under his arm, and a smile on his face.

"You know we couldn't get Garrick to leave Boston even if we drugged him, tied him up, and drove him across the border hidden in the bed of my truck, right?" he asked as he slung the massive pile of papers down on the kitchen island.

Rupert laughed. "You've obviously given this strategy some thought. And yes, I know."

"So, are you taking over?" Jack asked.

"What's this?" Alexei asked, pointing at the binder with one hand and slapping Jack's creeping fingers away from the pile of chopped peppers with the other.

Rupert flipped open the cover, revealing the project plan on top. "The construction project. Garrick was running it, then Callum took over. Now, it seems, it will fall to me until we can hire someone, I suppose."

Alexei leaned over for a closer look. "Can you do all this while you're managing the team?"

Rupert shrugged, because what choice did they have? He was saved from answering by the doorbell.

Who could possibly be coming over to coddle him and spoil his children now?

Reese, of course.

"Can I come in?" Reese asked in a dry voice while Rupert poked his head into the hallway to look for Hodges or Matilda.

"Yes, yes, of course. Come in," Rupert said, throwing the door wide. He checked the hallway again before closing it.

"I'm *alone*," Reese informed him, indignant.

"You were in Nova Scotia at lunch time. I know you were. We spoke on the phone. Did you drive yourself here?"

Reese rolled his eyes, which was fair. It *was* a stupid question. Reese hadn't driven once in the five years since he'd been run off the road by some lunatic. "Hodges brought me," he admitted snippily.

Rupert nodded. "Okay. Sorry. You know I worry."

"Yeah, well, you're not the only one," Reese said with a self-deprecating smile and a meaningful glance at the men in Rupert's kitchen.

Rupert smiled, then let out a loud *oof* as Reese yanked him hard against his chest.

"This hug thing still working?" asked Reese, holding tight.

Rather too well, in fact. Rupert allowed himself to wallow for a moment, letting Reese comfort him while reminding himself it would not do to let the kids see how upset he was. It was only their faces peering over the couch that held him in check.

"Rupert!" Alexei bellowed.

Rupert and Reese jumped apart.

"Yes, Alexei?" Rupert asked at an appropriate volume for speaking indoors.

"Mike and I can do this," Alexei announced, gesturing at the counter.

"Supper?" Rupert asked, confused. Wasn't that why they were there?

"No, the construction project. Mike and I can manage that."

Rupert honestly didn't know what to say to such a generous offer. But unlike Garrick and Callum, Mike and Alexei didn't own any part of the arena or the team.

Reese, as usual, dove right in at the brass tacks. "How would we pay you?"

Mike shrugged. "Hire Belvedoro to do it. Then you don't have to worry about it messing with our hockey contracts. You just pay the company like you would any other contractor and Alexei and I can sort it out on our end."

"You'll sort it out, you mean," Alexei said with a warm smile. "I suck at the books."

"Yeah, you do." Mike bent down to peck Alexei's lips then turned back to Reese. "The project is supposed to be done before the season starts, right?"

Reese smiled. "It damn well better be."

Mike and Alexei grinned back, obviously looking forward to the challenge. Rupert tried not to take it personally that Jack looked so relieved.

Dinner was a raucous affair, as per usual with Alexei involved. There was more than enough food to go around and *still* have leftovers, and, for a little while, Rupert's friends stopped looking at him like he was going to shatter into a million pieces.

Rupert just wished he didn't still feel that way.

His only solution was to focus on doing what needed to be done, for the team and for his boys. He was rather proud of how well the past three days had gone, with him juggling the logistics of having two children with wildly different needs and schedules, plus his own. He'd learned a lot from Callum, and no lesson was more important than there being no shame in asking for help.

Rupert looked around the table, smiling fondly at the odd collection of men laughing and teasing each other, cajoling Oliver to eat and asking Christian about his training. Reese caught his eye and grinned, and Rupert knew Reese understood.

There was nothing more important than family, whether chosen or born. Something else his time with Callum had taught him. How long would it be before it stopped feeling like such a big part of his family was missing?

Clearly, the men around him were determined to fill that role as much and as often as Rupert would allow, which was, honestly, quite a lot. They filled his home with laughter and love, and there was no imaginable reason to do anything but encourage it.

And if, at the end of the night, Rupert let Alexei pull him into a long, hard hug, there was no harm in that, either.

"You're going to be fine," Alexei said softly, just for Rupert to hear. "You're a really good father."

Michaela grabbed Callum's hand, stopping his incessant drumming on the center console of his car. He was fidgety and nervous, and had no idea why he'd let Michaela drag him out tonight.

He'd had a long day of training in the gym and on the ice. All he'd wanted to do was stay in his apartment, ice his knees, wonder if his coaches were trying to kill him, then go to bed early and do the same thing the next day. He'd found the relentless routine numbing, and had added as much to his days as his body could stand. He still hurt, in every possible way, but he was so exhausted by the time he climbed in bed at night that he could sometimes pass out before he had time to think. Before the ache in his heart made the rest of his pains seem like nothing in comparison.

"You've been moping for a week straight, Callum," Michaela said, still holding his hand. "Now you're acting like you want to crawl out of your own skin."

"I have not. I am not. I've just been busy."

"You've been brooding."

He had been, was the thing. He was gearing up for the new season, which should have been exciting. At some point, it would feel familiar again. He'd find his groove. And then maybe the vise around his chest would ease enough so he could take a full breath again.

The only bright spots had been his calls and Skype sessions with the boys. And Rupert.

Which was funny, since they were also agony. Callum hadn't been sure if Rupert would speak to him at all after he left. He would have understood if Rupert had wanted time and space. Callum probably should want the same, but he couldn't resist seeing Rupert and hearing his voice, his accent so crisp and ridiculous when he was worked up about something. They talked about the boys, the team, their friends, and it was if they'd never been apart. As if nothing had changed.

But, of course, everything had changed.

Rupert was paler than he'd been all summer, and Callum was too thin to be heading into the season. His coaches and the nutritionist were all over him about his diet and workouts, and he was trying to keep up, but it felt like his energy was slowly draining from him, no matter how hard he worked. Like he could eat and eat and eat and never be full enough.

He didn't talk to Rupert about that. Didn't mention how fucking much it hurt to see Rupert and to hear the boys laughing and to know that all of that was thousands of miles away. How Rupert could use Callum with so many of the plans and projects Rupert was involved in, but he wasn't there to help. It hovered between them, unspoken, a constant presence. Callum's guilt was a weight on his shoulders, pushing and pushing until he could barely breathe.

Maybe Rupert saw it. Maybe Rupert felt it, too. Because he always seemed to know when it was time to pass the iPad off to the boys, ending the game of emotional chicken before one of them cracked.

It was probably unhealthy and ridiculous and had to stop, but Callum couldn't bring himself to be the one to do it. He was too selfish. Too desperate for that tiny trickle of happiness seeing Rupert brought, even if it was buried under the flood of misery leaving Moncton had unleashed.

He turned into Mitch and Abby's driveway and parked next to the minivan under the basketball hoop. It occurred to Callum that there was room for a basketball court in the warehouse garage, the ceiling more than high enough to allow for a regulation hoop. Maybe he'd email Alexei later and suggest it. For Christian. And Oliver, one day. He tried to imagine Rupert playing basketball and smiled.

The pain in his chest got worse.

"Brooding," Michaela said with a sigh as she climbed out of the car.

She wasn't wrong. He was fucking pathetic with it.

By the time they stood at the front door, Callum had shaken the worst of it off. Or was doing a damn good impersonation of it. He even smiled when Mitch opened the door and waved them into the house.

From there it got easier. All three kids were still awake and tearing around the house, and Callum was more than happy to act as tea-party guest, Lego engineer, and jungle gym. He threw himself into it, and for an hour felt almost whole.

Mitch and Abby did a lousy job of hiding their surprise at his willingness to be adopted as Uncle Callum. Michaela just laughed and helped secure his tiara squarely on his head for the duration. She was a good friend like that.

He wanted to whine as loud and long as the children when

their mother announced it was time for them to go to bed. He gratefully accepted their hugs goodnight, and with each departure felt the yawning hole inside him open up a little further.

Michaela looked sorry for him. Mitch looked like he'd never seen him before. Callum turned away from Mitch's searching gaze and found himself face-to-face with a wedding picture. Two tuxedoed grooms and Mitch grinned at the camera from beneath a trellis, the ocean at their backs. Mitch's arm was around the one that had to be his brother, and he looked so fucking *proud*.

Callum swallowed the lump in his throat and quickly offered to help Abby in the kitchen.

Dinner was delicious and fun, and Callum tried to join the conversation. In all the years he'd been in Denver, he'd only ever accepted a handful of these invitations, preferring to stick to the team events and dinners when it came to socializing. He usually sat near or with Mitch at those, since he was happily married and less inclined to push Callum at every pretty girl in the bar. They'd talked a lot over the years, so they knew each other pretty well.

Except the part where Mitch didn't know Callum at all.

"I have something I want to tell you," Callum announced, grimacing when everyone looked at him with confusion, which was understandable given that he'd just interrupted a lively conversation about the local school system.

He grabbed Michaela's hand under the table and her eyes widened, but she held on tight.

She was a *really* good friend like that.

"What's up, Cal?" Mitch asked, giving him his full attention.

Mitch was a good guy, the kind of guy Callum would like to be good friends with, if he could. And that wasn't going to be possible unless he told Mitch the truth. Until Callum could be himself.

He clung to the idea that a real friendship was possible, even as his heart started to pound and his palms sweat. Maybe this would make Denver better. Home, again. A place he wanted to be and could relax and spend time with friends.

"I'm gay."

And, well, maybe he should have prefaced that with *something*. Mitch and Abby just stared at him, neither moving for what felt like a fucking eternity. Then Abby's eyes darted to Michaela, her lips turning down.

Mitch was still staring at him with a completely blank face.

Callum swallowed to wet his dry throat. "I'm sorry. I understand if you're angry. Of course you're angry. I'm an idiot. I understand if you can't forgive me. Michaela told me about your brother and, well, it made me feel stupid. I'm stupid. I should have told you years ago. When we first met, even. But back then—" He cut himself off from offering excuses. They didn't make sense to Callum anymore, he could hardly expect them to hold water with anyone else. "I just—I wanted you to know. I guess, I guess I needed you to know. And I'm sorry. About lying. About…everything," he finished lamely.

His hosts appeared stunned by that flood of inarticulate babbling. Michaela was squeezing Callum's hand so hard his fingers ached. Or maybe that was how hard he was holding onto her.

He tried to let her go, in case, but she wasn't having it.

"I've always known," Michaela offered in a calm, reassuring voice.

Mitch arched one eyebrow, but his gaze didn't leave Callum.

"It was my idea that we date," Michaela continued. "I thought it would give us both a reprieve from the press. The scrutiny. I didn't realize how easy it would be to let it go on for so long." She shrugged, her eyes pleading as she held Abby's gaze.

If he weren't such a self-absorbed asshole, Callum would have realized his declaration was going to impact Michaela's friendships with Mitch and Abby—particularly Abby—just as much as it would his own.

Callum lifted their joined hands to kiss the back of Michaela's. "She's my best friend. I would never do anything to hurt her," he promised, hoping Mitch and Abby believed him. "Neither of us could ever have fathomed how easy the lie would be. How quickly the press and the public would take to it. And then..."

He trailed off when Mitch started to nod, hoping that was some indication of acceptance. At this point, Callum was counting himself damn lucky he hadn't been punched in the face and tossed out on his ass.

"I get it," Mitch said, sounding surprised by that fact, but earnest.

"You do?" asked Callum. Would it be weird to ask Mitch to explain it to *him*?

"I was there, Callum. We were drafted the same year. If I'd been you, well...I get it. My brother didn't tell me until he was twenty-two. By that age you were in the big show, the entire world watching you."

"I still should have said something. To you, at least. Once we were friends."

Mitch frowned and looked at Abby, then down at his plate. "Let's be honest. Hockey is behind the times. It's getting better, but there's a reason you didn't know about my brother until Abby told Michaela. It's not that I'm ashamed. I'm not. I love Dave, and David, his husband, is one of my best friends. It's just—"

"I get it," Callum said firmly, a knot he'd carried for longer than he could remember loosening in his chest.

For a moment, no one said anything. Abby leaned across the table and took Michaela's hand. Michaela's relieved smile was wide, her grip on Callum's hand fierce.

Then Callum simply couldn't stand it. "Your brother's name is David, and he married a man named David?"

Mitch rolled his eyes, chuckling. "It turns out there are these rare, unexpected challenges to same-sex marriage."

Callum laughed as the tension around the table finally broke, the acceptance and warmth from the people around him making him lightheaded with relief.

He tried not to dwell on the fact that no matter how good this felt, how important it was, it hadn't done a damn thing to fill the hole in his heart.

Of all the lessons Rupert had learned about parenthood over the summer, he wondered how he'd forgotten, of all things, what a nightmare it was to travel with a small child.

Oliver was being really good, so Rupert shouldn't complain. Certainly he wasn't tantruming like the hell-born spawn who'd terrorized the entire Toronto Airport for the half hour they'd been waiting to board their flight to Boston.

And he had Christian, who'd been an enormous help the entire way, provided Rupert could ignore the constant fidgeting. Christian had probably burned off a day's worth of calories from leg-bouncing alone, but he'd also helped Rupert with the luggage and held Oliver's hand whenever Rupert needed to dig out documentation.

There'd been a moment in Toronto that he'd worried they weren't going to let him leave the country with Christian, but he'd presented the raft of paperwork his attorneys had promised would take care of things, and it had worked. Oliver was easier, since absolutely everyone assumed he was Rupert's son.

Christian only got more fidgety as the day went on, until finally, as their plane approached Logan Airport and the ocean was spread out beneath them, Rupert clamped a hand over Christian's knee.

"What's going on, kiddo?"

"Nothing. I'm fine." He couldn't have been less convincing if he'd tried.

"Do you not want to go?" A thought occurred to Rupert. "Are you upset at Callum?"

"No!"

"Okay. Good. Then tell me what's on your mind. You seem upset."

"I'm not upset," he said before worrying his lips between his teeth. "I guess I'm just nervous. I don't know anyone who's going to be there. And I've never been out of Canada before. Or on a plane," he mumbled at the end.

"What?"

He shrugged, as if it was nothing. "It's cool. I like it."

Well, that was something, but it didn't stop Rupert from feeling like a world-class idiot.

"I'm sorry, Christian. I didn't know. Why didn't you say anything?"

"I don't know. You made it all seem easy and I didn't want to seem stupid or whatever."

"You're not stupid."

Oliver's head popped up from where he was intensely focused on Rupert's iPad. "That's a bad word."

"Right," Rupert agreed. "We don't say stupid. We don't call other people stupid, and we *certainly* don't call ourselves that."

Christian nodded, still looking at his hands in his lap. Rupert jostled his knee until he looked up.

"Is that all that's bothering you?"

Christian shrugged, which Rupert took to mean it was not.

"You know, my dad never made me talk about stuff like this. He just ignored it."

Of course he had. "Well, that's not how I do things."

"Is it because you're gay?" Christian asked curiously.

Rupert used Christian's favorite weapon against him and rolled his eyes. "No. In fact, until this summer, I was really good at ignoring stuff like this, too. But that's not how this family operates any longer." Rupert ran a hand over Oliver's head.

"How come?"

"Because Callum pointed out that was…" Rupert struggled to find an appropriate word.

"Stupid?" Christian asked with a smirk.

"Yes, stupid," Rupert conceded. "And wrong. It certainly

wasn't going to make it any easier for Oliver to come live with me. Or you."

"Do you miss him?"

Rupert didn't have to ask who. "Yes. Very much." *Every day. All damn day.*

"Me, too," Christian said quietly.

Callum had Skyped with them for hours since he'd left. Rupert always answered his call and smiled and asked how things were going, and when he couldn't take it anymore, he'd pass the iPad to one of the boys so they could tear off to the couch together with it, tucking themselves close to each other so they could both be on the screen and see Callum.

It wasn't that he didn't want to see Callum more. To talk to him. But he could only take so much of his wan smile, the winces when he shifted his legs or rolled his shoulders, the haunted look in his eyes that Rupert knew was reflected back in his own. Eventually he'd beg to come to Denver, if even just for a visit. Or ask Callum when he was coming home.

This was going to be a very long weekend.

The sound of their landing gear dropping distracted Rupert and had Christian pressing his face to the window. It wasn't until the three of them were through Customs and Immigration and the baggage claim and possibly the sixth ring of hell that Rupert realized Christian had very effectively dodged the question of what else was bothering him.

Such a bright, dear, and sneaky boy.

Rupert promised himself he'd address it again later. For now, he needed to get them out of this airport. He'd intended to rent a car to drive the two hours to the northwest corner of Connecticut, but those plans had changed the second Garrick had heard. He, Savannah, and Rhian had *insisted* they could pick them up at the airport and deliver them to the family reunion.

The family reunion for the family they were not a part of.

He turned to ask Christian if this was part of what was bothering him, and found him watching Rupert closely.

"It going to be fine," Rupert said firmly.

Christian gave him a bland look. Rupert's efforts at confidence bolstering had obviously failed.

"Rupert!"

They turned to see Rhian jogging toward them, smiling and waving. When he dodged to the side, Rupert saw he towed Savannah in his wake, her hand clasped tightly in his.

Rupert grinned, relieved to see familiar faces, and such happy ones to boot. He put his hand on Christian's shoulder and checked that Christian still had a hold of Oliver's hand.

"Rhian. Savannah. I'd like you to meet my boys, Oliver and Christian."

Rupert didn't bother explaining the details, as he knew Callum had told his mother most of it, and had assured him the Morrison phone tree had probably been lit up like Christmas for the rest of the night after that.

Rhian smiled at them shyly, but Savannah stepped forward, shaking Christian's hand, then dropping to her knees to do the same with Oliver.

It was precisely what Callum would have done. Perhaps that was why Oliver slid forward and wrapped his arms around her neck. She hugged him back, her smile soft, expression delighted.

"This is nice. Thank you," she said warmly, pulling back to look into his face. She glanced up at Rupert. "The resemblance is remarkable."

"I'm Rupert's Mini-Me," Oliver declared.

"Oh, yeah?" Rhian asked.

"That's what Alexei always tells me," Oliver explained.

Rhian and Savannah laughed.

"We love Alexei. He's our friend, too," Savannah said with a big smile. Clearly this was all the character reference Oliver needed, given the way he beamed and put his hand in hers.

"You look just like Mimi," he announced, as if returning the favor of her compliment.

Savannah's smile froze for a moment before it bloomed into a full-blown grin.

"*Mimi*, huh?"

"Yeah, that's Callum's mum. Yours, too, right?"

"That's right," Savannah said as she stood, keeping hold of Oliver's hand. She glanced at Rupert, her eyes narrowing as she studied whatever she saw there. Then she smiled at Christian. "Well, I guess if she's already adopted all of you, it's my job to welcome you to the family."

"Thank you," Christian said, almost bashful.

Honestly, Rupert was falling in love, too, and Savannah was very much not his type.

Rhian squeezed Rupert's shoulder and winked down at Christian, confessing, "I'm adopted, too."

Christian gawped at the very handsome and young Rhian Savage, and—if Rupert had to guess—fell in love again, though perhaps in a slightly different way.

Christian had good taste in men already.

They grabbed their bags and found Garrick waiting at the curb in a minivan they'd apparently rented. Inside, there was a carseat waiting, and a collection of the kids' favorite snacks.

Callum's doing, Rupert could guess. What the hell Savannah, Garrick, and Rhian thought of all this, he couldn't imagine. Then again, Rupert thought as Savannah and her men clasped hands between the front seats for a moment, they weren't likely to judge.

The drive flew by, giving Garrick and Rupert time to catch up on all things Ice Cats related, and Savannah time to thoroughly captivate Rupert's children. The countryside was lovely, and Rupert made certain to point out the quaint villages as they rolled through. Oliver couldn't have cared less, but Christian seemed fascinated by the strange signs—"Why is everything in miles, not kilometers?"— and new sights. Rupert made a mental note to plan a trip somewhere soon. He wanted to show Christian the whole world, if he could.

Maybe starting with Denver.

Squashing that thought, Rupert gazed out the window and tried not to be nervous about their arrival.

Callum paced the length of Concourse C in the Denver Airport, gnashing his teeth. His flight had been delayed because of mechanical issues, and now cancelled for the same. Not that he was particularly eager to get on a malfunctioning plane, but this whole weekend had been highly ill-advised *before* Rupert had ended up at the mercy of Callum's entire family without him there as a buffer.

It was getting late, and the chances of his successfully getting on the already over-sold flight later that afternoon were slim. Slim enough that he'd booked a seat on the red-eye, just in case. That, though, wouldn't put him into New York until some god-awful hour of the morning, and then he'd have to drive two hours out of the city to get to his parents' house.

Leaving Rupert, alone and unprotected, with Callum's family for an entire afternoon and night.

He seriously considered calling Savannah and begging her to tuck Rupert and the boys into the Inn for the night without taking them to the house first, but knew that would be the equivalent of waving a red flag in the face of his bull-headed family. They would probably all decamp to the Inn immediately.

Callum ran his fingers through his hair, grabbing a good hank of it and tugging. When he turned, there was a young boy and his mother watching him. The boy stared up at him in awe.

Callum patted down his crazy hair and smiled. "Hello."

"Are you Callum Morrison?" the boy asked breathlessly.

Callum crouched down to his height and stuck out his hand. "I am. What's your name?"

"Dougie," he offered with a shy handshake.

"Hi, Dougie. How old are you? Four?"

His eyes went round. "How'd you know?"

"Well, I have a boy your age," he said without thinking. His heart sank. When he glanced up at Dougie's mom, she was staring down at him with a bemused expression on her face. "I mean, I have a friend. Who's a boy. Who's four."

Great. Now he sounded like an idiot or a creep.

He kept his smile firmly in place and chatted with Dougie for a while, keeping one ear out for announcements about his standby flight. He happily signed Dougie's hat, and a napkin from a nearby bar for Dougie to give to his father when they saw him next. And all the while, his heart ached for how much he missed Oliver. Dougie's high voice cut through the crowd noises the same way, his quick smile infectious. The way he glanced over his shoulder to check in with his mom because he wasn't sure about something or just because he wanted to know she was there.

That was what Oliver used to do. With Callum. And Callum hadn't appreciated how much it had meant until he'd lost it.

Another family came over, this one with two teenage boys who played hockey. Callum asked them about their teams, what positions they played, how their last season had gone. They hung on his every word, which had always made him feel awkward as hell, but this time was probably for the best. Because he could barely hear what they said back, instead watching how their parents hovered nearby, ready to protect. To scold and encourage. They were just so *present* and that, that right there, was what Christian needed. What he deserved.

And, god fucking damn it, what Callum wanted to give.

But couldn't.

Rupert felt a lot like a laboratory specimen. He'd been captured at the airport, caged in a minivan for two hours of subtle interrogation, and now he was under the microscope in a house full of men who looked hauntingly familiar.

Given the way Mary was eying him and the boys, Rupert was convinced dissection—metaphorically speaking—was still in store.

To be fair, the Morrisons were, to the last, charming and

kind. He and the boys had been welcomed with hugs and smiles and the promised chocolate chip cookies. Mary and Callum's father, Bruce, had sat with them in the kitchen, ignoring Rupert's protests while others unloaded the car and took their bags upstairs so that Garrick, Savannah, and Rhian could check in at the Inn down the street. No one said a word when those three didn't come back for over an hour, but their return was met with a burst of snickers and giggles from the Morrison brothers present.

The boys were to sleep in the twin beds in Savannah's room, while Rupert's bag had ended up in Callum's, much to his hot-cheeked horror when Mary, of all people, mentioned it.

Rupert wasn't sure Callum wanted Rupert to share his tiny full-sized bed to begin with, and he was completely certain it was a bad idea regardless. The last two weeks had been the longest of Rupert's life. Sleeping curled up with Callum would not help. Rupert was almost relieved when Callum's arrival was pushed back and Rupert learned he'd be spending the first night alone.

As to the second night, they would see. Rupert couldn't pretend he'd ask Callum to sleep elsewhere. Or offer to leave himself. That would all be up to Callum.

Bruce and Rupert spent a solid hour having tea—an excellent distraction from thoughts about sleeping arrangements—and talking about places in England and Scotland where they'd both been or lived. It was obvious Bruce missed his homeland, and was delighted to learn Rupert and Oliver had such close ties.

"Hey, Rupert, you don't play hockey, right?" asked Duncan when he came into the kitchen.

Rupert calmly took a sip of his tea. "No, I do not."

"I do," Christian offered quietly.

"Great!" Duncan said as he flopped into another chair at the table. He ruffled Oliver's hair. "You're too young to play with us, buddy. But you'll get there soon."

"I want to figure skate. Like Rupert."

"And are you going to make it all the way to the Olympics

like him, too?" Duncan teased, providing startling evidence of the Morrison phone tree's reach and depth of knowledge.

"Yes," Oliver stated, as if it were already fact.

Duncan grinned. "Good for you."

"But if I can't play, what will I do?" Oliver asked.

Mary scooped Oliver onto her lap. "You can sit with Mimi and watch, okay? Rhian's sister Chelsea doesn't play either. We'll have a grand time, I promise."

Oliver nodded eagerly, but Duncan looked positively aghast.

"But, Mom, you have to ref!"

Mary eyed Rupert. "Do I?"

Rupert had no idea why she was asking *him*. Unless... "Oh! I, you want me to—what? But, I've never—"

He shut his mouth when Mary patted his hand. "You don't have to. I just thought you might like to be out on the ice, and, given your current position, you probably have a good grasp of what's needed."

"It's not like a real game," Duncan added. "We don't fight—" Mary arched one eyebrow. "Uh, much. Hardly ever. It's mostly just off-sides and icing and stuff."

"And maybe a few penalties, here and there," Mary added dryly.

"Yeah, those, too," Duncan conceded.

Just then Kieran and his husband, Chance, exploded into the kitchen. "What are you all talking about?" Kieran asked, throwing himself into the chair next to Rupert's and practically into his lap. Kieran, Rupert had discovered, loved to flirt. A lot. And his husband, if the benign amusement on his face was any indication, wasn't bothered in the least by this.

"Your mother is suggesting I referee the big game tomorrow," Rupert supplied. He'd learned of the Morrison family tradition of a full hockey match long before he'd arrived this weekend. He'd been looking forward to watching, not *participating*.

"That's a great idea!" Kieran declared, bouncing right back out of his chair. "Let's go shopping!"

Rupert was beginning to accept that Kieran would always have him feeling a little off-kilter, like he was out on the ice with only one skate on.

"Shopping?" he asked nervously.

"Well, unless you happened to bring a black-and-white vertically striped shirt?" Kieran eyed Rupert's shoulders will ill-disguised admiration. "There's no way you can borrow Mom's."

"Oh, I suppose you're right? I mean…"

"Did you bring your skates?"

"Yes. Figure skates, though. And I haven't—"

"That's what Mom wears, too. Works great," Kieran assured him, dragging him from his chair.

Honestly, why did he even bother to argue? Kieran was already herding him out the door, announcing he knew just where to go and that they'd be back in time for dinner.

Rupert managed a weak wave to Oliver and Christian, neither of whom seemed concerned over his departure.

Chapter Twenty Two

Callum pulled into his parent's driveway just after eight o'clock the next morning, his eyes gritty from a long night, his knees and back sore from sitting up so long.

He'd managed, maybe, a total of five hours sleep between the waiting area in the airport and the flight to New York. That must be why now, having finally arrived, he decided it was a good time to panic.

Rupert was in the house. Waiting for him to arrive. The boys, too.

So why was he frozen in his seat?

He let out an embarrassing yelp when his car door flew open. Garrick, Savannah, and Rhian grinned down at him, their faces glowing with a sheen of perspiration. Shorts and running shoes clued Callum in.

"You ran over from the Inn?"

"Five miles, then here," Savannah explained. Not one of them appeared to be more than slightly winded.

His sister was obviously a terrible influence.

"You going to go in? They're dying to see you, Callum," Savannah said gently.

Oh god, he was dying to see them, too. Leaving his bags, his sister, her lovers, and the car door wide open in the driveway, Callum bolted up the front walk and through the front door.

"Anybody home?" he called, ignoring the half dozen or so members of his family sitting in the living room, staring at him.

"Callum!" came twin replies. Footsteps thundered across the kitchen and then the boys burst into the living room. Oliver's feet hardly touched the floor after that as he flew through the air and into Callum's arms. Christian slammed into them a second later.

Callum buried his face between their heads, taking what felt like the first full, deep, breath since he'd left Moncton. Oliver's arms almost strangled him as he babbled about how much he'd missed Callum, while Christian was completely silent, his face smashed to Callum's shoulder as he held on for dear life.

Callum peeked at the rest of the room. His family's expressions ranged from stunned to amused. Then his eyes settled on Rupert. Callum's breath left him again as the band around his chest constricted tighter than ever.

Rupert hovered in the kitchen door with a wobbly smile and a painfully uncertain expression. Callum wanted to demand he come over and join them. That he fling himself into Callum's arms and let Callum hold him, too. But, then, Callum didn't know if that was right. Or fair. To any of them.

With a last squeeze for the boys, Callum stood and smiled at his family.

"Sorry I'm late."

His mother was the first to recover, slipping past Rupert to come give Callum a hug and kiss. Then it was a free-for-all.

God, Callum loved these weekends home, looked forward to spending time with his family, but for the first time, instead of easing the lonely ache he'd carried with him so long, he felt worse. His father seemed to understand, giving Callum an extra-long hug and a long look Callum wasn't sure what to make of.

Once things settled down, Mary told Callum to go get his bags, and shooed the boys back into the kitchen. Rupert shuffled to the side to let them pass, his smile still uncertain.

"I'll help you with your things," he said and gestured to the door.

Callum nodded, and they made quick work of lugging his suitcase and gear bag up to his room. He was congratulating himself for not getting distracted by the view of Rupert above him on the stairs when he stuttered to a stop in the door to his room, instantly recognizing Rupert's pajamas draped over the footboard.

Rupert hovered nearby. "Is this okay?"

"Did my *mother* put you in here with me?"

"Um...yes?" Bright pink spots bloomed on Rupert's pale cheeks. "I wasn't sure if you'd mind, then when you didn't arrive last night, I thought I should just stay and see if you..."

Callum dropped his bags. "Come here," he said, his voice hoarse.

Rupert didn't hesitate, fingers threading into Callum's hair, mouths crashing together. Callum held Rupert as close as he could, until he could barely breathe as their tongues met and chased from one mouth to the other.

"God, I missed you," he whispered between kisses, reveling in the familiar scents and tastes of Rupert, even while he desperately tried to memorize them again.

"Me, too. God, Callum," Rupert said, wriggling until their hips were aligned and they were damn close to falling onto the bed.

Callum kissed Rupert until his lungs burned and his dick ached and his eyes stung. Until Rupert ended it with a gasp and Callum dropped his forehead onto Rupert's shoulder, shuddering, unwilling to loosen his hold.

"I've been miserable," he confessed. "I thought seeing you would help, that being here would make it better, but—"

"We can go."

"No!" Callum's heart stopped and he squeezed Rupert even tighter. "Please, don't go. I don't want you to go. Unless you feel like you have to. I don't have any right to ask you to stay, so I'll understand..." He couldn't finish the sentence, his voice going hoarse, then choking off entirely.

"I don't want to leave, Callum. I want you. However I can get you," Rupert admitted, and Callum knew how much courage it took for Rupert to admit that.

Callum lifted his head and looked directly into Rupert's eyes. "Good, because I want you here. So much." It didn't even begin to cover what Callum wanted. How much he wanted it and for how long. All things he couldn't say because he couldn't figure out how to make those dreams *possible*. He felt sick at the idea that he would hurt Rupert. Or worse, try to hide him and make him complicit in Callum's lies.

God, he was such a selfish bastard. Rupert deserved so much better.

Rupert's lips pressed gently to his, derailing Callum's thoughts in favor of long, slow kisses.

"Callum!" His mother's voice rang from the bottom of the stairs, jarring them apart. It was followed by the thud of footsteps too heavy and quick to belong to her. One of his nosey siblings, no doubt.

He stepped away from Rupert reluctantly, smoothing his hands through his disheveled hair a moment before Duncan came around the corner.

"Hey, Cal, breakfast is almost ready. And I don't know if Dad told you, but the game is right after lunch."

Shit. Right, the big game. He looked at Rupert apologetically, reminding him, "We have this thing—"

"Oh, I know," Rupert said with a laugh. "I've already been wrangled into service, don't you worry."

Callum was about to ask what that meant when Duncan said, "Come on. The boys are making you pancakes."

Callum hesitated. There was so much he wanted to say to Rupert, but he didn't even know if he could. Or should. It all felt so...unfinished, but he didn't have the right to ask for anything until he could figure out how to *give*.

Before he could begin to sort out any of that, Rupert slipped past him and followed Duncan down the stairs.

Rupert wasn't proud of himself for ducking out on Callum before they could talk more, but he'd been steadfastly fooling himself into believing that seeing Callum wouldn't be that hard, that it wouldn't make the last two weeks seem even more lonely and frustrating. That it wouldn't change anything about what he wanted and what he was willing to ask for.

Obviously, he was an idiot.

He took refuge in the kitchen, where he'd spent most of his visit thus far. Oliver tended to pop in and out with various members of the Morrison family, while Christian spent more time here, his gaze steady on Mary for long periods. The naked longing Rupert sometimes saw in Christian's face was heartbreaking.

Mary had proven endlessly patient with Rupert's questions. He'd hesitated to ask at first, but Mary was easy to talk to about his concerns over helping Christian balance school and his training, and how to pick the right school program for Oliver, and how to handle the travel once the season started. The latter discussion had to be conducted when Oliver wasn't within earshot. Christian tried hard to be casual about it, but any of the adults could see it was stressing him out, too.

Rupert wondered, as he tucked himself into the corner of the kitchen with Savannah and Murdoch to watch the boys and Mary cook breakfast for an army, how he'd ever thought he was a suitable guardian for these children who needed, who *deserved* so much.

The answer wandered through the door and sat down next to him.

Rupert couldn't decide if he wanted to shake Callum and scream, "Why, why, why?" or kiss him senseless to show him how grateful he was.

Mary smiled at her son and turned back to the stove, where she was supervising Christian in the scrambling and cooking of three dozen eggs. Oliver stood on a stepstool beside them, spatula in hand, watching the pancakes critically and glancing at Mary every few seconds to see if it was time to flip one.

"So, Christian, are you excited about going back to school?" Mary asked.

"Uh...I guess?" He cast a glance at Rupert, then Callum, before turning a single-minded focus to the pan of eggs.

Mary arched one delicate eyebrow, watching his face carefully. "What's your favorite subject?"

Christian shrugged. "Math, I guess. Maybe science, now that we're getting into the experiments and stuff."

"Just like my Murdoch," she said with a smile for her son,

who gave Christian a run for his money in the eye-roll department, even if his smile was fond. "Maybe you'll be a doctor like him someday, too."

"Yeah, I guess." Christian was obviously unconvinced.

"And what about after school? What do you do beside your figure skating?"

"Hockey," he mumbled.

"What's that, sweetie?" Mary asked.

"Hockey," Christian said more firmly. "I used to play a lot of hockey."

"Used to?" Savannah asked.

"He doesn't have to anymore," Rupert said, hoping to dispel Christian's rising tension.

"But he can if he wants to," Callum clarified. It garnered him an approving, if somewhat narrow-eyed look from his mother.

"Of course," Rupert agreed, reaching for Callum's hand, but pulling back at the last moment.

Christian sighed. "I don't know what I want."

"That's okay, too, kiddo," Callum said gently.

"My dad made me play," Christian explained to Mary. "He wouldn't let me quit. Said it would *make a man out of me*."

Savannah let out a bright laugh. "Look how well it worked for me!"

Christian looked stunned for a second, then giggled. "Yeah, I guess that's a pretty dumb thing to say."

No one bothered to defend Christian's father.

"I kind of like playing with my friends, though," Christian admitted with another glance at Rupert.

"Then you should," Rupert said.

Callum nodded encouragingly.

Mary's eyes narrowed on her son again.

"And what do you do when you're home? It's summer, so you don't have homework. Do you read?" Mary asked.

"Some, I guess."

"At least a half hour every day," Rupert affirmed.

"And I play video games and watch TV and stuff," Christian added.

"But only for an hour and a half max, right? That's what we agreed on," Callum reminded him.

"Until school starts," Rupert confirmed. "Then it's down to an hour at most of screen time."

"And none in the morning before school," Callum added.

Everyone around the table wore identical expressions of wonder as they stared at Callum. Rupert bit his lip to hide his smile. Callum didn't seem to notice the attention.

Christian rolled his eyes. "What if I don't have a lot of homework? Or practice?"

"Still then," Callum said firmly.

"Geez, you have a lot of rules," Christian muttered.

Rupert's heart clenched, but he forced back the worry. He and Callum agreed about these limitations. They'd spoken about them at length, consulted with Mary, the internet, and their consciences before deciding what was best. And it wasn't like the rules couldn't change. Rupert knew he would screw up sometimes, and then he'd correct. He had it on good authority from Mary that this was par for the parental course.

Perhaps with this in mind, Mary came to his defense. "It's about trying to be a good parent, Christian."

Christian smiled crookedly at Mary. "I know."

"It's not easy, believe me," she said.

"Yeah, but they don't have anything to worry about."

"*They* don't?" Mary asked, looking back at her son.

"Yeah. Ollie and I know we're really lucky," Christian said with a shrug. "We have more than most kids. We have *two* great dads."

It was for the best the boys couldn't see the look on Callum's face at that moment, or how it broke Rupert's heart.

No one said a word as Callum stood and quietly left the room.

By lunchtime, Callum had managed to hone his entire world down to thinking about only one thing—hockey. He couldn't begin to deal with what Christian had said, or Rupert's sad smile, so he spared not a single thought for anything but getting through the next few hours.

He loaded up on food at lunch to fuel what no doubt would be a grueling game. Goalies were the only players on a hockey team that regularly played the entire sixty minutes, but that didn't apply to a Morrison game. They'd draw teams and positions from a hat, putting Callum out of the net, in all likelihood. And with so few players, shift changes were rare or non-existent.

He helped Oliver cut up his food, and reminded Christian to drink his milk, and absolutely did not respond to the looks he was getting from virtually every single member of his family. They were confused. And concerned. And, if Callum wasn't mistaken, feeling increasingly protective of Rupert. Which was hilarious, actually, since those were pretty much the same feelings eating *him* alive, too.

When lunch was over, he suited up in his hockey gear and went down the hall to see if Christian needed any help. When Callum arrived in the door to the boys' room, he froze.

Goddamn his mother.

Oliver sat on the edge of his bed, bouncing up and down with excitement about his bright green Morrison hockey jersey, the name SMYTHE stamped across the back of his narrow shoulders. It was tiny and so fucking cute, the already fragile pieces of Callum's heart cracked in half.

Christian was also ready to go, already wearing his socks and pants, and, like Callum, was only in UnderArmor from the waist up. He held the white jersey between his hands, staring down at the SHAW printed there. Callum knew the green jersey would be the same, both with the Morrison crest on the chest.

"Just bring them both with you and we'll pick teams later," Callum said, his voice hoarse.

Christian looked up at him, still holding his shirt, and broke Callum's fucking heart all over again. "I wish it said Morrison."

Callum towed Christian in against his chest. "Me, too, kid. Me, too."

Once Callum could face his family without humiliating himself, he put Christian's hockey skates over his shoulder with his own and joined the stampede to the back door, making sure Christian had a hold of Oliver in the crush. The herd moved out for the rink, walking single-file through the woods at the back of the property, sticks laced with pads, and skates over their shoulders. Oliver rode on Callum's hip, Christian up with Angus and Duncan, laughing at something Callum could only hope was vaguely appropriate for a twelve year old to hear.

The Berkshire Academy Ice House was a familiar and welcome site. Almost as much a home to Callum as his parents' house. They all fit in a single locker room to draw teams and positions. Christian would play defense on the same team Callum would play right wing. Christian, who was used to playing forward, gamely took to his new position and huddled up with the rest of the green jerseys to plan their game.

Callum looked around the arena, searching for Rupert. His mother and Oliver sat in the stands, waving green and white pompoms. His brothers, Duncan and Lachlan, wrestled into goalie gear.

"Are you paying any attention?" Kieran jabbed a pointy elbow into Callum's gut. "I'm not going to be able to win this if my right wing's head isn't in the game."

"Where's Rupert?"

Kieran's smile was gleeful. "He's getting changed. Come on, he'll be out in a minute."

Callum's dad dumped a bag of pucks on the ice and the warm ups began with the scattering of little black biscuits across the ice. Callum stopped to double check Christian's helmet was fitted correctly, then sent him off and turned to start his skate.

He was arrested by the sight of Rupert practically running out of the locker room with the confident gait of a man long used to wearing skates, his smile wide as he burst through the open door and out onto the ice in his brand-new black-and-white-striped referee's shirt. As always, he was the embodiment of grace as he flew across the ice. Then he turned, executing a perfect pirouette, and Callum's mouth fell open.

"Jesus Christ," came Rhian's reverent whisper at Callum's elbow.

Callum could only nod and stare at Rupert's glorious, round, perfect, and, honestly, *enormous* butt in those tight black pants.

Savannah caught sight of Rupert and promptly tripped over a puck. Garrick caught her elbow, then he, too, froze. Callum's *mother* even stood up for a better view as Rupert flew past their seats.

Chance slid to a stop at Callum's side and spit his mouthguard into his glove. "That's the most beautiful thing I've ever seen," he said with frank admiration.

Callum growled, "Eyes to yourself," then glared daggers at Rhian, who was still watching Rupert with a slack jaw and zero shame.

"Eyes to yourself!"

Rhian managed to look chagrined even as he burst out laughing.

Rupert, apparently oblivious, executed a series of complicated steps, nimbly working his way around and over pucks as if they were a training exercise. Kieran sighed, audible from twenty feet away. Chance frowned and took off toward his husband.

Serves them both fucking right, Callum thought grimly. He had no doubt who was responsible for this. He'd heard all about the impromptu shopping expedition last night.

Garrick was the next to pull up to Callum's side. "I do believe," Garrick said thoughtfully, "that only Rupert could make polyester look that good."

Callum was about to tell Garrick to fuck off, but then Rupert bent at the waist to scoop a puck from the surface of the ice. Callum almost swallowed his tongue.

Garrick's knowing chuckle caught in his throat with a rough gurgle. "Holy shit."

"Yeah," Callum replied intelligently.

"Let's play!" Callum's dad shouted. He shook his head sadly at the group standing in the middle of the rink with their mouths hanging open. "*Now.*"

Everyone snapped out of their bubble-butt-induced stupors and quickly cleared the ice of extra pucks. Most of them had barely warmed up, but no one questioned the need for the game to get underway, least of all Callum, who was seriously considering breaking the no-checking rule the next time he caught someone leering at Rupert.

Rupert made a wide and graceful arc across the ice before coming to a stop on the red line between their two centers, Kieran and Chance. For a disgustingly happily married couple, these two were infamously hyper-competitive pricks when faced with each other on the ice. Now, though, instead of glaring each other down, they both leaned back a little, just to sneak another peek.

Callum whacked his brother on the ass with his stick. Hard.

Chance smirked until Rupert dropped the puck and Kieran won it cleanly.

For the sake of Callum's sanity, it was a good thing the game took over from there. He could admit that on a few occasions he mishandled the puck because at least half his brain was focused on the hope of handling something else in the very near future, but he didn't completely embarrass himself.

The best part, though, was watching Christian play for the first time without his father looking on. He laughed and scrambled and skated his damn heart out with a stamina Callum couldn't hope to emulate, and hadn't been close to since he was a teenager. Christian was a damn good hockey player, and every single person on the ice, whether teammate or opponent, made a point to tell him so at least once.

Callum really, really loved his family. The one he was born to, and the one he had made.

He'd clung to hockey for most of his life. Made it the most important thing, superseding all else. And it had been a wild and wonderful ride.

Perhaps that was why, right in the middle of a game, he figured out what he really wanted. And how to get it.

Rupert was perfectly aware that his trousers were too tight. Honestly, how could he not be, particularly with the disturbing presence of his first-ever jock strap and cup in there with his already admittedly over-sized bum.

He'd argued with Kieran in the sporting goods store, but had been foolish enough to let it go, figuring the fabric might stretch with wear. Having never worn such high polyester content in his life, he'd had no idea just how much it would continue to *cling.*

And Kieran, the sneaky devil, had assured him there was no reason to try on the cup with the pants in the store. Rupert had been so embarrassed by the entire purchasing process, and his ignorance around the equipment involved, that he hadn't argued. He'd been terrorized enough by Kieran asking if he needed a larger size.

Fortunately, it seemed Kieran was getting some of his own back—pardon the expression. Chance seemed rather enamored with the final results of his husband's trickery, and the longer he went on examining Rupert's *assets*, the more Kieran scowled. Rupert felt abundantly justified when he bent to pick up a puck and canted his arse in the general direction of Chance just a little more than was strictly necessary.

What Rupert hadn't counted on was Kieran blatantly hooking his stick around Chance's knee and sending him sailing right into the boards on his back.

Rupert whistled so loud and long, even his ears rang. With a stern frown for Kieran, he pointed at the penalty box.

Kieran opened his mouth to protest, but it was Chance, of all people, who leaped to his feet and his husband's defense.

"You can't give him a penalty!"

Rupert made a show of looking down at his black and white striped shirt, then back at Chance. "Oh yes, I can." And he'd enjoy the hell out of it, too.

Chance skated close, until he was looming over Rupert. He was a frightfully big man, almost six and a half feet with shoulders out to there. Rupert stuck his chin up and attempted to stare him down from below.

A skirmish broke out in his peripheral vision and Rupert glanced over to see Rhian and Garrick barreling down on them, ready to come to Rupert's defense. Callum stopped them with a hand on each.

"He's got this," Callum said.

Yes, Rupert sure as hell did. He raised his eyebrows at the husbands Morrison-McCormick then gave Kieran a pointed look.

"Get thee to the penalty box."

"For what?" Kieran cried, outraged. "He's not mad!"

"Oh, is that how it works now? He's not mad?"

"He didn't do anything," Chance announced.

"He didn't...*honestly*. He tripped you, while hooking *and* slashing. I'm not even sure which is the penalty best suited to this occasion. Maybe I should give him all three and add a boarding for good measure!"

"You will not," Chance said, looming larger, his scowl ferocious.

Rupert slammed his hands onto his hips. "How about you go with him for unsportsmanlike conduct?"

"You wouldn't dare."

"I bloody well would, you big oaf," Rupert snapped, pushing Chance back with both hands on his chest. "And you can bloody well give me some fadoodling space. I won't be bullied by the likes of you."

Chance wore a bemused smile. "Fadoodling?"

Kieran snorted and Rupert's shoulders dropped as a grin fought its way onto his face. He shot Kieran a look. "And fadoodle you, too."

Snickers from behind him caught his attention, and Rupert turned to see the rest of the Morrison family grinning at him.

"You're getting pretty bad-ass, Rupert. You've been spending too much time with hockey players," Savannah said.

"I suppose I have," Rupert conceded, noticing how Garrick studied him. The last time he'd seen Garrick, Rupert had practically thrown himself into his own filing cabinet in terror. Of Callum.

Too much time with hockey players, indeed. It turned out that not only were they not all that scary, a shocking number of them hid a soft and gooey center behind their scarred-up shells.

He almost wished Alexei were here to bellow something at him. He wondered if he'd succumbed to the hockey version of Stockholm syndrome.

He was interrupted from that thought by the loud crack of Callum's helmet hitting the ice, followed closely by his stick, gloves, and even his mouthguard—which, actually, was pretty gross.

What on earth was Callum doing?

Rupert stiffened, alarmed when Callum skated directly toward him. Rupert opened his mouth to protest whatever Callum was about to do, but then Callum's hands landed on his hips and pushed him backwards. Years of being forced to work with a partner kept Rupert on his skates as Callum threaded them between Kieran and Chance, picking up speed until, at the last moment, he cupped the back of Rupert's head and Rupert's back met the immovable surface of the boards.

Then Callum kissed him, long and deep and without a care for the catcalls and hoots of laughter surrounding them and echoing from the rafters. Rupert's hands flailed uselessly at his sides, his face on fire, until he finally gave in and kissed the stubborn, beautiful, ridiculous man back.

Honestly, he loved him so much.

By the time Callum removed his tongue from Rupert's mouth, there were cries of unfair advantage and conflict of interest. Rupert just sighed and stared into Callum's warm, smiling eyes.

He'd never felt safer. More cared for. Loved. And not just by Callum. Every shouted insult, accusation, and blatant innuendo warmed him.

Definitely hockey's version of Stockholm syndrome, then.

And there wasn't anything he wouldn't do to keep it. This. All of them.

"Callum, I—"

"All right, kids, back to work!" Bruce Morrison bellowed. "We still have twenty-two minutes of hockey to play."

Rupert looked over Callum's shoulder and burst into laughter. "Your father has his hand over his eyes."

Callum looked for himself and grinned. "Guess we better play before we scar the old man for life."

Rupert agreed, promising himself he'd come back to what he was going to say the moment they set foot back in the house, even if he had to drag Callum to the bedroom to do it. He could only imagine the commentary that would generate.

While Callum put himself back together, Rupert escorted a docile Kieran to the penalty box. He kept expecting him to argue, or for Chance to jump in again, but they couldn't seem to be bothered to do anything but smile at Rupert like he'd done something wonderful.

Chapter Twenty Three

Callum charged into his parents' house and up the stairs, desperate to strip off his gear and get into the shower. He didn't know what, exactly, he was going to say to Rupert, but he was going to be goddamn romantic about it. Which meant he shouldn't smell like old hockey socks and armpits. As a start, anyway.

By the time he'd made it back downstairs, Rupert and the boys had been pressed into service by his mother to help put out the snacks that his family was falling on like a pack of wild dogs. Hockey was hungry-making.

Callum munched on whatever was closest, which turned out to be peppers and hummus. He briefly considered running back upstairs to brush his teeth, since garlic breath didn't seem like much of an improvement over eau d' hockey, but then Christian was grabbing his arm and pulling him down to whisper in his ear urgently.

"Make them stop!" he hissed.

Callum looked around at his family, confused. They were loud, and ridiculous, and Angus had fewer manners than an orangutan when he was this hungry, but Callum couldn't understand what the problem was.

"Mom, what did you put in this guacamole? It's delicious," Duncan said.

"Oh, it's just something I fadoodled up," Mary said blithely.

Christian cringed like she'd run her nails down a chalkboard. "Oh, my god," he muttered.

Rupert came over and leaned in close. Callum barely resisted the urge to press his nose behind Rupert's ear and inhale deeply. God, he *needed* that.

"Is something wrong?" Rupert asked.

"I have no idea," Callum admitted. "Christian seems to have

taken a strong dislike to fadoodle."

Christian burst into hysterical giggles, further confusing Callum. "Stop it!"

"What? What on earth is the matter with you, Christian?" Rupert asked, apparently as bewildered as Callum.

"You have to make them stop saying it. You have to make *your mother* stop saying it," he hissed.

"Saying what?" Callum asked. "Fadoodle?"

"*Yes.*"

"Whatever for?" asked Rupert.

"Oh, my god. You don't know," Christian said, groaning into his hands.

"We don't know what?"

"I looked it up. I looked up fadoodle on the internet."

"Yes? So?"

Christian turned so vividly red, Callum could feel the heat coming off his cheeks. "It's old English. A fadoodle was a, you know…" Christian waved between their bodies. When he took in their blank looks, he rolled his eyes. "It means *penis.* And, you know, when you use it like an action, like a verb, it means you're, well, you know, *the same thing as the word you keep replacing it with.*"

"Oh, good god," Rupert muttered at the exact same time Callum's mother announced, "My goodness, I love a good fadoodling."

Christian groaned in horror. Callum absolutely cracked up.

Were it not for Rupert's steady grip on his flailing arm, Callum might have hit his head on the table as he doubled over with laughter, wheezing with it, until tears poured down his face.

His family looked on with shock and awe.

"Didn't he used to be the grouchy one?" Murdoch asked no one in particular.

He had! Callum had been the cranky sonofabitch no one wanted to be around because he was so miserable with himself.

But not anymore. Now he was so fucking happy, he was crying in his mother's kitchen.

Callum gasped for breath and held out a hand. "Come here, Oliver."

Oliver, to his credit as an intelligent boy, looked at Callum warily, but he slid off Savannah's lap and took Callum's hand. Callum gently nudged him to Rupert's side and put Oliver's hand into his brother's instead, so that both boys stood with Rupert.

Then Callum fell to one knee.

The room went completely still and silent.

"Rupert Douglas Macalister Smythe, you are the love of my life."

"*Holy shit,*" whispered someone at the table.

"There is nothing I want to do more," Callum continued, undaunted, "than spend the rest of my life taking care of you. All three of you." He looked at the boys, who both appeared as dumbstruck as Rupert. "I love you. I love our family. I want to be there for your first day of school and your obnoxious teenage years, and to show your first serious boyfriends or girlfriends embarrassing pictures of you." He met Rupert's gaze and hoped like hell those were tears of joy. "I want to grow old with you. I want to raise these kids as ours and maybe, someday, if it's okay with all of you, we can have a baby. Or seven. I'm sure Mike and Alexei can make room for us."

Callum paused. Maybe that was too much? Seven was a lot. Even his mom would say so.

"So, Rupert?" Callum asked, nervous and happy and so fadoodling terrified. "Will you marry me?"

Callum couldn't move, couldn't breathe, until Rupert's hand cupped his cheek. "You are crazy," he said quietly.

Which...wasn't a yes. But it wasn't a no, either.

Callum hung there, waiting. Heart pounding. Hands sweating. His cheek still nestled in Rupert's palm.

Rupert smiled.

A great cheer went up, and Oliver flung himself against

Callum's chest as chairs scrapped across the floor.

Then Rupert said, "But what about Denver?"

The room fell silent again.

Callum shrugged. "I'm going to retire."

"What?" Rupert gasped. "Can you just do that?"

"Yes, I can. And I want to. I've had a good run, but, god, what does it say that I won't even miss it? You can't leave Moncton and the Ice Cats, and the boys' home, *our* home is there. I refuse to spend another night away from you that I don't have to. My agent is a wizard. Anna will get it done and tie it all up with a bow."

"That's true," Duncan volunteered.

"It can be her wedding gift to us. What do you say we invite everyone we know and love up into these mountains and have a big party of a wedding?"

Now Rupert frowned. "Actually, we can't."

"What?" Kieran gasped, voicing Callum's horror exactly.

"We'll have to marry in England, I'm sorry to say," Rupert explained, and Callum's heart started beating again. "You are, after all, an unusual choice for the next Countess of Weckfordham. It will be interesting to present you to the Queen."

"Does he mean the Queen of *England*?" Rhian asked.

"I think he does," Lachlan whispered.

Callum swallowed hard. "Okay," he said weakly. This aspect of the whole thing hadn't really occurred to him.

"Rupert, lad," Callum's dad called out, "can we at least wear our kilts, then?"

Oliver peeked over Callum's shoulder. "Our cousin is the chief of the clan Macalister, Mr. Morrison. Of course we can."

Callum didn't think he'd ever seen a brighter smile on his father's face. "That's grandpa to you, young man."

Callum looked back up at Rupert. "So, what do you say, duchess?"

Rupert laughed and fell to his knees, and Christian fell along with him, leaving them in a tight knot in middle of his mother's kitchen floor.

Rupert pressed a sweet kiss to Callum's lips. "I love you. You've given me a gift I can never repay. My family. Our family. So, yes, Callum Morrison, I will definitely marry you."

This time, there was no stopping the cheers, or the pile-on as his family came to congratulate them.

About the Author

Samantha Wayland has always dreamed of being a novelist. She wrote her first book as an escape from the pressures of her day job. That fascinating piece of contemporary erotic mystery/suspense with elements of paranormal, international intrigue, and god only knows what else is safely tucked under her bed, where it will remain until hell freezes over. Since then, she's learned a lot about the craft and turned her attention to writing contemporary MM and MMF ménage erotic romance.

Sam lives with her family—of both the two and four-legged variety—outside of Boston. She used to spend her days toiling away in corporate nerdville but was recently sprung from that hell. Now when she's not locked away in her home office, she can generally be found tucked in the corner of the local Thai place with a few beloved friends (and fellow authors).

Her favorite things include mango martinis, tiny Chihuahuas with big attitude problems, and the Oxford comma.

Sam loves to hear from readers.

Email her at samantha@samanthawayland.com or find her on Facebook (Samantha Wayland) or Twitter (@SamWayland).

Also by Samantha Wayland

With Grace

A man yearning to explore his sexual tastes but afraid to turn up the heat, the woman who loves him but is hungry for more spice...and the chef who craves them both.

When Grace, Philip and Mark find a mobster's flash drive full of incriminating information, they are quickly embroiled in a dangerous situation. They stay together for safety, but proximity ignites the sparks they've long been fighting to ignore.

When three friends dare to succumb to their appetites, they find the perfect recipe for love.

Destiny Calls

Patrick didn't think it would be a big deal to kiss Brandon, his best friend and fellow police officer. Hell, they'd done crazier things to escape a bar fight. But then he had no way of knowing just how hot it would be.

Destiny Matthews is not a woman who is afraid to ask for what she wants, and when she sees her two best friends kissing, she knows just what she's going to ask for. Before she can convince Patrick that he's not as straight as he likes to protest, Brandon is attacked by an unknown enemy.

While they fight to protect each other's lives, they prove time and again that they're even better at protecting their own hearts.

Fair Play

Hat Trick Book One

Savannah Morrison is the new athletic trainer for the Moncton Ice Cats, a professional hockey team in the wilds of New Brunswick. It's a good thing she's got plenty of knowledge and grit, because as the only woman trainer in the league, she has to work twice as hard to win the players' respect. The last thing on earth she would do is date one of them.

Twelve year hockey veteran Garrick LeBlanc isn't ready to hang up his skates, particularly since he hasn't figured out what the hell he's planning to do next. He needs the new trainer to keep him fit to play, and she's got the skills to do it. Too bad he lost his mind and hit on her the day they met. Now she hates his guts and he's made an art of ignoring her.

When the team is put up for sale, Garrick and Savannah have to work together to save their jobs and their team. Somewhere along the way, they discover Garrick isn't just a hockey player, Savannah isn't only passionate about her work, and just maybe they've got more in common than they thought.

Two Man Advantage

Hat Trick Book Two

Rhian is working his way up the ranks of professional hockey, with the dream of making it to the NHL getting closer every day. He's doing it alone—no family, no friends—and that's the way he likes it. Then he arrives in New Brunswick, and meets the Moncton Ice Cats. Suddenly, he's got friends—and even something that might be an honest-to-god crush.

Garrick is lonely and counting the days until his last season with the Ice Cats is over and he can move to Boston. When his girlfriend suggests he take a lover—as long that lover is a man and Garrick tells her all about it—he laughs it off. But damned if his buddy Rhian doesn't take on the starring role in his fantasies. Good thing Rhian is way too young—and straight—for what Garrick has in mind.

Rhian takes a chance when Garrick's increasingly confusing signals start making sense, and soon discovers he's bitten off more than he can chew. Sex with strangers is simple. Sex with his best friend? Complicated.

End Game

Hat Trick Book Three

Garrick LeBlanc never intended to fall in love with two people, but he has, and now he has to figure out what to do about it. He wants to make them happy, but is afraid he's doing just the opposite. To make matters worse, he's trapped in New Brunswick until the end of the hockey season, while his lovers are both in Boston.

Savannah Morrison has no one but herself to blame for practically shoving her lover into the arms of another man. After all, it was her idea that Garrick take a lover while they are separated for the season. She loves Garrick with all her heart, but how the hell is she going to share him with Rhian?

Rhian Savage used to have such a simple life. Now he's in love, his dreams of skating on an NHL team are coming true, and he keeps spotting a strangely familiar face in the crowds. To top it all off, he has to see Savannah every day. He knows she's Garrick's real future, but he doesn't have the balls to do the right thing for all of them and end it—until his life goes sideways. As usual.

Now Rhian is alone, Garrick is heartbroken, and Savannah—the one person Rhian figured would celebrate his departure—is beating down his door. What the hell is up with that?

Crashing the Net

Mike comes to Moncton wanting nothing more than to play for the Ice Cats and finally live on his own terms. He's broke, bruised, and covered from head to toe in cheap lube, but he isn't going to let that stop him. All he needs is a place to live and some time to figure out how to reconcile who he really is with who everyone wants him to be.

Dumping three gallons of lube on the new kid is just another day at the office for Alexei. He knows exactly who he is: a goalie on the ice, a prankster in the locker room, and a man who knows better than to share his private life with anyone. He's let people in before and it's taught him that if he can't have what he really wants, it's better to be alone.

Despite their apparent differences, an unlikely friendship grows. Neither of them could ever have guessed how much they really have in common.

www.ingramcontent.com/pod-product-compliance
Lightning Source LLC
Chambersburg PA
CBHW050024030726
47506CB00001B/97